T0130571

TEMPTING LACHLAN

The ballroom was crowded, but predictably, everyone scurried out of Lachlan's way. Hyacinth had hardly caught her breath before he was standing before her.

He didn't say a word. He paused for a moment, his eyes on hers, and then his gaze drifted upward. A muscle in his jaw jerked as he took in her jeweled headband, the mass of fair ringlets gathered at the back of her head, and the long curls trailing down her face to brush her shoulders.

And then…and then, dear God, his gaze drifted downward.

Slowly, deliberately, those hazel eyes took her in, and he saw everything. The frantic pulse beating at the base of her throat, the flush spreading over her bare neck and shoulders. She'd been obliged to lace more tightly than usual to accommodate the snug fit of her bodice, and now his hot gaze lingered on the high curves of her breasts rising from the clinging violet silk.

Hyacinth couldn't prevent a soft gasp at this blatant appraisal, at the way his lips parted as he skimmed over the trim curve of her waist, the gentle swell of her hips, and lower, over the outline of her legs just visible through the filmy silk. He devoured every inch of her, leaving her breathless, and far warmer than she should be…

Books by Anna Bradley

LADY ELEANOR'S SEVENTH SUITOR

LADY CHARLOTTE'S FIRST LOVE

TWELFTH NIGHT WITH THE EARL

MORE OR LESS A MARCHIONESS

MORE OR LESS A COUNTESS

MORE OR LESS A TEMPTRESS

Published by Kensington Publishing Corporation

More or Less a Temptress

Anna Bradley

LYRICAL PRESS
Kensington Publishing Corp.
www.kensingtonbooks.com

LYRICAL PRESS BOOKS are published by

Kensington Publishing Corp.
119 West 40th Street
New York, NY 10018

All Kensington titles, imprints, and distributed lines are available at special quantity discounts for bulk purchases for sales promotion, premiums, fund-raising, educational, or institutional use.

Special book excerpts or customized printings can also be created to fit specific needs. For details, write or phone the office of the Kensington Sales Manager: Kensington Publishing Corp., 119 West 40th Street, New York, NY 10018. Attn. Sales Department. Phone: 1-800-221-2647.

Lyrical Press and Lyrical Press logo Reg. U.S. Pat. & TM Off.

First Electronic Edition: November 2018
eISBN-13: 978-1-5161-0534-2
eISBN-10: 1-5161-0534-6

First Print Edition: November 2018
ISBN-13: 978-1-5161-0537-3
ISBN-10: 1-5161-0537-0

Printed in the United States of America

For my daughter, Annabel. Keep putting kindness out into the world, sweet girl. We need it now more than ever.

Prologue

His mother was going to die.

Lachlan Ramsey stood beside her bed, staring down at her wasted face, and he knew this, as surely as he knew the sun would rise this morning, and again the morning after that.

She might not die today, or even tomorrow, but one day soon the sun would rise, and she wouldn't be here to see it.

Elizabeth Ramsey plucked at her bedclothes with pale, skeletal fingers. "What of Isobel Campbell? Surely *she* hasn't forsaken—"

"She has." Lachlan, unable to bear the pathetic hope on her face, cut in before she could finish speaking. "Isobel, and Ewan as well."

Isobel Campbell, his brother Ciaran's betrothed, and her brother Ewan, Lachlan's oldest friend. He hardly had a memory that didn't include Ewan Campbell. Tearing across the moors on their ponies as boys, brawling with the Fitzwilliam brothers as restless youths, and later, chasing redheaded Scottish lasses as randy young men—Ewan had been by his side for every bloody nose, every schoolboy infatuation. Less than a month ago, Lachlan wouldn't have believed Ewan could ever turn his back on him.

But he had. They all had.

"Isobel, and Ewan, too." Elizabeth closed her eyes for a long, quiet moment, and when she opened them again, they were bright with fevered determination. "It's over, Lachlan. There's nothing left for you here. Take Ciaran and Isla and leave this place, and once you've gone, never look back again."

"They could still change their minds."

"They won't. You know the people here—how stubborn they are, and how proud. They won't change their minds."

"We won't leave you—"

"There will be nothing left of me to leave. I'm dying, Lachlan. Let's not pretend otherwise."

He wanted to deny it—to rail at her—to storm through this castle's every room. He wanted to leave nothing but wreckage in his wake—anything to vent the impotent fury clawing at him, its talons ripping deep into his flesh.

But rage would do him no good. His mother was right. Elizabeth Ramsey had never been one to cheat the truth, no matter how painful it was. She would die, and they would leave her behind, buried in the cold ground, her grave the only evidence the Ramseys had ever been here at all.

"Where will we go?" He didn't say, *it doesn't matter where*, though it was true.

Elizabeth rolled her head on the pillow, and gestured weakly toward the small table beside her bed. "There, in the drawer. A key. Fetch it for me."

Lachlan fumbled through the drawer until his large fingers closed around a tiny silver key. "This?"

He held it up, and his mother nodded. "In my dressing closet, buried under a pile of quilts, there's a wooden box. Bring it to me."

Lachlan did as he was bid. The muted thud of his boots and the rattle of her labored breaths were the only sounds as he crossed the room and entered her dressing closet. He knelt down and shoved the blankets aside, but when he found the box, he paused, sitting back on his heels.

It was a plain wooden box, unremarkable in every way, and yet the moment he laid eyes on it, a shadow seemed to pass over the room. Lachlan couldn't have explained why, but everything inside him recoiled at the thought of opening that box.

"Lachlan?"

He turned at the sound of his mother's voice, then rose to his feet and hefted the box into his arms. No use hesitating now. Whatever it was, it couldn't be worse than what had already passed.

Much later, after his mother had revealed her secrets, and he, Ciaran and Isla were on the road to England, he'd think about this moment, and curse himself for a fool.

Things could always be worse.

"Put it here, on the bed." His mother was struggling to sit up, and Lachlan helped settle her against the pillows behind her. He tried not to notice how emaciated she was, but as he lifted her, a memory of a dead bird he'd found as a small child drifted through his mind. The dogs had killed it, and underneath the scattered feathers was a pile of tiny, fragile bones—white, impossibly thin, pathetically breakable.

His mother turned the key in the lock. Lachlan lifted the heavy lid and peered inside.

Papers—thin stacks lay neatly on top of each other. Most were letters, their seals broken. It looked as if a crest had been pressed into the dark red wax, but it had cracked and hardened over the years, and he couldn't make it out.

"The papers, Lachlan. Hand them to me, will you?"

Again, Lachlan did as his mother bid. Instead of reading them, his mother sagged against her pillows. Her thin fingers clutched at the yellowed sheets. "Perhaps I was wrong to keep this from you, but I've never had much use for regrets. They serve no purpose, and they won't do us any good now. When I die, Lachlan, I wish to be buried beside Niall Ramsey."

Niall Ramsey. Not 'your father,' but Niall Ramsey.

He should have anticipated what would come next, but he didn't.

He didn't, because how could he? How could anyone?

"Once I'm buried, you will take your sister and brother to Buckinghamshire—to an estate there called Huntington Lodge. Present yourself to Phineas Knight when you arrive. He's the Marquess of Huntington. He may not be pleased to see you—by all accounts, he's a proud, stern sort of man—but that doesn't matter. He can't refuse to acknowledge you."

Lachlan stared at her. "Acknowledge me as *what*?"

"As his brother." Her fingers tightened around the sheaf of papers in her hand. "The previous Marquess of Huntington recognizes you as his son in these letters. The current marquess, Phineas Knight, is your elder brother, Lachlan."

"Ciaran's my only brother." Dozens of confused images of Ciaran flooded his mind—Ciaran as an infant, cradled in their mother's arms, and later, Ciaran as a boy, always running after Lachlan on his stout little legs, tedious in his adoration, in the way of all younger brothers.

"No, Lachlan. Ciaran is your half-brother, and Isla your half-sister. Niall Ramsey is their father, but he…he's not yours. He loved you as his own—no man could have loved you more—but your real father is the late Marquess of Huntington, father to the current marquess."

Lachlan took the papers from her hand and stared at them blindly for a moment, then tossed them aside. Even if they did prove his claim to another life, he couldn't make them mean anything, or connect them to himself in any way. They were just marks on a page, rendered in fading black ink.

"I'm the bastard son of a marquess?" It was odd, how calm he sounded— almost as if his life hadn't just been torn apart, and the pieces rearranged in a pattern he didn't recognize.

"You're not a...I was married to Lord Huntington when you were conceived. When I met your fa—when I met Niall Ramsey, you were already growing in my belly."

Lachlan sucked in a quick, hard breath, as if he'd just taken a powerful blow to the stomach. "You fled your marriage, and left your first son behind? What kind of mother—"

What kind of mother leaves her son? What kind of father lets her go, knowing she's carrying his unborn child?

He bit down hard on the bitter words, because what did it matter what her reasons had been? There was no answer she could give that would make any of this right in his head, and recriminations were as useless as regrets.

Then something else occurred to him and his chest tightened with dread. "What about Ciaran and Isla? The Marquess of Huntington divorced you after you left him, didn't he?"

Because if he hadn't, if there'd been no divorce...

"No. He died several years later. I married Niall Ramsey then, but not before—"

"Not before Ciaran was born."

"Not before, no." There was no hesitation, and no shame—only determination. "You're my son, Lachlan, the legitimate son of the late Marquess of Huntington, and younger brother to the current marquess. Isla is my legitimate daughter with Niall Ramsey, and Ciaran—"

"Was born a bastard." Lachlan stared at the wooden box, half-expecting a nest of poisonous snakes to slither out. "It's dumb luck he's not a bastard still, and I'm...Jesus. I'm not even Scottish. I'm an Englishman."

He shook his head, dazed. Less than an hour ago, he'd entered this room as Lachlan Ramsey, son of Niall and Elizabeth Ramsey, brother to Ciaran and Isla.

Now he was someone else. Someone he didn't know, and didn't have the first bloody idea who to be.

"Not just an Englishman, but an English *lord*, son to a marquess. It's your birthright, and your future. Listen to me, Lachlan." His mother gripped his hand with surprising strength in one so ill. "When you leave Lochinver, you must leave your past here. Isla's...misfortune, and everything that followed it—you can't breathe a word of it to anyone. Promise me."

He jerked his hand away, repulsed by the touch of her cold, shrunken fingers. "More lies? Haven't they done enough damage?"

"Not nearly as much damage as the truth will do, should anyone in England discover it. You need look no further than Lochinver for proof of that. These people have known you your entire lives, and they've all turned their backs on you. Do you suppose strangers wouldn't do the same, if they knew the truth? I lived among the English aristocracy, Lachlan. I know them, how vicious they can be. The past must stay in the past. If it doesn't, Ciaran and Isla will be the ones to suffer for it."

And Ciaran and Isla have suffered enough.

His mother didn't say it, but she didn't need to. Lachlan had witnessed their pain. Their wounds had left scars on his own heart.

"Protect them, Lachlan. I'm begging you, on my deathbed, to keep the secret. Start a new life, without the burdens of the past weighing on you."

Wasn't a secret its own kind of burden? He laid a hand against the wooden box, and recalled how heavy it was.

Heavy with secrets and lies…

Tears stood in his mother's eyes. "Promise me, Lachlan."

Promise her, when she'd broken every promise she'd ever made to him, and to Ciaran and Isla, by keeping the truth hidden away in her dressing closet, locked inside a wooden box.

But she was his mother, and she was dying, so in the end, Lachlan gave her the promise she demanded. Not only because she'd begged him to, and because he loved her still, no matter what she'd done, but because he couldn't deny the truth of her words.

He couldn't trust anyone. Not those you believed to be your friends, or the man you'd called your father, and not your mother, who had secrets of her own, and would have seen them buried along with her, if she could have.

By the time the sun rose the following morning, Elizabeth Ramsey was dead. By the end of the week, they buried her. The flowers they placed on her grave were still fresh when Lachlan, Ciaran and Isla left for Buckinghamshire.

Their mother had warned them to forget their past, and they heeded her words. They left the only home they'd ever known, the only friends they'd ever had, and two cold, silent graves behind them.

Not a single one of them looked back.

There was no reason to. There was nothing left to see.

Chapter One

Aylesbury, England

Late January, 1818

Blood oozed from the corner of Lachlan's lip, trickled down his chin, and dripped onto the snowy white folds of his perfectly knotted cravat. *Damn it.* Another night, another brawl, and another ruined cravat. "Damn you to hell, Ciaran. Why do you always have to strike me in the mouth?"

Lachlan seized his younger brother by the neck of his shirt and shoved him backwards, and the two huge hands squeezing Lachlan's neck fell away as Ciaran stumbled against the railing behind him. He and Ciaran were of a similar size, so it was no easy feat to send his brother sprawling, but then Ciaran was already staggering before Lachlan laid a finger on him.

Drinking the better part of a bottle of whiskey could do that to a man.

Ciaran, who was far too drunk to know any better, staggered to his feet and lurched forward again. "It's not a proper brawl without blood, brother, and mouths bleed."

As if to prove his point, one of Ciaran's enormous fists came barreling straight for Lachlan's face, but before he could land the blow, Lachlan grabbed his hand, threw him off balance with a twist of his arm, and slammed his foot into the side of Ciaran's shin.

Ciaran dropped to his knees, and Lachlan was over him in a flash, his fingers gripping Ciaran's hair to keep him still as he lowered his nose to within an inch of his brother's. "Noses bleed, too. You're begging for my fist in yours, but I've no wish to spill your blood tonight."

He'd spilled Ciaran's blood the night before, and the one before that, but any hopes Lachlan had he wouldn't have to spill it again tonight vanished when a sudden blow to his ribs ripped the breath from his lungs.

"Oof!" He toppled sideways, and landed on the ground next to his brother, gasping for air. He rolled onto his back, but before he could scramble to his feet, Ciaran's knee landed in the center of his chest and pinned him to the ground.

"Aw, come on, Lach, you should have seen that one coming."

Lachlan only grunted in reply. He didn't have the breath to argue, and besides, it was true enough. He *should* have seen it coming. Even when they were boys Ciaran had always gone for the mouth first, then the ribs, and then—

Oh, Christ.

He didn't have time to spit the curse out before Ciaran's knuckles crashed into his jaw.

Mouth, ribs, jaw. Always the jaw.

"You're not even trying," Ciaran complained. He grabbed a fistful of Lachlan's hair, jerked his head up, and then dropped it back into the dirt with a hard thump. "It's no fun if you don't even *try*."

Lachlan *was* trying—trying to end this brawl without having to hurt his brother, but he'd relied too heavily on the whiskey to do the job he didn't want to do with his fists. "Damn it, how the devil are you still conscious, Ciaran?"

Ciaran grinned. "No bloody idea, but here we are, brother, and I doubt your face will be as pretty tomorrow as it was today."

Lachlan jerked and flailed like a fish on a hook, but trying to throw Ciaran off him was like trying to topple a horse. It would have to be a blow, then—either that, or he'd be leaving a puddle of his blood and maybe a tooth or two behind when he left this inn-yard.

Lachlan's arm tensed. He clenched his hand into a fist and waited, knuckles facing out. Ciaran liked his brawls bloody, so he'd go for the mouth again, or perhaps the nose, and when he did his body weight would shift ever so slightly, and...

Now.

Ciaran drew his fist back, but he didn't get a chance to strike before Lachlan's own fist shot up from the side, just far enough to the right so Ciaran never saw it coming. Lachlan winced at the crack of his knuckles against his brother's cheekbone, but the blow did the job. Ciaran listed sideways from the force of it, and before he could regain his balance,

Lachlan shoved the heels of his hands under Ciaran's knee, threw him flat onto his back, and leapt to his feet.

"You're set on more bloodshed tonight then, eh Ciaran?"

For a man so deep in his cups, Ciaran staggered back to his feet with impressive agility. "No need to spill another drop of yours. This isn't your fight, brother—not as long as you get out of my damned way."

But it *was* his fight. His and Ciaran's, just as every fight since they'd left Scotland had been their fight. Instead of accepting his fate, Ciaran's resentment was spreading like an infection from a festering wound.

Helped along by great quantities of whiskey, of course.

"If I was going to get out of your damned way, I would have done it by now." Lachlan turned in a slow circle, facing his brother as Ciaran closed in on him. "Now get up to your bedchamber before I knock that thick head of yours off your neck."

"No, I don't think I'll go up just yet. I fancy another drink."

"You've had enough to drink." If Ciaran returned to the inn and happened to come face to face with the Englishman he'd just accused of cheating at cards, he'd have far more to worry about than Lachlan's fist in his face.

The Englishman's ball between his eyes, for one.

Ciaran laughed, but there was an ugly edge to it. "A Scot who's trapped in England can't ever have enough to drink. But you wouldn't know anything about that, would you, *brother*, what with you being an Englishman now?"

Lachlan's hands curled into fists. Since they'd arrived on English soil nine days ago, he'd carved a dozen small half-moon scars into his palms. "I'm still Scot enough to knock you unconscious for the rest of the night."

Ciaran shrugged, then raised his fists. "Have it your way. First your blood, and then his."

"Get on with it, then." Lachlan dropped into a crouch, and waited for his brother to strike.

It was one o'clock in the morning, and so dark Lachlan could just make out Ciaran's face in the dim glow filtering into the yard from the inn's window. Ciaran was so drunk he likely wouldn't remember this encounter tomorrow, but Lachlan would still have to pummel his brother bloody before this would end tonight.

His stomach heaved in protest at the thought.

Didn't matter. He could heave all he liked, and it wouldn't make any difference. Whatever else might come of this evening, one thing was certain.

He and Ciaran were going to brawl.

Again.

* * * *

Two inches only. A mere sliver and no more than that. Two inches was all she dared.

Hyacinth Somerset scrambled to her knees on the window seat, pressed her cheek against the cold glass, and raised her chin so what little fresh air there was could drift across her open mouth.

It had come to this, then. Her world had been shrinking for weeks... no, longer than that. Months? A year? It had been narrowing, tightening, falling in on itself, and now she was to be smothered in an airless tomb, silent but for the low, continuous drone of impending doom buzzing in her ears, and—

"Hyacinth! What in the world are you doing, child? Close that window at once."

Hyacinth jumped at the sharp command, and her bottom hit the window seat with a hard thump.

Oh, very well, then. She *wasn't* trapped in an airless tomb, but in a cramped bedchamber at the Horse and Groom Inn. The drone *wasn't* so much impending doom as it was her grandmother's snoring.

At least it had been.

How in the world was her grandmother still conscious? Despite Hyacinth's warning, she'd dosed herself with enough laudanum to fell a horse.

"Oh, it's dreadful, traveling on country roads," Lady Chase fretted. "Hyacinth? Didn't you hear me? Close the window, and go to bed."

Hyacinth sucked in one last desperate breath of fresh air, and then closed the window with a defeated sigh. "I thought you were resting. Indeed, I'm certain you'd feel much better after a long, deep sleep."

A deep sleep, or a swoon—any form of unconsciousness would do. Hyacinth was an affectionate and dutiful granddaughter, but after hours trapped in a cramped carriage without a breath of fresh air, her patience was at an end.

She hurried across the room and perched on the edge of her grandmother's bed. "Now, lie back and close your eyes, won't you?"

Lady Chase rested the back of a feeble hand against her forehead. "I can't possibly sleep. All that dust and dirt has overset my nerves."

Hyacinth hadn't seen a particle of dust or a speck of dirt since they'd left Huntington Lodge, because her grandmother had insisted they seal the carriage up tighter than...well, than a tomb.

Still, she owed her grandmother's nerves a debt of gratitude. If it wasn't for their irascibility, they wouldn't have stopped at Aylesford on their way back to London, and Hyacinth would still be trapped in that coach. If only her grandmother's nerves would take the good lady off to sleep, Hyacinth would be grateful to them, indeed.

"Have you my vinaigrette, Hyacinth?"

Hyacinth pressed the bottle into her grandmother's hand, and tucked the coverlet under her chin. "Yes, here it is. Now, go to sleep, won't you?"

Lady Chase patted her hand. "I'll try. You're a good girl, my dear."

She *was* a good girl. So good—so docile and accommodating.

A sweet young lady, to be sure, and an heiress, of course, but there's no denying she's a bit odd, and meek to a fault. Indeed, you will not find a more timid young lady in all of London. It will be so diverting watching her attempt to survive her season, though indeed, it's unlikely the poor thing will make it through a single ball without fleeing to the ladies' retiring room and cowering there for the rest of the night.

Was this her own voice, taunting her in her head, or was she simply repeating the whispers she'd heard others murmur behind her back? Hyacinth had given up trying to work it out. In the end, it made no difference.

It wasn't, after all, as if the voice were wrong.

There was no sense in dwelling on that *now*, when her lungs were one gasp away from giving up entirely.

"You see how fragile Iris is, Hyacinth." Her grandmother straightened against her pillows as if she'd suddenly caught a second wind. "I doubt she'll be of much use to us this season."

Hyacinth's sister Iris and her husband Finn, the Marquess of Huntington, had accompanied them on the journey to London, and intended to remain in town for Hyacinth's season. Their other sister Violet and her husband Nick, the Earl of Dare, were on their way from Ashdown Park, as well.

And thank goodness for it, because Hyacinth would need every resource at her disposal if she were going to survive her season. If one was going into battle, her brother-in-law Finn was just the gentleman to lead the charge. Not just because the *ton* paid such deference to his rank, but because he was grand, stern, imposing, and fiercely protective.

Finn was, in short, rather terrifying. It was a useful quality, particularly when one must deal with the *ton*. "Finn will be there."

Lady Chase let out a heavy sigh. "Yes, yes, but men are never much help with such things, though I daresay he'll prove more useful than either Iris or Violet."

Her sisters were both *enceinte*, and suffered from extreme irritability—ah, that is, from *fatigue*. Yes, yes, that was the proper word for it. Even the short journey from Huntington Lodge had aggravated…that is, *exhausted*

Iris, and Finn had taken her away to the privacy of their room as soon as they'd arrived at the inn this evening.

"A child is a blessed event, to be sure, but I don't see why both your sisters must be blessed *now*. It's most inconvenient of them. I don't doubt I'll be left to manage your season myself. It's certain to take a toll on my health, but it can't be helped, and you know I never think of myself in these cases."

Hyacinth surreptitiously wiped her hands on her skirts. Her palms went damp when anyone so much as breathed a word about her upcoming season. There was no telling what wardrobe disaster might occur when she found herself trapped in the middle of a ballroom.

Flimsy silk was, alas, no match for sticky panic.

"I know, Grandmother, and it's your health I'm concerned with at the moment. You need to rest." Hyacinth tried to keep the desperation from her voice. "Consider your nerves."

"Yes, yes. I will." Lady Chase obediently closed her eyes, but before Hyacinth could draw a relieved breath, they popped open again. "That is, I'll try to rest, but I daresay I won't sleep a wink. Not a single wink, Hyacinth, until you're safely married. Another marquess, I think, or even a duke this time..."

Hyacinth watched her grandmother's lids grow heavier, then heavier still. Any moment now...

Lady Chase's eyelashes fluttered, and at last, she let out a long sigh. Her head lolled back against the pillow, and the buzz of a snore filled the room.

"Grandmother?" Hyacinth waited, breath held, for her grandmother's eyes to snap open again, but Lady Chase had succumbed to the laudanum at last.

Thank goodness.

Hyacinth loved her grandmother dearly, but the old lady was at her most cantankerous when her routine was disrupted. It was cause for concern, since Hyacinth's launch into the marriage mart was a mere week away, and certain to be a disruption.

At best.

At worst, it would be an utter catastrophe.

It wasn't as if she *wanted* a season. She didn't. The very idea of being on display for every aristocratic gentleman in London to gawk at made her stomach roil with nausea.

She wanted...something. Anything, really. She didn't much care what, as long as it made a tiny crack in the shell she'd built around herself.

The trouble was, she hadn't the faintest idea what that thing might be. A suitor, a courtship, a marriage—she didn't have much hope her season would bring her any of those things, but perhaps it would bring her something else.

Something I never could have imagined...

Before her sisters married, Hyacinth had told herself she'd be content to live out her days in her grandmother's Bedford Square house. After Iris and Violet were gone, the silence she'd once treasured became deafening, and her solitary peace an aching loneliness. With every day that passed the walls of that house pressed in upon her, closer and closer, and her world narrowed by another inch.

No one, not even she, could live within such a tiny sliver of space. So she'd agreed to a season, because she had, quite literally, nothing to lose.

Hyacinth rose from the bed and snatched her cloak from the back of a chair, but she paused when she caught sight of her reflection in the window, illuminated by the light from the lamp behind her.

She hesitated, her cloak clutched in her hand. She'd thought to take a quick turn around the inn-yard for some air, but it was darker than midnight outside. She didn't like to wander about an inn yard in the dark, but neither did she like to deprive her lungs of oxygen, and she'd been half-smothered all day.

She could open the window now, but the bite of cold air was sure to wake her grandmother. Perhaps she'd be better off simply going to bed. Surely, she could hold off on breathing for another eight to ten hours...

For pity's sake, you're frightened of the dark now? Has it come to this, then?

It was one thing to dread her season—seasons were dreadful, after all— but it was quite another to succumb to childish fears. If she kept on like this, what would be next? Ghosts? Thunderstorms? Large dogs? Spiders?

No. She wouldn't indulge it. It was utter nonsense. Well, all but the spiders, perhaps, because they were wretched, crawly things.

Hyacinth straightened her shoulders, pulled her hood low over her face, and tiptoed across the room and down the stairs. When they'd arrived at the Horse and Groom late this evening, the inn-yard had been crowded with carriages, but not a single soul graced the rows of wooden tables in the dining room now, and the entryway was eerily silent.

A strange shiver of apprehension shot down Hyacinth's spine at the stillness, but she shook it off and made her way toward the open space around the corner of the building, on the side removed from the stables.

She'd take a quick turn in the yard to get the blood flowing through her stiff limbs, and then she'd return to her bedchamber—

"...still Scot enough to knock you unconscious for the rest of the night."

Hyacinth turned her head toward the voice, confused, but as soon as she saw the two men, she went still.

They were standing just outside a faint pool of light spilling into the yard from the inn's dining-room window. Both of them were dark-haired, and...goodness, they were both giants, with shoulders that went on for miles and chests like stone walls. They'd tossed their coats aside and were circling each other in their shirtsleeves, but the fine cut and costly fabric marked them as gentlemen, not servants or stable-hands.

She ducked into the shadows at the side of the inn, some instinct warning her neither of these men would want a witness to whatever mayhem was about to occur between them.

The taller of the two of them was grim-faced, but the other's mouth was quirked at the corner with an insolent grin, as if he found something terribly amusing. It seemed to cost him an effort to remain upright, and Hyacinth guessed he was befuddled with drink, but he shrugged, undeterred by his companion's warning.

"Have it your way. First your blood, then his."

Even in the dim light, Hyacinth saw the taller man's shoulders go rigid. "Get on with it, then." He had a trace of an accent, but what might have been a pleasant lilt was spoiled by a tone so cold and hard it sounded as if he were spitting bits of chipped ice. There wasn't a hint of softness in his face, or a tremor of indecision.

Hyacinth stared at him, a sick feeling growing in the pit of her stomach. This man, with his steady hand and cold voice—he'd beat his opponent to unconsciousness without any hesitation, and without batting an eye.

She shook her head to clear a sudden dizziness as she gaped stupidly at the scene before her. They were seconds from attacking each other, right here behind the Horse and Groom Inn, and one had only to look at their faces to see the brawl would be an ugly one.

But...it was impossible, wasn't it? She watched them circle each other, her brain sluggish with shock. None of this made sense. Gentlemen didn't tear each other to pieces behind a public inn.

Except these two men, in this oddly quiet moment, half-hidden in the shadows...

They would. They *were*.

Even before either man made a move toward the other, Hyacinth could see this altercation between them was inevitable. Whatever had sent them careening to this point had them in its grip now, and like a heavy stone tipped over the edge of a cliff, it wouldn't end until it came to a crashing halt at the bottom.

A deadly hush fell over the two of them, and Hyacinth just had time to wish with everything inside her she'd remained in her room with her grandmother before a ferocious grin split the second man's lips, wide and ghastly, and he lunged.

The other man's arm shot forward so quickly Hyacinth didn't realize he'd struck until she heard a sickening crunch. The first man's head snapped to the side, and he staggered backwards. He stumbled a few steps before he righted himself, and when he did...

Oh, dear God.

Hyacinth pressed her hand against her mouth until her teeth cut into the inside of her bottom lip. His face was covered in blood. It gushed in a flood of red from his nose, spattering his white shirtfront. He lifted his forearm to his face to staunch the flow. When he pulled it away a few moments later, his sleeve was streaked with gore.

"End it here, brother." The first man spoke calmly, for all the world as if he hadn't just broken the other man's nose. He was facing away from Hyacinth now, and she could see his hard muscles rippling and stretching beneath his linen shirt. The rigid line of his shoulders had loosened, and he appeared relaxed, as if...

As if he were enjoying himself.

Her stomach lurched, and she lowered her hand from her mouth to press it there, afraid she'd be sick.

"End it?" The other man spat a mouthful of blood onto the dirt at his feet. He raised his head to face his opponent, and laughed.

Laughed.

Blood was dripping off his chin, and he was laughing. "Oh, no. We've just begun."

He raised his fists and lunged again. This time he managed to land a blow to the other man's face, near his eye, and then a second brutal blow to the man's ribs, which sent him reeling backwards.

Hyacinth sucked in a sharp breath, her knees shaking with dread. Surely, that would be the end of it? No man could withstand blows like that and remain on his feet—

Before she could finish that thought, the first man regained his balance with a few agile steps, and with one graceful leap, he closed the distance between himself and his opponent, and landed two sharp blows to the other man's stomach.

His opponent doubled over with a pained grunt, and then he retched, and was sick all over his boots.

The first man was holding his arm tight against his side, but otherwise he showed no sign he was hurt. "Enough?" His voice was tight and strained this time, every hint of casual politeness gone. His shirt was transparent with sweat, and his chest heaving.

The other man was struggling to crawl to his knees. The fight was over, but to Hyacinth's horror, instead of surrendering, a vile string of curses fell from the downed man's lips, and he lashed out with one leg and struck a blow to the back of his rival's knees.

This time the taller man did crash to the ground, but he was up again in a flash, and when he struck again, it was clear he intended to end the fight once and for all. This time, he showed the other man no mercy.

After that, it was over in seconds, but they were the longest seconds of Hyacinth's life.

He grabbed him by the neck of his shirt, hauled him to his feet with one mighty wrench, and then landed a blow to his jaw that should have sent the man back to his knees, except his opponent didn't allow it. He gripped his shirt in a merciless fist and held him upright as he crashed his fist into the man's face a second time.

At last, the hapless victim slumped forward and lay unmoving on the ground, his jaw slack with unconsciousness.

Was he only unconscious, or...

Hyacinth stared at his battered face, at the blood spattered everywhere, and the pool of vomit soaking into the dirt beside him. He was so pale, the streaked blood standing out in sharp relief against a face that had turned whiter than his shirt.

She clutched her stomach and doubled over as if she'd been struck herself. Bile threatened to gag her, but she choked it back down, terrified if she made a noise the man would come for her, drag her from the shadows, and...and...

Oh, God. Had he seen her? Her breath seized in her throat as his head jerked in her direction, his eyes narrowing as he peered into the gloom. She shrank back against the wall, her lips moving in a silent prayer.

Please don't let him see me. Please...

There was no telling what such a man would do if he discovered her. She'd just witnessed a bloody, brutal beating.

A beating or a murder.

Her stricken gaze fixed on the man still slumped in the dirt, then darted back to the other man, her breath whooshing from her lungs when he turned away from her and brought his attention back to the motionless body at his feet.

He ran a hand through his damp hair, as if he were trying to decide what to do.

In the end, he did what every murderer does.

Hid the body.

He leaned down, grasped the prone man under his arms, and dragged him from the inn-yard.

For a long time after he'd disappeared, Hyacinth was too terrified to move. She flattened herself against the building at her back, shaking, and gulped down one shallow, panicked breath after another. Her brain was so fuzzy with shock; she began to wonder if she hadn't imagined the whole thing. But she could see the blood, the pool of vomit, and the two tracks the defeated man's boots made in the dirt when he'd been dragged away. She could see them with her own eyes, and there were two coats as well, tossed to one side of the yard.

Two coats.

If she hadn't happened to notice the coats, she might have remained there for hours, her limbs frozen with panic, but the realization that the man might return for them made her tear herself from her hiding place. Pounding blood and her own frantic gasps echoed in her ears as she fled for her room. Once she reached it, she darted inside, slammed the door, and fell back against it, nearly sobbing with relief.

"Hyacinth? Is that you?" Her grandmother rolled over in the bed to peer at her with sleepy, unfocused eyes. "Goodness, child. You look as if you've seen a ghost."

"N-no, I'm quite all right, I-I-I..." Her denial faded to horrified silence as the truth crept over her, leaving raised hairs and gooseflesh in its wake.

I might well have just seen a ghost.

Or at the very least, a man on his way to becoming one.

"Hyacinth?"

"It's all r-right, Grandmother. I j-just...I-I had a b-bad dream, that's all. Go back to sleep."

Her grandmother muttered something, and then rolled over. Within seconds, she was snoring again, but Hyacinth never closed her eyes that night. She wasn't sure she even blinked. She lay in her bed; her shaking arms wrapped tightly around herself, and stared at the fire for hours, tears streaming from her eyes as she thought about that man slumped in the dirt, reduced to a bleeding pulp.

Not half an hour before he'd been beaten, she'd wished for something to happen.

Anything.

She squeezed her eyes closed, and longed with all her heart she'd been far, far more careful what she'd wished for.

Chapter Two

The First Ball
Lord and Lady Huntington request the pleasure of
Your company at a ball held in
Miss Hyacinth Somerset's honor,
At 7:00 o'clock in the evening
Saturday, January 24
10 Grosvenor Street

"If you insist on hiding behind that column, Hyacinth, you won't be asked to dance at all this evening."

Hyacinth peeked around the white marble column she'd ducked behind to find Iris lying in wait for her, ready to drag her out of what had, until now, been a perfectly good hiding place.

"The gentlemen can't put their names on your dance card if they can't find you, can they?" added Violet, who was peering at her over Iris's shoulder.

No, and that was rather the point.

Finn and Iris's ballroom was massive, and Hyacinth had taken care to tuck herself behind the most inconspicuous column she could find, in a quiet corner at the very back of the room, but here were both of her sisters, like two homing pigeons descending on their nest. For pity's sake, what use were dozens of immense marble columns if they couldn't even hide one small lady?

Hyacinth made an attempt at a carefree shrug. "Oh, well, I don't care to dance tonight." To dance, to flirt, to speak, or to be noticed in any way. Not by any gentleman, and not by her sisters either, if the truth were told.

Iris and Violet exchanged glances. Some sort of mysterious communication must have passed between them, because they pasted identical bright smiles on their mouths, grasped Hyacinth by her elbows, and without further ado, dragged her out from behind her column.

"Of course you'll dance, dear. It's the opening ball of your very first season, and Iris and Finn have gone to such trouble to make it special for you." Violet patted her hand, but her grip on Hyacinth's elbow was relentless. "You don't want to disappoint them, do you?"

"Or Grandmother, either." Iris clutched Hyacinth's other elbow. "She has her heart set on your catching a duke, you know."

Hyacinth snorted. A duke, indeed. There would be no duke, nor a marquess, an earl, a viscount, or a baron. She'd be fortunate if she managed to land a stable boy, and it was best for all concerned if they didn't expect more of her than that. A lady who cowered behind a column didn't become the belle of her season, and she didn't make a brilliant match. That Hyacinth seemed to be the only one who understood this was either terribly flattering, or utterly terrifying.

"A duke? I'm far more likely to catch a consumption." Still, Hyacinth dragged herself from her hiding place, because—short of throwing her arms around the column and clinging to it for dear life—she didn't have much choice.

"There, that's better." Violet fussed with the folds of Hyacinth's skirt, then stood back to study the effect. "I don't see why you shouldn't have a duke. That gown is worthy of any duchess, and you look lovely in it."

Hyacinth glanced down at her gown. It was white, of course—her grandmother had insisted on white for her first ball—with short, puffed lace sleeves and a subtle pattern of vines and flowers worked into the bodice and around the hem.

It was a beautiful gown, if less elaborate than many of the other gowns on display tonight, but the simplicity of it suited Hyacinth. She'd even felt a little thrill of girlish anticipation when she'd donned the gown in the privacy of her bedchamber this evening.

Now she just felt exposed, particularly her bosom. A low décolletage was a drafty business. "Perhaps a season wasn't such a good idea, after all." Hyacinth gazed at the crowds of people swarming the ballroom, their bright jewels flashing, and her stomach knotted with anxiety.

"Oh, my dear." Iris squeezed Hyacinth's cold fingers. "We know this isn't easy for you, but I confess I didn't think you'd find it *quite* so difficult, especially with all of us here to support you."

Violet's brow creased with a worried frown. "You've been more anxious than usual these past few days. Is something troubling you, aside from the start of your season? If there is, you must tell us at once. Perhaps we can help."

A ripple of fear darted down Hyacinth's back, and she sucked in a quick breath of air. She'd tried again and again over the past few days to tell someone—anyone—about the horrific scene she'd witnessed at the Horse and Groom Inn but every time she tried to speak, she pictured that man lying in the dirt, covered in blood, and her throat collapsed around the words.

She'd looked for him, before they'd left the inn the next day, but there'd been no sign of the beaten man, or the man with the dark, glittering eyes who'd struck him down. Even if she had found them, there was little she could do. She'd been the only witness, and the crown tended to turn a blind eye to an affair of honor between two gentlemen.

So she tried to forget it, but no sooner would she find a moment of peace than the memory of that man crawling in the dirt would come upon her unawares, and she'd be a shivering wreck once again.

"There's nothing to tell. I'm quite well. Just anxious about my season, that's all." She forced a smile for her sisters' sakes, and vowed once again to put the incident from her mind.

"It will be all right." Violet linked her arm with Hyacinth's. "Iris and I won't leave your side tonight. Will we, Iris?"

"Indeed we won't. Not for the entire season, if you need us, and if you truly don't care to dance with any gentlemen you don't know, then you needn't do so. Finn or Nick will lead you out if you wish to dance."

It didn't seem a good time to confess she found her brothers-in-law nearly as frightening as every other gentlemen—especially Finn, who was a trifle forbidding—so Hyacinth offered Iris a wan smile instead. "Very well, then. I'm ready."

She cast one last longing look at her column, and then she drew a deep breath and turned resolutely back to face the ballroom. She didn't need the column. She was in Iris's home, and no matter what happened tonight, her family was here to support her.

Nothing will happen.

She was perfectly safe.

* * * *

"You don't suppose Lord Huntington owns dozens of carriages, do you?"

Ciaran jerked his chin toward the Grosvenor Street mansion. Light spilled from every window, and even from the street, they could plainly hear the strains of a waltz.

"No, I think not." Their sister Isla watched as a fine, black carriage stopped in front of the house and disgorged a trio of ladies half-smothered in silks and costly jewels. "It seems we've arrived in the middle of a ball. A grand one, too."

"Bloody inconvenient timing," Ciaran drawled.

Lachlan stared at the house, his lips tight. It was a damned sight worse than inconvenient. Lord Huntington wasn't likely to be pleased to see them on any day, but it couldn't get much worse than interrupting the man while he was hosting a ball.

"But wait. Perhaps all this fanfare is for *you*, Lach." Ciaran turned to him with a smirk. "Did you tell his lordship you were arriving this evening? After all, it's not every day a man gains a brother."

Lachlan's mouth tightened further, but he didn't reply.

"Stop nettling Lachlan, Ciaran." Isla frowned at her brother. "It's not as if we're here just for him."

Ciaran laughed, but his obvious resentment robbed the sound of any humor. "We may not be here only for Lachlan, but there's no question we're here *because* of him."

Lachlan's hands fisted, and he carved another crescent-shaped scar into his palm.

A penance, for all the good it did him. For all the good it did any of them.

"We might have been here a day earlier if you'd been able to sit a horse yesterday." Despite his cool tone, guilt burned in Lachlan's belly. Ciaran had been in no shape to ride after their brawl, and they'd been obliged to remain at the Horse and Groom for a second night so he could recover.

Ciaran snorted. "Yes, it's a terrible pity. Just think, Isla. If we'd arrived yesterday, you could be dancing with some grand English lord even now. Either that or the exalted Lord Huntington would have already tossed us out on our arses, and we'd be on our way back to Scotland by now."

"We're not going back to Scotland." Lachlan's voice was hard. "No matter what happens with Lord Huntington. The sooner you accept that, Ciaran, the better."

Ciaran's brow lowered, and his jaw twitched with anger. "Perhaps *you're* not going back."

Lachlan glanced down at the pristine white cravat he'd just knotted, and shot his brother a warning glance. "None of us are going back, and before you get it into your fool head to drag me from my horse for another brawl, keep in mind this isn't some filthy inn-yard. It's Grosvenor Square. And that, right there?" He jerked his chin toward the elegant mansion. "It's not some country inn. It's Lord Huntington's home."

An ugly sneer twisted Ciaran's lips. "I know where we are, Lachlan. Christ, how could I forget it? I feel like a bloody Highland sheep dropped in the middle of a herd of overbred stallions."

"This isn't the place for another drunken brawl. Or do you think it will improve our chances with Lord Huntington if we show up in his ballroom with blackened eyes and bloodstained cravats?"

Ciaran didn't answer, only gave him a sullen look.

Lachlan sighed, and made an effort to lighten his tone. "Behave yourself, Ciaran, and maybe Isla will find herself a duke with deep pockets who'll keep you in wagering and whiskey."

"She doesn't want some bloody Englishman, do you, Isla?"

Ciaran's tone was defiant, but Lachlan saw the bleakness in his brother's eyes, and he jabbed his fingernails into his palms again. "She doesn't know what she wants anymore."

A sharp bark of laughter burst from Ciaran's chest. "Jesus, Lach. Have you only just met Isla? She's a Ramsey, isn't she? She was born knowing what she wants. The fact she can't have it anymore doesn't change a damned thing."

Isla let out a weary sigh. "I beg your pardon, but in case you've both forgotten, I'm right here. Kindly stop talking about me as if I can't hear every word you're saying. You do realize, Ciaran, you're only making this harder."

"Harder for who? Lachlan? You forget, Isla, he's Lord Lachlan now. I'd say things are a good deal easier for him than they've ever been before."

The way Lachlan saw it, there was nothing easy about becoming an English lord, but he didn't deny things were a damn sight easier for him than they were for Ciaran. His brother didn't mention Isobel Campbell, but Lachlan heard the echo of her name in every word Ciaran spoke, just as clearly as if Ciaran had said her name aloud.

Isla glanced at Lachlan, and her face softened. "Lachlan might be younger brother to a marquess, but as far as I'm concerned he's a Ramsey, the same as you and me. He's still *our* brother too, Ciaran, and he always will be."

"Half-brother."

Lachlan flinched as if Ciaran had struck him, but he remained silent.

Ciaran glanced at him, and blew out a quiet breath. "Then again, you're still the same arrogant, overbearing arse you've always been, Lach, and I'd still choose to pummel the life out of you as soon as look at you. I guess that makes you my brother right enough, same as always."

Lachlan shook his head, but a corner of his lip twitched. That was Ciaran. Stubbornly loyal, even when he'd rather beat you bloody.

"We're going to have a devil of a time with these upright English sticks." Ciaran pointed at his battered face. "Lachlan and I look like a couple of savages. Even if we do get past Lord Huntington, we're sure to frighten away any of Isla's future delicate English suitors."

Isla grimaced. "Not so delicate as all that, I hope."

"Of course they're delicate. They're English, aren't they?" Ciaran straightened his coat, smoothed his cravat, and tried to tame his wild mess of dark hair. "There. Do I look fine enough to meet a marquess?"

"No. You look like a savage who's been brawling in an inn-yard, but it's too late to fix you now." Lachlan glanced back toward the house. Damn it, brother or not, he didn't care for the idea of confronting the Marquess of Huntington in a crowded ballroom, with every aristocrat in London gaping at him, but they'd come this far, and he wasn't going to wait any longer. "How the devil will I find him? It looks like a crush, and I don't even know what he looks like."

"Like an English lord, I imagine." Ciaran raised an eyebrow at Lachlan. "Whatever you do, try and scrape together a smile. You won't get anywhere with your usual black scowl."

Lachlan grunted. "I don't scowl."

Both Ciaran and Isla laughed. "Oh, of course not," Isla said. "You're not at all *scowlish*. You're the very picture of good humor, Lachlan."

Despite his denial, Lachlan felt a scowl creep over his face. "*Scowlish* isn't even a word."

"Well, it bloody well should be. Look, Lach, if you can't find the lord, look for Lady Huntington. The housekeeper at their country seat said she's a beautiful blue-eyed blonde—a perfect English rose."

"That's no help," Lachlan grumbled. "I doubt a man can move a damned inch in a London ballroom without stepping on some fair-haired English rose. There's bound to be dozens of them in there."

"Ah, but not a single raven-haired Scottish lass. Poor Isla. If the English are as enamored of blue-eyed blondes are they're rumored to be, you'll end a spinster."

Isla only shrugged, but Lachlan frowned at Ciaran. Isla, a spinster? No, he wouldn't allow that to happen. He'd see to it she got back everything she'd lost, and an English lord into the bargain, if she wanted one. "Isla was the belle of every ball in Scotland. She'll have her pick of English lords, too."

That is, if he got past Lord Huntington's butler. He dismounted and tossed his reins to Ciaran. "I'll go in alone first, and then come back for you when I've settled things with Lord Huntington."

Ciaran nodded. "One Scottish savage at a time? Very wise."

Lachlan thought so, too, but Lord Huntington's butler seemed to think one Scottish savage was one too many, because he stopped Lachlan before he'd taken two steps into the entryway. "How may I help?"

Lachlan's scowl deepened at the butler's lofty tone. "I'm here to see Lord Huntington."

"Are you an invited guest of his lordship?"

Lachlan gave the man a thin smile. "You could say that."

The butler cast him a disdainful look, sniffing at Lachlan's travel-stained clothing, his muddy boots, and most particularly his black eye. "Lord Huntington is not seeing any tradesmen tonight. You may return to speak with the housekeeper tomorrow, and be sure to use the entrance in the mews when you do."

The butler swept a hand toward the door, as if he could sweep Lachlan away like the dust from his lordship's stairs.

"I'm not a tradesman." Lachlan took a step toward the butler. "And I'll see Lord Huntington right now."

"Impossible. His lordship is—"

"Get his lordship, or I'll do it myself." Lachlan smiled, but it was feral baring of teeth, and decidedly unfriendly. "I've no quarrel going through you to get to him." He stared down his nose at the man, who was two heads shorter, and not half his width.

The butler blanched. "I—I'll fetch him right now, sir."

"Good. I'll wait here."

"Yes, sir. I won't be a moment, sir." The butler backed away slowly, as if Lachlan were a bull about to charge, and crept down the hallway in the direction of the music and light.

Well, he'd return either with Lord Huntington or with a pistol—it was anyone's guess which. Lachlan folded his arms across his chest and strode from one end of the entryway to the other, but when he'd been back and forth several dozen times without any sign of the butler, Lord Huntington, or a pistol, he ran out of patience and stalked down the hallway to have a look for himself.

He stopped when he reached the double doors leading into the ballroom, his eyebrows shooting up. Good Lord. The room was enormous, and stuffed to the rafters with overdressed English aristocrats. And damned if all the ladies didn't look alike, just as he'd suspected they would. He'd never seen so much pink silk in his life, and how many variations on the color white *were* there? He was looking out on a sea of pink and white English roses, every one of them a pale-faced, flaxen-haired version of the others.

He couldn't have told one simpering chit from the next if someone had pressed a blade to his throat and demanded it, and the gentlemen weren't much better. All of them wore the same fitted black breeches and perfectly tailored coats, and each masculine neck sported a spotless white cravat—no blood on *that* linen—many adorned with fussy jeweled pins.

A highland sheep among overbred stallions.

This is what Ciaran meant. Nothing but English blood flowed through Lachlan's veins, and yet he was as Scottish as a man could be, and these fine lords didn't need to look too closely to see it. He towered over most of the other gentlemen in the room, and no amount of expensive, elaborate clothing could disguise the uncouth enormity of him, the rough brawn and raw edges that defined him as clearly as if he'd charged into the ballroom with a claymore in his hand, and a kilt around his waist.

He didn't belong here.

He didn't belong in Scotland anymore, either, and neither did Isla or Ciaran. Their former friends had made that bloody clear enough. There was nothing for them there. Likely as not, there was nothing for them here, either, but at least here they had a chance. It was a damn sight more than they'd had in Scotland.

He wandered the outskirts of the ballroom, squinting at one elegant aristocrat after another, hoping he'd recognize his own features in one of their faces. It stood to reason he and Huntington would look alike—they were blood brothers, after all—but three turns around the ballroom didn't reveal a more lordly-looking version of himself, and his eyes were crossing from studying the parade of dark-haired gentlemen.

None of them looked anything like him.

Lachlan dragged a hand down his face. This was absurd. He'd never find Huntington. The ballroom was crawling with English lords, and he'd be damned if he could tell a viscount from a marquess.

He turned and stalked back toward the entryway to wait for the butler, peering at every fair-haired lady he passed, stupidly hoping one of them might leap from the crowd and identify herself as Lady Huntington.

He'd made it nearly to the entryway when he came to an abrupt halt, his feet frozen to the floor, every thought in his head scattering as his gaze fell on a young lady half-hidden behind a column on the other side of the ballroom, directly across from him.

He stared, his mouth going as dry as dust. Had it only been a few moments ago he'd thought all English ladies looked alike?

His first confused thought was she was Lady Huntington, but he'd never met the marchioness, and this lady...

Hadn't he seen her before?

Her face...he couldn't have said why, but there was something familiar about her face that tugged at him, that drew and held his gaze. The delicate arch of her cheekbones, the swell of her bottom lip, the way she lowered her eyelashes to hide her expression...

Her eyes were blue. He couldn't see them, but somehow, he knew they were blue. Not an ordinary blue, and not a bright blue like a sun-filled sky, but a deeper blue, like the darkest sapphire.

Her hair was gathered into a knot at the back of her head and held in place by a plain blue silk band, but a few loose curls escaped to brush her forehead and the sides of her face. It was simply done—plain even, compared to the other young ladies in the room—but even the modest style couldn't disguise the lush beauty of that mass of gilded waves.

A strange sensation welled inside him as he stared at her. Had he seen her in a dream? No, that was impossible, but he was certain he'd caught a glimpse of her face before—just a fleeting impression, enough to recognize the shy, wide-set eyes, the curve of her chin.

Wherever it was he'd seen her before, she hadn't been smiling.

Had he already passed by her tonight without noticing her? Is that why she looked so familiar? Now he'd seen her, he couldn't believe he could have overlooked her, but then she was lingering beside that pillar, almost as if she were trying to disappear behind it.

Lachlan took in every curve and line of her, from the top of her head to the toes of her slippers, which were peeking out from beneath the hem of her white skirts. Her gown was very fine, but like her hair, it was simple. Aside from a few bits of lace here and there, and a wide silk ribbon around her narrow waist, it was unadorned.

He watched as she melted back against the column, her white gown disappearing into the curved white marble. She'd found a way to vanish, right here in plain sight. Everything about her, from her hair to her gown, to her hiding place beside the column was calculated to avoid attention.

That was why he hadn't noticed her before. She was doing everything she could *not* to be noticed.

Yet despite these efforts, she had Lachlan's attention.

All of his attention. He couldn't take his eyes off her.

Aingeal.

The pale, fine skin, the golden hair, the sweet curves of her face...
She looks like an angel.
Lachlan shook his head to clear it. What the devil? He wasn't the sort
of man to fall into raptures over a pretty face. Romantic fancies were for
English lords with nothing better to do. He had no business standing here
and gawking at her while his brother and sister waited outside on the street.

He began to weave through the crowd, his brow lowering with annoyance
as the people in his path scurried nervously out of his way. Did they suppose
he'd toss them aside with a swipe of his enormous paw if they didn't move?
Christ, he hoped all Englishmen weren't as timid as these. He couldn't let
his sister marry a coward.

He was halfway across the ballroom when the murmur rising in his wake
caught the young lady's attention, and she glanced up. Her gaze caught
his, and her brow creased with a frown, as if she thought she recognized
him, but couldn't quite place his face.

He paused, almost certain now they must have met. Remembering
Ciaran's warning about his black scowl, he forced the corners of his lips
to curve in an unfamiliar, upward direction.

He must have done it wrong, because she did *not* smile back.

Her mouth dropped open, and she raised one gloved hand to her lips to
cover it. Her eyes widened, and the blood drained from her face, leaving
her as white as her gown.

Lachlan's half-smile faded, and he hesitated in the middle of the ballroom,
confused by her reaction. Had he scowled at her, without realizing it? If
so, his scowl must be as black as Ciaran claimed, because she looked as
if she were about to collapse with terror.

He tried again, but she went paler still, and reached out a shaking hand
to grasp the back of the chair next to her.

"Hyacinth?" The gray-haired lady who was seated there braced her
cane on the floor and half-rose, her own face going pale when she saw the
young lady's expression. "My dear, whatever is the matter? Are you ill?"

The young lady didn't answer, but continued to stare at him, her lovely
face twisted with horror. She tried to back away from him, her panicked
gaze darting everywhere, as if she were planning an escape, but she was
hemmed in on all sides by the crowd. She jerked her head back to face
him, and raised her hand in front of her as if to keep him back. "Don't
come near me."

Lachlan stared at her, astonished. He glanced behind him, certain he'd
find an ogre or a monster lurking there, but she dispelled that notion at

once by pointing her finger directly at his face. "You." Her voice was pitched unnaturally high. "I saw you."

Lachlan shook his head. "I don't think so. I've only just arrived in London—"

He broke off, his body going rigid with dread. Oh, God. Could she mean she knew him from Scotland, from Lochinver? He stared at her, into her angelic face, and saw his family's future collapsing with a few words from those perfect pink lips. "You've mistaken me for someone else," he said, his voice cold. He turned abruptly on his heel, but her shaking voice brought him to a halt.

"*No*. I s-s-saw you. I s-saw what you d-did." Her chest rose and fell in shallow, panicked gasps, and her entire body was trembling.

What the devil was happening?

"Hyacinth? Who is this man?" The young lady's panic had by now spread to the gray-haired lady, whose voice rose with each syllable until she was shrieking. "What did he do?"

By now the scene had caught the attention of the people nearest them. They crowded around, and the rumble of feet scrambling across the floor echoed in Lachlan's head as people rushed from every corner of the ballroom, all eager to witness whatever scandal was unfolding.

"That m-man, at the inn in Aylesbury. Y-you b-beat him, and his f-face… it was covered in b-b-blood." She dragged her hand down her own face, as if she were trying to wipe away imaginary blood.

Aylesbury? What—

Ciaran. The fight at the Horse and Groom, two nights ago.

Relief flooded through Lachlan, so profound his knees shook. He took a step toward the young lady, his hands held out in front of him. "This is a misunderstanding—"

"You beat him until h-he fell down, and he di-di-didn't get up again, and there w-was so much b-blood…"

She couldn't catch her breath, and Lachlan froze, afraid if he moved any closer to her, she'd swoon.

As soon as the word "blood" reached the crowd's ears, the mood grew instantly darker, and the murmurs grew louder and more ominous. They moved in closer, crowding in on Lachlan.

"You…you k-killed him. You're a m-m-murderer."

The crowd gasped, but his accuser, the lady who looked so much like an angel she'd nearly stopped his breath in his chest, didn't hear them. With these damning words still on her lips, she fainted dead away.

A shocked silence fell, and then…

Chaos erupted.

Ladies collapsed, and gentlemen leapt forward to catch them. The whispers began, and before Lachlan could draw a breath, the words "killer" and "murderer" spread like wildfire, from every pair of lips to every ear.

Just as they had in Scotland.

Within moments, he'd been tried and convicted. In the middle of a ballroom, in less time than it took to dance a reel.

A group of men broke free of the crowd and took threatening steps toward Lachlan.

They aren't all cowards after all, then.

This was, oddly, his first thought, but he didn't move, or make any effort to evade them, because his second thought came with startlingly clarity, and it snapped his spine straight.

He'd been called a killer and a murderer before, but even as this scene unfolded with sickening familiarity, it wasn't the same at all.

This time, it wasn't true.

Chapter Three

Something soft and white was floating around her, tickling her eyelids. Perhaps it was clouds, or something even nicer, like the petals of hundreds of white daisies, or the sweet, fluffy wool of a new spring lamb.

Goodness, whatever it was, it was lovely. Hyacinth wanted to sink deeper into it, wrap it around herself, curl up in it—

"Take your bloody hands off me. I've told you over and over again, she's made a mistake!"

There was a crash, as if a chair had been overturned, the sound of a brief scuffle, and then Finn's voice, low and breathless. "Good God, he's stronger than a team of oxen. Dare, help me subdue him."

Hyacinth frowned. For pity's sake, it wasn't as if she had a chance to float on a cloud every day, and here they were, ruining it for her with their shouting.

"Stop thrashing, damn you." A string of muttered curses followed this command, and then Nick's voice rose to a bellow. "Now keep still, or we'll tie your hands, you blackguard! Violet, have Jameson fetch the magistrate."

"The magistrate? Christ, this is absurd."

There was a shocked gasp. "A murderer *and* a blasphemer!" It was her grandmother speaking, but there was an odd, fluttery quality to her voice, as if she were about to succumb to a fit of hysteria.

Something awful had happened. Hyacinth couldn't quite remember what, but as she drifted back toward wakefulness, dread seeped into the blurry edges of her consciousness.

"For God's sake, will you allow me to explain myself? The lady's mistaken. I didn't beat a man to death at an inn in Aylesbury!" It was more of an angry growl than a voice, and strangely familiar. Hyacinth's sluggish brain groped for the memory, but it hovered just out of reach.

"My sister-in-law says you did. Why should she say it if it's not true?"

A brief silence fell, then it was broken by a man's bitter laugh. "Scores of high-strung chits in that ballroom, and the one who accuses me of murder is Huntington's sister-in-law. Bloody perfect. Well, wake her up, and make her explain herself."

"*She* explain herself!" It was Finn, and his voice was shaking with fury. "It's *you* who owes the explanation, sir. I've never laid eyes on you before, and I can't think of any innocent reason why you'd be skulking about my ballroom uninvited. But you'll have ample time to explain it when the magistrate arrives."

"Finn, wait." It was Iris's voice, but it was faint, as if her sister were speaking from a great distance away. "What sort of murderer confronts a witness to his crime in the middle of a crowded ballroom?"

Nick snorted. "A remarkably foolish one?"

"No. Something isn't right about this." It was Iris again, her voice still distant. "I think we need to do as this, ah...gentleman asks, and wake Hyacinth."

Hyacinth's frown deepened. Why, what a traitor Iris was.

She didn't want to wake up. She wanted to stay where she was, gliding about on this soft cloud. Hyacinth's fingers twitched as she tried to grasp at the cool, floating mist; desperate to hold onto unconsciousness just a little while longer, but as she began to drift off again, the acrid scent of smelling salts burned her nose.

"Hyacinth?" Cool fingers brushed her forehead. "Open your eyes, dearest."

Hyacinth jerked her head away, but it was too late. The fog was dissipating. A faint moan of protest left her lips, but whoever wielded the smelling bottle waved it under her nose again. The last few shreds of that blessed, numbing fog slipped through her fingers.

She peeled her eyes open to find she was in a dimly-lit room. The walls were spinning in dizzying circles around her, but she thought she was lying on a sofa in Finn's study, her head in someone's lap. Iris, Violet and Lady Chase were leaning over her, peering anxiously down into her face.

"She's waking up." Iris patted her cheek, and some of the tension eased from her face when Hyacinth's eyes opened wide. "Ah, much better. We're going to sit you up, all right? Violet, take her hands."

They eased her limp body upright and propped her against the back of the sofa. Lady Chase wrapped cold fingers around Hyacinth's hand, and the rest of her family gathered in a protective circle around her.

"What happened?" Hyacinth blinked up at the faces surrounding her.

They all looked at each other with blank expressions, then Violet said, "We're not sure, dear. A man none of us recognizes approached you in the ballroom just now. For some reason he gave you a fright, and—"

"And you called him a murderer, then fell into a swoon without explaining yourself."

The voice was deep and clipped, slightly accented, but with the lilt shorn off at the edges.

I'm still Scot enough to knock you unconscious...

Hyacinth's entire body went rigid as memories slammed into her, all at once, one after the next. The blood gushing from that man's nose, the dark red stains on his white cravat. The sickening crack of a fist meeting bone, the hard wall of the inn digging into her spine as she shrank back against it, clinging to the shadows.

The man, lying still and lifeless on the ground, his face covered with blood.

Without warning, Hyacinth shot to her feet. Dizziness swamped her, but she struggled against the swoon that threatened.

"Hyacinth!" Iris leapt up and gripped her arm, but Hyacinth shook her off, and took two steps toward the fireplace, from where the voice had come. When she emerged from the shadows and he got a look at her, a scowl blacker than death itself fell over his face.

Oh, dear God.

She'd thought him terrifying enough when she saw him beat another man to a bloody pulp, but he was far more frightening up close. He was the most enormous man she'd ever seen—a veritable giant—with shoulders wider than a doorway, straining at the seams of his coat, a wild shock of inky black hair, and hands the size of horse's hooves.

"You...w-why did you c-come here? W-wh-what do you want of me?"

His hard mouth pulled into a grim line, and icy hazel eyes narrowed on her face. "Not a damn thing until you began shrieking about murder. Would you be so kind as to explain yourself, before someone slips a noose around my neck?"

Violet came up beside her and grasped her hand. "Is it possible you've made some sort of mistake, Hyacinth?"

"No! Do you think I'd accuse a man of such an awful c-crime if I weren't certain of his guilt? There's no m-mistake. I saw him do it with my own eyes, the n-night before last."

"I don't recall beating a man to death the night before last. You'd think I would, wouldn't you?" He smiled, but it was the cold smile of a thief just before he wields a blade. "You've made a mistake—"

"*No!* Y-you were in Aylesbury, at the Horse and Groom Inn, f-f-fighting with another man in the yard behind the stable." Hyacinth's voice rose, every syllable ringing with panic. "You beat him unconscious, and there was b-blood everywhere, and he never got back up again, and then you dragged him away, and—"

"Just look at her, will you, Lord Huntington? She's frightened to death!" Lady Chase hurried across the room and wrapped her arm around Hyacinth's shoulder. "Why, this man must be a cold-blooded killer, just as Hyacinth claims he is. You and Lord Dare must take him to the magistrate, and see him hanged at once, before he murders us all."

"For pity's sake, Grandmother, you can't simply hang a man without a trial—"

Iris didn't get any further, because the giant man interrupted her. "I was at the Horse and Groom Inn in Aylesbury the night before last. She's right about that, if nothing else."

Finn turned to Hyacinth, his face puzzled. "I didn't see this man that night, and if a murder did take place, it was a remarkably quiet one. I never heard a thing."

"There was nothing to hear." The stranger muttered a curse under his breath. "She did see something, but it wasn't a murder, and I can prove it."

"Well, let's see it then, man, so we can put an end to this, and I can take my wife home. She's upset, and no wonder." Lord Dare raised an eyebrow at Finn. "Beg your pardon for saying so, Huntington, but this is the least enjoyable ball I've ever attended."

"You'll get no argument from me," Finn muttered.

"My brother and sister are in front of your house right now, waiting for me," the man said to Finn. "Send a servant to fetch them here, and we'll explain everything."

Finn didn't move. "Why the devil should your brother and sister be standing in front of my house?"

The giant gave Finn a tight smile. "One interrogation at a time, Lord Huntington, and I'd just as soon save my neck first, if it's all the same to you."

Finn hesitated, but then he blew out a breath and crossed the room to ring the bell. When the servant appeared, he murmured a few words to him, then sent him off.

Then they waited, not one of them uttering a single word.

Hyacinth sank down next to Lady Chase on the sofa, but she couldn't keep her gaze from wandering toward the black-haired giant, who now stood in front of the fireplace, his legs spread wide, and his hands clasped behind his back. He didn't spare Hyacinth a glance, but instead watched Finn with a strange, fixed attention—at odds with his expressionless face.

She was still staring at him when the door to the study opened and the servant ushered a slender, dark-haired young lady into the room, and behind her...

Hyacinth choked out a gasp, her blood freezing in her veins when she got a good look at the man who strolled into the room. A black mark shadowed his left eye, his lip was cut and swollen, and a large bruise covered his jaw, but there was no mistaking his face.

It was the man from the inn-yard, and he was...well, he appeared to be very much alive.

He stopped in the middle of the room, summed up the situation with one quick glance, and to Hyacinth's astonishment, barked out a laugh. "Well, it looks as if everything is going just as we hoped it would. Well done, Lachlan."

Lachlan—for that was presumably the giant's name—ignored this, and pointed at Hyacinth. "This lady has accused me of beating a man to death at the Horse and Groom Inn two nights ago."

The man blinked in surprise, but then his lips curved in a grin. "Has she indeed? How peculiar."

Lachlan crossed his huge arms over his chest. "Tell her she's mistaken."

"Hmm. I wish I could, but I can't say what happened with any certainty. I was unconscious, if you recall."

Lachlan took a threatening step toward the other man. "I said, tell her she's mistaken, Ciaran."

The man gave him a wide-eyed, innocent look. "But I don't like to lie to these good people, Lachlan, and for all I know you *did* beat a man to death, after you'd finished with me. I do remember you being quite angry."

A low, warning growl rumbled from Lachlan's chest. "Damn it, Ciaran."

"Oh, no. He looks as if he might do someone an injury." The man— Ciaran—nodded toward Lord Dare and Lord Huntington. "Perhaps you two gentlemen had better restrain him, just to be safe. Tie him to a chair, or—"

"Oh, for pity's sake, Ciaran. Hush, will you?" The dark-haired young lady had been watching the scene unfold, but now she stepped forward and silenced the man with a single, quelling look.

"This isn't some bloody game, Ciaran—"

The young lady cut him off. "Quiet, Lachlan. You're as bad as he is, and it looks as if you've made a grand mess of this. No doubt it was that black scowl of yours that started it all."

Lachlan jerked his chin toward Hyacinth. "I wasn't scowling until she accused me of murder."

The young lady dismissed this with a wave of her pretty fingers. "Certainly you were scowling. You always do."

Hyacinth stared at the lady, amazed. She had the loveliest voice— feminine, but slightly husky, with a pleasant lilt and a smooth, low-timbered quality to it. To hear her was rather like listening to music, yet for all its sweetness, the entire room fell silent when she spoke.

"My name is Isla Ramsey." She offered the company a polite curtsey, then straightened, and tossed a disgusted look toward the two men behind her. "As much as I might wish to disown them at the moment, these two scoundrels are my brothers, Lachlan and Ciaran Ramsey. I beg your pardon, Lord and Lady Huntington, for bursting upon you so rudely."

"Well, I...that is, thank you, Miss Ramsey." Iris looked as if she were at a loss as to what to think, but she managed to give Miss Ramsey a gracious nod. Finn said nothing, but stood frozen, staring at Isla Ramsey as if she were a ghost just risen from the grave.

If Miss Ramsey noticed Finn's pointed stare, she chose to ignore it. "My brothers had a bit of a set to the night before last. Ciaran had the worst of it, and he was, ah...a trifle *messy* by the time it was over. I'm afraid this lady," she nodded toward Hyacinth, who sat speechless on the settee. "She must have seen them brawling, and assumed the worst."

Lachlan glanced at Hyacinth, scorn written plainly on his face. "A few blows, and a few drops of blood, nothing more. Who could mistake such a minor scuffle for a murder?"

Isla Ramsey turned on her brother, her lips pinched into a stern line. "Why, an English lady who's not accustomed to seeing two thick-headed ruffians pummel each other, of course. For goodness's sake, Lachlan. You must see how it would have looked to her. Ciaran was unconscious by the time you'd finished with him."

"Not from my fists. The bottle of whiskey he drank was what finished him. Christ, he was so far in his cups he accused some lordling of cheating at cards. I dragged him out to the yard to keep a bullet from landing between his eyes."

Lady Chase gasped, but before she could say a single word, a hearty laugh rang out, and every head in the room turned toward the fireplace, where Ciaran Ramsey was wiping tears of merriment from his eyes. "Really, it's too delicious this lady happened to be at the Horse and Groom Inn the night before last. Jesus, what are the odds?"

Lachlan Ramsay didn't seem to find it nearly as amusing as his brother did. He jerked his head toward Hyacinth and snapped, "Enough, Ciaran. Introduce yourself to her so she can see you're still breathing."

"With pleasure." Ciaran Ramsey strolled across the room and stopped in front of the settee. He bowed to Lady Chase, then turned to Hyacinth, captured the tips of her fingers in his enormous hand, and dropped a chaste kiss on the back of her glove. "How do you do, miss? Allow me to offer my appreciation for your concern over my murder."

Lachlan Ramsey raised an eyebrow at Hyacinth, his face hard. "Is this your dead man?"

Hyacinth swallowed. "Yes."

"I thought so. Not so dead after all, is he?" He could have said it as a jest, an attempt to break the tension, but there wasn't a trace of humor in his voice, or a hint of softness in his face.

Hyacinth lowered her gaze to her lap, her cheeks burning with shame. "No. I—it seems you were right after all. I did make a mistake. I beg your pardon, Mr. Ramsey."

He grunted. "It's too late for apologies. The entire ballroom heard you. My family is ruined, thanks to your hysteria."

"Watch yourself, Ramsey—"

"Why, how *dare* you—"

"She's *not* hysterical, only a trifle nervous—"

Lady Chase, Iris, Violet and Lord Dare all leapt at once to Hyacinth's defense, but Isla Ramsey, turning to her brother with a scowl as black as his own, drowned out their protests. "Shame on you, Lachlan Ramsey! None of this is her fault. If you and Ciaran hadn't been brawling, this never would have happened."

"And we did warn you not to scowl, Lach," Ciaran Ramsey added. "The English get nervous when they see a man your size with a scowl on his face."

Isla turned and jabbed her finger into Ciaran's chest. "You may as well wipe that smirk off your face at once, sir, because this is *your* fault, as well. Goodness knows when you and Lachlan brawl you come close enough to killing each other."

Hyacinth stared at this forbidding creature with awe. She looked like an ocean tempest, with her fiery blue eyes and the midnight blue skirts of her riding habit swirling around her ankles. She was a tiny, slender thing, no more threatening than a woodland sprite, with her narrow, delicate face and cloud of dark hair, and yet there she stood, her hands on her hips, scolding her enormous, wild-looking brothers, either of whom could crush her under a boot heel in a single step.

She's not afraid.

What would it be like, not to be afraid? To feel words tumble off the edge of your tongue without a stammer, and without a single moment's hesitation?

"That's enough, Isla."

Lachlan's harsh tone was enough to make Hyacinth shrink back, but Isla Ramsey dismissed his warning with a toss of her head, and turned to Hyacinth. "I beg your pardon for my brother's behavior, miss, ah…miss…"

"Somerset. Hyacinth Somerset. I'm Lady Huntington's sister."

"Lady Huntington's sister!" Ciaran Ramsey let out a peal of laughter. "Good Lord. That's cursed bad luck, that is."

Miss Ramsey took Hyacinth's hand. "How do you do? Oh, dear. Your fingers are so cold, Miss Somerset. Perhaps you'd better lie down again."

"No, I…no. You're very kind, but I'm quite all right now, thank you."

"No, you're not, child." Lady Chase struggled to her feet. "You seem a nice enough young lady, Miss Ramsey, but these brothers of yours." She pointed her cane first at Ciaran, and then at Lachlan Ramsey. "Beatings and murders, and blood and whiskey—scoundrels, the both of them. I'm taking my granddaughter home. She's had a terrible fright tonight, and she suffers from delicate nerves—"

"Wait, Lady Chase."

Finn hadn't moved or spoken since Miss Ramsey came into the room, but now he came forward, and Hyacinth was shocked to see his face had drained of color. He pointed at Isla Ramsay. "Who are you?"

Iris frowned, and laid a hand on her husband's arm. "Are you quite all right, Finn? They've just told us who they are—"

"No." Finn shook his head, but his gaze never left Isla Ramsey's face. *"Who are you?"*

Iris, Violet, Nick and Lady Chase exchanged puzzled glances, but Hyacinth was watching Lachlan Ramsey. A chill shot through her when she noticed he didn't look at all confused. Indeed, all three of the Ramseys seemed to know exactly what Finn was asking.

Iris, who was truly alarmed now, tugged at Finn's sleeve. "They're the Ramseys, just come to London from...from...where did you say you came from?"

"Scotland." Finn's voice was hoarse. "They came from Scotland."

* * * *

Lachlan had seen this moment unfold over and over again in his mind. Ever since he'd learned the truth about his birth, he'd agonized over how best to break what was sure to be unwelcome news to the Marquess of Huntington.

The scene had played out any number of ways, but not once had Lachlan imagined he'd have to defend himself against a murder charge moments before he was introduced to his long-lost brother.

Ciaran was right. He'd made a mess of this.

No, I didn't. Hyacinth Somerset did.

He shot her a resentful look. She noticed, and her face paled as if he were a wild beast about to lunge for her throat.

Timid thing. Excitable, too. Possibly mad.

Hyacinth Somerset might look like an angel, but celestial beings were useless enough, and beautiful women were always more trouble than they were worth. He should have known she'd prove difficult as soon as he saw her face.

It was too late now. The damage was done. Scotland, and now England... Everywhere they turned they found only wreckage, and now they'd run out of places to go.

"This young lady, she..."

Lachlan raised his head to see Lord Huntington had ventured a step closer to Isla. He studied her face, his gaze lingering on each of her features. "She looks just like my mother."

"Your mother?" Lady Huntington paled, and reached down to grip her husband's hand. "But that's...so strange. You don't remember what she looked like, do you?"

"Not much, no. I only recall the outlines of her face, but my father commissioned a portrait of her several years before she ran away, and her resemblance to this young lady, the dark hair, the shape of her face, the eyes and mouth..." Lord Huntington shook his head, stunned. "She could be my mother's daughter. My God. Who are you?"

Isla was a brave little thing, but even she was faltering under Lord Huntington's intense stare. "Lord Huntington, I—"

"It's all right, Isla. Go sit down." Lachlan gave her a gentle push in the direction of the settee, and this time she didn't argue, but crossed the room and sank down onto it.

Lachlan drew a deep breath, and faced Lord Huntington. For good or ill, this was it. They'd come all the way from Scotland for this moment. "Isla is your half-sister, my lord, and Ciaran your half-brother. The four of us share a mother."

"Half-brother and sister?" Lord Huntington drew his wife to his side, and held her tightly against him. He was shaking his head, but he seemed to be trying to make sense of Lachlan's words rather than denying them. "I'd heard rumors, of course...whispers about siblings in Scotland, but I never truly believed it." He turned to Lachlan. "If this is your brother and sister, then aren't you my half-brother, too?"

"No, I'm..." God, he wanted this moment over with, but as badly as he wished it done, Lachlan was finding it far more difficult than he'd expected to say what had to be said.

He'd never been a man of many words, but *these* words, these confessions...

I'm not Niall Ramsey's son. For twenty-eight years I've believed I was a Ramsey, but I'm not, and I never was.

He was an Englishman, with an English father, and not just *any* English father. No, he was the legitimate son of the Marquess of Huntington. The son of a man he'd never met, and couldn't imagine, and younger brother to the man who was standing before him now.

The moment had come. For the first time Lachlan wondered if it would be as hard for him to say these words aloud as it would be for Lord Huntington to hear them. What must it be like for him, to be one moment dancing a carefree quadrille with his wife, and in the next to find himself a brother to three strangers?

He cleared his throat. "I'm your younger brother. Not your half-brother, Lord Huntington. Just...your brother."

Lady Huntington gasped, but Lord Huntington only repeated faintly, "My brother?"

He was gaping at Lachlan in shock, unable to utter another word, and Lachlan's chest tightened. That baffled, lost look on Huntington's face... was that how *he'd* looked, the day he'd found out everything he'd believed to be true about himself and his family was nothing but a mountain of lies?

"I should have written, but I didn't know about you until a few weeks ago, when my mother..." Lachlan cleared his throat. "That is, *our* mother, confessed the truth, just before she died. I've brought letters that prove..."

Lachlan trailed off, his throat closing. Prove what? That they'd all been victims of a lie that had dragged out over decades?

A deafening silence fell over the room, and they might have sat there for hours, all of them staring stupidly at each other, if the old lady sitting beside Hyacinth Somerset hadn't broken the silence with a sudden, sharp outburst. "But this is outrageous! Brothers don't simply fall down from the sky, Mr. Ramsey, and drop without warning into the middle of a London ballroom!"

Ciaran's lips quirked, and he turned to offer her ladyship a mocking bow. "We came from Scotland, ma'am, by way of the Great North Road. The sky had nothing to do with it."

"I'm the younger son, with no claim to the Huntington title, or the fortune or properties. Isla's the youngest, our only sister, daughter to our mother and Niall Ramsey. Ciaran..." Lachlan swallowed the bitterness in his throat. "Ciaran's birth wasn't as tidy as Isla's, but our mother and Niall Ramsey *did* marry, as I've said. We'll leave it there."

No one in the room could possibly mistake his meaning, and another tense silence fell over them all. Even the old lady sitting next to Hyacinth Somerset didn't say a word, though she did take a healthy sniff from her smelling bottle.

The moment stretched on until Lachlan turned to Lady Huntington with an awkward bow. "I suppose this means you're my sister-in-law, Lady Huntington."

"Indeed it does." Ciaran bowed to Lady Huntington. "And Miss Hyacinth our sister-in-law of a sort, too. A large, happy family, and all of us overjoyed to be so, I'm sure. Pity, though, that business about Lachlan killing me." He turned to Hyacinth Somerset with a wicked grin. "I daresay you agree with me, Miss Somerset, when I say it's a deuced awkward thing, accusing your brother-in-law of murder."

Chapter Four

If Lord Huntington was about to throw the Ramseys onto their arses in the street, he'd better call his burliest footmen to do the job, because Ciaran wasn't likely to go quietly.

Lachlan, who was sprawled in a deep leather chair in his new brother's study, had opened his mouth to offer this advice when Lord Huntington turned abruptly away from the window, and fixed Lachlan with an intense hazel gaze that was at once both alien, and disturbingly familiar.

Lachlan recognized that gaze. He'd seen it hundreds of times before, staring out at him from his mirror. He and his new brother didn't look much alike, though. Not really. They were both large men, but Lord Huntington was fairer, his features smoother and more refined, and he looked like what he was—a marquess. He had a sort of easy aristocratic elegance that would forever elude a rough devil like Lachlan.

The eyes, though, the shifting shades of brown and green, each color fighting for supremacy—there was no mistaking the eyes.

They were their mother's eyes.

"What was she like?"

Lachlan jerked in surprise at the question. He'd been prepared for a flood of words to spew from his lordship's lips—words like *leave, and never return*—but not this.

Lord Huntington stood in front of the window, his hands braced on the sill behind him, waiting. He didn't clarify who "she" was, and Lachlan didn't ask him to. There was no need.

"She was…complicated." Even as he chose that word with care, Lachlan wasn't sure it was the truth. Maybe their mother had been simple enough, and it was only his feelings for her that were complicated. "You have no memory of her?"

"Hazy images, but not much else. I was very young when she left. I do remember she smelled sweet, like flowers. Or perhaps it was citrus. I couldn't say for certain."

"Orange blossoms." A faint smile curved Lachlan's mouth.

"Was that it?"

"Yes. Sweet, but with a tart edge to it. It suited her."

"I'll have to trust your opinion on that." Lord Huntington drew away from the window and wandered to the middle of the room, but once he was there, he seemed not to know what to do with himself, and he turned back to Lachlan. "I don't remember her voice, or much else about her, but I remember that scent." He paused, then, "The first year after she left, when I still believed she'd come home, I waited for her, every moment of every day. At night, I used to dream she'd come into my bedchamber, and tuck my blankets around me, but a dream was all it ever was. She never came."

"No." That one word wasn't enough, but neither would a thousand words be enough, so Lachlan kept quiet.

"I used to wish for siblings, too—brothers, or perhaps a younger sister or two. But my—*our*—father died when I was eight, and after that, well..." Lord Huntington shrugged. "There wasn't much point in wishing anymore. My childhood was a lonely one. It's odd now to discover that all those years I spent longing for siblings I had three of them, living just a few hundred miles north. I don't know...forgive me, Mr. Ramsey, but I don't know how to feel about that."

Lachlan tensed. For the past two days he, Ciaran and Isla had been staying in Grosvenor Square, at Lord and Lady Huntington's invitation. They'd been treated with careful courtesy during that time, but this...this wasn't distant politeness.

This was something else.

An apology, maybe, or an explanation.

A dismissal.

Whatever it was, Lord Huntington spoke like a man who'd made a decision. Either he'd accept the Ramseys into his family, or he'd tell them to leave, and never return. Lachlan had already made up his mind to accept whatever decision his lordship made, but it was difficult to sit here and wait while another man decided his family's fate.

After a long silence, Lord Huntington cleared his throat. "The papers you brought—the letters exchanged between our parents, the miniature of our mother, the timing of your birth...I believe you're telling me the truth,

Mr. Ramsey. But then, I would have believed it if you'd arrived here with a story and nothing else. Your sister's face is all the proof I need."

Without realizing he did it, Lachlan rose to his feet.

"I know the value of family, Mr. Ramsey, likely because I didn't have much of one growing up. I don't pretend it isn't damned odd for me to have ready-made brothers and a sister arrive on my doorstep like the morning post, but I've spoken to Lady Huntington, and we've agreed to acknowledge you all as our family."

Lachlan stood there stupidly, shock rendering him silent. It wasn't until Lord Huntington spoke that Lachlan understood he'd expected to be sent away, and warned to stay away. That this man would accept them into his home—into his *family*—with so little hesitation, when the friends they'd known their entire lives had tossed them aside without a backward glance, seemed nothing short of miraculous.

He stared at Lord Huntington—no, at his *brother*, and couldn't say a word.

Lord Huntington offered him a tentative smile. "Shall I call you Lord Lachlan now? It's your rightful title, as the second son of a marquess."

At last, Lachlan found his tongue. "Call me what you like, but I doubt I'll answer to Lord Lachlan."

Lord Huntington chuckled. "Perhaps just Lachlan then, at least for now, and you must call me Finn, as a brother would. I'm afraid I'll make an indifferent brother, however. I haven't the vaguest notion how to go about it."

One corner of Lachlan's lip quirked. "Mostly it's just brawling. At least, Ciaran and I spend more time bloodying each other's noses than anything else."

"Yes, I gathered that." Finn's voice was dry. "I'd like to have a word with you about that incident the other night, with Hyacinth."

Lachlan hid his grimace. He'd known the issue of Hyacinth Somerset's hysterical outburst would come up again. He wasn't looking forward to this, but the sooner they had it out, the sooner he could forget her entirely.

Finn waved Lachlan to a chair in front of the fire, and then crossed to a sideboard with a neat row of crystal decanters arranged across the top. "Hyacinth's…well, she's unusual."

Unusual. That was one word for it—a generous one, in Lachlan's opinion.

"My wife's parents died when Hyacinth was only fifteen years of age. The loss was sudden and tragic, and Hyacinth, being the youngest of the five sisters, had the hardest time of it. Lady Huntington tells me Hyacinth was painfully shy even before their deaths, but it grew worse afterwards. I'm afraid it grows more so every year."

"That's unfortunate." It was, and Lachlan felt a twinge of pity for Miss Somerset, but he'd just as soon stay clear of the girl before she succumbed to another hysterical fit, and accused him of something worse than murder.

Finn handed Lachlan a glass of Scotch, then settled into the chair across from him. "Yes, it is. I've never known a lady who suffers with such crippling anxiety as Hyacinth does. The *ton* gossips about her, about her timidity, which of course only makes it worse."

Lachlan took an uneasy swallow of his whiskey. He wasn't sure why Finn was telling him this, but he'd likely need more whiskey before it was over.

"I was stunned speechless when Hyacinth agreed to a season," Finn went on. "I never dared hope she'd venture into society, but it's the very thing she needs. There's a great deal more to Hyacinth than meets the eye—that is, one need only look at her face to see her sweetness, but she possesses a strength she's wholly unaware of."

Lachlan turned his glass in his hands. No doubt, the girl was sweet enough, but if she did have reserves of strength, she did a damn good job of hiding it.

"Unfortunately, my wife, Lady Dare and Lady Chase are far too overprotective of Hyacinth. They fuss over her for the most affectionate reasons, but they underestimate her, and Hyacinth doubts herself. I've spoken to Lady Huntington about it, but she insists Hyacinth is delicate, and her health is fragile. There's not a damn thing wrong with Hyacinth's health, or with Hyacinth herself, but I can't blame my wife for her concern. We never see our own family as clearly as others see them, do we?"

Lachlan thought of his mother, of all the secrets she'd kept—secrets he'd never guessed at. "No, we don't."

"Because of that incident at the ball, and the scandal that's sure to follow, her sisters and grandmother want to put an immediate end to Hyacinth's season. They intend to pack her off to Brighton for a restorative holiday."

Privately Lachlan thought it was just as well if Miss Somerset did go off to Brighton. Even without the scandal, odds were she wouldn't have made it through her season. "And you don't want her to go?"

Finn tossed the rest of his whiskey back. "No. I want her to see out her season, if only to prove to herself she can. What kind of life will she have if she runs away every time there's some sort of unpleasantness?"

That question cut closer to the bone than Lachlan liked, and he flinched away from the sharp prick of his conscience. "Order her to finish her season, then."

"That won't do. It will only make her miserable if I force her into it, and I don't wish to upset my wife, either, especially given her delicate condition. No, Hyacinth has to choose it herself." Finn leaned back in his chair, his empty glass dangling from his fingers, his eyes on Lachlan. "I did have one idea."

Ah. Here it was. "Which is?"

"What if our sister were to debut with her? It would be much easier for Hyacinth if she had a friend by her side, and Miss Ramsey—Isla—seems a sturdy, resolute sort of young lady. If Isla has a season, we may be able to persuade Hyacinth to join her."

Lachlan drained his whiskey to smother the immediate refusal that rushed to his lips. "Isla can't debut. All of London thinks her brother's a murderer."

Finn shrugged. "There are ways around that."

Lachlan gave an incredulous laugh. "Ways around a murder accusation?"

"A *false* murder accusation. I don't pretend it will be easy, but you forget I'm a marquess. We're permitted a certain amount of latitude with the *ton*. Isla is vivacious and beautiful, and she's a Huntington now, and a lady of fortune—"

"Not by English standards, she isn't."

Finn looked surprised. "What, do you suppose I won't dower her?"

"*Dower her?*" Lachlan stared at him in astonishment.

"She's my *sister*, Lachlan, just as she is yours. Of course, I'll settle money on her—on all of you, though we needn't discuss that now. But you sound as if you don't like the idea of Isla having a season."

"It's not that. I just…I never thought of it."

He'd never dreamed of it, more like. Never dared to.

Since they'd left Scotland, Isla didn't smile anymore. It had broken her heart when her dearest friends had turned their backs on her, and Lachlan hadn't been able to do a damn thing to help her. He could only watch while it happened, a bitter, helpless fury writhing in his chest.

But a season, and all it entailed—balls and gowns, dancing, perhaps a suitor, and even a marriage—he'd do whatever it took give Isla this chance to gain back everything she'd lost, even if it meant putting up with Hyacinth Somerset.

"I know how to manage the *ton*, Lachlan. I've been doing it all my life. You may trust me when I say we'll find a way around the scandal."

"I do." *As much as I trust anyone.* "As long as she's not scorned by the *ton*, I don't object to Isla having a debut."

"Excellent. Is there anything else I should know, before we send the young ladies off to wreak havoc on the hearts of every gentleman in London?"

There is.

A secret, buried deep—so deep it would stay buried unless Lachlan chose to drag it into the light.

If he'd ever owed the truth to anyone, he owed it to Finn, who'd brought them into his family without question, as if they belonged here.

Who'd treated him like a brother did.

The truth crept to the tip of his tongue, and he wanted to speak it into words, and be free of the burden of a secret he should never have vowed to keep, but as it hovered on the edge of his lips, his mother's warning rushed into his head.

The past must stay in the past...Isla and Ciaran will suffer...promise me, Lachlan.

"No, nothing."

And with those words, it wasn't his mother's secret any longer.

It was his now, and the lie tasted like ashes in his mouth.

* * * *

"Good afternoon, Miss Hyacinth! Have you come for your punishment?"

It was an unusually clear day for London in January, and Hyacinth had ventured into the gardens hoping for a quiet ramble to calm her nerves before the dreaded confrontation with Lachlan Ramsey, but she whirled at the sound of her name, and saw Isla and Ciaran Ramsey wandering toward her along one of the gravel pathways.

Ciaran snatched his hat off and waved it over his head, beckoning to her. "Come walk with us!"

Hyacinth blinked in surprise at the warm greeting, given that just two nights ago she'd falsely accused their brother of murder, but she made her way down the pathway, and caught up to them at the fountain in the center, where the walkways converged.

"Good afternoon, Miss Hyacinth. See, Isla? I told you she'd come. One can't hide from family forever, no matter how much they might wish to."

"Oh, no. I wasn't hiding, Mr. Ramsey. I was just, ah...well..."

She trailed off, her cheeks burning with embarrassment. Of course, she *had* been hiding. Judging by the teasing glint in Ciaran Ramsey's eyes, he knew it.

"You're a terrible liar, Miss Hyacinth. But come now, there's no need for such a furious blush. I'm only teasing. You looked so serious and earnest as you approached us, I couldn't resist."

"Oh." Hyacinth gave him a shy glance. Ciaran Ramsey was nearly as big as his brother, and the bruises still visible on his face made him look a bit sinister, but it was difficult to be afraid of a man with such a playful grin. "Well, then. I'm come to beg your pardon for my behavior the other night, and to take my punishment."

Ciaran's brow quirked with surprise. "Well, how gratifying to be administering a punishment at last, instead of receiving one. All right then, Miss Hyacinth, what would you like for your punishment?"

Hyacinth smiled. "If it's something I like, then it's not a punishment at all, is it?"

"Oh, right. Well, you see I'm not very good at this. Perhaps we'll just forego the punishment entirely, and simply start fresh, as if none of it happened."

Hyacinth curtsied. "Thank you. You're very kind."

Isla Ramsey's dark eyes twinkled with humor as she linked arms with Hyacinth. "I warn you, Miss Somerset, not to let down your guard. Ciaran can be charming when he wishes, but he's also a merciless tease."

"Oh, no. I'm sure Mr. Ramsey can't be so wicked as that."

Isla let out a short laugh. "Indeed he is. You don't have brothers, Miss Somerset, but you may trust me when I say they're all horrid, teasing things."

"All of them? Even your eldest brother?" Lachlan Ramsey hadn't struck Hyacinth as a carefree, lighthearted tease, but then she'd been wrong about him being a murderer. Perhaps she was wrong about this, too.

"Lachlan? Oh, Good Lord, no." Ciaran was loping along behind them, swinging his hat by the brim. "You see, Miss Somerset, teasing leads to smiling, and even—heaven forbid—laughter, and Lachlan doesn't do either of those things. He's more the grim, menacing sort of brother."

Menacing? Hyacinth choked back a surge of panic. She owed Lachlan Ramsey an apology, and she'd give him one, no matter that the thought of facing that black scowl made her quake in her slippers. "Is he…is Mr. Lachlan Ramsey about? I must offer my apologies to him, as well."

"Apologize, to Lachlan?" Ciaran gave a low whistle. "There's your punishment."

Hyacinth bit her lip. In truth, the only thing she wanted to offer Lachlan Ramsey was a wide berth, but she'd publically accused the man of a murder he didn't commit. It wasn't the sort of thing one could pretend hadn't happened. "It's not such a daunting task as that, is it?"

"No, no. Of course not." Miss Ramsey frowned at Ciaran. "Lachlan went riding, but he may be back by now. You could check the stables."

"Yes. I will. Thank you."

Hyacinth wandered off in the direction of the stables, her feet dragging with every step. Why did it have to be the stables? No one would hear her scream from *there*, and weren't there pitchforks in the stables?

"Good luck!"

Hyacinth turned back to see them waving gaily at her, but she couldn't help but notice Isla's brow was furrowed with concern, and Ciaran was fingering his black eye, as if he'd just recalled what Lachlan was capable of.

Hyacinth slipped as quietly as she could into the cool, dim interior of the stables. She'd far rather catch Lachlan by surprise than the other way around, but aside from the dust motes floating in the weak sunlight, the stables were empty.

Perhaps he'd already come and gone, or given up the idea of riding altogether. Well, it was an awful pity, but she *had* done her best to find him. She could always beg his pardon later, in the drawing room after dinner this evening, perhaps, when there were witnesses present—

"Riding out, Miss Somerset?"

Hyacinth was halfway through the stable door, mere feet away from a timely escape, but she whirled around at once to face the owner of that low, mocking voice. It had to be Lachlan—no one but a giant had a voice that deep—and the last thing she wanted was a giant sneaking up behind her in a dark barn.

"You forgot your riding habit." He came around to the front of the stables, a cloth in his hand, and a heavy saddle slung over one arm.

Hyacinth stared at him, a peculiar sensation fluttering in her belly. He wasn't wearing a hat or a coat—just a white linen shirt open at the neck, and pair of buckskin breeches so snug, she fancied a closer inspection would reveal…well, the sorts of masculine things a lady was obliged to overlook.

Not that she intended to get any closer.

Except she couldn't help but notice the dark bristles shadowing his cheeks and jaw, or the tousled mass of thick hair falling over his forehead. It was damp with sweat, and his shirt was so transparent she could see the muscles in his back ripple as he tossed the saddle onto a rack at the end of the front row of stalls, as if it weighed no more than a handkerchief.

Goodness. She'd never seen a more, ah…*manly* sort of man in her life. He put her in mind of a coiled spring just before it exploded into action. His entire body hummed with restlessness, and he looked as if every inch of him was about to burst through the seams of his clothing. He was all long legs and undulating, flexing bits—

"You're staring at me, Miss Somerset, as if I were the elephant at the Royal Menagerie."

The elephant? What nonsense. If he were anything, he'd be the Bengal lion, prowling about his cage, stalking his prey.

"Should I duck into one of the stalls?" he asked. "That way you could peer over the edge, and it would be more like the Menagerie."

Well. It seemed Lachlan Ramsey did know how to tease, despite what his brother had said. But this wasn't a friendly tease. He wasn't smiling, and there was more than a little mockery in his voice.

She jerked her gaze away from the hint of his chest revealed by the loose neck of his shirt. "No, I, ah—no, of course n-not. I didn't c-come to stare. I mean r-ride. I didn't come to *ride*. I w-was looking for y-you."

Hyacinth cringed as the words caught on her lips, then flushed with humiliation when they stumbled in fits and starts from her mouth. She didn't often stutter these days, but when she did, it was always at the worst possible moment.

If he noticed her embarrassment, he didn't show it. He simply stared at her, his face devoid of expression. "Well, what do you want?"

Hyacinth twisted her fingers in her skirts, flustered at his clipped tone. "Well, I-I thought I'd…t-t-that is, I just w-wanted to…" Dash it, must she stutter through the entire thing? Lachlan Ramsey no doubt already thought her a hysterical half-wit.

She drew a deep breath to calm herself, and get her mouth around her syllables. "I came to beg your pardon, for…"

She fell silent again, her mind going blank as she struggled to find a way to say it without inflaming the situation further. How did one apologize for such a thing?

I beg your pardon for my unjustified murder accusation? I regret I called you a killer in front of all of London?

Neither seemed quite the thing, so Hyacinth settled on the blandest words she could think of. "I apologize f-for the misunderstanding last night. I sincerely beg your pardon, Mr. Ramsey."

This was met with a long, tense silence, until at last, one of his eyebrows rose. "Misunderstanding? Is that what you'd call it?"

Dash it. She'd managed to spit out a word at last, and it was the wrong one. "Well, I thought—"

"I doubt the London gossips will call it a *misunderstanding*."

His voice was cold, inflectionless, but his hazel eyes were flickering with some sort of suppressed emotion, and she'd seen for herself what a formidable temper he had…

She edged closer to the stable door. "No, I'm afraid they won't, but—"

"No. When they repeat it to their friends—and they *will* repeat it—they'll call it an accusation. But call it a *misunderstanding*, if it comforts you."

Despite all appearances to the contrary, Hyacinth had a bit of a temper of her own. She never indulged it, of course—anger led to all sorts of unpleasantness—but a hint of irritation rippled up her spine at this cool speech.

He was awfully self-righteous for a man with a black eye.

The unfortunate truth was that Lachlan Ramsey *had* engaged in a bloody brawl in a public inn-yard, where anyone could have seen him. It was cursed bad luck that she'd been the one who had, but given those circumstances, her assumptions about him hadn't been entirely out of line. He wasn't, after all, completely innocent in this.

Still, it seemed wiser not to dwell on sensitive issues like truth and guilt while she was trapped in the stables alone with him. "I can assure you, Mr. Ramsey, nothing about this situation is comfortable for me, but—"

"Why not? All of London doesn't believe *you* to be a murderer."

"It wasn't *all* of London. Lady Atherton wasn't there, or Lord and Lady Herbert, or—"

"You managed to do enough damage, just the same," he interrupted, with another arch of that infuriating black eyebrow.

Hyacinth blew out a breath. "I realize that, and that's why I came to say—"

She didn't get any further, because he turned and strode away from her without another word. Hyacinth stood there, watching his broad back as he walked away, and tried to recall a time when she'd felt as utterly invisible as she did right now. It was as if he'd snapped his fingers, and she'd disappeared in a puff of smoke.

She should have been glad for it. She'd apologized, just as she'd intended, and she hadn't wept, or cast up her accounts, or fallen into a swoon. She hadn't done anything she need be embarrassed about, aside from the stammering.

All and all, it had gone far better than she'd dared hope.

Then why wasn't she flying out the stable doors, muttering prayers of thanks to heaven for granting her such an easy escape? Or perhaps the better question was, why was she going after Lachlan Ramsey, and stopping him with a hand on his forearm?

She didn't have time to answer these questions, because he whirled around at her touch, astonishment plain on his face. His hard muscles jerked under her fingertips, a trace of black hair tickled her palm, and for a moment, Hyacinth could only stare up him, strangely breathless.

"What the devil—" he began.

"Not *everyone* in London believes you a murderer, Mr. Ramsey. Finn doesn't believe it, and neither does Iris, or Lord and Lady Dare. Even my grandmother has admitted, albeit grudgingly, that she isn't quite ready to condemn you to the noose. Surely these are the people who truly matter?"

"What about you?" He took two long strides forward, until he was towering over her.

Hyacinth's hand dropped away, and every muscle in her body urged her to back up, or to flee, but some latent streak of stubbornness made her hold her ground. "Me? What about me?"

"Don't you matter?"

For the first time Hyacinth noticed his eyes were an unusual greenish brown color. Hazel, just like Finn's. "Of course I believe you innocent, Mr. Ramsey. How could I not? I think we can all agree your brother is very much alive."

Lachlan grunted. "For now he is."

For now? Oh, dear. Surely that was a joke? A nervous giggle escaped her, but he only stared down at her without a trace of humor in his hard face.

Hyacinth swallowed. "Yes, well….um, my point is, if you wish to take a place in London society, Finn and Iris will do whatever is necessary to see that it happens. As the Marquess and Marchioness of Huntington, they hold considerable influence over the *ton*."

"What about you?" He repeated a second time.

She snorted. "I hold no sway over the *ton* whatsoever, I'm afraid."

"I mean, Miss Somerset, what will *you* do to ensure I'm able to take a place in London society?"

Hyacinth blinked up at him. Was it possible he didn't understand of how little consequence she was? She would have thought it was obvious, but then he was new to London, and might not recognize social obscurity when he saw it. "When I said I regret my actions of the other night, I meant it, Mr. Ramsey. I wish to make whatever amends I can, but I've no power over the *ton*, despite my aristocratic connections. I'll be of very little use to you, I'm afraid."

Before she could say another word, the black scowl she recalled from the other night returned. "It's more convenient for you that way, I think."

Her mouth dropped open. "What in the world does that mean? It sounds as if you're accusing me of something."

His face hardened. "*Me*, accuse *you*? Is that a joke?"

"No! I don't…I only meant—"

"Don't trouble yourself about me, Miss Somerset. The best way for you to make amends is to stay away from me, before some other *misfortune* occurs. Now, is that all? Or do you have something else to say to me?"

"No." In fact, Hyacinth suddenly had quite a lot to say to him, and none of it pleasant, but of course she'd never *dare*—

"Good, because there's no point in arguing. You said yourself you'd be little help, and I agree."

Then again, perhaps she *did* dare, after all.

Hyacinth drew herself up to her full height, which was, admittedly, not quite as high as his shoulder, and met his cool gaze with a furious one of her own. "Is this how you accept a lady's apology, Mr. Ramsey? By insulting her?"

He shrugged. "I'm sorry you find the truth insulting, but that's nothing to do with me."

"Oh, you're a dreadful man!" She was so angry, she actually stamped her foot. "You were right the first time, Mr. Ramsey. You *do* belong in the Royal Menagerie. What a pity they already have—"

Oh, no. No, no, no. I can't say that.

She bit down hard on her tongue, and stopped herself just in time. And thank heaven for it, because what she'd been about to say…well, she couldn't say it.

No matter how much she wanted to.

And she *did* want to.

Badly.

Even now, the words were trying to leap off her tongue.

Lachlan Ramsey, who hadn't bothered to hide his boredom during her apology, was now looking down at her with a great deal more interest, his hazel eyes glittering. "I think you do have something else to say to me, after all. Go on, then. The Royal Menagerie already *what*?"

"They already have an ass!"

Oh, dear God.

Hyacinth slapped a hand over her mouth, but it was too late. She'd actually said it. She'd called Lachlan Ramsey an ass.

Dizziness threatened as the word echoed in her head, and her knees were quaking under her skirts as she waited to see what he'd do. Would he wrap his huge paws around her neck and squeeze the life out of her? Toss her over his shoulder and drop her into one of the horse stalls? Skewer her with a pitchfork?

He didn't do any of those things. Instead, something else happened. She watched, dumbfounded, as his black scowl faded, and one tiny twitch at a time, the corner of his mouth quirked.

Then the last thing in the world she would ever have expected to happen…

Happened.

Lachlan Ramsey smiled.

Chapter Five

"Did you just call me an ass?"

Lachlan crossed his arms over his chest and waited, but Miss Somerset's face had gone scarlet, and instead of answering, her pink lips opened and closed helplessly, like a fish trying to dislodge a hook.

For God's sake. At this rate, she'd swoon before she managed to squeak out a word. "Did you, or did you not, just call me an ass, Miss Somerset?" He thought she had, but it could have been his conscience shouting at him, since he had, in fact, been acting like an ass.

"Well, yes, I, ah, I did call you that, and I…" she swallowed. "Perhaps I shouldn't have been quite so…descriptive. I beg your—"

"No." He held up his hand, the half-smile still tugging at the corner of his lips. "Don't take it back *now*. You'll ruin it."

He'd watched her creep into the stables half an hour ago, looking like a guilty child due for a thrashing, and he'd known she'd come for him. He'd expected her to apologize, and she had. He'd expected that apology to be tedious, and it was. He'd expected at some point he'd get too close to her, or sigh too loudly, or blink too aggressively, and she'd scurry off like a terrified little mouse.

Instead, she'd surprised him. She was still here, and this apology was turning out to be far more interesting than he'd expected.

The lady had a temper. Oh, she kept it under tight control, but under that sweet angel's face, behind the blushes and timid stammering was a lady with the word "ass" just waiting to spring from her lips, and it hadn't taken much goading on his part to set it free.

Not so angelic, after all.

"What do you mean, I'll *ruin* it?" She braced her hands on her hips. "Do you mean to say you enjoy being called as ass?"

"No, but I like it when someone surprises me, and you're not the sort of lady I'd expect to call me an ass."

She let out a heavy sigh. "Do you expect *other* sorts of ladies to call you an ass, then?"

His lips twitched again. "Just Isla. She does so regularly."

"The more I hear of Miss Ramsey, the fonder I become of her." She paused, and her eyes narrowed suspiciously, as if she weren't quite sure she could trust his smile. "Well, then. Do you accept my apology?"

He couldn't very well refuse her. She was Lady Huntington's sister, and Finn had made it clear enough he wanted Hyacinth to finish her season. Lachlan still didn't think she'd make it through to the end—no doubt she'd take fright again, or fall into another swoon over some foolish thing, but he kept these thoughts to himself.

"Your apology and your offer to make amends." He bowed, then held out his hand to her, and after another brief hesitation, she rested the daintiest fingers he'd ever seen in his palm. His hand swallowed hers up, right down to her wrist, like a pelican scooping up an entire fish in a single gulp.

"Thank you. I'll make whatever amends I can, but as I said before—"

"Lachlan?" Ciaran wandered into the stables, squinting into the gloom. "Lord Huntington is...oh, there you are, Miss Somerset. Your sisters have been searching for you this half hour. Lord Huntington wishes to see everyone in the drawing room."

They followed Ciaran out, and when they entered the drawing room they found the entire family assembled, and Lady Huntington serving tea from a low table in front of the settee.

Lady Chase was sitting next to her, nibbling on a biscuit and fretting over someone named Lady Bagshot. "I'm telling you, that wretched woman will have tattled this business from one end of London to the other by now. Oh, what a pity you invited her to the ball at all, Iris! But I suppose it's too late to do anything about that *now*."

"I had to invite her, Grandmother. I couldn't snub her without risking a return snub, and you know all the *ton* clamors for an invitation to her annual ball."

"Yes, yes, I know." Lady Chase took up another biscuit from the tray and snapped its head off with one bite. "Though I don't see why. It's the dullest affair in London, and her refreshments are a disgrace. I've had better cake at Almack's, and as you know, their cake tastes like dry toast."

Lord Huntington entered the drawing room then. He closed the door behind him, took a place at the head of the room, and got right to the point. "I don't need to explain to any of you the change in our family's circumstances. We're all aware the Ramseys have come, and that they intend to make their home in England now."

Lachlan glanced around the room. He half-expected to see everyone rise up in open rebellion at the thought of welcoming the previous Marchioness of Huntington's scandalous offspring into their family. Despite Finn's assurances, Lachlan was still amazed his new brother intended to publicly acknowledge them. As for the rest of the family, he doubted they'd be overjoyed at the prospect of the scandal. After all, the Ramseys had no claim on Lord and Lady Dare, or on Lady Chase.

No one batted an eye. They sat quietly, munching their biscuits and sipping their tea, their attention on Finn as they waited for him to continue.

"There's a great deal that needs to be sorted out, of course, and it will take time, but there is one immediate question we must answer at once. What do we intend to do about Hyacinth's season?"

"I don't see what can be done," Lady Chase said, with an air of doom. "It's already caused an uproar, and soon all of London will have heard of it. Lady Bagshot was sitting right beside me when poor Hyacinth took such a fright, and you all know what an awful gossip she is."

"Now, Lady Chase," Finn said in a soothing tone. "It's not as bad as all that."

Lady Dare shook her head. "Bad enough. An unfounded murder accusation, Finn? A dramatic swoon in the middle of the ballroom, with all the *ton* looking on? I agree with Grandmother. I don't see how we recover from this."

Hyacinth dropped onto the settee, her shoulders slumped as if the weight of the scandal had just crashed down upon them. Whatever spirit she'd shown in the stables seemed to drain out of her, leaving her pale and deflated. "Dear God. It's a disaster, isn't it?"

Finn blew out a breath. "It's not a disaster unless we let it be so. You made a mistake, Hyacinth—an unfortunate one, yes, but a simple, forgivable mistake nonetheless. There may yet be a way to repair the damage."

Lady Chase snorted. "I've never known the *ton* to be very forgiving."

"How is it to be repaired, Finn?" Lady Huntington gave her husband a sharp look. "No, I think it would be best if you withdraw from your season at once, Hyacinth. The other night was…well, Violet and I are concerned the strain will be too much for you, and Grandmother thought—"

"I thought perhaps we'd take a holiday to Brighton instead." Lady Chase gave Hyacinth a bright smile. "You have delicate sensibilities, dear. Worry or anxiety of any sort may make you ill. Such a pity to see all those lovely gowns go to waste, but no matter. It's not to be thought of, when weighed against your health."

"Miss Somerset doesn't look ill." Lachlan's voice was harsher than he intended, but damn it, not half an hour ago Hyacinth Somerset had been well enough to call him an ass. It wasn't until she'd entered the room that she began to look like a crushed flower trapped under a muddy boot heel. If they kept on like this, they'd have her convinced she had the plague.

"She doesn't look ill to me, either. Quite the opposite," Ciaran said, with a flirtatious smile at Hyacinth.

Pink washed over her cheeks, and she looked away, as if she was flustered by Ciaran's compliment. Lachlan frowned. A beauty like that, and she didn't know how to flirt? For God's sake, her grandmother and sisters must keep her wrapped in cotton wool.

"She's not ill, only delicate, and easily overwrought." Lady Dare frowned at Ciaran. "It isn't good for her to remain in London at the mercy of all the gossips."

Overwrought, delicate, ill...

Lachlan rolled his eyes. Jesus, he'd never heard such nonsense in his life. "Surely Miss Somerset isn't as fragile as all that."

Lady Dare took Hyacinth's hand and cradled it gently in hers. "You did enjoy your holiday in Brighton last year, dear, and the sea air did you a world of good. You were so refreshed when you returned to London. Wouldn't you like to go again?"

"Well, of course Brighton is...that is, the sea air..." Hyacinth looked down at her hands. "It's just...I didn't expect much from my season, but I hadn't imagined it would be over in a single night."

Lachlan glanced from Lady Huntington to Lady Dare, and then to Lady Chase, but none of them seemed to notice Hyacinth was shrinking right before their very eyes. The more they fussed over her, the smaller she became, as if their suggestion she were ill was enough to make her believe it herself.

"But of course I'll go, if you all think it best," Hyacinth said at last, her eyes downcast.

"We do." Lady Dare breathed out a sigh of relief, and patted Hyacinth's hand. "And there's no reason why we can't revisit the idea of a season next year."

Next year? Lachlan restrained an impatient growl. Bloody nonsense. Finn was right. If Hyacinth didn't debut this year, she never would.

Finn cleared his throat. "Before you make a decision, Hyacinth, you should know Lachlan and I have agreed we'll bring Isla out this season."

Isla had remained quiet during the discussion about Brighton, but now she glanced up, and a smile lit her face. "A London season? Truly?"

"If you'd like it, then yes, of course." Finn looked pleased at her reaction. "We'll have a job managing the *ton*, but it will be a great deal easier if you and Hyacinth have each other for support."

"Oh!" Isla clapped her hands together with delight. "I should love that above all things! What fun we'd have, Miss Somerset!"

"I wouldn't suggest it if I didn't think you could manage it," Finn added gently to Hyacinth. "I don't say it won't be a challenge, but I've no doubt you have the strength to rise and meet it, especially if you have a friend by your side."

A tense silence descended on the room. Lady Dare and Lady Chase traded uneasy glances, and Lady Huntington was looking at her husband as if she wished to box his ears, but Lachlan only spared them the briefest glance.

He was watching Hyacinth.

A look of intense longing crossed her face, a look so poignant, so heartbreaking, it made his breath seize in his chest. She was frightened, yes—of the *ton* and the gossip, of the damage done by the scandal, and she was concerned she'd worry her sisters and grandmother by remaining in London—but even so, and despite her doubts about herself, a part of Hyacinth Somerset desperately wanted her season.

Then, in the next breath, the look of yearning was gone, and in its place was a blank face, one that gave nothing away. "I thank you, Finn, for the kind suggestion, but I think...I think I prefer to go to Brighton."

Finn's face fell. "Hyacinth—"

"It's for the best, Lord Huntington." Lady Chase levered herself up from the sofa with the help of her cane, and held out her hand for her granddaughter. "Well, come along, Hyacinth. You look fatigued. It's time we went home, my dear."

"Wait, Grandmother." Hyacinth ignored her grandmother's hand, and instead crossed the room to where Isla sat. "Forgive me, Miss Ramsey, for not joining you this season, but I hope you'll tell me how else I can help you before my grandmother and I leave for Brighton."

Lachlan could see Isla was disappointed, but she hid it under a smile. "How kind. I confess I'm a trifle apprehensive about a London season. I got a glimpse of the ladies' gowns when we passed by the ballroom the other night, and I already know mine won't do."

Hyacinth was quiet for a moment, her face thoughtful. "Perhaps all my gowns needn't go to waste, after all. Because of my grandmother's generosity, I have enough gowns squeezed into my closet to dress a dozen ladies for an entire season. I'm certain you'd find something there to suit you. We're close enough in size it won't take any time at all to have some of my gowns made over for you."

Isla's eyes went wide. "Oh no, I couldn't ask that of you."

Hyacinth smiled. "You didn't ask. I offered. Please do let me help you, Miss Ramsey. Nothing would make me happier."

"Why, how generous you are!"

Isla looked as if she wanted to say more, but Hyacinth's cheeks colored, and she hastily interrupted her. "Will you come to Bedford Square some afternoon this week? We'll send for Madame Bell, you can choose which gowns you like, and we'll have a fitting of sorts. You'll need a ball gown right away, because Lady Bagshot's ball is the week after next, and it's very grand, and..." Hyacinth trailed off, biting her lip. "Oh, dear. We haven't yet worked out how to secure the Ramseys an invitation to Lady Bagshot's ball, have we?"

Iris shook her head. "No, I'm afraid not. It's lovely of you to offer your gowns to Isla, Hyacinth, truly it is, but as of yet, she has no place to wear them. Even under the best of circumstances Isla's debut would be tricky, and these are not the best of circumstances."

A brief silence fell as they all considered this, then Lady Chase gave a great sniff. "What a pity it has to be Lady Bagshot, of all people."

"Indeed." Lady Dare seated herself on a sofa beside her husband. "But if Lady Bagshot snubs Isla, she won't be invited anywhere else. However we proceed, we'll have to prepare for gossip. God knows the *ton* is vicious when it comes to scandal."

"Not all of the *ton*," Finn said, with a calm sip of his tea.

Lady Chase snorted. "I hope you don't mean to try and persuade us Lady Bagshot isn't vicious. Why, I've known her for years, and she's always been as mean as a snake."

"No, she's vicious enough, but there are a few kind, decent souls to be found tucked into the corners of the English aristocracy. Among all of us, we know most of them. There's no way around the gossip, but it isn't as if we don't have any resources at our disposal." Finn looked around the room. "Dare. You know the Worthingtons fairly well, don't you?"

Nick nodded. "Andrew Worthington and I have known each other for years, and my aunt, Lady Westcott, is dear friends with his parents."

"Is Lady Atherton in town?" Finn turned to Lady Chase. "I understand she spends a good deal of time in Bath."

"She does, the poor dear. Ill health, you know. But she's well enough now, and in town for the remainder of the season."

Iris tapped her lip, thinking. "Lady Bagshot's ball is next week, and then Lord and Lady Hayhurst's ball is after that." Iris turned to Isla. "Lady Hayhurst is my friend, and a dear, kind thing. If I ask her to, I'm certain she'll invite you to her ball. That alone will go a long way toward ensuring your acceptance with the *ton.*"

"Well, that's one problem solved. Now if we can only get Lady Bagshot, as well as the Hayhursts." Lady Dare stirred three lumps of sugar into her tea, then set her spoon aside. "Hyacinth might be able to persuade her. She's always been rather a favorite of Lady Bagshot's."

"Yes, that's true. Lady Bagshot fancies herself a great judge of music, and admires Hyacinth's skill on the pianoforte." Lady Chase smiled proudly at her granddaughter. "You do play like an angel, dear. It's the one point on which Lady Bagshot and I agree."

"There it is, then. Miss Somerset will call on Lady Bagshot and influence her in the Ramseys' favor. Of course, you'll have to delay your trip to Brighton for a few days." Lachlan raised a meaningful eyebrow at Finn.

He caught on at once. "Brilliant idea, Lachlan. She'll receive *you,* Hyacinth, even if it's only to get the gossip firsthand. Do you suppose you can put off the trip to Brighton for a week or so? Do you feel well enough?"

Hyacinth gave her sisters an uncertain look. "I don't suppose an extra week in London will hasten my demise."

"I don't think—" Iris began.

Lachlan interrupted her, his gaze on Hyacinth. "You told me you wished to make amends, Miss Somerset. Here's your chance. Your gowns won't be of much use to Isla if she's not invited anywhere."

"And I daresay you're safe enough for a few more days. For the entire season, really," Finn added.

Hyacinth hesitated, then glanced at Isla with a shy smile. "Perhaps we could call on Lady Bagshot together, Miss Ramsey, and see if we can't win her over. It will help your cause a great deal if we can. Lady Bagshot is rather a favorite with the *ton.*"

"Nonsense. She's as dreadful an old dragon as you'll ever meet." Lady Chase pursed her lips. "But she *does* have a weakness for quiet, well-behaved young ladies."

"I suppose a few extra days won't do any harm," Iris admitted reluctantly. "Violet, you and Nick should call on the Worthingtons, and Grandmother, you must go see Lady Atherton. We'll have you all put it about the unfortunate, ah...*incident* the other night was a simple misunderstanding, and drop a hint or two about the Ramseys' relationship to Lord Huntington."

"Yes, that's very good. Oh, I do love it when a plan falls logically into place." Lady Dare rubbed her hands together.

Everyone began chattering about Lady Bagshot, and the Hayhursts' ball, and Lady Atherton's chest complaints, but Lachlan remained silent, his gaze on Hyacinth.

It was a few days' delay only. If he and Finn couldn't persuade her to go ahead with her season, Hyacinth Somerset would be off to Brighton with her grandmother before the ink dried on Lady Bagshot's ball invitation.

The thought bothered him more than it should.

The gowns—it was the damn gowns that had done it. What sort of lady offered all her pretty ball gowns to another lady she hardly knew, one who was going to debut in her place?

Hyacinth Somerset was kind. Truly kind, just as Finn had said she was. It wasn't right she should be left to languish on the sidelines, as if she were no more than a lonely spectator in her own life.

There was a brief lull in the conversation, and Lady Chase rose to her feet. "Come along, Hyacinth. I daresay you'd like a rest, wouldn't you? You look a bit pale. I hope you haven't exhausted yourself today."

Lachlan snapped back to attention just as Miss Somerset accepted her shawl from Lady Dare. She wrapped it around her shoulders, and tucked Lady Chase's hand into her elbow. "I'll see you soon, Miss Ramsey? Shall I send a note round once we've secured an appointment with the modiste, Madame Bell?"

Isla stood, curtsied to Lady Chase, and held out her hand to Hyacinth. "Yes, of course. I'm looking forward to it."

Before he knew what he intended to do, Lachlan jumped to his feet. "May I see you to your carriage?"

"Um...of course. Thank you, Mr. Ramsey." Miss Somerset looked surprised at his offer, but she took his arm and let him escort her out to the drive.

"Lady Chase." He bowed, then handed her into the carriage, and while the old lady fussed with the cushions and carriage rugs, he took Miss Somerset aside. "They don't have an ass at the Royal Menagerie."

Her cheeks flooded with color. "I—it was a figure of speech. I do beg your par—"

"No, don't beg my pardon. I've never been to the Royal Menagerie, but I've heard they have a Persian lioness. Have you seen her? Fiercely protective animals. Rather like brothers. If you did change your mind about your season, you'd have nothing to fear, Miss Somerset. Not from anyone."

She blinked. "Are you trying to say you'd protect me from the *ton*, Mr. Ramsey?"

"Just as I would Isla. As if you were my own sister. I won't let anyone hurt you."

"That's very..." She trailed off, as if she couldn't determine *what* that was. "But my sisters and grandmother wish me to go to Brighton. I doubt I'll change my mind."

"Pity." Lachlan didn't argue with her—not this time—but led her to the carriage, and handed her in. "I wish you a pleasant afternoon, Lady Chase. Miss Somerset? Enjoy your rest."

Chapter Six

"Tell me, Miss Somerset. How will you persuade Lady Bagshot I'm not a murderer?"

Lachlan Ramsey sat across from her in Lady Chase's carriage, his enormous hands folded over the head of his walking stick, doubt written in every line of his handsome face—

Handsome face?

Hyacinth blinked. Lachlan Ramsey was imposing, yes. Frightening, certainly. But handsome? Perhaps some ladies might think so—the sort of ladies who found a dark scowl attractive, for instance, but—

"You may be a favorite with her, but that alone won't be enough. You have less than half an hour today to make her invite us to her ball, reveal Lord Huntington is our brother, and persuade her I'm not a murderer."

Hyacinth twisted her hands in her lap and tried to breathe through her rising panic. How in the world would she manage to stammer her way through all of that without making a mess of it? The minute Lady Bagshot's beady eye was upon her, she was sure to collapse like a house of sand—

"Well, Miss Somerset?"

Hyacinth frowned at him. Was this why he'd insisted on accompanying her and Isla to Lady Bagshot's townhouse? So he could quiz her in the carriage, and then prevent them from making the call if he didn't care for her answers?

And he *didn't* care for them—that much was plain to see. The black scowl was already gathering on his brow like an incoming thunderstorm. "I, ah, thought I'd determine the best way to proceed once we arrived."

Lachlan drummed his fingers against the head of his walking stick, his face grim. "But what if you become...how did your sister put it? *Overwrought*? If you get nervous or hesitate, it could make things worse."

Hyacinth arched a brow. "Lady Bagshot thinks you're a murderer, Mr. Ramsey. I don't see how it could get any worse."

"It can always get worse." He shifted his attention to Isla, who sat next to Hyacinth. "This isn't a good idea."

Isla's mouth pinched with annoyance. "Nonsense. I trust Hyacinth. Stop teasing, Lachlan."

"We have no choice but to make the call, Mr. Ramsey." Hyacinth winced when her voice emerged in a timid squeak. Dash it, how could she sound so confident in her own head, but just like a mouse with a boot crushing its tail once the words left her lips?

Lachlan's dark gaze narrowed on her face, but whatever he saw there didn't seem to interest him, because his eyes flicked away again at once. "We should wait until Lady Huntington can do it."

Was that disdain curling his lower lip?

"Even Lady Chase might be a better choice," he muttered.

Not quietly enough, however, because Hyacinth heard him, and anger began to churn in her stomach. "My grandmother wouldn't make it past the butler, Mr. Ramsey. She and Lady Bagshot despise each other, and have for years."

"One of your sisters, then. They're both calm, steady sorts."

By that, Hyacinth supposed she was meant to infer she was hysterical and unsteady. But then Lachlan Ramsey certainly had reason to think so, didn't he? That pricked at her far more than it should, and for reasons she didn't understand. It wasn't, after all, as if everyone in London didn't share his opinion. Even *she* shared it, but somehow it niggled at her that *he* should find her lacking.

Well then, give him a reason to think otherwise.

She drew in a quick breath, and then turned away from the window to face him. "My family asked me to make this call for a reason, Mr. Ramsey. I'm her ladyship's favorite, and more likely than anyone else to be received by her."

He shrugged. "That makes sense. An arrogant countess like Lady Bagshot is far more likely to favor a quiet, accommodating young lady like yourself."

Hyacinth's teeth clenched. "I didn't become Lady Bagshot's favorite by being quiet and accommodating. I became her favorite because I know how to manage her. That's one advantage to being quiet, Mr. Ramsey.

I'm not so preoccupied telling everyone else how to behave that I'm too busy to listen."

Isla laughed. "Bravo, Hyacinth! Well said."

Hyacinth smiled at her, then darted a look at Lachlan Ramsey to see how he'd taken this set down. She was rather proud of it, really. It wasn't every day she managed to put a short-tempered giant in his place.

His dark brows lowered, and the scowl his brow had only hinted at earlier had crept over the rest of his face. He might have looked menacing, indeed, but for the hint of appreciation in his eyes.

"Very well said. We'll see soon enough if your managing skills are as sharp as your tongue."

Hyacinth only raised her chin in reply, but underneath her cloak, she crossed her fingers.

* * * *

"Her ladyship isn't receiving calls today, Miss Somerset."

Lady Bagshot's butler, Forbes, peered down his long nose at Hyacinth without a flicker of recognition on his face, despite the fact she'd faithfully called on Lady Bagshot once a week since last spring.

"Not at home?" It was nonsense, of course. Lady Bagshot was *always* at home. The *ton* brought the choicest gossip to her doorstep every day during calling hours. There wasn't a chance her ladyship would risk missing a single morsel.

Forbes shoved the silver tray under their noses. "As I said, Miss Somerset. Would you care to leave your cards?"

Hyacinth pressed her lips together to smother a sharp retort. Lady Bagshot *was* at home. Even now, the bothersome old thing was likely listening to this very conversation through a crack in her drawing room door.

Hyacinth tried to force a reassuring smile for Isla's sake, but this didn't look at all promising. Lady Bagshot had never before refused to receive her. That she would do so now could only mean one thing.

She'd already made up her mind about the scandal, the Ramseys, and Hyacinth herself, and her friends would follow her ladyship's lead, just as they always did. Once Lady Bagshot condemned you, social ruin was the inevitable result, and her ladyship never offered second chances, not unless...

Not unless the gossip was so delicious she simply couldn't resist.

Hyacinth's heart started to pound as a terribly foolish, but undeniably ingenious idea began to take root in her mind.

No, it was far too risky. She'd never pull it off. It would backfire and explode right in her face, and she wasn't a lady who enjoyed explosions. Or risk.

Then again, after that speech she'd made about her grandmother never getting past Lady Bagshot's butler, did she really want to slink back to the carriage and admit to Lachlan Ramsey *she* couldn't get past Lady Bagshot's butler, either?

No. Almost anything was preferable to *that*.

The idea began to sound more and more plausible as she allowed it to take up space in her head, and really, what other choice did they have at this point? She could tackle Forbes about the knees and storm Lady Bagshot's drawing room, or she could offer up the tastiest morsel of gossip in London to her ladyship, and see if that wouldn't get them through the door.

How fortunate the tastiest morsel in London just happened to be waiting in their carriage.

"No, we won't leave our cards. Thank you, Forbes. Come, Miss Ramsey." Hyacinth gave the butler a pleasant smile, then drew Isla's hand through her elbow and led her down the steps.

"Oh, dear. I don't suppose that was a good sign, was it?" Isla glanced back at Lady Bagshot's door with a forlorn sigh. "Well, perhaps Lord and Lady Huntington will have better success with the Hayhurst's."

"Oh, no worries there. They'll have success. Iris and Lady Hayhurst have been friends since we came to London. But I'm not quite ready to give up on Lady Bagshot yet." They'd reached the street, but Hyacinth motioned for the driver to remain on the box, and opened the door to the carriage. "Mr. Ramsey. We'll need you to come with us to call on Lady Bagshot."

Both Lachlan and Isla looked at her as if she'd lost her wits.

"Have you gone mad? Lachlan can't pay calls, he's…well, everyone thinks he's…" Isla darted a look at Hyacinth, bit her lip, and trailed off into silence.

"Everyone in London think I'm a murderer," Lachlan said, his tone matter-of-fact. "Or have you forgotten?"

Hyacinth's face heated at the reminder. "No, and I'm not likely to, but Mr. Ramsey's reputation for, um…lawlessness is precisely what will get us through the door."

Lachlan pinched the bridge of his nose between his fingers, as if she were giving him a headache. "Does Lady Bagshot regularly welcome murderers into her drawing room?"

"No, but only because no murderers ever call on her. Don't you see? It's easy enough for Lady Bagshot to turn Isla and me away, but she'll never be able to resist the chance to entertain *you*, Mr. Ramsey. Why, you're London's most notorious gentleman at the moment."

"Not by choice."

"Well, no," Hyacinth admitted. "But that's neither here nor there. Perhaps you need to know Lady Bagshot as I do to understand, but you may trust me when I say she loves gossip above all things. Do you suppose she'll give up the chance to be the first lady in London to get the story from the so-called murderer's own lips? She'll be crowing about it in every drawing room in London."

Lachlan gave her a long, hard look, as if he'd never seen her before now. "That's diabolical, Miss Somerset. I wouldn't have guessed you had such a fiendish side. What other surprises are you hiding under that angelic face?"

If he'd said the word "angelic" with even a hint of admiration it likely would have tied Hyacinth's tongue for a week, but he sounded more suspicious than appreciative, and since she wasn't certain if it were an accusation or a compliment, she decided to ignore it. "Will you come?"

"Arrogant countesses, gossip, ball invitations." He slid across the seat with a sigh, stepped onto the street, and closed the carriage door behind him. "It's tedious, being a murderer."

Hyacinth's lips quirked. "If all goes well, you won't have to be one for much longer."

As they made their way back down the street toward Lady Bagshot's townhouse, Hyacinth couldn't help but think he looked...oh, not like a murderer, of course, but his was an intimidating figure. He was so large and broad, and everything about him spoke of barely leashed power. His enormous hand on the head of his walking stick, the way he strode down the street—even his dark cloak billowed behind him with authority.

Lachlan Ramsey wasn't a murderer, but Lady Bagshot's butler, Forbes didn't know that, and when he opened the door to them the second time and got a look at Mr. Ramsey, he blanched.

"Good afternoon, Forbes." Hyacinth gave no indication she and Isla had been here not five minutes earlier, but offered only a bland smile. "Miss Somerset, Miss Ramsey, and Mr. *Lachlan Ramsey* to see Lady Bagshot."

There was no sign of the silver tray this time. Forbes scurried off down the hallway toward the drawing room as if Prinny himself were standing at the door.

Forbes was gone for quite a while, and Hyacinth held her breath and crossed her fingers the entire time. If this didn't work—if Lady Bagshot refused to see them—then there was an end to Isla's season. If her chances should be ruined, it would be Hyacinth's fault, and—

"Lady Bagshot is pleased to see you."

Oh, bless you, Lady Bagshot, you incorrigible gossip!

As Forbes took their wraps and led them down the hall, Hyacinth released the breath she'd been holding in a silent sigh. They'd made it as far as the drawing room, but that was only the outermost circle of these particular circles of hell. Limbo, as it were. She'd have to handle the situation with the utmost care if she intended to get any further—

"Miss Somerset. How delightful to see you. Why, I don't believe I've ever seen you look so well."

Hyacinth resisted the urge to point out Lady Bagshot wasn't looking at her at all, but at Lachlan Ramsey, her beady eyes wide open with horrified relish. Instead, Hyacinth bit her tongue, and offered her ladyship a polite smile. "Good afternoon, my lady. How kind you are."

Lady Bagshot dragged her gaze to Hyacinth's face with an effort. "Yes, well, I was terribly concerned for you, after that unfortunate incident at Lord and Lady Huntington's ball. Such a dreadful business! Why, I can't imagine what it all meant, but you're very kind, my dear, to come and tell me all about it, and reassure me."

Hyacinth's smile remained fixed to her face, but she felt it growing a bit brittle around the edges. Lady Bagshot intended to have the whole story before they left her drawing room, no matter how unsubtle she had to be to get it. That was how the *ton* worked. Lady Bagshot had permitted them to enter, and now it was Hyacinth's turn to uphold her end of the bargain.

"But then you've always been a favorite of mine, as you well know, dear," Lady Bagshot added, her avid gaze darting between Isla and Lachlan.

"You've always paid me that compliment, my lady, and that's why I've come straight to you. I haven't called on a single soul since that ball, because I knew I could trust no one but you with the *true story.*"

Hyacinth hid her smile as Lady Bagshot let out a delighted little gasp. Yes, that was very good. Flattery, followed at once by the promise of exclusive gossip. Unless she missed her mark, it was the perfect approach to take with Lady Bagshot.

She hadn't missed her mark. Her ladyship's eyes were already gleaming with greedy anticipation.

"Oh my, yes, my dear," Lady Bagshot breathed. "I won't repeat a word of it to anyone. As you know, I'm the very soul of discretion."

"I do know that, my lady. May I present my friends? But oh, dear, I'm afraid I've…well, perhaps I've mislead you, because they're really not my *friends* at all. They're much more than that. They're my *family.*"

Hyacinth lowered her eyes with becoming confusion, but she peeked through her lashes at Lady Bagshot, and saw the final word of that sentence had had just the effect she wished for.

Lady Bagshot's eyes and mouth went wide, and she patted her fingertips rapidly against her chest. "Family? My dear Miss Somerset, did you say *family?*"

"I did, indeed. That is, they're not my direct family, but my brother-in-law, Lord Huntington's family. Lady Bagshot, may I present Miss Ramsey, and Mr. Lachlan Ramsey, Lord Huntington's sister and brother? They've another brother, as well—Mr. Ciaran Ramsey—but he and Lord and Lady Huntington are calling on Lady Hayhurst this afternoon."

"Sister and…" Lady Bagshot clutched at the arms of her chair, breathless with ecstasy. And no wonder. This was far better than just a plain murderer. A brother and sister, popping up out of nowhere? The brother and sister of the Marquess of Huntington, no less? Why, there were bound to be all sorts unsavory details tied up in this business. Secrets, lies, adultery, and—if London was lucky—the stain of illegitimacy.

"Brother, my lady. I'm Lord Huntington's younger brother."

Lachlan stepped forward and bowed with surprising smoothness over Lady Bagshot's hand. His mouth was tight, and Hyacinth could see he was disgusted by the whole business, but he held himself carefully in check, and Lady Bagshot didn't seem to notice.

"Mr. Ramsey. My goodness." Lady Bagshot gaped up at Lachlan as if she'd never seen anything like him before. "That is, I'm pleased to make your acquaintance, Mr. Ramsey, and Miss Ramsey." Lady Bagshot nodded at Isla. "Well. Lord Huntington's brother and sister. Well, my heavens, how extraordinary. Was Lord Huntington expecting your arrival in London?"

"He was not," Hyacinth said, before Lachlan or Isla could say a word. "It's all been quite a surprise, but Lord Huntington couldn't be more pleased by it, and of course Lady Chase, and Lord and Lady Dare and I are equally delighted to welcome the Ramseys into our family."

Hyacinth paused to let Lady Bagshot absorb her meaning. *My entire family intends to support the Ramseys.*

"I see. Well, how…wonderful for you all."

Hyacinth allowed herself just the tiniest breath then—just a small sip of oxygen to calm her pounding heart.

There. That part was done.

When Lady Bagshot carried this tale into the next drawing room, she'd be certain to make it clear the Ramseys were not without friends in

London. If the *ton* intended to cut the Ramseys, they'd also have to cut the Huntingtons, the Dares, Lady Chase, and all their friends, as well.

"But there's something I still don't understand, Miss Somerset." Lady Bagshot arched an eyebrow at Hyacinth. "Surely Lord Huntington's own brother isn't a murderer?"

Hyacinth hid her hands in her skirts to cover their trembling. This part was a trifle more difficult to explain. "Mr. Ramsey, a murderer? Oh, no, my lady. Of course not. That was an unfortunate—"

"Because I distinctly recall you accusing him of that crime, my dear. I was sitting right next to Lady Chase when Mr. Ramsey approached you, and I heard every word that passed between you. I hope you don't mean to say I can't trust the evidence of my own ears?"

Hyacinth glanced at Lachlan Ramsey, but he simply raised one dark eyebrow at her, as if he were as curious as Lady Bagshot to hear her explanation.

"N-no. As I-I said, it was an unfortunate m-m-mistake on m-my part—"

"Mistake? My dear Miss Somerset, how in the world could you possibly mistake an innocent man for a murderer?" Lady Bagshot sat back, her lips curling with satisfaction.

Once again, Hyacinth caught herself glancing at the Ramseys. Isla slid to the edge of her seat, her expression anxious, and Lachlan...

He'd thrown an arm over the back of the settee, crossed one leg over his knee, and was casually examining the tip of his boot, but his jaw was tense, and Hyacinth knew he was listening intently to every word.

"A c-curious series of events led to my m-mistake. A few nights before the ball, I happened to witness a...well, I beg your pardon, Lady Bagshot, but there's no other way to say this. I witnessed a violent brawl at an inn on the way back to London from Huntington Lodge. One of the men was badly beaten."

"My dear, how shocking!"

"It was, especially for a lady like myself—that is, a lady with delicate nerves." As she spoke, Hyacinth's voice grew stronger. "I was very upset by it. It was still much on my mind the night of the ball, and when Mr. Ramsey approached me—I hadn't yet met him at that time, and didn't know his connection to Lord Huntington—I made a dreadful mistake and mistook him for the man I'd seen at the inn several nights before. Their countenances are similar, you see, though I confess not so similar it justifies my error."

This explanation was met with a long silence while Lady Bagshot regarded Hyacinth with narrow-eyed suspicion. It was plain she didn't entirely believe the tale, but it wasn't so far out of probability she could challenge it outright.

At last, she gave a reluctant nod. "Well, that is a rather...*curious* series of events, isn't it, my dear?"

"Yes. You can't know how deeply I regret it, my lady."

"I should say so." Lady Bagshot turned to Lachlan. "Well, Mr. Ramsey. I'm very sorry our dear Miss Somerset should have made such a grievous error, but she's always been a bit high strung, I'm afraid."

Lachlan was staring at Hyacinth with an unreadable expression, but now he turned and nodded to Lady Bagshot. "You're very kind, my lady."

Lady Bagshot rattled on for another five minutes about their common acquaintances in London, dropping bits of gossip here and there like a trail of breadcrumbs, but Hyacinth had said what she'd come to say, and she and the Ramseys took their leave soon afterwards.

Isla chatted happily away on the drive from Lady Bagshot's back to Grosvenor Square, prattling about how well Hyacinth had managed her ladyship, and making plans for the Hayhursts' ball, but Lachlan only nodded now and again in reply.

Hyacinth didn't say a word, but kept her face turned toward the glass, and watched the London streets pass by her window, her heart still pounding.

She could scarcely believe how well she'd done. Oh, she didn't fool herself into thinking this would put an end to the gossip. The *ton* would continue to speculate, but she'd explained her actions, made her family's position regarding the Ramseys perfectly clear, and discouraged further questions.

It just might do.

"Oh, look! Lord and Lady Huntington are back." Isla nodded at their carriage, which was sitting in the drive. "Shall we go find Ciaran, Hyacinth, and tell him what happened with Lady Bagshot? He'll laugh, of course, and poke fun at us, but he'll like it."

Isla didn't wait for an answer, but leapt from the carriage as soon as it stopped, and ran across the drive toward the house. Hyacinth slid across the seat, intending to follow her, but Lachlan Ramsey stopped her with a hand on her arm.

"Wait. I want to talk to you, Miss Somerset."

Hyacinth glanced back at him. Her gaze caught on his hard mouth, on the hazel gleam of his eyes, and sudden heat washed over her, leaving flushed, prickling skin in its wake. His gaze followed the pink wave over her cheeks and down her throat, his eyes darkening as they drifted over her neck.

A strange warmth pooled in Hyacinth's belly, part alarm, and part... well, she didn't know what, but she was quite sure it wasn't proper. She snatched her arm away, suddenly panicked. "Can't it wait? I...I'm f-fatigued, Mr. Ramsey."

"It won't take long." He didn't attempt to touch her again, but he studied her so intently he may as well have slid his fingertips over her skin.

"I beg your pardon," he murmured at last. "You told me you knew how to manage Lady Bagshot, and you did. It was cleverly done. Masterful, even."

Hyacinth's eyes went wide. She hadn't expected an apology from Lachlan Ramsey, but then, was it really an apology? It sounded more like a scold disguised as an apology. "I, ah...well, thank you."

I think.

"Now, if you'll excuse me—"

"No." He shifted slightly, so she'd have to brush against him if she wished to exit the carriage. "Not yet." His voice had dropped to a murmur, as if were sharing a secret with her, or coaxing her to share one with him. "You're not delicate, Miss Somerset. Shy, yes, and timid on occasion, but you're stronger than your family thinks you are. Stay in London, and finish your season. Your health isn't at risk. You don't need to be shuffled off to Brighton, and you know it, don't you?"

Hyacinth stared into his burning eyes, and a nameless fear clutched at her throat. "Do you pretend to know more about me than my own family? We've only just met. You don't...you d-don't know anything a-about me."

She jerked her gaze from his, and reached for the door latch. She was getting out of this carriage, even if she had to crawl over his lap to do it—

"You lied to Lady Bagshot." He caught her wrist, and this time, he didn't let go. "You told her you made a mistake about the man you saw that night at the inn, but we both know you didn't. You took all the blame onto yourself, instead of telling her the truth about my fight with Ciaran."

He wasn't holding her tightly. On the contrary, his huge hands were careful, his thick fingers gentle, but the warmth of his skin against hers was so distracting, she wished he'd squeeze her hard, and remind her who he was. "Yes."

"Why?"

"That fight would do you no credit with the *ton*, Mr. Ramsey." She risked a glance at his face, but her gaze skittered away the moment she met his eyes. "And because I deserve the blame. This whole mess is my fault."

"Not just yours. Don't...don't *ever* sacrifice yourself for me again, Hyacinth."

His words were harsh, but there was a pleading look on his face she'd never seen before. The way he uttered her name—in that low, hoarse voice—sent another unexpected rush of heat through her.

And with it, a question she hadn't allowed herself to ask.

Did I do it for him?

That lie she'd told Lady Bagshot—had she told it for *him*?

"I didn't. I—I wouldn't." She swallowed. "I did it for Isla."

He didn't reply, but his gaze dropped to her hand. His eyelids went heavy over his dark eyes, and as if he were in a trance, he leaned forward and brushed his fingertips across the pale skin of her wrist, then lower, stroking over the sensitive flesh of her palm.

The heat that had been gathering in her belly forked into a streak of lightning, and struck straight at her core. Hyacinth gasped, and snatched her hand away. She fumbled for the door latch, and this time he let her go.

But as she scrambled out of the carriage and ran for the house, her hand closed into a fist, to keep the memory of his touch tight against her palm.

Chapter Seven

Lachlan had made two discoveries this afternoon.

The first was that Hyacinth Somerset had the softest skin he'd ever touched. He didn't know why this surprised him. He had only to look at her hands; at that fine tracing of blue veins and those long, delicate fingers to know her skin would be nothing less than perfection.

He turned over his hand and studied his own fingers, but they were the same blunt, rough, coarse things they'd always been. He'd half-expected to find she'd left some mark on him—some imprint or evidence to prove that glide of warm satin under his fingertips had been real, and not just his imagination.

There was nothing, but she *had* left something else behind.

Questions.

He'd seen a hint of her temper in the stables the other day when she'd called him an ass, but he'd thought it was a thing of the moment only, a brief flare of courage that would vanish as quickly as it appeared.

He'd been wrong.

Underneath that delicate skin, that angel's face and those downcast eyes, she was hiding another lady—one of great cleverness and conviction, with a thread of steel in her spine, and a devil of a sharp tongue.

He liked it. He liked *her*.

That was his second discovery this afternoon.

Finn had insisted there was a great deal more to her than anyone suspected, but Lachlan had shrugged this off as the ramblings of a fond brother-in-law. She was a sweet lass, and she'd been kind to his sister, but Lachlan had been relieved when she'd refused Finn's offer to continue with her season.

Hyacinth Somerset was no match for the English *ton*. The sooner Lady Chase took her off to Brighton, the better.

Or so he'd thought, until this afternoon.

Even getting access to Lady Bagshot had been a devil of a thing, but it was nothing compared to Miss Somerset's performance once they'd gained the drawing room. She'd doled out the gossip to Lady Bagshot the way a nun deals out bowls of gruel to her orphan charges. Stingily, careful to stretch every meagre spoonful to feed as many gaping mouths as possible.

To make it count.

Lady Bagshot had swallowed every drop, and the old lady would no doubt cast it back up again, right into the *ton*'s ears, just as Miss Somerset meant her to.

Damned if he saw any sign of the "delicate nerves" he kept hearing about.

That lie she'd told, about his fight with Ciaran? If he'd known she intended to lie he'd have put a stop to it, but he'd never imagined she'd put her own neck on the block to protect a rough devil like him—

"Lachlan! For goodness' sakes, why are you sitting alone in the carriage, talking to yourself?" Isla was peering at him through the carriage window. "Come inside. Lord Huntington has called us all in."

Once again, they found the party assembled in the drawing room.

"Well?" Lachlan asked Ciaran, as he settled beside him on the settee. "Did you get the invitation from Lady Hayhurst?"

Ciaran rolled his eyes, as if it were a foolish question. "Of course. You forget how charming I can be, Lach. Lady Hayhurst was quite taken with me."

Lachlan suspected their success had more to do with Lady Huntington than Ciaran, but he didn't bother to argue the point. They'd gotten both the invitations they needed, and with it a chance at a successful London season for Isla. That was all that mattered. Lachlan glanced at his sister's glowing face, and for the first time since they'd left Scotland, a glimmer of hope rose in his chest.

She might yet get all she ever wanted—all she deserved.

Now if he could only find a way to help Ciaran. He didn't have much hope his brother would fall in love again—not after his bitter disappointment with Isobel Campbell—but there were many pretty girls in London. Maybe one of them would catch Ciaran's eye this season—

"Lord and Lady Dare are occupied with a messenger from Ashdown Park at the moment," Finn said, hurrying into the room. "But they've assured me the Worthingtons have agreed to throw their support behind the Ramseys. How did you do with Lady Atherton, Lady Chase?"

"Well, I won't pretend Lady Atherton wasn't shocked by the rumors she'd heard, but we've been friends for years now, and she wouldn't dream of denying any request of *mine*. She assures me she'll be pleased to make the Ramseys acquaintance."

Finn looked relieved. "That's very good, my lady. What of Lady Bagshot, Hyacinth?"

"Yes, tell us how you managed the old dragon." Ciaran grinned at Miss Somerset. "Isla says you prodded and squeezed until she finally spat out an invitation."

"Mr. Ciaran Ramsey, your manners leave a great deal to be desired." Lady Chase attempted to turn her most severe frown on Ciaran, but she couldn't quite hide her glee at hearing her nemesis maligned.

Ciaran's grin widened. "Beg pardon, my lady."

"Humph. Still, Lady Bagshot *is* our greatest concern. How did she behave, Hyacinth? I daresay she refused to receive you."

"No." Hyacinth shook her head. "She received us, and she was…quite gracious."

Lachlan's head snapped up at this brazen lie. Lady Bagshot *had* refused their call, and when she'd admitted them at last, she'd been about as gracious as a Seven Dials cutpurse.

Lachlan scowled at Hyacinth, but she avoided his gaze.

Lady Chase, however, was as skeptical of this story as Lachlan, and she didn't hesitate to say so. "Gracious? Why, that woman's never been gracious about anything in her life. I don't believe a word of it."

"Well, perhaps I should say she was as gracious as Lady Bagshot ever is. She'll spend the next week spreading gossip about us all over London, of course, but that was to be expected, and at least now, she'll repeat our preferred version of events. More or less."

"Oh, yes!" Isla beamed at Miss Somerset. "Hyacinth was ever so clever about it all. She had Lady Bagshot right on the edge of her chair. At one point I thought her ladyship was going to have an apoplexy from the suspense."

Lady Huntington laughed. "Hyacinth's very good at managing Lady Bagshot. I don't know how you do it, Hyacinth. She's an awful old thing, but somehow you always contrive to get around her."

Lady Chase gave her skirts a sharp tug. "Why you can't contrive to give her a *real* apoplexy, Hyacinth, I'll never know. I assure you all of London would thank you for it."

Lachlan said nothing, but he watched Miss Somerset, curious to see what she'd do as they all sang her praises. Her cheeks flushed, and she looked increasingly nervous with every compliment, until at last she interrupted them in a high, thin voice.

"Is it warm in here?"

Lady Chase turned to her granddaughter, noticed her change in color, and began at once to fuss over her. "Are you overwarm, child? I hope you aren't getting a fever. Oh, dear. You're bound to be weakened after that swoon the other night."

Lady Huntington rushed to put a screen in front of the fire, to divert the heat away from her sister. "There. Is that better? It *is* rather close in here."

"I'm fine, really. Just a trifle warm—"

"Let me just take your shawl." Lady Huntington drew the shawl off her sister's shoulders. "There. Just a bit of air, I think. Tell me if you feel at all chilled, Hyacinth."

Lachlan watched this little drama unfold with tight lips. It was plain to see Miss Somerset's family cared deeply for her. As they scurried about to make her comfortable, their faces were twisted with a tender anxiety that was difficult to witness.

And yet...

Miss Somerset was a trifle warm, nothing more. What would they do if she took a chill? Set the sofa ablaze?

Lachlan glanced at Finn. He seemed to understand exactly what Lachlan was thinking, and raised an eloquent eyebrow at him.

Lachlan let his gaze drift back to Miss Somerset. Damn it, not one hour ago she'd played Lady Bagshot like a virtuoso plays a violin. She knew just how to pluck every string, coax every note, but here she was now, acting as if she were a porcelain vase about to tip sideways and shatter onto the floor.

It was the columns all over again.

The first time he'd seen her, she'd been tucked out of sight behind that column in Lord Huntington's ballroom. Her gown, her hair, and her behavior that evening—she'd been doing everything she could to go unnoticed.

She'd been hiding, and she was doing it again, right now. Hiding her cleverness. As soon as they thought she might be feverish, her family had forgotten all about her triumph with Lady Bagshot.

Being underestimated provided a certain paltry freedom, he supposed. No one expected much of an invalid.

But every escape came with a price.

Did she even know she was paying it? Did she realize the light in her face grew dim, and then dimmer still as she sat quietly in the midst of all the fuss surrounding her? With every ray that was extinguished, Lachlan's chest grew tighter and tighter, until he couldn't stand to watch another moment of it. "You mentioned something about your gowns the other day, Miss Somerset," he blurted, his voice louder than he'd intended.

She turned to him in surprise. "Oh, yes. Thank you, Mr. Ramsey. I thought I'd...yes, please, Iris, I'll have my shawl back."

Hyacinth let Lady Huntington drape the shawl about her shoulders, then turned to Isla with one of her shy smiles. "We have just over a week before Lady Bagshot's ball. We'll have to go through my gowns, find those that flatter you, and have them altered to fit you. Do you suppose we can have Madame Bell in this week, grandmother?"

"Yes, I daresay she'll come on short notice. It's lovely of you, dear, to offer your gowns to Miss Ramsey." Lady Chase patted Hyacinth's hand. "You're a good girl."

Lachlan's teeth clenched. Oh, Miss Somerset was *good*, all right—as good at managing her grandmother as she was Lady Bagshot. Good at managing everyone, in fact.

"Shall we go upstairs and see if any of your own gowns will do for the season, Miss Ramsey? It will help us to decide what you still need. Iris, you'll come up too, won't you?"

"Yes, of course." Lady Huntington gave her husband's hand an affectionate squeeze, then rose from the settee to follow them.

But before they could leave the room, Lady Dare burst through the door. "Oh, dear. It's the most dreadful news. Poor Lady Westcott has had a fall, and broken her leg!"

Lady Huntington gasped. "Oh, no, Violet. Will she be all right?"

Lady Dare's face was pale, and she was wringing her hands. "The doctor says she will be. He says it was a clean break, whatever that means. He's set the bone, and made Lady Westcott comfortable, but Nick is beside himself. He's gone to fetch the servants to pack our trunks. We must return to Ashdown Park at once."

"Of course, you must," Hyacinth said, her brow creased with concern. "Poor Lady Westcott! What can we do to help?"

"I'm too scattered to tell. Oh, Miss Ramsey!" Lady Dare spun toward Isla and grasped her hand, her face a picture of distress. "I'm so terribly sorry, but it seems we won't be able to assist with your London season, after all. Oh, it's the worst timing, truly! I realize you were counting on our support."

"Oh, please don't think of it, Lady Dare," Isla said. "We'll miss your company, but of course, you must go at once."

"Lady Westcott is Lord Dare's aunt, you know, and his only living relative. She's a most beloved member of our family, and we can't bear to think of her alone at Ashdown Park with only the servants to tend to her."

Lady Dare gazed at Isla for a moment, her brow furrowed with concern. "But perhaps Lord Dare can go without me. I could remain in London, just for a few weeks, until the worst of the gossip dies down, and—"

"No indeed, Lady Dare," Ciaran interrupted, shaking his head. "It's kind of you to offer, but we won't hear of it, will we, Lachlan?" He gave Lachlan a sharp nudge.

"No, no. Not a word. You must go to your aunt at once," Lachlan said, but his jaw had gone tight. He wished Lord Dare's aunt a quick recovery, but he couldn't help cursing the timing. Isla needed as many earls and countesses as they could get to support her claim to London society. Losing Lord and Lady Dare was a blow.

But there was nothing to be done for it. Within the hour, the servants had loaded their trunks onto their carriage, and they were on their way to Lord Dare's estate in West Sussex.

Everyone stood about the drive for a moment after the carriage disappeared, then Lady Huntington said, "Shall we go upstairs and see Isla's gowns now?"

Lachlan smothered a derisive snort.

Gowns, for God's sake. If only it were as simple as a few pretty ball gowns.

Fashionable clothing would do Isla little good if she didn't also have an army of aristocrats standing beside her when she faced the *ton*. Unless Miss Somerset had some magical corsets and petticoats secreted away in her closet, or a few earls and a duke hidden among her underclothes, Isla's success in London had just become a great deal less certain.

"Ball gowns are beyond my area of expertise." Finn paused to kiss his wife's hand, then clapped a hand on Lachlan's shoulder. "Fancy a drink?"

"I bloody do," Ciaran muttered, wandering off down the hallway toward Finn's study.

"I'll come in a moment." Lachlan gestured for Finn to go ahead, as well. "I need some air first."

Finn shrugged. "Very well."

Lachlan waited until Finn and Ciaran disappeared behind the study doors, then he went up the stairs after the ladies. He caught up to them on the second floor, cupped Miss Somerset's elbow in his palm and, before she could do more than gasp in surprise, he drew her around a corner and into a shallow alcove at the end of the hallway.

"Mr. Ramsey! W-what do you think you're—"

"Do you want to help my sister, Miss Somerset?"

"Why, of course I do. What kind of question—"

"Isla is much worse off without Lord and Lady Dare's support, but you and Lady Chase could offset their absence. If you want to help Isla, you'll stay in London for the season with her, instead of going to Brighton." They needed a spare aristocrat, and Lady Chase was a countess. As far as Lachlan was concerned, one aristocrat was as good as any other.

"I can't stay in London without risking my health, Mr. Ramsey. My grandmother and sisters won't hear of it."

His gaze roamed over her face, taking in the fresh glow of her skin, the becoming flush of her cheeks. Damned if she didn't look the picture of health to him. "They hover over you as if you'll crumble to dust in a vigorous wind, but I didn't see any sign of feebleness when you were jerking Lady Bagshot about as if she were a marionette dangling from a string."

Her eyes flickered with surprise. "That's different. That was...I was—"

"And the other day, in the stables, when you called me an ass, and told me I should be on display at the Royal Menagerie. Now I think on it, I've only ever seen you overwrought twice. The night of Lord and Lady Huntington's ball, and just now, in the drawing room, when you wanted to distract your family from your success with Lady Bagshot."

She bit nervously at her lower lip. "That's nonsense, Mr. Ramsey. Why should I want to distract them?"

Lachlan dragged his gaze away from the temptation of her mouth, now pink and swollen from the punishment her teeth had inflicted. He met her eyes. "Because you're hiding."

She dismissed this with an awkward laugh. "Am I? Hiding from who?"

Despite the laugh, her eyes had gone wary, and Lachlan could see he was distressing her. The thread of gentlemanliness still buried deep inside him regretted it, but the other part of him—the rough part that lurked far closer to the surface—told him a little distress might move her in a way all the coddling in the world never would.

He moved closer to her, and his voice dropped to a murmur. "From your family, Hyacinth, and from yourself."

She stared at him, her chest rising and falling rapidly. "How dare you? You've known me for less than a week, and you presume to tell me—"

"Such a waste. She's remarkable, that lady underneath the one you pretend to be. So clever, such a razor-sharp wit hidden behind that sweet angel's face."

Her eyes went wide. "I'm not—I don't pretend at anything, Mr. Ramsey."

"Yes, you do. You're not fragile or weak, except when it suits you. Maybe you were delicate at one time, when you were younger, but you're not anymore."

She sucked in a sharp breath, and an angry wash of red stained her cheeks. "Are you accusing me of pretending to ill health to manipulate my family? You must think me a monster indeed, Mr. Ramsey, if you believe I'd do something so underhanded."

It was quite a speech, and Lachlan couldn't help noticing she didn't stammer once.

He wrapped his hand around her upper arm and lowered his face to hers, because he wanted her to look at him, to *hear* him. "I would never accuse you of such low behavior. It's not manipulation, but instinct—a way to protect yourself. It's easier that way. Easier if no one expects much from you."

She yanked her arm away. "*You* expect a great deal from me, I think, and you're not even honest about it. You don't truly believe I'm remarkable, but you'd try and convince me you do, to drag me through a season and smooth Isla's way with the *ton*."

"I don't deny it started that way, but now, I just…I don't want to see you cheat yourself this way." Lachlan blinked, surprised to find it was true. Somehow, after their call this afternoon, his feelings for Hyacinth Somerset had become more complicated.

Her eyes narrowed to blue slits. "I don't believe you. Ass is too kind a word for you, Mr. Ramsey. That is, you *are* an ass, but you're a scoundrel, as well!"

"I don't deny that, either." Maybe he was a scoundrel, because instead of the regret he should feel at having provoked her into a fury, fierce satisfaction shot through Lachlan. "You've a quick temper, Miss Somerset. What happens when it's unleashed? Whatever it is, I doubt it's *delicate*."

Her hands clenched into fists. "Whatever you may think, I'd never lie to my family, or hurt them in such an unforgiveable way."

"No. Anyone can see how much you care for them. But you'd hurt yourself. You'd lie to yourself."

As soon as he said them, Lachlan could see she recognized his words as the truth. The angry color faded from her cheeks, leaving her alarmingly pale. *Damn it.* He dragged his hand through his hair, regret heavy inside his chest. He hadn't meant to hurt her, only to make her understand. "I beg your pardon. I shouldn't have said—"

He wouldn't have believed she could move so quickly. One moment she was standing with her back to the wall, staring up at him with burning eyes, and the next she'd skirted around him, and darted out of the alcove.

He caught her arm, alarmed at the bleak expression on her face, and eased her back against the wall. "Listen to me. I should never have said that. I'm sorry I did." But he didn't take it back, and he didn't say he hadn't meant it. He wasn't going to lie to her. "I'd take care of you," he murmured. "If you did go ahead with your season. I'd take care of you."

She let out a bitter laugh. "I don't even know what that means, Mr. Ramsey."

"I mean in the same way I take care of Isla." His feelings for Hyacinth Somerset weren't what he'd call *brotherly*, but it didn't matter. He had no intention of acting on them. "I may be an ass and a scoundrel, but like most brothers, I'm protective of my sister. Maybe more so than most brothers. Just ask Isla."

She shook her head, her mouth tight. "I don't need your protection. I have Finn."

"You can't have too many protectors. If you do this for Isla, in turn I swear to protect you from whatever it is you're afraid of."

She looked into his eyes then, and hers were shadowed with an emotion that tugged at something deep inside his chest. "I'm afraid of everything, Mr. Ramsey, including myself. How do you intend to protect me from that?"

The sadness in her voice made his breath catch. An unfamiliar urge to soothe her made him move closer—so close he inhaled each of her frantic breaths into his own lungs.

Or maybe it wasn't about soothing her. Maybe he just wanted to touch her again. He reached out to stroke her cheek, or caress the curve of her lower lip, but as his hand drew closer to her face, her eyes widened with alarm. "Mr. Ramsey?"

He forced his hand back down to his side.

Brotherly.

It was better if he forgot her skin was even softer than it looked, better if he didn't know if her lips would feel like velvet under his thumb.

When he made no further move toward her, she slid a few inches away from him, her back still pressed to the wall. "Even if you could protect me, I wouldn't accept your help. I don't trust you."

Lachlan said nothing to this, because there was nothing he *could* say. He knew well enough he hadn't given her any reason to trust him.

So he did the only thing he could do. He stepped aside to let her pass.

She darted away from him and hurried down the hallway, her skirts billowing out behind her. Lachlan watched her go, half-hoping…

But in the next breath she'd disappeared around the corner, without looking back.

Chapter Eight

Hyacinth tucked a fold of the pale blue silk between her thumb and finger and held it against Isla's waist. "An inch at least, I think." She cocked her head from one side to the other, assessing the bodice of the gown with a critical eye. "Perhaps an inch and a half, but no more than that, or she won't be able to breathe."

Madame Bell made the sort of derisive noise only London's most sought-after French modiste could get away with, and marched toward Isla with an air of ruthless determination. "*Non*. Two inches." She plucked at the back of the gown, pinching until she found another scant half inch of loose silk. "The gown must be tight here, see? Mademoiselle can breathe after the ball has ended."

Hyacinth gave Isla a wry smile, then turned to her grandmother, who was ensconced in her favorite chair, with a tufted ottoman under her feet and a plate of biscuits at her elbow. "What's your opinion, Grandmother? A comfortable inch and a half for Miss Ramsey's bodice, or two inches, and a fainting fit before supper is served?"

Lady Chase popped a biscuit into her mouth. "I advise you to listen to Madame Bell. She knows what she's about, and in any case, Miss Ramsey's corset will be tighter than *that*."

"Welcome to the London season, Miss Ramsey," Hyacinth murmured, so only Isla could hear her. "Where fashion takes precedence over respiration, every time."

"Perhaps I can learn to breathe through my ears," Isla murmured back with a grin.

"We must make the most of her figure." Lady Chase pointed at Isla, the biscuit still clutched in her hand. "Such a tiny waist you have, Miss Ramsey!

Oh, I remember those days. Did you know, Hyacinth, your grandfather could span my waist with his hands when we were courting?" She stuffed the biscuit into her mouth with a dramatic sigh. "Oh, my, yes. I had the narrowest waist in London in my day."

Madame Bell stuck a few last pins into the bodice of the gown, then stood back and assessed her handiwork with a satisfied smile. "Ah, such a gown!"

"Such a gown!" Lady Chase, Hyacinth and Isla echoed the sentiment with rapturous sighs, because there was no denying the gown was a masterpiece—a young lady's dream come true. It was a symphony, an aria, a shimmering confection in the finest silk, every line of it so graceful a lady's heart ached to behold it, and the color just as glorious as the cut and fabric. It was the softest sky blue imaginable, and trimmed with Belgian lace so delicate it could bring a lady to tears.

Hyacinth fluffed a stray fold of the skirt and indulged in a private little sigh of her own. She didn't regret not having a season—of course she didn't, she was *quite* reconciled to it—but she couldn't help a quiet sigh of yearning for all the beautiful gowns she'd never have the chance to wear. Her youthful heart delighted in fine silks and brightly-colored satin ribbons as much as the next young lady's did, and this gown in particular, oh, that delicious blue! It looked like a slice of the morning sky, and the lace, so dainty, like woven threads of gossamer. It was quite simply the most perfect gown she'd ever beheld, and she had the dearest little blue slippers to match it—

"What are all those scraps of white at the neckline? They're all over the waist, too. They look like bits of those old lace caps Mrs. McGurty, our housekeeper in Lochinver used to wear. Don't they, Lach?"

Lachlan only grunted, but Madame Bell's assistant, Eliza, who was on her knees pinning the hem of the gown let out an appalled gasp, and Hyacinth, Isla, Lady Chase and Madame Bell all whipped their heads around to gape at Ciaran Ramsey, their mouths open in identical expressions of feminine outrage.

Ciaran, who didn't seem to have the faintest idea of the devastation he'd wrought, stepped closer to peer at Isla's gown, then drew back with a cheerful laugh. "Good Lord, I'd forgotten all about those lace caps until now. Poor Mrs. McGurty. She was a kind old soul, but I used to have nightmares about her when I was a boy."

"Lace caps?" Madame Bell staggered backwards, her hand pressed to her chest as if to keep her heart from bursting out of her bodice. "*Housekeeper?*"

"Scraps of white?" Lady Chase's face had gone purple. "Those *scraps*, Mr. Ciaran Ramsey, happen to be the finest Belgian lace that can be had in London!"

Hyacinth squeezed her eyes closed. After a great deal of effort she'd almost managed to forget Ciaran and Lachlan were here at all, but now Ciaran had gone and given Madame Bell an apoplexy, and her grandmother looked as if she were about to collapse face first into her plate of biscuits.

"Ciaran Ramsey!" Isla turned a furious gaze on her brother, who was poking cautiously at the lace trim with the tip of his finger, as if he thought it might rear up and bite him.

Ciaran gave her a surprised look. "Why, Isla, what's made you so cross?"

Isla slapped his hand away. "You and Lachlan promised you'd remain *utterly silent* if I didn't fuss about your coming with me today."

"I have been silent. Mostly. Why, I'm sure you hardly knew I was here."

Isla planted her hands on her hips. "Do you call chattering on about white strings and lace caps being *silent*, Ciaran?"

Ciaran turned to Lachlan with a helpless look. "What did I do?"

Lachlan had hardly spoken a word since he arrived, but now he roused himself for long enough to scowl at Ciaran. "Never mind him, Isla. Just go on with your fitting as if neither of us are here."

Hyacinth couldn't prevent her soft snort of disbelief. Weren't here, indeed. One was as likely to forget Lachlan Ramsey as they were to forget a lion pacing from one end of the room to the other. The sprawl of his long, muscular legs in those tight blue breeches seemed to take up every spare inch of floor space, and the way he kept fondling the head of his walking stick with those enormous hands was so distracting Hyacinth wanted to snatch it away from him and hurl it into the fire.

Whatever she might think of Lachlan Ramsey, there was no *forgetting* him.

After their argument in the hallway yesterday, she hadn't expected to see him again until she returned from Brighton. For pity's sake, what gentleman insisted on sitting through an entire afternoon of gown fittings?

But here he was, his hazel eyes following her every move.

If she spoke, he sat up in his chair to hear what she said. If she sighed, his gaze jerked toward her to see why. If she so much as stroked a fold of silk or fingered a ribbon, he noticed it. She'd been so disconcerted by him she'd pricked herself at least a dozen times with Madame Bell's pins. Her poor fingertips looked like pincushions.

"I've got it, Lach!" Ciaran had gone back to studying Isla's lace, and now he turned to his brother with a triumphant smile. "It's the same as the lace on Mrs. McGurty's night rails!"

"Madame Bell!" Hyacinth leapt forward, caught the modiste, and hurried her to a chair just as the poor lady's legs gave out beneath her.

Ciaran attempted to give the lace another poke, but Isla slapped at him again, and he jerked his hand away. "Ow! That stung. Good Lord, Isla. All this fuss to protect you from the *ton*, when it's the *ton* who needs protection from *you*."

Isla pointed toward the door. "Out. Both of you. This instant."

"Why? What did we do?" Ciaran looked from one outraged lady to another with a baffled expression. "It wasn't the *lace* that gave me nightmares. It was Mrs. McGurty."

Isla stamped her foot. "Never mind Mrs. McGurty! I don't want to hear another word about her. I want you to *go*, right this second. I don't know why you insisted on coming. You're both obviously bored to tears."

Lachlan didn't deign to explain himself, but rose to his feet and approached Isla, his eyes narrowing on the blue gown. "This isn't the gown you intend to wear to Lady Bagshot's ball, is it?"

"I'd thought to, yes. Why, don't you like it?"

Lachlan's gaze shifted to Hyacinth, who was standing behind Isla, then back to his sister. "Not for you, no."

Isla ran a reverent hand over the skirt of the sky blue gown. "Well, it's up to Lady Chase and Hyacinth, not me."

"What's wrong with the white one? It'll do—" Lachlan began.

"Of course you should have it." Hyacinth was aware of Lachlan's gaze fixed on her, and she forced a smile, ignoring the pang in her chest at the thought of losing the blue gown. "You look lovely in it. Doesn't she, Grandmother?"

Lady Chase's eyes were misty. "Do you recall your final fitting for this gown, Hyacinth? I do. You reminded me so much of your mother that day. She used to wear that shade of blue. Well, well, Miss Ramsey must have it, of course. Such a lovely gown must be worn, mustn't it? I don't mind saying I did long to see you dance in it, Hyacinth, but there, never mind my sentimental ramblings."

Hyacinth turned hastily away to hide the sudden tears pricking her eyes. *It's just a gown. It doesn't matter.*

But the whisper she'd been trying to silence ever since she'd agreed to go to Brighton insisted she hadn't just given up a gown.

She'd given up her season. Perhaps her future.

"There will be other gowns," Hyacinth murmured, though she wasn't certain if she meant to reassure her grandmother, or herself. "Can you alter it to fit Miss Ramsey in time for Lady Bagshot's ball, Madame Bell?"

That poor lady was still trying to recover from Ciaran's slur about the lace caps, but she rose from her chair, drew herself up with as much dignity as she could muster, and nodded to Lady Chase. "Because Madame is such a valued client, I will forget the grievous insult dealt me today. Send the gown to my shop in Bond Street, and it will be done." She snapped a finger at the footman, who'd been stationed by the door. "See my carriage is fetched at once. Come, Eliza."

"And *you*, Mr. Ciaran Ramsey." Lady Chase pointed the tip of her cane at Ciaran. "You will escort Madame Bell to her carriage, and beg her pardon for your unspeakable rudeness today. Lace caps, indeed."

"Yes, ma'am." Ciaran offered Lady Chase a meek bow. "I can't imagine why you should all be in such a fuss over Mrs. McGurty, but I can safely promise you, Isla, never to attend another dress fitting as long as I live. I'll save my energies for ladies without gowns." Ciaran frowned. "That's not *quite* what I meant to say, but it's, ah…something like that."

Isla groaned. "For pity's sake, Ciaran, will you hush?"

Hyacinth, who thought it wise to separate Ciaran and Madame Bell as soon as possible, gathered up the measuring tapes and pins still scattered across the floor, handed them to Madame Bell's assistant, then followed them all down the hallway and saw them safely turned over to Lady Chase's butler, Eddesley.

When she returned to the parlor, she found Isla Ramsey wringing her hands, her face flushed with embarrassment. "I beg your pardon, Hyacinth. Ciaran is…well, he nearly killed your modiste, didn't he? I'm not sure how one begs pardon for that."

"No, me either." But Hyacinth couldn't quite resist the smile tugging at the corners of her lips. Ciaran Ramsey was an awful tease, but there was no denying he was entertaining. "Oh, never mind, Isla. Gentlemen are notoriously ill behaved at dress fittings. Perhaps next time we'll make Ciaran hold the pins, and stick him with one every time he misbehaves."

Isla laughed. "He'd be bled into a swoon before midafternoon."

"Lady Chase." Lachlan had been standing with his back to the company, looking out a window, but now he turned and bowed to Lady Chase. "I see there are a series of pathways off the terrace that wind around behind those hedges. It's a dry day, and warm enough. May Ciaran and I escort you for a walk while Miss Somerset takes Isla upstairs to change? The ladies can join us when they're ready."

"Yes, all right." Lady Chase pushed the ottoman aside with her cane and got to her feet. "Miss Ramsey, please do join us when you're ready, but Hyacinth, you look weary, dear." Lady Chase tutted, and patted Hyacinth's cheek. "A short rest will put some roses back in your cheeks."

Hyacinth thought she heard Lachlan Ramsey make a soft, impatient sound, but when she risked a glance at him, his face was expressionless.

"Mr. Ramsey." She curtsied to him, and then to Ciaran, who'd wandered back into the drawing room, looking rather chastened. "And Mr. Ciaran. Thank you for your...lively company this afternoon. Grandmother, I'll come to you after I've rested."

Hyacinth's maid, Jenny, accompanied them upstairs to help Isla out of the blue gown without upsetting the pins. Isla was quiet as Jenny laced her back into her own gown. Isla's face was thoughtful, and once she was tucked back into her day dress, she took Hyacinth's hand in hers. "Forgive me, but I must ask. Are you certain you wish to give up the blue gown? You looked at it so wistfully while it was being pinned."

They both turned to look at the blue gown, which Jenny had laid carefully over Hyacinth's bed, along with a few dinner gowns, and another cream-colored ball gown Isla had chosen. Hyacinth's chest swelled with another pang of regret, but she shook her head as she turned back to Isla. "That gown was made to be worn, and for the lady who wears it to be admired. It was made to be danced in."

"Yes, it was. By *you*, Hyacinth, not me. Any one of your other ball gowns would do for me, but that one...well. It's *yours*, isn't it?"

"Not anymore. If you don't wear it, Isla, it will only go to waste."

"It doesn't have to. Wear it yourself, Hyacinth. Come to Lady Bagshot's ball with me, and dance in it."

Hyacinth didn't answer, because how could she explain to a lady like Isla—a lady confident enough to hold her own with her two giant brothers, a lady brave enough to face down the *ton* after a scandal—that even if she did wear the gown to Lady Bagshot's ball, she wouldn't dance in it. No, she'd hide behind a column, or cower in the ladies' retiring room.

After a moment, Isla squeezed her hand. "Just think about it, won't you?" She didn't wait for an answer, but went out the door, closing it quietly behind her. Once she was gone, Hyacinth turned back to the bed to find Jenny was collecting the gowns Isla had chosen, to take them downstairs.

The maid took up the sky blue gown, draped it over her arm, and—

"Leave the blue, Jenny."

Hyacinth covered her mouth with her hand, her eyes wide. The words had rushed from her lips before she realized she was going to say them. "No, I mean, of course you should take it—"

"No, no. I can't carry them all at once, miss. I'll just come back for it later, shall I?" Jenny smiled, then hurried out the door before Hyacinth could argue, leaving the blue gown spread out across the bed.

Hyacinth stared at it for a long moment, then reached out and ran one finger down the gleaming silk folds of the skirt. It felt like a dream under her fingertip, as if the strains of a waltz had been woven into the fabric.

But then it was a dream, wasn't it? That was all a gown like this could ever be to her.

Hyacinth dragged the back of her hand across her eyes. Such foolishness, to fuss over a gown she'd never wear, and really, it wasn't so very special, was it? It was a blue silk ball gown, nothing more. Just one of at least five such gowns in her closet.

But even as she lectured herself for her selfishness, Hyacinth caught up the gown and crossed to the mirror. She wouldn't put it on, of course—she didn't fancy being stuck with dozens of pins—but if she just held it up in front of her, perhaps that would ease the longing ache in her chest. Then she'd see at once it wasn't as special as she imagined it was, or meant for her alone to wear—

"You're not giving that gown to my sister."

For an instant Hyacinth froze, her eyes closing as the low, deep voice stroked across her nerve endings, but then she whirled around, and her heart leapt from her chest.

Lachlan Ramsey was standing in the doorway.

On the *inside* of her bedchamber.

"My goodness! Mr. Ramsey, what are you...this is my bedchamber! You can't be in here with me." She stared at him, aghast. "You can't be in here *without* me, either! You just...you can't be in here at all!"

Hyacinth was so shocked she hardly knew what she said, but Lachlan Ramsey eyed her calmly, and then, as cool as you please, he closed the door behind him, crossed the room, and took the gown out of her hands.

The slippery material slid through her nerveless fingers. "How did you know where my bedchamber was?" There were at least a dozen things—of far greater importance—she should have asked. For some reason, this question rose to her lips.

"I followed you upstairs, waited around the corner until your maid left the room, and now here I am. Nothing so remarkable in it."

Hyacinth felt her eyes go so wide she was afraid they were about to fall out of her head. He said it so casually, as if he made a habit of sneaking about hallways and following young ladies into their bedchambers.

Then again, perhaps he did.

"But my grandmother! She'll have seen you!" If Lady Chase should find Lachlan Ramsey in her bedchamber—dear God, either it would put a period to that dear lady's existence, or else Hyacinth would find herself wed to the man within a fortnight.

"You *cannot* be in my bedchamber, Mr. Ramsey! You must leave, at once." Without thinking, she hurried across the room, braced her hands against his chest, and tried to shove him toward the door.

He didn't move a single inch. Hyacinth planted her feet on the floor and shoved harder, putting all her strength behind it, but it was no use. She'd have more success trying to knock over a stone wall.

He sighed, as if she were making a great fuss over nothing. "Your grandmother is in the garden with Ciaran and Isla. I told her I wanted a look into the library, and so they went on without me. We don't have long, however, so let me make myself understood. You will not give this gown to Isla. I forbid it."

He *forbid* it? *He* forbid it!

Why, it was no wonder Isla knew how to deal out a stinging slap when the situation demanded it. With her brothers, she'd had no choice but to learn to assert herself.

"*You* forbid it? You haven't any right to forbid me anything, Mr. Ramsey."

Hyacinth wasn't sure what response she'd expected, but it wasn't the twitch of his lips, or the ghost of a grin that followed it.

"What's wrong, Miss Somerset? Are you *overwrought*?"

She threw her hands in the air. "You lied to my grandmother, followed my maid up the stairs, sneaked into my bedchamber, and snatched my gown away from me. Yes, Mr. Ramsey. I think it's fair to say I'm *overwrought*."

"I thought you might be. But it's curious. Didn't you say your grandmother and sisters worry for your health when you become overwrought? Because you look very well at the moment." His gaze roamed over her face, lingering on her eyes and mouth. "Sparkling eyes, pink cheeks…perhaps you should become overwrought more often."

Hyacinth gaped at him. Well. She hadn't the faintest idea what to say to *that*.

He didn't seem to expect her to say anything, because he shifted his attention back to the gown. "I agree with Ciaran about the white scraps."

He shook it a bit, as if he could force it to explain itself. "But no matter. Choose another gown for Isla. You said yourself you have dozens of them."

"But *why*? We went through my ball gowns already, Mr. Ramsey, and your sister chose this one." By this point, Hyacinth was truly baffled. "Why shouldn't she have it?"

He gazed down at her, his expression unreadable. "Because it's yours."

"Strictly speaking, they're *all* mine."

"No. Not like this one."

"This one's no different than any of the others." She tried not to sneak a last look at the gown, but it was no use. Her eyes darted toward it, and her heart sank in her chest.

He noticed, and his eyes narrowed to dark green slits. "Yes, it is. You care about this one."

Hyacinth fell back a step, closing her hands into fists to stop their sudden trembling. He'd been watching her all afternoon—every time she turned around she found his gaze on her, studying her, assessing every fleeting expression on her face.

He'd seen her.

All she had to do was glance at his face, into his eyes, and she knew he'd seen it all. The yearning she kept hidden. The regret and the disappointment. Not at losing the gown, but the disappointment in herself. How had it happened, that he should be the one to strip away all her protective layers? It made her feel...

Exposed.

Panic curled in her stomach, and as any frightened animal would, she lashed out. "This is absurd. I gave that gown to your sister, and I don't intend to take it back now."

"I'll explain it to Isla. She'll understand."

Hyacinth knew very well Isla already understood, but she stubbornly held her tongue. "There's no time to do another fitting before Lady Bagshot's ball, so...Mr. Ramsey! Stop that!"

He'd laid the gown over his arm, and now he was pulling all the pins out, one by one.

"No!" She leapt forward to snatch the gown away from him, but of course, it was no use. She might as well have tried tackling a tree. He easily held it out of her reach. Once he'd pulled every pin free, he reached around her and placed them carefully on her dressing-table, then draped the blue gown over the chair.

"It looks as if we'll have to make time for another fitting. Another gown, Miss Somerset?"

Hyacinth gazed at the blue gown for a moment, then turned to look up at him. He stared calmly back at her, his face composed. Someone who didn't know him might even think he was bored, but she'd seen that determined glint in his eyes before—yesterday, when he'd told her Isla needed her, and asked her to help his sister.

He promised he'd take care of her.

But she didn't want to think of all the ways she was disappointing Isla, and disappointing herself. She'd already packed her trunks for Brighton, and they would leave the day after tomorrow. It was too late to change her mind.

Now, all she wanted was to be done—with talk of her season, with these blasted ball gowns, and with Lachlan Ramsey. The easiest way to rid herself of him was to give him what he wanted. She could argue with the man for the rest of the afternoon, but it wouldn't do a bit of good, and in the meantime, her grandmother would be wondering where he was.

She crossed the room to her closet and began snatching down ball gowns. "Isla likes this pale yellow one, and I thought this ice pink looked very well on her." She tried to hand the gowns to him, but to her surprise, he was staring at the array of gowns with a frown.

"Why are they all so pale? Don't English ladies like bold colors?"

Hyacinth sighed. She was partial to bright colors, but even if they were proper, she still wouldn't have worn them. A lady couldn't disappear behind a white marble column if she were wearing a bright green gown. "Bold colors aren't proper for young ladies just coming out."

Lachlan grunted. "What about this one? It's bold enough." He pulled out a gown of a deep violet color, and held it up for Hyacinth to see.

"Oh, I forgot about that gown." Hyacinth caught a fold of the bright silk between her fingers. It was a glorious gown, but between the color and the low-cut bodice, it was far too daring for an unmarried young lady. "It belongs to Iris. She intended to wear it this season—it's proper for a married lady to wear such a color—but now she's, ah, *enceinte,* it no longer fits her. She knew I admired it, so she left it with me. Silly of her, since I'll never wear it."

He assessed the gown, his gaze lingering on the low-cut neckline, then he glanced at her. "Pity. It would suit you."

Something about his expression and the husky pitch of his voice made Hyacinth's face and chest explode with heat. She stared up at him, her heart beating a wild tattoo against her breastbone.

"I'll take the yellow," he murmured, holding her gaze.

"The, ah…what?"

A small smile quirked his lips. "The yellow gown, Miss Somerset. For my sister. I'll take her to Madame Bell's shop tomorrow and have it fitted."

"Oh, y-yes. Of course, the yellow gown." She handed it to him, then turned and hurried from the closet to hide her flushed cheeks.

He tucked the yellow gown under his arm, then offered her a polite bow, which seemed a bit absurd to Hyacinth, given they'd spent a scandalous twenty minutes alone in her bedchamber.

"I beg your pardon for disturbing you this afternoon, Miss Somerset."

"Why did you?"

He'd turned to leave, but now he paused, and turned back to her. "Why did I what?"

"Disturb me." She waved a hand toward the sky blue gown hanging over the dressing-table chair. "Why should you care which gown I give away? Why go to all this bother?"

He looked at her for a long moment, then he put the yellow gown aside on the bed, approached her, and held out his hand.

For reasons Hyacinth couldn't explain, she took it, and let him lead her to her dressing-table. He took her shoulders in his hands and positioned her in front of the mirror, then moved behind her. The edges of his coat brushed her back and the rasp of his breath stirred the loose tendrils of hair against her neck.

Her gaze met his in the mirror. His eyes had darkened to a deep brown-green, and a hint of softness, rare for him, played about his lips. He took up the blue gown, held it up in front of her, and then leaned down, his lips nearly touching her ear.

"Look."

Hyacinth shifted her gaze from his face to hers, then back again. "What am I looking at? It's just me, in a blue gown—a gown much like every other."

His big fingers touched her jaw, and he held her still with her face centered in the looking glass. "No. *Look.*"

Hyacinth never lingered over her glass, but now, with his warm, gentle fingers holding her, she met her mirror reflection, and for perhaps the first time in her life, she truly looked.

She looked for so long, and so hard, that after a time her face stopped making sense. Her brow, her eyes, her nose and mouth—they became shapes only, with no meaning attached to them—hers, and not hers at once.

Then he stroked his thumb over her jaw, and gradually the shapes changed, transformed, melted back into the face she'd seen in her glass thousands of times before, and it was *her* face—her brow, and her eyes, her nose and mouth, but somehow the sum of the parts now seemed to equal a different whole…

"This gown is *yours*. No one but you should dance in it." He brushed a stray curl away from her ear, leaned closer, and whispered, "That's why."

Then he was gone, and she was holding handfuls of sky-blue silk, staring at herself in the mirror, and wondering if she'd imagined the entire thing.

Chapter Nine

Lady Chase hadn't yet had her morning chocolate.

The very first lesson Hyacinth and her sisters had learned when they arrived in London was one didn't annoy Lady Chase when she hadn't yet had her morning chocolate, because until she had, she could be a bit—

"What does Lord Huntington mean, rousting us out of bed at such an hour? Why, I don't think I exaggerate, Hyacinth, when I say it's indecent! I can't imagine what could be so important we must be dragged from our beds. Indeed, I can't account for his behavior at all."

"It might be Iris who sent for us, Grandmother. The servant didn't say it was Finn."

"Well," then, I daresay all this fuss is over something to do with Miss Ramsey's gowns. Oh, I do hope Madame Bell hasn't gotten into a temper, and sent them back unaltered. I wouldn't half blame her if she did, after that scoundrel insulted her so infamously. White scraps, indeed!"

Hyacinth doubted this mysterious morning summons had anything to do with Isla's gowns, unless Iris had worked herself into a sudden, inexplicable panic over them. Unlike Hyacinth, Iris had never been the sort of lady who was prone to fits of anxiety, but her calm demeanor seemed to be giving way to nervous agitation the further she got into her pregnancy.

Poor Iris. She'd been in quite a lather since the Ramseys arrived in London. She was so determined to make society accept them—both for their own sakes, and for Finn's—she'd exhausted herself with her efforts.

"It's the gowns. You may count upon that, Hyacinth. Madame Bell's sent them back. She has an artist's delicate temperament, you see, and that rogue Ciaran Ramsey has tipped it all askew."

The worry fluttering like manic butterflies in Hyacinth's belly began to calm. Perhaps her grandmother was right, and it was just the gowns, after all. Perhaps Isla didn't care for the yellow gown, or the color didn't flatter her, and she wished to change it again.

Well, this was what came of allowing Lachlan Ramsey to fuss about in her dressing closet. What did *he* know about ladies' ball gowns? Why, nothing at all. No man did.

Except...

This gown is yours. No one but you should dance in it.

His whisper, his warm breath against her ear—she'd dreamed of it, and of the softness in his eyes when they met hers in the glass.

It made her yearn for things she could never have.

"I blame those brothers of hers," Lady Chase declared. "Scoundrels, the both of them. Oh, I imagine scoundrels do well enough in Scotland, but those brothers don't know how to behave in proper society."

Hyacinth sighed. She never should have let Lachlan Ramsey tempt her with the sky blue gown. If she'd sent him away as she should have, she wouldn't be trapped in this carriage with her grandmother, and Lady Chase as bad-tempered as a bear with a thorn in its paw.

Or a bear deprived of its morning chocolate.

"Now Miss Ramsey is a sweet child, and genteel enough, but the elder brother, Hyacinth! Why, what need is there for him to be so large? And always with that frightening glower on his face! Well, well. I don't wonder you mistook him for a murderer, dear. He has a felonious look about him."

Lady Chase chattered on about Lachlan Ramsey's scandalous proportions until they'd reached Grosvenor Square. Hyacinth half-expected to see Madame Bell's carriage parked in the drive, and Madame's assistant, Eliza, rushing about with pins in her mouth, carrying armfuls of silk, but the Grosvenor Street house was quiet.

Oddly so. An oppressive hush hung over everything, as if the house and all its inhabitants had taken a deep breath, then been frozen in place before they could release it. Finn's carriage was in the drive, but there was no sign of him, and no servants wandering about, either.

All was still, and ominously silent.

Uneasiness shivered up Hyacinth's spine. Something was wrong, and whatever it was, it went beyond an irate modiste, or an unflattering gown. "It's too quiet. Come, Grandmother. Let's see if we can't find Iris."

But it wasn't Iris who was waiting for them in the entryway. It was Finn, his face so pale and drawn an involuntary cry tore from Hyacinth's lips. "Finn? Oh, dear God, something's happened, hasn't it? Is it...it's not Iris?"

He shook his head, but his lips remained white with strain. "At the moment, Iris is well."

At the moment?

"Finn, the...the child?"

He hesitated, and Hyacinth's stomach gave a sickening lurch.

"Iris awoke early this morning with pains. I feared..." Finn swallowed. "I feared the worst, and sent for the doctor right away. He's been here all night. The pains have subsided, and Iris is resting."

"Thank God," Hyacinth whispered, reaching out to clutch her grandmother's hand.

"The doctor believes Iris is perfectly well for the moment, but he can't assure us this, ah..." Finn flushed a little. "This irritation of the abdomen won't happen again. He advises rest and uninterrupted quiet until Iris is brought to bed."

"Yes, yes, of course, she must rest," Hyacinth said. "We must do just what the doctor says."

"I want to take Iris back to Huntington Lodge at once." Finn's troubled gaze met Hyacinth's. "There's certain to be a good deal of disruption here with Isla's season, and London is loud and dirty. Iris will be much better off in Buckinghamshire."

Hyacinth's manic butterflies were back, but this time their wings felt like tiny whips cracking against her ribs. "But it can't be safe for her to travel, can it?"

"The doctor thinks she's safe enough if we take the trip slowly, with plenty of stops for rest. But if we're to go, we must go at once. The risk increases as the child grows. If we don't go soon, we won't be able to go at all."

"Then you must go." Hyacinth attempted a reassuring smile. "Iris says you were born at Huntington Lodge, and your father before you. She's told me over and over again she wishes to continue that tradition with your child."

"Yes, she's said the same to me, many times, and yet now she's refusing to leave."

"What?" Lady Chase's shrill voice echoed in the empty entryway. "Why should she refuse?"

Finn let out a short bark of laughter, but there was an edge of panic in it. "Because she's the most stubborn, willful woman in England."

"It's the Ramseys, isn't it?" Hyacinth pressed her palm to her forehead. "If you leave London, it puts an end to Isla's season. She can't go forward without a single member of the family here to support her, not after that scandal."

"No, she can't." Finn's face was grim. "Iris is insisting we both remain in London, or that she goes ahead to Huntington Lodge without me, but I won't let her go alone."

"No, of course not. You'd go mad here in London, worrying about her." Hyacinth was patting her palm against her forehead, as if she could shake loose a solution. "And Isla's debut can't be put off, either."

Isla couldn't withdraw from her season now—not after they'd gone to such lengths to persuade the *ton* to overlook the scandal. A retreat at this point would be disastrous. The *ton* had deigned to give the Ramseys a second chance. To squander it was a grave social offence, at best. At worst, it was an admission of wrongdoing.

Finn, who'd no doubt reached the same conclusion, was shaking his head. "No. I'm afraid it's too late to withdraw now. Either she debuts this season, or not at all."

"Surely something can be done?" But what? Hyacinth's brain was spinning, and catching her thoughts was like trying to catch a carriage wheel broken loose from its axle.

She knew only one thing.

Iris loved Finn with all her heart, and Isla was Finn's sister. His *sister*. Lachlan and Ciaran—they were his brothers. His *family*. A family he'd always wanted, always wished for, ever since he was a child. It would break Finn's heart to fail the Ramseys, and if Finn's heart were broken, Iris's heart would be, as well.

All this was to say nothing of Isla, who would be bitterly disappointed.

Hyacinth touched Finn's arm. "Let me speak with Iris. I may be able to persuade her."

Then I'll work on persuading myself...

She had an idea, but it would mean week after week of balls and dinners, routs and musical evenings, lectures and art exhibits, and the entire *ton* staring at her, whispering behind her back. And they *would* be whispering. She was, after all, the only debutante in London who'd publicly accused a man of murder.

If she went ahead with her season, there wouldn't be enough columns in all of London to hide her.

* * * *

It had been one of the longest days of Lachlan's life, and it was only nine o'clock in the morning.

Isla's season was over before it could begin, and Ciaran, who'd been tormented all night with dreams of Isabel Campbell, had sought to soothe his anger and despair by brawling with Lachlan in the grotto behind the rose garden.

Then there was Finn, who was so sick with worry over his wife he'd spent the past three hours hovering outside her bedchamber door, unwilling to enter because he didn't wish to wake her, but also unable to stay away.

Lachlan pressed his arm tight against his side, and paced back and forth in front of the fireplace in the drawing room. He needed to think what to do, but the blow Ciaran had landed on his ribs hurt like the devil, and his head was cloudy.

He ran a weary hand through his hair. Maybe they shouldn't have come to London at all. There wasn't anything left for them in Lochinver, but maybe he should have let Ciaran figure that out for himself. At least then there wouldn't be this anger and bitterness between them—

"Oh, Mr. Ramsey. I beg your pardon."

Lachlan turned, and despite the burning pain in his ribs, he couldn't help the grin that curled his lips at the sight of Hyacinth Somerset.

She was wearing the most ridiculous gown he'd ever seen.

He'd seen for himself she had dozens of pretty gowns in her closet, but she'd chosen to wear a gray, shapeless thing, the neckline so high and tight she was risking another swoon, this time from lack of oxygen. If that weren't bad enough, it was finished with a frill of lace that swallowed her chin. No doubt the sleeves were as tight and smothering as the neck, but he couldn't be sure, because she'd finished her ensemble with some sort of short coat that looked so dark and heavy she seemed to be sagging under the weight of it.

He couldn't see a single sliver of the pale, fine skin he'd admired yesterday, and not a single golden hair escaped the prison of pins jabbed into her skull. Every curve and edge and loose end of her had been trimmed, buttoned and tucked away.

She looked like a shorn sheep.

And still, he couldn't take his eyes off her.

"No, don't go," he said, when she turned to leave. "How does your sister do?"

"My sister?" She gave him a blank look, as if she couldn't quite recall having a sister, and wandered into the drawing room in a daze.

"Yes. Your *sister*, Miss Somerset. Lady Huntington."

"She's, ah…Finn is right about her, you know. She's the most stubborn, willful woman in England. Yet she's agreed, just the same." Hyacinth let out a strange little laugh. "I suppose I didn't think she would, but now she has, well...I'll have to go through with it, won't I?"

Lachlan frowned. What the devil was wrong with her? She wasn't making any sense, and her face was leached of color. "Sit down, Miss Somerset." He took her arm and led her to the sofa. "Now, what has Lady Huntington agreed to?"

She turned to him in surprise, as if she'd just recalled he was there. "Oh, you don't know? She and Finn are to go to Huntington Lodge. The servants are packing their things."

"I see." It was the right decision, and Lachlan was relieved for his brother's sake, but a heaviness settled on his chest as Isla's season vanished like a cloud of smoke before his eyes. "And you and Lady Chase leave for Brighton tomorrow?"

"Brighton?" Hyacinth folded her hands neatly in her lap like a schoolgirl about to recite her lessons, but Lachlan noticed her knuckles were white. "Oh, no. We're not going to Brighton."

"Not going? Why—"

"Did you mean what you said the other day?" she asked suddenly, her blue eyes so bright she looked almost feverish.

He shrugged. "I say a good many things. Odds are I mean some of them."

"You said if I went ahead with my season, you'd consider it your responsibility to look after me, just as you do with Isla."

Lachlan's heart began to pound with hope. "I did mean it. Every word."

She studied his face for a long moment without speaking, as if trying to gauge his sincerity. "I don't want to do it, you know. My season. I never did, not even before the scandal, when all my family was here to help me along. Even then, I predicted it would be a disaster, but now..." She looked down, as if she were ashamed, and whispered, "I'm afraid."

He moved closer, and took her hand in his. "I know you are, but I swear I won't let anyone hurt you. Will you trust me?"

She glanced down at his large, rough fingers wrapped around her dainty white ones. What did she see when she looked at his hands? Did she see a fist crashing into his brother's face, his knuckles smeared with blood? Did she imagine him grasping Ciaran by his collar with one hand while he bloodied his nose and blackened his eyes with the other? He'd always been a harsh, rough sort of man, but that *she* should have seen him that way, when he was at his most brutal, filled him with shame.

After a long silence she sighed, and raised her gaze to his. "I'll have to trust you if I'm to go ahead with my season, won't I?"

He hadn't given her one reason to trust him, and more than one not to, but here she was, with her big, blue eyes fixed on his face, offering him something he'd denied to her. He was repaying her trust with secrets and lies.

Not just her, but Finn, and Lady Huntington—all of them. The thought made his gut twist with misery. Surely he could trust them with the truth? They'd welcomed him and Ciaran and Isla into their family, shown them nothing but kindness.

But then their friends in Lochinver had offered their kindness, their friendship, too—right up until they hadn't anymore. He'd trusted before, and it had been a deadly mistake. If it should happen a second time, and they found themselves adrift again, he wasn't sure Ciaran and Isla would survive it.

Ciaran and Isla will be the ones to suffer.

"...warn you not to hope for much. I'm hardly a replacement for the Marchioness of Huntington."

Lachlan brought his attention back to Hyacinth.

"The *ton* may yet laugh us out of Lady Bagshot's ballroom before the master of ceremonies introduces Isla, and we still need Lady Chase to agree to sponsor her. Iris is speaking with her now, but my grandmother may insist on taking me off to Brighton, regardless of my wishes. This might not work."

No. It might not work, but it was a chance, and that was more than Isla had ten minutes ago. "Isla will be pleased." He was a good deal more than pleased, but he wasn't sure how to thank her, so he only tightened his fingers around hers.

She gave him a self-conscious smile. "I may disappear behind a column as soon as we enter the ballroom, or worse, fall into a swoon the moment some grand lord asks me for a dance."

"You'll dance the first dance with me, then." The first hour of the ball would be the most difficult one for her, what with everyone gaping and whispering. He could shield her from the worst of it if they were dancing, and she couldn't vanish behind a column if he was holding her in his arms.

What would it feel like, to hold her in his arms? To gather her soft body against his, and urge her closer with his hand on her waist? Damn, it was too bad the first dance was never a waltz.

"It will be my first dance of the season, and it would certainly send a clear message to the *ton* if I danced it with you. After all, if you were truly a murderer I wouldn't dare, would I?"

Lachlan went still, the pretty illusions he'd spun splintering into shards.

No, you wouldn't.

If she knew who he really was, and what he'd really done, she wouldn't allow him to touch her. She wouldn't dare to be alone in the same room with him.

He'd do well to remember that. A devil had no business trifling with an angel.

Lachlan dropped her hand and rose from the sofa. "I'm certain you'll have dozens of better offers—"

"Hyacinth? Where are you, child?"

Lachlan turned at the sound of shuffling feet, and the muted thump of the tip of a cane on each stair.

"Oh, for goodness' sakes. Why must Iris have so many stairs?"

Lachlan strode into the hallway. "May I help you, Lady Chase?"

Thump. "No indeed, Mr. Ramsey. You'll only make me nervous. Just tell me where my granddaughter is, if you please."

"Just here, in the drawing room. We were discussing—"

Thump. "Yes, yes. I know very well what you were discussing. I don't know what you did to coax my granddaughter into this foolishness, Mr. Ramsey, but if she should die of a consumption because she didn't go to Brighton, you may comfort yourself with the knowledge it was all done in service to *you.*"

"This was my idea, Grandmother, not Mr. Ramsey's." Miss Somerset came up beside him, and offered her arm to Lady Chase, who'd at last made it to the bottom of the stairs. "You spoke with Iris?"

"I did, indeed, and she's as foolish as you are."

"Then you know she's refused to go to Buckinghamshire unless you agree to sponsor Miss Ramsey, and remain in London so the two of us can debut together?"

"I know it all, but you needn't pretend Iris approves of this business. She isn't any happier about this idea than I am. She wants you to go to Brighton."

"Yet she did agree to it, nonetheless, and I'm sure you don't wish her to stay in London, or go to Huntington Lodge without Finn."

"Humph." Lady Chase glared at Lachlan.

Hyacinth led her grandmother into the drawing room and settled her on a sofa close to the fire. "Does that mean you agree?"

"But what of Brighton, Hyacinth?" Lady Chase rapped on the floor with her cane. "What if you should become overwrought, and contract some dreadful disease?"

It took all Lachlan's powers of restraint not to snort. Damn it, he was starting to despise the word *overwrought.*

Miss Somerset hesitated for a fraction of a second—just long enough for his breath to stop with dread—but then she shook her head. "If I start to feel myself weakening, we can always go to Brighton then."

Lady Chase regard her for a long moment, then let out a deep sigh. "Well, Hyacinth, I know you're fond of Miss Ramsey, and you've always been a tender-hearted thing. But are you certain you wish to do this?" She cast a dubious look at Lachlan Ramsay. "I daresay it won't be at all pleasant."

Another slight hesitation, then, "I'm certain."

"You don't have any obligations in this, my dear. The Ramseys are Lord Huntington's family, not ours." Lady Chase held up a hand to stop her granddaughter from interrupting. "I know it sounds selfish to say it, but there it is."

"Come now, Grandmother." Miss Somerset sat down on the settee next to Lady Chase. "You know I don't make those sorts of distinctions. Finn's family is our family."

Lachlan stared at her. Her blue eyes had gone soft, and even in that ungodly sack of a dress...

Aingeal.

Lady Chase sighed, then she patted her granddaughter's cheek, and there was no mistaking the pride and affection in her face. "Well, well. You've a kind heart, Hyacinth. Always have."

Lachlan had begun to back out of the room to give them privacy, but before he could reach the door, Isla and Ciaran burst in.

"Lord Huntington is carrying Lady Huntington down the stairs!" Isla announced breathlessly. "I mean, Finn is carrying Iris...oh, bother! You all know who I mean!" With that, she darted back into the hallway, presumably to watch this momentous event.

"Lady Huntington's mad as a hornet about it!" Ciaran seemed to have put aside his anger of this morning, and was now wearing a gleeful grin. "She fussed and protested until Lord Huntington lost patience, wrapped her up in a blanket and scooped her into his arms like she was a sack of potatoes. By God, I like our brother, Lachlan. I thought he was going to be a stiff, proper, deadly dull English peer, but he's a great deal more fun than I expected."

Ciaran strode into the hallway after Isla, and the rest of the party followed him, just in time to see Finn turn on the landing and start down the final flight of stairs. He was clutching Iris to his chest, his mouth a grim, determined line. Iris had her arms wrapped around his neck, and she was looking up into her husband's face, her expression an odd combination of irritation and amusement.

"This is absurd, my lord. I'm perfectly capable of walking...oh, Mr. Ramsey!" Iris called, when she spotted Lachlan at the bottom of the stairs. "Will you attend me to the carriage? I'd like a word."

Lachlan blinked in surprise, but he followed them out to the carriage, and stood by while Finn deposited his wife gently on the seat, and arranged half a dozen cushions around her. "I'm going to fetch another blanket."

"There are five here already, but if you insist, then by all means fetch another one." Once Finn had disappeared into the house, Iris turned her attention to Lachlan, and she didn't mince words. "My parents died when Hyacinth was fifteen years old. Both of them at once, in a dreadful carriage accident. Did you know that, Mr. Ramsey?"

Lachlan's eyebrows shot up, and he fumbled for a response. "Ah, Lord Huntington mentioned it, yes."

"Hyacinth was always a quiet child. Even before we lost our parents, she was painfully shy, and then the other children teased her because of her stammer, which only made things worse. She'd largely outgrown her difficulty with speech by the time she was fifteen, but after my parents' sudden deaths she stopped speaking altogether. We feared she'd never... she'd never..."

Lady Huntington choked on her words, then fell into a pained silence, but Lachlan didn't need to hear any more. He could already see Hyacinth in his mind's eye—a fair-haired girl with an angel's face, so devastated by grief she retreated inside herself, lost and silent.

"We're all very protective of her, Mr. Ramsey—perhaps too much so, but I couldn't leave without making sure you understand how difficult undertaking a London season is for her. Indeed, I think it's far, far more difficult than either you or I can possibly imagine."

"I understand," he murmured hoarsely. His chest was tight, so tight...

"We're trusting you to take care of her. Promise me you will." Lady Huntington reached for his hand, and looked straight into his eyes as she held it between her own.

He was a liar. Some claimed he was a murderer, as well. There were a dozen different reasons why Lady Huntington shouldn't trust him.

But in this...in this, he would not fail.

No matter what else happened, no one was going to hurt Hyacinth Somerset.

"I will, Lady Huntington. I swear it."

Chapter Ten

The Second Ball
Her Ladyship, the Countess of Bagshot
Requests Miss Hyacinth Somerset's presence
At an elegant evening party at Orchards Park
Tuesday, Feb. 3rd, 8:00 o'clock in the evening
S. Audley Street, Mayfair.

Hyacinth had already predicted there'd be a shocking lack of columns in Lady Bagshot's ballroom. What she hadn't guessed was there wouldn't be any columns at all.

Alcoves. That was it, and they were shallow ones, at that. What good were shallow alcoves to her? Paltry, insufficient things—

"You're anxious. Your hands are trembling."

Hyacinth shifted her attention from the alcoves to Lachlan Ramsey's steady hazel eyes. There was no sense in denying it, not when her fingernails were even now tearing a hole in the arm of his coat. "It's the columns."

He glanced around the ballroom. "There are no columns."

"Yes, I know. That's why I'm anxious."

His lips quirked. A bolt of pleasure shot through Hyacinth, and for a moment she forgot all about columns and alcoves, and let happiness sweep over her. Lachlan rarely smiled, but when he did, she felt it all the way down to the soles of her slippers.

"There's nothing to be anxious about. You look..." He waved his hand toward her gown. "Very well," he finished gruffly.

Very well.

It was a proper, brotherly sentiment, but the way his eyes darkened to that hot, intense green when he looked at her...

It wasn't brotherly. That is, Hyacinth didn't think it was. She didn't have brothers, but she'd never seen any of her acquaintances' brothers look at their sisters the way Lachlan Ramsey was looking at her right now.

He cleared his throat. "The color suits you."

Hyacinth let a fold of the pale blue silk drift through her fingers. The gown had lived up to every one of her girlish fantasies. It was divine, and if it was the only good thing that came of an otherwise disastrous evening, at least she'd gotten the chance to wear it.

"I think I understand the white bits now." Ciaran was standing next to Lachlan, with Isla on his arm. "They make more sense now you're wearing the gown. They, ah...well, they enhance the..." He made a vague gesture toward Hyacinth's bosom. "That is, they call attention to the—"

"For God's sake, Ciaran." Lachlan's smile was swallowed by his usual dark scowl as he eyed his brother.

"What? That's what the white bits are for, isn't it?"

Lachlan didn't answer, but continued to glower at him until Ciaran gave a helpless shrug. "Well then, I'll simply say all three ladies look lovely tonight. Your turban, Lady Chase, is an exceedingly good one. I didn't realize feathers of such a spectacular green existed in nature."

"Never mind my feathers, you young rogue. Make yourself useful, and take me over to Lady Atherton. She's just there on the other side of the ballroom, chatting with Lady Eustace."

"Who are all those young ladies hanging about the alcoves?" Ciaran asked, peering across the ballroom at a cluster of grim-faced debutantes.

Lady Chase squinted at the ladies through her quizzing glass. "Wallflowers. Well, it's disgraceful any young lady should be neglected, with all these gentlemen wandering about. Shockingly bad manners on their part."

"Wallflowers?" Ciaran looked appalled. "But they're lovely!"

"Amiable, too, most of them." Lady Chase lowered the glass with a sigh. "Oh, look, Hyacinth—poor Miss Atkinson is back for a third season. Well, it's a pity. She's a sweet thing, but no money, you know, so what's to be done?"

"Why don't you invite her to dance, Ciaran?" Isla suggested.

"Perhaps I will. Perhaps I'll make myself useful, just as Lady Chase commands, and invite them *all* to dance."

Lady Chase nodded approvingly at him. "Very gentlemanly of you, Mr. Ramsey. Now, Hyacinth, my dear. Don't fret. You've never looked lovelier, but do stop biting your lip, won't you? Miss Ramsey, come along, and I'll introduce you to Lady Eustace and her son. Perhaps he'll invite you to dance. He isn't handsome, and he's an atrocious dancer, but you have to start somewhere."

"Yes, my lady." With a last wide-eyed look at Hyacinth, Isla let Lady Chase and Ciaran drag her to the other side of the ballroom.

Hyacinth watched them go. Ciaran's coat was a bit rumpled, his hair was tousled, and he was pushing his way through the crowd with a bit more energy than was strictly polite, but his height and dark good looks were striking. Hyacinth noticed more than one pair of appreciative feminine eyes following his progress across the ballroom. "It looks as if the *ton* will welcome Ciaran warmly enough."

"The female half, yes, though I don't know why. He looks like a blackguard."

"He does a bit, but it suits him. The young ladies here seem inclined to admire him."

"The Scottish lasses did, as well. No need to worry about Ciaran. He can take care of himself, and Lady Chase has Isla well in hand. Will you dance, Miss Somerset?"

Her nervous gaze roamed the ballroom. They'd attracted more than one curious glance when they were announced, and even now she saw a number of speculative faces pointed in her direction, but it was nothing to the stares and whispers that would commence once she and Lachlan danced together.

"Tell me about Ciaran's Scottish lasses first."

He let out a surprised laugh. "Tell tales on Ciaran? All right. He's a rogue. I can't say any more than that without shocking you."

Hyacinth was absurdly gratified to have made him laugh, and her lips curved in an answering smile. "Indeed? How intriguing. What has he done?"

His eyes narrowed. "One tale about one lass. Then we dance."

"Yes, all right." She'd have to dance sooner or later, and perhaps it was a nice long tale.

"Ciaran's first love was a red-headed lass named Fiona. She didn't return his affection, so he tried to woo her by bringing her a gift—a fish he'd caught, which was still thrashing and flopping when he dropped it in her lap. She screamed and ran away from him, and Ciaran's heart was broken."

Hyacinth laughed, delighted. "Oh, poor Ciaran. How old was he?"

"Seven. He's better at wooing now."

"Did he win the affections of his second love?"

"One tale about one lass, Miss Somerset. It's time for our dance."

Dread rolled through Hyacinth as the couples on the floor moved through the final figures of the quadrille. "Perhaps we should wait just a bit longer, until..."

Until I'm not about to cast up my accounts all over your shoes. "Hyacinth."

Hyacinth's gaze darted to his face. She'd never heard that soft inflection in his voice before.

"There's nothing for you to be afraid of." He held out his hand to her as the first notes of a waltz drifted across the ballroom. "Come. You'll feel better when it's over."

There was a breathless pause as the quadrille ended, and the company watched him lead her to the center of the floor.

Then the whispers began.

She could see the faces of the company watching them from both sides of the ballroom. She'd known they'd all stare at her, and she'd expected the ladies would whisper and smirk from behind their fans. She'd known there would be tittering and gossip, wide eyes and even wider mouths, greedily repeating every tidbit of information. She'd known they'd be curious— had prepared herself for it—but this wasn't mere curiosity. There was a darkness to it, an edge of malicious glee she never could have predicted, even in her worst nightmares.

She missed a step, and stumbled against Lachlan. His hand curved more firmly around her waist. "Don't look at them, Hyacinth. Look at me."

Yes. That was a good idea. Surely she could manage that much. He *was* far larger than anyone else in the room.

"Good," he murmured, when she lifted her face to his. "Is that better?"

"Yes." And it was better, for a moment or two, until her frantic gaze wandered back to the press of bodies surrounding them. Dear God, they looked as if they'd moved closer, as if they were trapping her in a tight circle from which there'd be no escape. Her head began to spin, and her stomach dropped, just as it had the other night, right before she'd swooned—

"Ciaran did win over his second love," Lachlan said suddenly. "Her name was Catriona, and she was also a red-headed lass."

That caught Hyacinth's attention. The crowd around them blurred into the background again, and she was able to gather her wits enough to ask, "Does Ciaran only fancy redheads?"

"Not anymore. He was more discriminating then. Now he fancies everything in skirts."

Well. That was a highly improper thing to say, and yet despite the heat in her cheeks, Hyacinth couldn't help being diverted. "Catriona returned his affections?"

"Yes. I caught him kissing her behind the stables one day. I was so jealous I jumped on his back and held his face to the ground until he was so filthy Catriona refused to kiss him anymore."

"But that's awful! Why would you do that? Did you fancy Catriona yourself?"

"No. I was jealous because he was only nine at the time, and I was already eleven, and I'd never kissed a lass. I was older, and my pride wouldn't allow him to kiss one before I did."

Any lingering awareness of the sneering faces surrounding them faded from her consciousness at this fascinating detail. Hyacinth tried to picture Lachlan as a dark-haired eleven-year old boy, seething with jealousy over his younger brother's romance. "So you tried to drown him in the mud? That doesn't seem fair."

"No, but neither of us cared about what was fair. Ciaran and I spent most of our childhood beating each other bloody. I didn't break his nose that time, though. In any case, he got me back."

"He did? How? What did he do?"

"When I was twelve I was mad for a lass named Mary Mackenzie, and used to show off for her by doing tricks on my horse. One day I tried to impress her with some foolish stunt, and I split the seat of my breeches. Mary saw my bare bottom, was disgusted, and never spoke to me again. I found out later Ciaran had picked apart the seams of every single pair of my breeches. He'd been waiting a week for one of them to split."

Hyacinth laughed so hard she missed another step in the waltz. "Did you break his nose that time?"

"No. He broke mine, and I blacked his eye, and then we decided lasses were too much trouble to bother with, and we went off fishing together."

"Oh, my! It sounds as if it must be much more entertaining to have brothers than sisters. My sisters and I never brawled, or broke each other's noses, or picked each other's seams loose. Was Mary Mackenzie a red-head?"

She peeked up at him through her eyelashes, her lip caught between her teeth, far more interested than she should be in his reply.

"No." That rare smile twitched at his lips. "She had fair hair, and blue eyes."

He stopped moving then, but his smile scattered her wits, and she hardly noticed.

Goodness. What in the world was wrong with Mary Mackenzie that she'd walk away from a man with such a smile as that, over a pair of split breeches?

"Miss Somerset?"

"Yes?"

"The dance is finished."

* * * *

Lachlan had endured any number of awkward experiences in his life.

Mary Mackenzie and the split breeches was only one example. There was the time he'd emptied an entire bottle of his father's best whiskey down his throat, and woken the next morning with his face in a puddle of his own sick. Or the afternoon he'd stumbled upon Ciaran with a girl from the village, and witnessed a feat of anatomy that still made him cringe when he thought about it.

But nothing was more excruciating than leading Hyacinth Somerset through a dance while every damned aristocrat in London gawked at them, as if this were a bloody cockfight instead of a waltz. At one point, when her fingers had gone slack in his hand, he'd been certain he was going to lose her to another swoon.

Lachlan glanced down at the top of her shining head, and waited for the last note of the waltz to fade before he released her, and drew back a fraction so he could get a better look at her.

Golden hair. Fine, pale skin. A slender, graceful figure, and curved lips so pink and plump they made a man's mouth water. Columns or no columns, these Englishmen were daft if they could overlook a lady with such a face.

Aingeal.

But he didn't have any business lingering over her face. Her face, or any other part of her, no matter how tempting those parts were. He'd sworn he'd treat her just as he treated Isla—that he'd take care of her for the duration of the season as if she were his own sister. He wasn't her suitor or her lover, but her *brother*, and from this point on, he'd allow himself to think only brotherly thoughts about her.

And no more sneaking glances at her bosom, either.

He cleared his throat, and offered her his arm. "Shall I take you back to Lady Chase?"

She rested her fingertips on his coat. "Yes, I think that would be best. I wish I had more acquaintances in London to introduce to Isla, but between my grandmother and I, we should be able to ensure she isn't obliged to sit out a dance, and—oh! Look, Mr. Ramsey."

They'd reached the edge of the ballroom, but she'd turned back to look at the couples assembling for a country dance. Lachlan followed her gaze to find a tall, aristocratic-looking gentleman taking his place opposite Isla in the set.

"He's Lord Sydney," Hyacinth murmured. "The Earl of Sydney, that is."

Lachlan studied the man with narrowed eyes. "He's a decent sort?"

"Oh, yes, and quite respectable. I believe this is his first ball since his father died last year."

"What kind of man is he?"

"I don't know him well, but he's always been friendly to me. He's rather lively, and very fashionable, but not at all affected, like so many gentlemen of the *ton*."

They all looked affected to Lachlan—the gentlemen, and the ladies. He watched the couples twirling across the floor, and wondered idly which of these chits was this season's belle.

Whoever she was, she didn't compare to Hyacinth.

He glanced over the crowd, but not a single one of them stood out. It was like looking over a meadow of white daisies. They were pretty enough, but unremarkable, and each indistinguishable from the next in their pale-colored gowns. There was one auburn-haired young lady who'd do for the belle, or perhaps that girl in yellow, with the chestnut-colored hair. She looked likely enough, but none of them were anywhere near as beautiful as—

"Miss Somerset. How do you do this evening?"

Lachlan and Hyacinth both turned at the low, throaty voice.

A young lady with sparkling dark eyes and gleaming ebony locks piled atop her head offered Miss Somerset a shallow curtsey, but when she raised her eyes, she wasn't looking at Hyacinth at all.

She was looking at Lachlan, her full lips tilted into an inviting smile.

Lachlan quirked an eyebrow at her. No pale daisy here, but a showy rose in full flower, the single bloom that stole all the water and sunlight until every other flower withered on the vine. Curved red lips, white shoulders rising from the low neckline of a pale pink gown...

She was the belle.

"How do you do, Lady Joanna?" Hyacinth's tone was perfectly courteous, her curtsey proper and polite, but the flatness in her voice gave her away.

Hyacinth didn't like Lady Joanna.

Lady Joanna either didn't notice, or didn't care. Her gaze was fixed on *him*, and she hardly spared Miss Somerset a glance.

Whatever Hyacinth might feel about Lady Joanna, she was far too polite to fail to make the introductions. "Mr. Ramsay, may I present Lady Joanna Claire? Mr. Ramsey is recently arrived in London from Scotland."

Lady Joanna dipped into a graceful curtsey. "I daresay you didn't receive *quite* the welcome you expected when you arrived, Mr. Ramsey. May I take it from your being here tonight you aren't, after all, a murderer?"

Lachlan stared at her. *Christ.* That was plain enough. He was tempted to tell Lady Joanna she could take his presence however she liked, but any rudeness on his part would reflect on them all, so instead he forced a tight smile. "You may."

This short reply was just on the edge of incivility, but Lady Joanna shrugged it off. "But Miss Somerset doesn't defend you, sir. I do hope she doesn't mean to imply with her silence that you have, in fact, committed a murder?"

Hyacinth paled, and sucked in a quick breath. "No. Not at all. I, ah... made an unfortunate mistake the other evening."

Lady Joanna's eyes narrowed. "Pity you should have said such a thing in front of all of London then, isn't it? One would think, Miss Somerset, you'd be certain before you made such a grave accusation."

Hyacinth's fingertips dug into his arm, and she had that stunned, frozen look of a fox who realizes it's been cornered, right before the hounds tear it to shreds.

She didn't offer a word in her own defense.

"It was a misunderstanding, nothing more," Lachlan said evenly. "Anyone else might have made the same mistake. Even you, Lady Joanna."

"Oh, I doubt it." Lady Joanna tittered. "But you're very kind to defend Miss Somerset, Mr. Ramsay. For as long as I've known her, Miss Somerset has been rather a slave to overactive nerves. A bit of a frenzied imagination, I think." She tapped Hyacinth's arm playfully with her fan, as if they were the best of friends. "I've never seen it cross into outright hysteria as it did the other evening, though. Are you quite well, Miss Somerset? You look a bit peaked, even now."

"Very well, yes." But Hyacinth's voice was faint, and her gaze was darting around the ballroom, as if she were looking for an escape.

"I'm vastly relieved to hear it. You're so pale. I thought you might be on the verge of a swoon. *Another* one, that is."

Lachlan's jaw went hard. Lady Joanna put him in mind of a lazy, malicious cat, taking one swipe after another at a nervous mouse, toying mercilessly with it before ending it with a single deadly slice of its sharp claws.

With a little effort, even the most timid mouse could sink a tooth into its tormentor, but he could see by Hyacinth's blank expression she'd already retreated into herself. She held her tongue, and like all cats, Lady Joanna grew bored of her game when her prey ceased to squirm. "Is that your sister, dancing with Lord Sydney?" she asked, turning back to Lachlan.

"It is."

"Yes, I thought so. And that must be your brother, on the other side of the ballroom, with Lady Chase and Lady Atherton. My goodness, Mr. Ramsey. If you were an affectionate brother, you'd save him from such an awful fate as that."

Lachlan gave her a cold look. "You're aware Lady Chase is Miss Somerset's grandmother?"

"Oh, I'm aware, and of course Lady Chase is excessively diverting, but surely your brother would rather dance than stand about chatting with old ladies and wallflowers." She let out a tinkling, brittle laugh that made Lachlan think of glass shattering. "Do call him over, Mr. Ramsey. Oh, and look, here are my dear friends Miss Barton and Miss Tilbury, so anxious to meet you and your brother."

The two simpering misses who'd joined Lady Joanna batted their eyelashes at him, but aside from brief nods in her direction, they both ignored Hyacinth. Before long, it became clear to Lachlan that Lady Joanna and her gaggle of dim-witted friends were intentionally excluding her.

The longer it went on, the more furious Lachlan grew. A few more gentlemen and ladies joined them, but they took their cue from Lady Joanna as well, and after a few shallow bows and cool smiles, they also dismissed Hyacinth, chatting and laughing with each other as if she weren't there.

Lady Joanna kept him engaged with an endless stream of blather, but at last Lachlan managed to free himself for long enough to take Hyacinth's arm and draw her aside. "What the devil is going on?"

"Nothing. That is, it's all right. Just take me back to Lady Chase, won't you?" She didn't meet his eyes, and her cheeks were flushed with embarrassment and misery.

"Hyacinth, tell me why they're being so rude to you."

She glanced fearfully back at the knot of people behind them, which was growing larger by the second. "I can't explain it all now, but Lady Joanna bears a grudge against Iris for some business that happened last season. It seems she's decided to vent her ire on me in Iris's stead."

"Then we'll both return to Lady Chase at once, and stay there."

He drew her arm through his elbow and tried to lead her away, but she dug her heels in to stop him. "No! Listen to me, Lachlan. Lady Joanna is the belle of the season, and her friends—they're the most fashionable young aristocrats of the *ton*. All of Isla's best prospects move in Lady Joanna's set, including Lord Sydney. You can't afford to alienate them. Just take me to Lady Chase and fetch Ciaran to come back here with you."

Lachlan didn't give a bloody damn who they were. "No. I won't just abandon you—"

"Please, Lachlan. I…I prefer it, really." Her blue eyes were pleading. "I d-don't want…I-I c-can't stay here another moment."

Lachlan ran an agitated hand through his hair. Damn it, he didn't like this, but she looked frantic, her stammer had returned, and she was growing more agitated by the moment. "It's all right. I'll take you back to Lady Chase, if you wish."

"T-thank you." She was trembling as he escorted her across the ballroom to her grandmother. He laid his hand over hers, and even through their gloves, he could feel the iciness of her skin.

"Ah, my dear. There you are. Lady Atherton was just telling me…" Lady Chase's voice faded as she got a close look at her granddaughter's face. "Hyacinth? Are you unwell?"

"N-no. Just fatigued, Grandmother. Mr. Ramsey was kind enough to escort me back to you to rest. I see Isla's found a partner, and Lady Joanna has asked for an introduction to Ciaran. It's all going very well, I think." She managed a wan smile. "Mr. Ramsey, won't you introduce Ciaran to your new friends?"

Friends? They were no friends of his. "I don't want—"

"Go on, Mr. Ramsey." Lady Chase waved him off. "The dance is over, and Lord Sydney is leading your sister off the floor. He's an earl, you know, and it looks like he admires her. You must go and make his acquaintance at once."

Lady Atherton was staring curiously at him, and they'd attracted the attention of Ciaran's wallflowers, as well. Lachlan had no choice but to bow, and lead his brother off to meet Lady Joanna's fashionable set of featherbrains and peahens.

The evening dragged on endlessly, but never more so than when Lachlan was obliged to invite Lady Joanna to dance. Ciaran was charming to everyone, but much to Miss Tilbury's and Miss Barton's disappointment, he danced only with those ladies who'd been obliged to sit out. Isla danced every dance, and was singled out for Lord Sydney's exclusive and admiring attention.

Hyacinth didn't dance again. Not even with Lachlan or Ciaran, though they both pressed her to. No other gentleman asked her. All three of the

Ramseys made a point of returning to her side throughout the ball, but no one else approached her in her solitary corner.

Then, she disappeared entirely.

Lachlan searched the ballroom for her, and had Isla check the ladies' retiring room, but they didn't see Hyacinth again until the end of the evening, when Lady Chase appeared with her hand tucked into her granddaughter's arm, and informed them she'd called for the carriage to take them all home.

Hyacinth hadn't needed any columns. She'd found another place to hide.

Chapter Eleven

Hyacinth knew how to disappear. She'd had many years of practice.

But when she crept back into Lady Bagshot's ballroom at the end of the evening and saw Lachlan Ramsey's scowl when he caught sight of her, she knew she was about to face a reckoning. When he gruffly informed her he'd sent Isla and Ciaran ahead in Lady Atherton's carriage, she realized it was coming sooner rather than later.

Good Lord, he looked grim. She'd rather face a dozen Lady Joannas than that black scowl.

"Where is my grandmother?" She tried to suppress a shiver as he settled her wrap around her, and his big fingers brushed her shoulders. "Surely she didn't leave the ball without me?" Her grandmother could hardly be persuaded to leave a *room* without her, much less Lady Bagshot's ball.

"She's in the carriage, waiting for us. She's fatigued. I tried to send her with Lady Atherton, but she refused." His tone was clipped.

Hyacinth let out a relieved breath. She wouldn't be alone with him for the drive home, then. There was one witness, at least.

But when Lachlan handed her into the carriage, Hyacinth found her one witness half-asleep, the green feathers in her turban fluttering wildly with each nod of her head. By the time they drew away from the curb, Lady Chase was snoring contentedly.

Lachlan looked anything but content. His jaw was hard, his mouth tight. He'd crossed one long leg over the other and thrown a massive arm across the back of the seat, but his casual posture didn't reassure Hyacinth.

This was not the man who'd led her so carefully through the waltz this evening—the man who'd made her laugh with his stories about his boyhood with his brother. No, right now he looked more like the man who'd used that same brother's face as his punching bag on a dark night in an Aylesbury inn-yard.

Hyacinth squirmed in her seat. Goodness, this was awful. Not just because he looked angry. That is, he *did* look angry, but he also looked... Troubled. Disappointed, even.

Well, that made two of them, but then she was so accustomed to that vague, niggling discontent whenever she went into company, she hardly even noticed it anymore.

Except tonight. Tonight, she noticed it.

It had been a long time since she'd had anyone in her life to disappoint. Her family had long since accepted her shortcomings as simply the way she was, and she had, too, but now...

Was it *his* disappointment in her that hurt the most, or her disappointment in herself?

A chill washed over her, and Hyacinth gathered her heavy wrap tighter around her neck. She turned to look out the window so she wouldn't have to see the disillusionment on Lachlan's face, but despite her efforts, her gaze was drawn back to him again and again, until she could stand it no longer. "Mr. Ramsey, I believe I owe you an explanation for my—"

He silenced her with a single shake of his head. He didn't say a word for the rest of the ride to Bedford Square, but he never took his eyes off her. When the carriage rolled up in front of the entryway, he opened the door without waiting for the driver, descended, and held out his hand to her.

Hyacinth hesitated, but his eyebrows shot up in challenge, as if he were perfectly willing to throw her over his shoulder and carry her to...well, she didn't know where he'd carry her, but it didn't seem wise to find out.

She laid her fingers in his gloved palm and let him help her from the carriage. He closed the door quietly behind her, then led her by the hand through the front door and into the entryway.

Hyacinth drew in a deep breath. It was as good a place as any to explain herself. She'd never once heard Lachlan raise his voice, but if he *did* have a mind to shout at her, it wasn't as if he do it in the middle of her grandmother's entryway. "Lachlan, I—"

She gasped as he backed her up against the door behind her, and moved so close she could see the tiny gold flecks in his eyes. "Where did you disappear to tonight, Hyacinth?"

"Disappear?" She cringed at the telltale croak in her voice. "I didn't—"

He took her by the shoulders. "Yes, you did. You stayed with your grandmother and Lady Atherton for a while, but by the time I returned from my second dance with Lady Joanna, you were gone."

"Yes, well no good ever came from dancing with Lady Joanna."

Oh, no. Dash it, she'd gone and blurted that aloud, like a jealous, sniping shrew. Her eyes went wide as that thought took hold.

Am I jealous, over Lachlan Ramsey?

No, surely not. That is, her belly did leap with joy when she coaxed a smile from his lips, and perhaps once or twice she'd imagined what it might be like to kiss him, but that didn't prove a blessed thing. She thought of him as a brother, nothing more, and he'd made it clear he regarded her as a sister, so there could be no question of jealousy between them.

No question at all.

That elusive smile of his twitched at the corners of his lips at her unexpected outburst, and a peculiar, fluttering weakness rose from her knees to her belly—

No, no. This wouldn't do. Her feelings for him were *sisterly.* No question about that, and it was delightful, really, because hadn't she always wanted a brother?

His hands tightened on her shoulders. "You didn't answer my question. Where did you go? I know you weren't in the ladies' retiring room, because I sent Isla to look for you there."

He had? That was…surprising. He took his role as protective brother more seriously than she'd thought. "Yes, all right. It's nothing so awful. I went and rested in Lady Bagshot's library for a little while."

It was a trick she'd learned from Violet, who'd spent a good part of her own season hiding in one library or another. Even now, Violet insisted one could discover a great deal about a person from snooping through their books.

Hyacinth expected this information to soothe Lachlan, but he was frowning down at her, looking anything but soothed. "You went to the library alone? That's not safe."

"Not safe? That's absurd. What place could be safer than a library?"

"You can't be as naïve as that. Do you think there wasn't a single rake among all those fine English peers at the ball tonight? What if one of them had followed you? No one knew where you were, and no one would have heard you if you cried out."

Rakes, stalking young ladies, then leaping upon them in dusty libraries? It sounded a bit far-fetched to Hyacinth. "My grandmother knew where I was—"

"But *I* didn't know. I had no idea where you were, and Lady Chase had gone off to the supper room by the time I missed you. Anything could have happened to you in that amount of time."

Hyacinth stared at him in shock. He'd released her shoulders and was pacing from one end of the entryway to the other, his hand gripping his hair in agitation. "I—I'm sorry. I n-never meant to worry you. I suppose I wasn't th-thinking."

He stopped in front of her and grasped her shoulders again. "I told you I'd watch over you this season. Did you think I didn't mean it?"

"No, of course not. I just didn't think…" she trailed off, not sure how to finish that sentence.

I didn't think you'd notice if I was gone.

That he *had* noticed felt strange, and not in a way she'd ever experienced before. She couldn't say what the fluttery feeling in her chest meant, but it didn't feel *sisterly.*

"Before Lady Huntington left for Buckinghamshire, I promised her I'd take care of you. I made you the same promise. Do you think I'm not a man of my word?"

Hyacinth laid a hand on his arm, appalled to see he looked offended, or worse, hurt. "No, of course I don't think that. I'm sorry, Lachlan. Truly. I won't disappear again."

After a pause he nodded, and then they stood for an endless moment in an awkward silence, until Lachlan released a heavy sigh. "That business with Lady Joanna—what was that about? I could tell you weren't prepared for her attack."

She was quiet for a moment, then, "No, but perhaps I should have been. I knew the *ton* would punish *someone* for the scandal. Now I think on it, it makes sense it would be me, as I was the one who made the false accusation. If Lady Joanna hadn't tormented me, someone else would have."

"Is Lady Joanna that spiteful with everyone?"

"I won't *quite* say that, but she's not precisely delightful company, either. She dislikes all the Somersets, but her particular grudge is with Iris."

"For what?"

Hyacinth sighed. "Iris was the undisputed belle of her season, and many young ladies felt eclipsed by her, Lady Joanna among them. Then Iris had the temerity to go on to become the Marchioness of Huntington. Unforgivable, especially for a lady new to London, and one without a title."

"Is that all?" Lachlan's lip curled. "Lady Joanna nearly took your head off because Iris was a belle, and married a marquess?"

"No, there was something else to it, as well—something to do with Finn thrashing Lady Joanna's brother."

"Finn thrashed her brother?" Lachlan's eyebrows shot up. "Two English noblemen, rolling about in the dust? I wish I'd seen that. Why did he thrash him?"

Hyacinth tapped her lip, thinking. "I'm not entirely sure. I was in Brighton with my grandmother at the time, so I didn't see it, but it was something to do with Iris and a horse race. Lord Claire nearly unseated Iris, and Finn fell into a fury and thrashed Lord Claire. Now I think on it, no one ever explained to me what happened."

That was a common enough occurrence. Her sisters and grandmother tended to avoid telling her any news they thought would distress her. She didn't recall it ever bothering her before, but for pity's sake, marquesses didn't thrash earls every day, did they? How was it she hadn't demanded more details?

"But why should Lady Joanna punish you for something to do with Iris?" Lachlan asked. "You had nothing to do with it."

"Well, she has to punish someone, and Iris would never allow..."

Iris would never allow Lady Joanna to belittle her.

But Hyacinth would. She *had.*

Lady Joanna would never have dared to be as vicious to Iris as she'd been to Hyacinth tonight, and yet Hyacinth hadn't said a word to defend herself.

"Iris would never have allowed what?"

Lachlan was so close now she had to tilt her head back to look into his eyes, and she could see by the intent way he held her gaze he already knew the answer. "You know what."

"I want you to say it."

She pushed out a sigh so deep it burned as it left her chest. "Iris would never allow anyone to speak to her in such a way, and Lady Joanna knows very well how to choose her victim."

He looked down at her for a long moment, then gave a slow shake of his head. "She can't make you her victim unless you let her, Hyacinth."

There it was again, written plainly across his face.

Disappointment.

"I kept waiting for you to stand up for yourself, but you never did."

"I don't remember how, or...perhaps I never knew." Hyacinth's gaze dropped to the floor, her cheeks burning with shame. Her struggle tonight hadn't really been against Lady Joanna. It had been against herself. She'd lost similar battles before, but somehow this failure cut more deeply than the others, because for the first time in as long as she could remember, someone had expected more from her, and she'd disappointed him.

He tipped her face up to his with a finger under her chin. "Lady Huntington told me you were shy even as a child, but it's more than shyness now, isn't it?"

Hyacinth stared up into those knowing hazel eyes, and wondered why Lachlan Ramsey, of all people, should be the only person to understand this about her. Her sisters, her grandmother, her own family—none of them ever questioned her failings. They simply worked around them, and she'd learned to do the same. She no longer knew anymore whether she'd taught them to expect so little of her, or if they'd taught her to expect so little of herself.

But it hardly mattered, did it? Either way, the result was the same.

Two inches of space. No more than that, and it was growing narrower every day. Her life was being whittled down to a sliver while she was ducking behind columns and hiding in libraries.

"Yes, it's more than shyness. I don't know how it happened, or why, or even when, but for as long as I can remember, I've felt like two people. There's the timid Hyacinth everyone knows, and then the other, braver Hyacinth."

His lips quirked. "I know her. She's the one who called me an ass."

Hyacinth's cheeks heated. "Yes, she did. She's...a trifle unruly, I'm afraid."

That Hyacinth had ideas. She had opinions. *That* Hyacinth had a quick temper, and a wicked sense of humor, and she had mouthfuls of words. But it had always been so difficult to say them—such a struggle to get her words past her stammer, at some point she'd simply stopped trying, until *that* Hyacinth had been reduced to nothing more than a voice in her head.

How long would it be, before she disappeared entirely?

"But then that's the way of things, isn't it?" She whispered the words aloud, but she was talking to herself more than Lachlan. "We lose ourselves along the way. At first it's just a small thing—a tiny wager, a single coin. But then it becomes another, and then another, and it happens so slowly— just one coin at a time—by the time you realize your danger, it's too late. You've given it all up, and all your coins are gone."

His fingers tightened on her chin. "Not always. Sometimes a risk pays off, and you get back something you need."

Something you need...

Gold-flecked hazel eyes. A warm, rough fingertip against her skin. An elusive, surprisingly vulnerable, hide-and-seek smile.

Or something you want.

Hyacinth stared up at him, mesmerized. Did he realize the gold flecks in his eyes glowed when he was agitated? Or that the fall of his dark hair over his brow made him look almost boyish, despite his intimidating size, and the way he vibrated with raw intensity?

Did he know he made her entire body vibrate in response?

Perhaps he did, because as he stared down at her, there was a subtle shift in his expression. It might have been imperceptible to anyone else, but Hyacinth saw it. His mouth softened, and his eyelids grew heavy over eyes gone suddenly dark.

Her breath caught in her throat.

Then, slowly—oh, so agonizingly slowly she wasn't sure he was moving at all until she felt his touch—he slid his hands over her neck and stroked the rough pads of his thumbs across her jaw.

She sighed softly. His gaze dropped to her parted lips, and then he was moving closer, his mouth descending toward hers, and she was trembling in anticipation, her eyes drifting closed…

Oh, so soft. His lips were so much softer than she'd dreamed they'd be. Because she *had* dreamed of them. Of him, and his kiss. She hadn't admitted it to herself until the moment his lips met hers, so careful at first, so gentle, just the lightest brush against one corner of her mouth, then the other. They were tiny, restrained kisses, but they deepened when a whimper tore from her throat, and she rose onto her tiptoes to wrap her arms around his neck.

"Hyacinth…" A hoarse whisper in her ear, her name both a plea and a warning at once, but she didn't heed it. She held him tightly, stroking her lips over his again and again until at last he let out a tortured moan, and took her mouth harder, teasing the tip of his tongue at the seam of her lips until she opened for him.

A low growl rumbled in his chest as he dragged her closer, his mouth plundering hers. His tongue was hot and demanding as he stroked into all the empty spaces inside her—the ones she knew about, and the ones she didn't. She clung to him, her knees weak, and her belly quivering with desire.

He dragged his lips over her throat, her neck, across the tops of her breasts. His kisses were desperate, as if he thought she'd be torn from his arms at any moment, and wanted to taste every inch of her skin while he still had the chance. But even as he devoured her, he was whispering to her, his voice strained, breathless, "Hyacinth, we can't…"

Her heart gave a fierce throb of protest as he began to pull away from her. She buried her hands in his hair, but it did no good. He raised his head, and her eyes popped open just as he took a step back, away from her.

And dear God, she'd never been so disappointed in her entire life. Her heart, bursting with hope only moments before, dropped like a wounded bird into the pit of her stomach.

No, don't stop. I don't want a brother, after all.

But Lachlan had already drawn away, so far away even one of his long arms couldn't stretch across the chasm he'd put between them, and the boldness that had made her demand his kiss curled in on itself, and burned into nothingness.

* * * *

Whatever cold, black remnant of his heart remained, Hyacinth Somerset was breaking it.

He couldn't bear to see her always hovering on the edges, like a shivering, hungry child standing on a freezing sidewalk, her nose pressed against the window, looking in on a room filled with the warmth and light of a roaring fire—a child who wanted to come inside, but couldn't quite find her way. What kind of hard-hearted scoundrel could stand about and do nothing while a child froze to death?

Not him. As little as a week ago Lachlan would have said he was just the scoundrel for the job, but she'd made that shriveled organ in his chest creak to life again, shuddering and protesting with every beat.

But Hyacinth Somerset was no child.

She was a woman—a woman with wide blue eyes and soft, plump pink lips, with skin that begged to be touched, and curves that pleaded for the stroke of a man's hands.

His hands.

How like him, to want to steal all her sweetness for himself. A sweetness he had no right to, and didn't deserve. He'd done wicked things in his life before—things he regretted, and things he was ashamed of, but to take something so sweet...

It was unforgivable, like ripping the wings off an angel.

An angel who also happened to be his new brother's sister-in-law. A new brother Lachlan was growing fond of, and one who, apparently, wouldn't hesitate to thrash him if he laid one finger on Hyacinth.

It wouldn't be one finger, either. No, it would be all his fingers, and fingers would lead to other appendages, because once he touched her, he wouldn't be able to stop. Hyacinth wasn't Mary Mackenzie, and he was no longer a twelve-year old boy. He was a man, well past the point of an innocent flirtation, and God knew there was nothing about Hyacinth that made him feel innocent.

Christ. He'd *kissed* her, and she needed to be kissed more than any woman he'd ever known. Kissed and stroked and treasured, until she saw herself as he saw her.

Perfect. Beautiful.

He wasn't the scoundrel for that job, either, but the thought of anyone else kissing her made him want to rip a gaping hole in the sky.

In every way in which it was possible for a woman to be untouchable, Hyacinth Somerset was untouchable to him, and yet he couldn't just avoid her. No, in a vicious twist of fate that was no doubt a punishment for his many sins, the only lady he couldn't touch—the one lady who tempted him more than any other lady ever had—was the same lady he'd vowed to protect.

Even if it meant protecting her from himself.

For an entire season. Weeks of dancing with her at balls, and riding with her in close carriages. Weeks of gazing into those dark blue eyes, and weeks of trying not to gaze at those maddening lips.

Weeks of sensual torture.

And he'd bear it. He suppress every lustful urge, and he'd do it without a word of complaint. She'd been forced to put up with Lady Joanna's insults tonight because of *him*. He'd coaxed her into going ahead with her season, and he wasn't going to abandon her now.

"Lachlan? My grandmother is still in the carriage."

Lachlan jerked his attention back to Hyacinth, suddenly aware he hadn't said a single word in more than five minutes. He ached to take her in his arms again. Even now his eyes refused to leave her face, and his body wouldn't obey his command to back further away from her. Jesus, at this rate he'd tip over into madness before the end of the season. "No more hiding in the library, Hyacinth, and no more surrendering to Lady Joanna. Promise it."

Lachlan winced at the hard edge in his voice. He hadn't meant to sound so severe, but there was safety in retreating into the roughness he knew so well.

Her eyes went wide, but then she dropped her gaze entirely. When she spoke, her voice sounded small. "I promise. I-I think we'd better fetch my g-grandmother from the carriage now."

Lachlan dragged a hand down his face, remorse washing through him when he heard her stammer. She'd had a miserable evening, and he wasn't sure how he'd prevent it from happening again. He understood fists and blood, and how to bring a man to his knees with a single blow, but whispers and sneers, and the *ton*'s sophisticated malice? He hadn't any idea how to protect her from that sort of cruelty.

"I'll go at once." He strode outside to the carriage, roused Lady Chase and escorted her into the entryway.

"Oh, there you are, dear." Lady Chase released Lachlan's arm and took Hyacinth's elbow. "Well, well. I don't know how Lady Bagshot always contrives to have such exhausting balls, but there it is. Good night, Mr. Ramsey."

"Good night, Lady Chase, Miss Somerset."

Hyacinth didn't reply, and when he straightened from his bow, she'd already turned away, and was leading her grandmother up the stairs. She looked smaller to him, as if the massive staircase were swallowing her, and her frame seemed too slight to bear Lady Chase's weight. A surge of sudden, fierce protectiveness shot through him, and before he was aware of what he was doing, he'd climbed half a dozen stairs after her. He made it to the first landing before he came back to his senses, and trudged back down to the entryway, and outside into the cold.

It was late. A fine, wet mist hung over the drive, and the coachman was waiting to take him back to Grosvenor Street, but Lachlan took a moment to lean back against the closed door, and draw a few cold breaths of air into his lungs.

He'd never felt anything like that sudden, mindless stab of emotion in his stomach when he'd charged up the stairs after Hyacinth. Reason had abandoned him, pushed aside by pure instinct.

Whatever he'd been feeling in that moment, it wasn't brotherly.

But it would be. He'd make it be, no matter what he had to do.

Only a devil ripped the wings off an angel.

Chapter Twelve

The Third Ball
Lord and Lady Hayhurst
Request Miss Hyacinth Somerset's company
At a pleasure ball on Tuesday, February 10th
At 7:00 o'clock in the evening
33 Charles Street
Berkeley Square

"It's insupportable you shouldn't have danced at all tonight, Hyacinth. Every single gentleman in this ballroom should be horsewhipped."

Isla flopped onto one of the tiny gilt chairs lined up on the side of the Hayhursts' ballroom, but jumped up again at once, and turned around to glare at it. "My goodness. That's the most uncomfortable chair I've ever sat on."

Hyacinth sighed. It was even more uncomfortable if you'd been sitting on it all night, as she had. "Perhaps the chairs are Lady Hayhurst's way of encouraging the young ladies to dance."

Isla snorted. "Or to punish them for being wallflowers."

Hyacinth glanced down the long row of chairs lined up along the wall, many of which held a glum-looking young lady. "One would think being a wallflower would be punishment enough. I don't think any of us would choose to be here if we could help it."

Isla plopped back down into the chair with a long sigh of her own. "No, I suppose not. These English gentlemen are easily intimidated, aren't they? Why, if we were in Scotland, you wouldn't be permitted to sit out a single dance, no matter what scandal followed you."

That the scandal *was* following Hyacinth was now beyond question. If she'd held out any hope Lady Bagshot's ball was an aberration, it was dashed the moment she set foot in Lord Hayhurst's ballroom this evening. Aside from the sneers and whispers, the *ton* had made a great show of ignoring her.

But then *someone* must be punished for the scandal, mustn't they? One couldn't simply go about accusing innocent gentlemen of murder and face no consequences for it. Wasn't there something, well…*unseemly* about that youngest Somerset girl's hysterical swoon?

No, it simply wouldn't do.

The *ton* was obliged to take someone to task for the debacle. It stood to reason it would be the Somerset chit. If Lord Huntington and Lord Dare weren't in London to witness the girl's disgrace, so much the better. One didn't like to make an enemy of them—if one could avoid it—but the way was conveniently clear in that regard.

Hyacinth was still invited everywhere, but once she arrived, she was roundly shunned. Not just by Lady Joanna and her set, but by all of London.

She'd been a fool not to have seen at once how it would be. After all, all the signs were there. No one had spoken a word to her at Lady Lovell's musical evening two nights ago, and she hadn't been invited to play at bowls or shuttlecock with all the other young people at Lady Otis's picnic yesterday.

It wasn't until tonight, however, that she'd been made aware of the extent of her punishment.

Fully, painfully aware.

It might have been bearable if everyone had simply dismissed her, but she wasn't even permitted to suffer her disgrace in private. Her skin was crawling from all the cold stares aimed in her direction, and her ears burning from the scathing comments whispered behind her back.

She was both spurned and notorious at once. It was her worst nightmare.

"Now the Scottish lads," Isla was saying. "They know a worthy lass when they see one, but *this* lot." She waved a disdainful hand toward the dance floor. "Honestly, they only need the white woolly bits to be mistaken for a herd of sheep."

Both Isla and Hyacinth burst into a fit of giggles. It was the first time Hyacinth had laughed all night.

Thank goodness for Isla.

It would have been easy enough for all of the Ramseys to forget her entirely. She was isolated in a lonely corner of the ballroom with all the other wallflowers and spinsters, whereas they were welcome in Lady

Joanna's much livelier crowd of fashionable young people on the other side of the room, closer to the dancing.

Much to Lady Joanna's dismay, Ciaran didn't seem at all interested in being fashionable. He'd spent most of his evening wandering from one tiny gilt chair to the next, and leading each neglected young lady to the center of the ballroom for a dance. When he wasn't dancing, he chatted and laughed with these forgotten ladies, and made himself so charming and agreeable he was earning a heroic reputation among London's wallflowers.

All three of the Ramseys had been unfailingly loyal to Hyacinth. Isla popped in every chance she could to entertain her with some amusing nonsense or other, and Lachlan prowled about like an overprotective bear, turning that black scowl of his on anyone who dared glance twice at her.

She'd danced twice with him this evening.

Of course, he'd also danced twice with Lady Joanna.

Not that Hyacinth was keeping track of his dances. Because she wasn't. Lachlan could do as he pleased, and after all, it was hardly a surprise he admired Lady Joanna. She was beautiful and clever and audacious—just the sort of lady a vigorous man like Lachlan should admire.

The fact that she was also a poisonous viper was neither here nor there—

"Of course, there are worse things than being a wallflower," Isla murmured, with a quick glance at Lady Chase to make certain she wasn't overheard. Lady Chase was on Hyacinth's other side, well within eavesdropping distance, but she was busy chatting with Lady Atherton. "Much worse things," Isla added, with a meaningful raise of her eyebrows.

"What sorts of things?" What could be worse than being a wallflower and a scandal at once?

Isla lowered her voice. "Well, for instance, I'd prefer an entire evening of being perched on this unfortunate chair to another dance with Lord Clement."

"Oh? What's wrong with Lord Clement?"

"He condescends to the ladies, and he has no conversation that doesn't involve either his matched set of grays or his phaeton. He's also wearing a canary yellow waistcoat this evening. Didn't you notice it?"

"Well, yes." There was no overlooking that waistcoat. "But surely he's not as bad as all that?"

"He *is* as bad. He's a fop and a dandy, but without the wit. He nearly fell into a faint when Ciaran mentioned the bloody nose Lachlan gave him. Now, I'll grant you Ciaran and Lachlan discuss bloody noses *far* too often, but what sort of man faints at the mere mention of blood?"

Hyacinth choked back a laugh. Oh, dear. Poor Lord Clement. "Not the sort of man who'd suit you, I daresay, but my goodness, Isla. I never would have guessed you weren't enthralled with him. The smiles, and the laughing and flirting your fan—that's all feigned?"

"I'm afraid so. Now, before you think me very wicked, I can assure you Lord Clement doesn't give a fig about me. He wants Lady Joanna, and pays attention to me only to irk her. Not that it does the least bit of good, because Lady Joanna is too busy flirting with Lachlan to even notice Lord Clement."

Hyacinth thought of Lady Joanna's laughing red mouth, and her stomach tied itself into a tight knot. "D-does Lachlan flirt back?"

"No. He scowls darkly at her, just like he does everyone else. I adore Lachlan, but he's *not* charming, you know. But then that's what Lady Joanna likes about him."

"I—what do you mean? Why should Lady Joanna like to be scowled at?" Hyacinth preferred his smiles to this scowls, though he'd been so distant with her since their kiss, at this point she'd take either.

"She likes him because he's enormous, and dark and rough and scowlish, and—"

"Scowlish? Is that a word?"

"Not a real one." Isla shot her a mischievous smile. "Ciaran and I made it up years ago, just for Lachlan. It comes in quite handy. Anyway, Lachlan's scowlish, and he doesn't have the least interest in impressing Lady Joanna. That's why she likes him. Well, that and because he's brother to a wealthy marquess."

Hyacinth managed to hold her tongue, but she was quite indignant on Lachlan's behalf. He *was* dark and rough, and perhaps he was even scowlish, but there was far more to Lachlan Ramsey than that. If Lady Joanna couldn't see it, then she didn't deserve his scowls, or his smiles.

"Does...do you suppose Lachlan cares for Lady Joanna?" Hyacinth asked, her heart pounding painfully in her chest.

Isla shrugged. "I'm not sure. It's difficult to tell with Lachlan, but something is certainly distracting him."

Hyacinth's heart sank. Lady Joanna was what was distracting him. What else could it be?

Isla dragged her chair closer to Hyacinth's. "Otherwise he'd have noticed at once how shamelessly Lord Sydney's been flirting with me. But for the moment it suits me for Lachlan to remain distracted."

Hyacinth didn't want to hear anything more about Lachlan and Lady Joanna, and she leapt at the chance to change the subject. "Why, are you flirting back? I wouldn't blame you if you were. I've always liked Lord Sydney. He's very handsome and gentlemanly without being dull."

"Oh my, yes. Lord Sydney is lovely, and great fun, too. I like him very much, but there is another gentleman..."

"Indeed?" Hyacinth tilted her head closer to Isla's. "Who?"

A becoming flush rose in Isla's cheeks. "Lord Pierce. I don't know him well," she rushed on, before Hyacinth could interrupt. "He's not one of Lady Joanna's set—though not from lack of effort on her part—but he's friends with one or two of the gentlemen who are, so he comes over now and again. He's quite...arresting, isn't he?"

Arresting. Yes, that was a good word for Lord Pierce. He was a marquess, for one, which was quite good enough for the *ton* to approve of him, but he also happened to be very tall, very broad-shouldered, and very handsome. More than one young lady in the Hayhursts ballroom tonight was angling for his attention.

"He is, yes, but he's so..." Hyacinth hesitated.

"What? Do you know something to his discredit?" Isla clutched at Hyacinth's hand with such sudden energy, Hyacinth had to wonder if her friend found Lord Pierce a great deal more than just *arresting*.

"No, not at all. Quite the opposite. He's a well-respected, honorable gentleman. It's only that he's a bit...stern? No, that's not quite right, but he's very serious, and a trifle forbidding. Perhaps he should smile more."

Then again, Lachlan rarely smiled, and it hadn't done much to deter *her*, had it? It only made his smiles more precious, and made her more determined to coax them loose.

"Oh, I don't know. I like his stern countenance. He has the most deliciously firm lips. They're shown to best advantage when he doesn't smile."

"Isla!" Hyacinth laughed. "My goodness. Don't say you stare at his lips!"

"I do indeed, and since he disapproves of me and never smiles at me, I've had quite a lot of time to study his frowns. I've decided they suit him."

"Why should he disapprove of you?" Hyacinth asked, with a touch of pique. No one was lovelier than Isla.

"Well, it's rather foolish, really, but we had a bit of an argument about propriety at Lady Bagshot's ball the other night. Miss Tilbury said something about ladies not being permitted to walk or drive down St. James's Street. I said I thought it an absurd rule, and so it is, Hyacinth. I don't see why the ladies' freedom should be curtailed because the gentlemen drink too much at White's, and then loll about in the bow window, gawking at passersby, and forgetting their manners. Anyway, Lord Piece gave me quite a lecture over it."

"I wish I'd heard that conversation. Lord Pierce *is* very proper. What did he say?"

"Oh, some tripe about it being for the ladies' own good, but I don't believe that's the real reason. I think it's so the gentlemen can behave as badly as they like, without anyone about to take them to task for it. I didn't hesitate to say so, and I'm afraid I was a bit, ah...*lively* with him, but I do so hate to be lectured, and I particularly hate being told things are being done for my own good."

"I wonder you came away from this discussion with a liking for Lord Pierce." Hyacinth gave her a teasing smile. "I would have thought it would be just the opposite."

Isla grinned back. "Not at all. I was so tremendously relieved to find an Englishman who wasn't a biddable sheep like all the others, I found myself quite taken with Lord Pierce. He's dreadfully stiff and correct, but I fancy there's some unruliness lurking under his lordship's propriety."

If Lord Pierce had an unruly side, Hyacinth had never seen it, but she kept this observation to herself. "It's a pity Finn isn't here. Lord Pierce owns the neighboring estate to Huntington Lodge, and Finn knows him rather well, I believe."

"Yes, that would have been helpful, but for the moment I'll go on as I have been, poking at Lord Pierce every now and again." Isla gave Hyacinth a cheeky wink, then rose from her chair. "I'd quite like to see what's under there."

Hyacinth laughed. "And what of Lord Clement? What if he falls in love with you, and asks Lachlan for your hand, and Lachlan commands you to marry him?"

The hem of Isla's gown swept dramatically over the floor as she turned around to face Hyacinth, a grin on her lips. "I'm afraid I've never been very good at doing what I'm told."

* * * *

The darker Lachlan's scowl became, the more Lady Joanna seemed to admire him.

Foolish chit.

"Tell me more about your life in Scotland, Mr. Ramsey. Do the women really drink whiskey, and the men carry swords everywhere? Is it true the entire country is overrun with sheep?"

The ladies and gentlemen surrounding Lady Joanna tittered, but Lachlan was occupied with looking over her shoulder at Hyacinth, and he ignored Lady Joanna entirely.

That lady wasn't accustomed to being ignored, and she stepped several inches to the right, so her face was directly in Lachlan's sight line. "But you don't seem amused, Mr. Ramsey. I'm afraid you're distracted this evening." She flicked a glance over her shoulder. "Oh, dear. It's poor Miss Somerset, isn't it?"

Another titter went around the group at Hyacinth's name, and Lady Joanna's malicious smile widened.

Lachlan gave her a bored look. "Miss Somerset looks happy enough to me. She doesn't need or want your pity, Lady Joanna."

"How silly you are, Mr. Ramsey." Lady Joanna let out a tinkling laugh, but her dark eyes narrowed. "No young lady who's obliged to spend an entire ball watching other young ladies dance while she herself is ignored can possibly be happy."

Ignored? If only that were the case. Every aristocrat in this bloody ballroom had spent the entire evening gawking at her. The gossip had reached such a fever pitch Lachlan had even considered taking her into Lord Hayhurst's library himself. At least then she'd be shielded from vultures like Lady Joanna.

"Poor thing. Such a sad state of affairs." Lady Joanna shook her head in mock sympathy, her eyes gleaming with satisfaction. "There must be something we can do to assist her. Don't you agree, Miss Tilbury?"

Miss Tilbury, who always agreed with Lady Joanna, no matter what nonsense she spouted, gave the required answer. "Oh, yes! Of course. But what?"

"Hmmm." Lady Joanna tapped her fan against her lips. "Well, it's rather difficult, given Miss Somerset's pitiable situation, but there must be something…oh, I have it! Lord Chester, why don't you invite Miss Somerset to dance?"

"Yes, you must, my lord!" Miss Tilbury looked as if she were trying to smother a sudden burst of laughter. "What a wonderful idea. I don't know why we didn't think of it before."

A suspicious frown creased Lachlan's brow as he turned to the young man in question. Lady Joanna and Miss Tilbury looked far too delighted for Lachlan to be easy about this suggestion, but he couldn't find any reasonable objection to Lord Chester. He was younger than the other gentlemen, and hung about on the fringes of Lady Joanna's set. God knew the boy was awkward and bumbling, but he seemed decent enough.

"I, ah, well, I'm certain Miss Somerset wouldn't care to dance with me." The young man's face had gone scarlet, and he plucked nervously at his cravat. "I'm not a very accomplished—"

"Why, what nonsense! Of course she'll dance with you." Lady Joanna gave Lord Chester a little push forward. "She's hardly danced all night, and is in no position to refuse you. Indeed, my lord, you'd be doing her a kindness."

"Well, of course I'd be delighted to dance with Miss Somerset, if you think it a good idea." Lord Chester bowed to Lady Joanna, but his face was pinched with worry. "If she agrees, that is."

"Oh, she will." Lady Joanna gave him another shove, her eyes gleaming. "Go on, then."

Lachlan watched the lad make his way across the ballroom and bow to Hyacinth. Damn it, he didn't like this. Lady Joanna was far too gleeful, but short of tackling Lord Chester to the floor, there wasn't much he could do to stop it.

From across the ballroom Lachlan saw Hyacinth nod her head, and the red-faced young lord took her arm and led her to the center of the ballroom.

"Will you dance, Miss Taylor?" Lachlan hastily turned toward the least objectionable of Lady Joanna's friends, and offered her his arm. He didn't have any interest in dancing with her, but he hadn't liked the look on Lady Joanna's face just now. If she intended to cause Hyacinth some mischief, he wanted to be nearby to put a stop to it.

Miss Taylor simpered her agreement and took his arm, and Lachlan led her out to the floor. They took up positions behind Miss Tilbury and her partner, who were placed just behind Lady Joanna and Lord Sydney, who were at the top of the set. Hyacinth and Lord Chester were several places below him.

Lady Joanna called a country dance, the music swelled, and Lord Sydney led Lady Joanna in a series of lively steps down the long line of couples. When Miss Tilbury and her partner went down the line, Lachlan could see that lady's face was alight with spiteful anticipation, but he still didn't see anything amiss. It appeared to be a typical country dance.

That is, it did until Lord Chester led Hyacinth down the row.

That was when Lachlan saw it.

Everyone saw it.

Lachlan's chest tightened with impotent fury as the young lord, his face red with shame, trod on Hyacinth's feet not once, not twice, but three times as they made their way through the set.

The boy couldn't seem to take a step without crushing her slippers under his pumps. The couples along the line noticed and began to titter at his clumsiness. He grew more nervous, and it made matters worse.

Lady Joanna and Miss Tilbury tripped lightly down the row, their faces wreathed in smiles. Both of them were clearly well pleased with their plot, but by the time Lord Chester had taken Hyacinth down the line three times, he looked as if he were ready to burst into tears.

And the dance wasn't nearly over. Given the number of couples in the line, it could easily go on for half an hour or more. There wasn't a damn thing Lachlan could do except watch, his entire body stiff with rage, as Hyacinth's dainty feet were battered. He struggled to hold himself in check, but when Lord Chester's pump snagged the edge of her gown and ripped a long tear in her hem, he'd had enough. He started forward, ready to lunge for Hyacinth and carry her off the floor, but he'd hardly moved a single step toward her when she caught his eye.

She stopped him with a tiny shake of her head, imperceptible to anyone but him, but a world of understanding passed between them in that single gesture.

Don't interfere.

Her gaze had met his for a single instant only before it slid away, but it was enough.

Lachlan obeyed her silent command, but Christ, it was torture. Pure torture, to be forced to watch as she was hurt over and over again, without being able to do a damn thing about it. There was only one person more wretched than he was, and that was Lord Chester, who saw, too late, that he never should have allowed himself to be goaded into such a cruel prank.

But Hyacinth...

She never flinched.

Not once, as Lord Chester continued to make mincemeat of her feet, did she ever acknowledge by word or expression that anything was wrong. She didn't miss a single step, and her resolve never faltered. She looked up into her partner's face as she went through the figures of the dance, her hand clasped loosely in his, her lips curved in a tight smile.

Helpless anger, regret, and guilt gathered like a storm in Lachlan's chest as the dance dragged on and on, until he was sucked into such a whirlwind of confused emotions he couldn't tell how he felt, or who he was angry at anymore.

He knew only that this dance was endless.

At last the music faded, and the gentlemen bowed to their partners. Hyacinth dipped into a graceful curtsey in front of Lord Chester, for all the world as if she'd never enjoyed a more pleasant dance in her life.

Lachlan stared after them as a grim-faced Lord Chester took Hyacinth's arm and escorted her through the crowd, but he lost sight of them in the crush as couples streamed off the floor, and others moved to take their places. He hurried to deliver Miss Taylor to her mother, then ran across the ballroom toward Lady Chase.

But when he came to a breathless halt beside her, Hyacinth wasn't there. "Where is she?"

Lady Chase was wringing her hands. "She went to the ladies' retiring room. Oh, Mr. Ramsey! I tried to accompany her, but she wouldn't allow it. I daresay she didn't want me to see how bad it was—"

"I'll go, and wait for her in the hallway."

"Yes. Hurry, won't you?"

Lachlan tore through the ballroom. More than one head turned to follow his progress, but Lachlan ignored them all, his gaze fixed on the double doors that led into the long hallway beyond. Only one person mattered to him, and nothing in the world could have stopped him from going after her.

Chapter Thirteen

Hyacinth didn't allow herself a wince or a limp until she'd left the ballroom and all the prying eyes behind. Once she was alone in the dim hallway, she braced her hand against the wall and made her slow, painful way toward the ladies' retiring room, her feet howling in protest with every step.

It felt as if the bones in her toes had been crushed to a powder, but it couldn't possibly be as bad as that. Surely no bones were broken. Her toes were a bit mangled, yes, and her slippers were certainly ruined, but nothing worse.

She gritted her teeth against the pain and hobbled down the hallway, but when she neared the ladies' retiring room she became aware of a babble of female voices drifting out into the hallway, punctuated by an occasional shriek of laughter.

Hyacinth hesitated outside the door, leaning against the wall for support. She couldn't be sure they were laughing at *her*, but the high-pitched titters and squeals had an ugly, mocking edge to them. In any case, she couldn't inspect her injuries with every gossip in London hanging over her shoulder—not without giving them the opportunity to describe her bruises and gashes to the *ton* in thrilling detail as soon as they returned to the ballroom.

Her lips pulled into a grimace as she straightened from the wall and wobbled to the end of the hallway on her battered feet. She opened the first door she found, and slipped inside.

Cool darkness enveloped her. Hyacinth pulled in a deep breath and let it out in a long sigh as she began to pick her way over to the nearest sofa. She'd promised Lachlan she'd avoid deserted libraries for the rest of the season, but she'd made that promise before her toes were trampled to mush under Lord Chester's pumps. Surely bodily injury was an exception—

Hyacinth froze at the soft click of the door opening behind her, then closing again, and the muted thud of footsteps at her back. She tried to whirl around to face her pursuer, her heart crashing against her ribs, but her feet chose that moment to fail her. She stumbled, but before she could fall to her knees, a strong, hard arm wrapped around her waist.

Oh, dear God. It was one of those dreadful library rakes Lachlan had warned her about, and she couldn't properly defend herself from any improper advances, because her toes were crushed.

"Unhand me at once, you blackguard!" She struggled against his hold, beating her palms against his shoulders. In some dim part of her brain she realized only two gentlemen in the ballroom this evening had shoulders as broad as these, but panic had her in its grip now, and she continued to fight instinctively, like a trapped animal.

"It's all right. It's only me."

Lachlan's calm, quiet voice pierced her haze of panic. He held her against his hard, enormous chest until she stilled, and he felt so good, so safe Hyacinth didn't even stop to consider what she was doing, but twined her arms around his neck, sagged against him, and pressed her face into his waistcoat.

A low, comforting rumble rose from his chest. He swept her up as if she weighed no more than a feather, cradling her in his arms with such gentleness she let herself nuzzle deeper against him with a sigh. Oh, how had she ever believed this man was dangerous, or that he relished brawling and violence? His fists may be the size of a horse's hooves, and he knew how to use them, but no man who touched a lady with such tender care would ever needlessly hurt someone.

If Lachlan used his fists, it was because he felt he had no other choice.

He carried her over to a long leather sofa, laid her carefully against one end, and then smoothed her skirts over her legs before seating himself on the other. His face was half-lost in shadows, but he was watching her—she could feel the weight of those dark hazel eyes on her face as if his fingers were stroking her cheek.

He didn't say a single word, but sat quietly, waiting.

Hyacinth twisted her fingers together in her lap. "It wasn't as awful as it looked."

The words had hardly left her mouth before he contradicted her, his voice flat. "Yes, it was."

"No, I-I wasn't badly hurt, really."

"Yes, you were." Again, no hesitation, and even in the cool dimness of the library, his eyes seemed to burn right through her. "I saw you limp into the library from the other end of the hallway. You could hardly walk."

"Of course I can walk! It's not as terrible as you're making it out to be. It wasn't anything, really. Just a dance, and not that many people noticed it—"

"Everyone noticed it, or if they didn't, they'll hear about it soon enough. Don't pretend it was nothing, and don't lie to me."

"I'm not lying!" she protested, her voice a touch higher than normal, as it always was when she lied. "I admit it wasn't the most pleasant country dance I've ever had, but it wasn't the disaster you make it out to be—"

"Let me see your feet, then."

He reached for the heel of her slipper, but she jerked her foot away before he could take it off. "No."

Oh, God—it *was* as bad as Lachlan thought it was. Worse, if the throbbing in her toes was any indication. There would be bruises and cuts, and likely blood and swelling, and if she let him take off her slippers he'd see it, and...

And she didn't want him to, because somehow, in a way she couldn't explain, she was ashamed of herself. Ashamed of being an object of ridicule, and ashamed of getting hurt.

"Hyacinth." His voice was grim with warning.

"No! Just help me get to the carriage, then fetch Lady Chase, won't you? I want to go home." Oh, how she despised the wobble in her voice just then!

He heard it, and his hands clenched into fists. "I should never have asked you to do this. This is your last ball, Hyacinth. Your season ends tonight."

Hyacinth stared at him, dumbfounded into silence. This was the reprieve she'd been longing for since Lady Joanna had mocked her at Lady Bagshot's ball. This was her chance to escape the *ton*'s censure without disappointing anyone—her chance to fade back into comfortable obscurity, where no one laughed at her, and she could be certain each hour would mirror the one before it.

It should have made her happy. As little as a week ago, it would have. But now, well...everything had changed, hadn't it?

Lachlan had urged her to stand up for herself. He'd told her she could do it—she could show the *ton* they couldn't intimidate her into running away. She'd looked into his eyes, and she'd searched those fierce hazel depths, and she hadn't seen a single shred of doubt there. He'd believed in her, and because of that, for the first time in as long as she could remember, she'd believed in herself.

She wasn't going to give that up for anything, not even if all ten of her toes were broken, and she'd left a trail of bloody footprints on Lord and Lady Hayhurst's pristine ballroom floor.

Not for anything, or anyone, not even Lachlan. He might think her too weak to fight her way to the end of her season. He might not believe in her anymore, but she was no longer that same lady she'd been just a week ago. There was no going back. Not now. Not ever.

Now, nothing in the world mattered as much to her as proving him wrong. Proving them all wrong.

She *could* make it through her season. She *would* make it, despite Lady Joanna's attacks and Lord Chester's pumps and the *ton*'s gossip and smirking.

Because if she didn't...if she didn't...

Where would it end? Where would *she* end? In her grandmother's townhouse, wandering from room to room, her footsteps echoing in the emptiness. In Brighton with the other invalids, her grandmother hovering over her, fearing the worst each time she coughed, or showed even the slightest hint of low spirits.

No. There had to be more than that. She needed more, and she deserved more, and if she was the only one left who believed she could have it, well...

Then so be it. She met Lachlan's eyes, and slowly shook her head. "No. I'm not giving up. I promised I'd finish the season with Isla, and that's what I intend to do. You said...just last week you urged me to stand up for myself. You said no one could make me a victim without my consent. Was that just talk, Lachlan? Because nothing's changed since then."

His face darkened. "Everything's changed! Tonight it wasn't just a few snide words from Lady Joanna. They've *hurt* you, and I couldn't stop it. I couldn't protect you from it."

"You think this is *your* fault?" Hyacinth gaped at him, stunned. For the first time she noticed the bleakness in his face, the way his hand shook as he dragged it through his hair.

He didn't see this as her failing. He saw it as *his*.

"Lachlan." She reached for his hand and held it between her own. "There was no way you could have known this would happen. Even *I* didn't know poor Lord Chester was such a danger on the dance floor, and he and I have been friends for several years. You've been in London for less than three weeks. How could you possibly know?"

"I knew something was wrong. Lady Joanna was giddy at the thought of you dancing with Lord Chester, and so was that half-wit, Miss Tilbury. I should have seen it, and put a stop to it before—"

"How could you have put a stop to it, Lachlan, without causing a scene and making it worse? Would you have chased poor Lord Chester out of the ballroom when he stepped on my foot? Thrown me over your shoulder and carried me off the floor?" She squeezed his hand, and offered him a cautious smile. "At one point I thought you might do just that, and I'm very glad you didn't. There's quite enough gossip about me already."

She'd hoped for a smile in return, but his lips remained tight. "I should have warned you something was wrong before he led you out to the floor."

"Even if you had warned me, it wouldn't have done any good." She released his hand and fell back against the sofa with a sigh. "As I said, I've known Lord Chester for several years. Even if I'd known he'd step on my toes, I wouldn't have refused to dance with him."

"Damn it, Hyacinth." The bleakness on his face dissolved into anger. "Is that your idea of standing up for yourself? Letting some gawky, tongue-tied lord crush you under his feet?"

Hyacinth flinched at his ugly words. She didn't answer right away, but watched him in silence for a long moment. "No," she whispered at last. "That's what I call being a friend."

A harsh sound tore from his throat. "A man who'd let Lady Joanna coax him into trampling you isn't your friend."

"He didn't set out to hurt me, Lachlan. He wouldn't. I don't know what happened with Lady Joanna, but I know Lord Chester. He wouldn't do that."

"He *did* do it!" He yanked the hem of her skirt back to reveal her slippers, but the anger on his face transformed into horror when he saw the blood seeping through the white satin covering her toes. "Hyacinth…oh, God, look what he did to you."

His voice broke on the last word, and Hyacinth jerked her skirts down over her slippers to hide them, then pulled her knees up and wrapped her arms around them to keep them hidden. "Listen to me, Lachlan. Lady Joanna is…"

But she hadn't any words for Lady Joanna. That kind of vindictiveness was wholly outside her experience. She didn't understand it, and she didn't want to. "Lady Joanna is one thing, but Lord Chester…"

Oh, how to make him understand?

She drew in a deep breath. "Lord Chester was one of the first gentlemen I met when I arrived in London. His grandmother, Lady Dale, is friends with my grandmother, and a dear, sweet lady. I was just sixteen when I came to live with my grandmother, and a hopeless, bumbling country girl. My parents had died the year before, you see, and I'd never been to London. I was…quite lost."

She peeked at him through her lashes, half-afraid he'd be glowering at her, or worse, yawning with boredom, but he was watching her face with such attentive intensity, heat washed over her cheeks.

"Lady Dale used to bring Lord Chester with her when she came to visit my grandmother, and he was...oh, he was the kindest young man. Awkward, to be sure, and shy, but then so was I. Still, between the two of us we somehow managed to put our self-consciousness aside, and we became friends. I told him all about the life I'd left behind in Surrey, and he confided in me about his father's illness. Sometimes we'd walk in the gardens, and he'd give me the scientific names for all the plants. He's fond of botany, and has a great deal of knowledge about it, and—"

"He's your friend. I understand that. But that doesn't mean you have to let him hurt you, whether he meant to or not. You should have let me escort you off the dance floor."

She shook her head. Lachlan said he understood, but he didn't. Not really. "If I'd let you escort me off the dance floor, and we'd left Lord Chester there alone, in the middle of a set, how do you think he'd have felt, Lachlan?"

She was watching him closely, and as soon as she asked, she saw it hadn't even occurred to him how Lord Chester might feel. Which was all well and good, because Lachlan didn't owe Lord Chester a thing.

But *she* did. She owed him her friendship. It was as simple as that. To her, it made all the difference.

"He would have been dreadfully embarrassed. Shamed and humiliated. Don't you see, Lachlan? Lady Joanna tried to make a fool of Lord Chester tonight, just as she did me—she was as cruel to him as she was to me. If I'd gotten angry with him, or cried out, or walked away, it would have hurt him terribly and, well...I daresay Lord Chester's feelings are more sensitive than my toes." She looked away, down at her hands twisted in her lap, and added quietly, "I don't call hurting my friend standing up for myself. If it is, then I suppose I won't ever be able to stand up for myself, after all."

She continued to pluck at the folds of her gown with nervous fingers, avoiding his eyes, but when he said nothing, and the silence had stretched so long she'd nearly ripped a hole in her skirts, she risked a glance at him.

His dark gaze met hers, and the look in those hazel depths made her breath stop in her chest.

* * * *

This woman. God in heaven, *this woman.*

When he'd first seen Hyacinth Somerset, he'd thought she looked like an angel. After she'd accused him of murder, he'd thought her mad. Then he'd believed her sane enough, but too fragile to be of much use to anyone, and he'd decided they'd all be better off once her grandmother took her away to Brighton.

But then he'd caught a glimpse of all she kept hidden. Cleverness. Determination. And a hesitant sort of bravery she'd only just begun to understand.

And when he looked at her now...

Lachlan gazed into her wide blue eyes—eyes that were pleading with him to hear her, to understand—and he found he couldn't say a word. His mouth was dry, his breathing labored, and his heart...it was shuddering and jerking and swelling inside him as if it were about to crash through his ribcage.

He'd been right, all those weeks ago. She was an angel.

Not because of her beauty. No, he'd been wrong about that. Her blue eyes, golden hair, and soft, smooth skin would distract any man, but dozens of ladies in the ballroom tonight had golden hair and blue eyes, and not one of them made his heart swell. None of them made him want to sink to his knees.

Not a single one of them was the angel *she* was.

Her eyes and her hair, her skin and her smile—it caught people's eyes, and turned their heads, but her beauty didn't end there.

It didn't begin there, either.

It began in her heart.

Her pure, true kindness was rarer and more precious than any gem. Her kindness *was* her strength. He thought of her feet—of the blood staining the white satin—and of her face as it had been in the ballroom, when every dancer in the set was laughing at her.

She'd looked into Lord Chester's face and smiled at him. She'd finished the dance, her head high.

That was strength, and it came from the deepest part of her.

And her smile...dear God. She had the sweetest smile he'd ever seen.

After the trouble in Scotland, he'd vowed he'd never put faith in loyalty or kindness again. They were lies, nothing more. People liked to pretend they existed, but they didn't. Not really.

But here they were deep inside the heart of this little English lass, with her timid stammer and sweet smile, and her wide, anxious eyes.

She was waiting for him to say something, but Lachlan had no words for her. Nothing he said could explain how he felt at this moment. He'd never been the sort of man who could magically spin his feelings into pretty words. He was rough and hard and more likely to scowl than smile, but he did know how make his actions say what he couldn't.

He reached for her slowly, and then, as gently as his big hands would allow, he wrapped his fingers around one of her slender ankles. She stiffened at once as if to pull away, but he stopped her with a soft murmur. "Let me see your feet, *aingeal*. I won't hurt you."

She hesitated, then gave a brief nod.

He shifted closer to her, slid his hand under the hem of her skirts, and carefully drew out one of her feet, then the other, and laid them both gently across his thighs.

Lachlan had seen more than his fair share of bloody noses. He'd *had* more than his fair share of them, as well, along with the usual gashes and punctures and a variety of other gaping, seeping wounds one would expect of a boy raised in the Scottish Highlands. His body was a roadmap of nicks and scars.

He'd never in his life recoiled from the sight of blood.

Not until it was *hers*.

The toes of her white satin slippers and her fine white stockings were smeared with ugly red stains. "I don't want to hurt you, but I need to take your slippers off, and your feet have swollen to twice their size." Damn it, her toes could be crushed.

"It looks worse than it is, I'm sure."

But her voice was shaky, and when Lachlan glanced at her face, he could see she'd gone pale. His jaw went hard and his thighs tensed, and she must have noticed it, because she tried to slide her feet off his lap. "You look angry. Perhaps this isn't a good idea, Lachlan."

He cupped one of her heels in his palm to still her. "It's all right. I'm not angry. I won't even scowl."

He *was* angry. He was bloody furious, but she didn't need him falling into a rage right now. She was hurt, and in more pain than she was letting on. He wasn't calm, gentle or patient, but for Hyacinth, he'd do his best.

"Settle back against the sofa, and try and relax. I know it's difficult." He rubbed his palm back and forth across one of her ankles in a slow, soothing motion until he felt some of the tension drain from her. "There. That's better."

She sighed, and let her head fall back against the sofa's arm. "That feels...nice."

Lachlan thought so, too. Far *too* nice.

He cleared his throat. "I want to take off your slippers before your feet swell any more. Will you let me do that? You'll feel better when the silk isn't cutting into your skin, but it's, ah...it's going to hurt when I take them off."

"It already hurts." She lifted her head and gave him a wan smile. "So you may as well go ahead."

He nodded. "Rest your head against the sofa again, and close your eyes."

She obeyed, and after a brief struggle, Lachlan managed to slip the tip of his finger between her heel and the back of her slipper. He slid it down as gently as he could, then nudged the top loose to free her toes. A small gasp of pain escaped her, but then she clamped her lips shut. Lachlan had the distinct impression she was trying to be quiet to make this easier on *him*.

"There. That's the worst of that foot done." He resumed his steady, rhythmic stroking of her ankle until her breathing steadied. "One more, *aingeal*. Lie back again, and close your eyes."

By the time he slid the second slipper free, his hands were shaking. Perspiration misted her face and neck, and she was so white, alarm shot through Lachlan. "It's all done now. Take a deep breath."

"Are they...how bad is it?" Her eyes were tightly closed still, as if she were afraid to look.

Lachlan studied her feet, but he couldn't see much. "I can't tell. Your stockings. Can you remove them?"

"Yes, all right." She sat up, but then lay back down immediately, and what was left of the color in her face drained away entirely. "In a moment, perhaps. I'm a bit dizzy."

"I'll do it. That is, with your permission, I'll take them off for you. I don't have to lift your skirts to do it, but just slide my hands under..."

Lift your skirts? Slide my hands under?

Christ. Did he have to sound so eager?

"Yes, I—I think that would be best. That is, it's a bit awkward for both of us, but if you're willing..."

Willing? There wasn't a man alive who wouldn't be willing to slide his hands under her skirts. He was more willing than any of them, which was precisely the reason he shouldn't be doing it.

"I wouldn't suggest such a thing, but if the blood dries the silk will stick to it, and it will be much more painful to remove them," she added, her cheeks reddening.

"Right, of course." For God's sake, she wasn't his lover, and this wasn't some bloody seduction. She was hurt, her head dizzy with pain, and he was sitting here like a scoundrel, thinking about untying her garters.

"Lachlan? If you'd rather not, then—"

"No, I will. You're right. We don't want the blood to dry. All right, then. Lie back, and..."

No! Don't lie back. There would be no lying back of any kind while he was foraging around under her skirts for her garters.

"This will only take a moment." He fumbled about, his fingers clumsy, but at last he managed to slide his hands under her hems. Smooth silk over warm skin filled his palms, and her legs, the slender, sweet curve of her calves...

The longest moment of my life.

Chapter Fourteen

If anyone had told Hyacinth this evening would end with Lachlan Ramsey's hands under her skirts, she would have denied the charge most vehemently. She would have said she'd never allow such a thing. She'd have insisted they were mad.

Then she would have spent the rest of the evening wondering what those huge hands might feel like, sliding over her legs, his rough fingertips catching on the delicate silk...

Divine. She'd never had a man's hands under her skirts before, but now she had, she understood perfectly how it was young ladies could end up ruined.

Or was it just this man's hands that were so delicious? Was it only his touch that made her eyelids drift closed, and her chest rise and fall like a bellows with each panting breath? Dear God, her bosom was actually heaving. She'd heard whispers about heaving bosoms. She'd always thought it was mere exaggeration, but here she was...

Heaving.

It was so divine she forgot the awful throbbing in her toes and the sharp stab of pain in the arch of her left foot. With a tiny sigh she gave herself over to the seductive stroke of his palm over the back of her knee.

"Damn it. I can't get the bow loose." He fumbled at her garters, and Hyacinth let out a soft gasp as his thick fingers grazed the bare skin at the top of her stockings.

His gaze jerked to her face. "Hyacinth? Are you dizzy still? Are you going to swoon?"

Swoon? And miss this? No, indeed.

"No, no, don't stop…I mean, I'm quite all right, and not the least bit dizzy anymore." A lie, of course. She *was* dizzy, but for an entirely different reason now.

He gave her a doubtful look, but he continued his fumbling, and after a moment he managed to grasp one end of the ribbon. He gave it a quick tug to loosen it. "There. Got it. I'm going to, um…slide the stocking down your leg now."

She nodded, bracing herself, but when he dipped his fingers under the top edge of the stocking, it took all of her concentration not to whimper at the seductive glide of his palms over the bare skin of her leg.

My goodness. The shy, prim, reserved Hyacinth Somerset, a wanton? Why, how shameful, or…something else. Delightful?

"There. Just one more to go."

Hyacinth's eyes were still closed, but she opened them again at the strained, tortured note in Lachlan's voice. It was so low and gravelly he sounded like a great, predatory lion, unable to make up his mind whether to growl or purr.

She rose onto her elbows, her brow creased with concern as she studied him. He'd taken great care to keep her skirts pulled down and arranged modestly over her legs, and his gaze was firmly fixed on something over her left shoulder. All very proper, of course, but the fact that he refused to look at her meant he spent a great deal more time foraging around under her skirts than he would have otherwise.

"You can raise my skirts a bit," she offered. "Just enough so you can see what you're—"

"No!" The word flew from his lips like a shot from a rifle.

Hyacinth's eyebrows shot up. "Very well. Are you…are you quite all right?"

"Yes."

He didn't look it. He drew his arm across his forehead to wipe away beads of sweat, and when he turned his attention back to her skirts, he wore the same look of grim determination her brother-in law Nick wore whenever Violet dragged him off to the opera.

"Just one more to go," he muttered again, gritting his teeth, and delving under her skirts a second time. This time he did all he could to keep from touching her, but, alas, the ribbons on her garters wouldn't untie themselves.

His palm stroking over her calf, the brush of his fingers against her thigh—it was all Hyacinth could do not to stretch and writhe like a lazy cat under his touch, as he left dozens of burning fingerprints on her skin.

a hint of some flavor in it that reminded her, strangely enough, of treacle. "Mmmm."

She took another, deeper sip, and Lachlan gave her one of his rare grins. "Drink your whiskey. That's a good lass." He removed his coat, tucked it around her, and then unwound his cravat.

"Why are you removing your clothing?" My, this whiskey was nice, and if it made him wish to undress, well, that was nice, too.

"Just my coat and cravat. I'll keep the rest on."

Well, that was rather a pity. Hyacinth took another deep swallow of her drink.

"I'll wrap your feet with this." He ripped a hole into his cravat with his teeth, then tore the long length of white linen straight down the middle.

"Oh, dear. What a waste of a perfectly good cravat."

He shrugged. "I don't have much luck with cravats. Somehow they always end up stained with blood. Usually Ciaran's."

"Or yours, I imagine." Hyacinth burrowed into his coat, which was so large she could go swimming inside it, and followed him with sleepy eyes as he returned to his seat at the end of the sofa and gathered her feet into his lap again.

She winced a little when he touched her, but the worst of the throbbing pain had ebbed, and she was able to watch with steady nerves as he wrapped her foot in his cravat.

Such large hands—who ever could have guessed a man with that black a scowl and such rough, enormous hands could have such a gentle touch? That a man could who could bloody a nose, or black an eye with one mighty blow from a gigantic fist could be so careful, so tender?

She watched his hands, mesmerized.

After a moment, he began to murmur to her, his voice gruff and mild in turns as he scolded and then soothed her. He ordered her never to be as foolish again as she'd been tonight. He said he was sorry, so sorry she'd been hurt, and he promised her she'd heal quickly.

He told her she was brave.

The strength of his hands, the curl and glide and pluck of his fingers and the husky rasp of his voice cast a spell over her. She lay back against the sofa, transfixed by him. What would it feel like, to have those hands move over her body? To hear that hoarse whisper in her ear as he touched her? Would he caress her with slow, gentle strokes as he was now, or would passion make him rough, demanding?

Both. He'd be gentle and demanding, but he'd *never* hurt her. She knew this without any question, as surely as she knew no matter how he touched her, she'd sigh and writhe and cry out for him. He'd be like the whiskey she could still taste on her tongue. First a bite—a tiny, stinging nip, but underneath...

Smooth, dark, seductive heat.

Hyacinth shivered, and Lachlan, misinterpreting it, curled his hand around the heel of her foot. "Shhh. The worst is over. I've finished wrapping them, and now we only need to get you home. I met Ciaran in the hall earlier, and he went to fetch the carriage. They'll be waiting for us by now."

He slid out from under her feet and went to her, but before he could lift her into his arms, Hyacinth stopped him with a hand on his cheek. "Lachlan, wait."

His hand covered hers, and for one brief, delirious moment his eyes flashed a dark, hot green as he held it against his cheek.She brushed the pads of her fingers over his face, reveling in the prickle of his emerging beard. "You're a good man. The best of men."

His forehead met hers, and his eyes drifted closed. "No, I'm not, *aingeal*. You don't know what I've done. All I've done..."

His words died on his lips as she drew closer, so close their warm breath mingled, and then her lips met his. He tasted of whiskey, wild and dark.

Then neither of them spoke at all.

* * * *

He'd dreamt of her kiss a hundred times since the night he'd first tasted her—the softness of her lips under his, the slow, tempting glide of her tongue—but even in his most fevered dreams, when he was lost in the deepest slumber, he'd never dared dream of such tenderness as this.

How could a man dream of something he'd never had? Something he hadn't believed existed, until her lips touched his?

He tried to make himself release her, but his arms tightened around her, gathering her tighter against his chest, and he sank to his knees beside the sofa.

God, the sweetness of her, the shy innocence of her kiss, wasted on a man so utterly unworthy of it. He didn't deserve her sweetness, but like the blackguard he was, he'd take it from her. As soon as her palm cupped his face and she whispered his name, he no longer had a choice.

She let out a soft sigh, as if his arms were the only place she wanted to be. "I, ah...I'm not very good at this. Am I...do you like this?" She pressed a tiny kiss to his jaw, then drew back, an anxious furrow between her brows.

Lachlan leaned toward her and dropped a kiss on one corner of her mouth, then the other, a smile tugging at his lips. He was a scoundrel and a devil, but God, how could any man resist her? That tiny crease between her brows, the hesitant nibble on those plump pink lips—she was the sweetest thing he'd ever held in his arms, and the thought of letting her go made everything inside him howl in protest.

"Your kiss couldn't ever be wrong." Lachlan dragged his thumb across the seam of her lips, his breath snagging in his chest when they parted. "That's it, *leannan*. Open for me."

Deep pink color washed over her cheeks as he caressed her mouth. "What does that word mean? *Leannan?*"

He traced the outline of her lips with his thumb, then tugged gently on her lower lip and drew closer, so his mouth was hovering over hers. "It means sweetheart," he murmured, just before he claimed her mouth with his.

Her first shy, innocent kiss had made his heart race, but this kiss...

It set his body on fire.

The way she welcomed him into her wet heat, the tip of her tongue teasing his, the soft nip of her teeth on his lower lip, her fingers tightening in his hair—within seconds every promise he'd made himself regarding Hyacinth Somerset fled, and he was lost in her. He kissed her and kissed her, his mouth ravenous and demanding, and she twined her arms around his neck and urged him on with an eager passion that thrilled him.

She's innocent...never even kissed a man...

The thought penetrated the fog of his desire, but it was there and then gone, chased away by the hot press of her mouth on his, the seductive strokes of her tongue. Hers wasn't a maiden's kiss, but the kiss of woman who knew her own desires, and somehow, despite her inexperience, knew *his*, as well. Every brush of her lips, every stroke of her tongue, the maddening drag of her fingertips down his neck...

God, he was wild for her—so aroused he was moaning, his shaft swollen and surging against his falls. It was as if she knew just how to touch him, just what to do to make him pant for her, as if she'd been made for him.

No. She isn't mine, and she never can be.

But she *was* his, for now, while she was in his arms, with her breasts crushed against his chest and her soft gasps and whimpers in his ears. She was his, and he wanted her with a fierce desire he'd never felt for any woman before her. He wanted to touch her everywhere, with his hands and his mouth—to make her wet for him, only him, and then bury himself inside her until she shuddered with pleasure, and he spilled into her arching, writhing body.

He tore his mouth from hers, then nudged her onto her back on the sofa and leaned over her to trail hot, open-mouthed kisses over her throat and neck. She gave a sharp cry when his teeth closed over her earlobe, and the desire curling in his stomach sparked at the needy sound and blazed through him, reducing his control to ashes.

He nipped at her again, triumph swelling inside him at her soft moan. "Do you like that?" He reached behind his neck to unclasp her hands and hold them above her head, his fingers wrapped lightly around her wrists.

"Yes." She arched into him, rubbing her breasts against his chest.

He buried his face in the curve of her neck, growling as he sucked at the soft skin there, out of his mind with desire, his cock straining against his breeches.

She was still wrapped in his coat, and he worked his other hand under the edge of it, stroking his palm over the curve of her hip. Then he moved higher to brush his fingers against her collarbones and the upper swells of her breasts, desperate to feel her bare skin. "Tell me what else you like, *aingeal.*"

She gazed up at him for a long moment without answering, then her lips curved in a dreamy smile. "Why do you call me *aingeal*? I'm not one, you know. Not even close."

Lachlan looked down at her face, at her sweet, guileless smile. "You're the closest thing to an angel I've ever seen."

And the closest I'll ever get to one.

A sudden chill crept over him at the thought, chasing away the haze of his desire. He stared down at her, and all at once everything snapped into sharp, painful clarity.

He was on top of her, one of his hands mere inches from cupping her breast. Her lips were pink and swollen from his kisses, and there were half a dozen tiny red marks on her neck where his teeth had grazed her tender flesh.

Jesus. What was he doing? He was pawing at her as if she were some doxy he'd found in a brothel on London's West End, instead of his brother's sister-in-law. She was young, naïve, and untouched, and she was...

Lachlan closed his eyes as shame washed over him.

She was *injured.*

If she knew what he truly was, what he'd done, the secrets he was keeping from her, she'd never let him lay a finger on her. Perhaps she wasn't an angel, just as she said, but she deserved far better than to be touched with hands as bloody as his. He yanked them away from her, horrified, then stumbled to his feet and backed away, putting space between them.

"Lachlan?" She rose up onto her elbows, her puzzled gaze searching his face. "What's wrong?"

He dragged both hands through his hair. "We can't...this was a mistake. I shouldn't have touched you. I can't...this can never happen again."

Her mouth opened, then closed, and she pulled his coat tighter around her in an unconscious effort to protect herself. "I don't understand."

Lachlan blew out a harsh breath. No, she didn't understand, and why would she? One moment he was kissing and touching her as if she were London's merriest widow, and now he was so ashamed he couldn't even look at her.

"Your sister is married to my brother, Hyacinth. I swore to her I'd protect you, and I made the same promise to you. I said I'd take care of you just as I do Isla, as if you were my own..." He trailed off with a swallow.

My own sister.

It was absurd, given what had just happened between them.

She flushed, and her eyes dropped to her lap. "I—t-this isn't your f-fault. I k-kissed *you*, and I s-s-see I shouldn't have."

He recoiled from the pain and confusion on her face. He wanted to take her hands, to reassure her she hadn't done anything wrong, but he didn't trust himself to touch her. "It *is* my fault. You're an innocent, and I'm..."

A scoundrel, a liar, a murderer...

He blew out a hard breath. "I know better than to toy with a naïve girl."

She flinched. "Yes, well...I suppose a gentleman like you prefers more sophisticated ladies, like Lady Joanna."

Lady Joanna? Lachlan started at her, too shocked to answer. How could Hyacinth ever believe he'd prefer Lady Joanna to *her*?

"I daresay Lady Joanna isn't obliged to rush off to Brighton every time her nerves are overset," she added, with a forlorn little laugh.

The forced half-smile trembling on her lips made him want to tear his hair out with frustration. Did she actually believe *she* wasn't good enough for *him*? That he didn't want her?

He did want her, so desperately he wasn't sure he could stay away from her. "I want you and your grandmother to go to Brighton."

She started, and her face paled. "B-Brighton? But—"

"As soon as you can ready yourselves." Lachlan forced his face into an expressionless mask, even as he dug new half-moon scars into his palms.

"No, Lachlan. I'm not going to Brighton. I told you—"

"Yes, you are. We're only a few weeks into the season, and you've already been hurt." He jerked his chin toward her feet. "It's only a matter of time before something worse happens. Your sisters and grandmother were right. London, the season, Lady Joanna and the *ton*—it's too much for you." *Too much for both of us.*

If she was within his reach, and they lost control again as they'd done tonight, she'd be the one who paid for it. She'd be forced to marry him—to tie herself forever to man with nothing but ugly secrets and a dark past to offer her. A man she'd despise, once she knew the truth about him.

A scoundrel, a liar, a murderer...

"N-no, it's not. I can do it, Lachlan. I can make it through—"

"No, you can't." Lachlan choked the words past the bitter regret lodged in his throat. God, he hated himself for hurting her, for making her doubt herself, but he'd sworn to protect her, and there was nothing but heartbreak for her in London. "It's best this way, Hyacinth."

She didn't answer, only gazed up at him, her eyes two wide, dark blue pools of hurt.

Lachlan turned away, unable to bear the pain and betrayal on her face. "I'll get Ciaran and have him carry you to the carriage."

"All right," she agreed, her voice dull.

He crossed the room and opened the door, but stopped before going out. He told himself not to look back, not to look at her, but if was as if his feet were frozen in place.

His head turned.

She was huddled on the sofa, half-buried in his coat, her cheek resting on her bent knees, and her shoulders hunched. Her face was turned away from him, but there was no mistaking the way she'd curled into herself, as if she could fight back the pain by making herself smaller.

Despair washed over Lachlan, but he didn't linger.

There wasn't any point. It was done.

Chapter Fifteen

The Fourth Ball
Lord and Lady Sedley
Request the honor of Miss Hyacinth Somerset's presence
At an evening ball on Thursday, February 19th
At 6:00 o'clock, 40 Upper Brook Street
Grosvenor Square
Dancing to commence at 8:00 o'clock in the evening

Hyacinth stared at her reflection in the glass, her elbow propped on her dressing-table, and her chin resting on her hand.

Had it truly been only a matter of weeks since Lachlan had stood behind her at this very mirror, held the pale blue gown in front of her, and challenged her to face her reflection? Had it only been a matter of weeks since he'd insisted only *she* could wear that gown? That only *she* could dance in it?

It was astounding, how much could change in such a short time.

She no longer knew whether he'd meant the words he'd whispered in her ear that day, or indeed, any of the words he'd said to her since the night he arrived in London. His kisses, his promises, his murmured endearments—all those *aingeals* and *leannans*—perhaps it had all been a ploy from the start to coax her into a season, and smooth Isla's way.

Hyacinth didn't know what to think anymore, but she did know one thing, beyond any doubt or hesitation.

She wasn't going to Brighton.

No, she was going to the Sedleys' ball, and to Lord Pomeroy's ball next week, and to every other tedious, wretched ball she was invited to attend, right through to the end of the season, just as she'd planned.

Lachlan was under the mistaken impression she and Lady Chase had left for Brighton this morning. How he'd been so misinformed, Hyacinth hadn't the least idea. That is, she *may* have said something about Brighton to Isla, who'd come by yesterday afternoon to fetch some ribbons, and Isla *may* have repeated it to Lachlan, but then bits of gossip like that often got muddled in the retelling.

What she'd told Isla was she *didn't* intend to go to Brighton. If Lachlan had heard something else, well…that was unfortunate, but hardly Hyacinth's fault. If he'd truly been concerned about her plans, he could have called on her, and asked her himself.

But he hadn't. He'd kept away from her since their passionate encounter in Lord Hayhurst's library last week. Indeed, he'd made his feelings regarding their tryst perfectly clear, and there was nothing for her to do but accept it, and try and forget the kiss had ever happened. Rather difficult, when every moment of that kiss haunted her dreams—both the sleeping and waking ones.

But not tonight. Tonight she was tired of it all—tired of mooning over a kiss, and tired of pale silk gowns and bland hairstyles. Tired of the *ton*'s vicious gossip, and tired of fruitless yearning.

Tired of Lachlan Ramsey.

"Shall I arrange your hair in the usual style, miss?" Hyacinth's maid stood behind her chair, a pair of hot tongs in her hand and a resigned expression on her face. Jenny's fingers itched to work her hair into the kind of sophisticated, curled, bejeweled affair worn by all the other young ladies, and it irked her to no end Hyacinth insisted on such understated, simple styles.

But tonight, Hyacinth was tired of the usual style. What good had it done her to try and fade into the background? She'd been bounced from one humiliation to the next since the season began, and she was sick to death of feeling like a billiard ball careening wildly around the baize as the *ton* struck at her from all sides.

"This gown is dreadful on me, isn't it?" She lifted a fold of the pale yellow silk, and met Jenny's eyes in the mirror. "The color isn't flattering, and the cut is better suited to the schoolroom than the ballroom. It makes me look like an infant. Besides, Miss Ramsey is wearing a yellow gown this evening. I want a different gown. Something brighter, Jenny."

Jenny went still, like a predator who longs to pounce, but is afraid of charging too quickly and scaring off her prey. "The blossom pink satin with the white lace, or the pale blue?" she asked, carefully assessing Hyacinth's reaction in the glass. "The cream-colored one, with the tiny pearls?"

Pearls. Hyacinth's mouth twisted with distaste. "I suppose the cream will have to do."

Jenny regarded her for another moment, then she turned and disappeared into the wardrobe. In a few moments she returned, a triumphant smile on her face, and waved Iris's violet gown in front of Hyacinth with a dramatic flourish.

Hyacinth's eyes widened. "No, Jenny. I couldn't possibly wear something so...well, it's far too daring, isn't it? What will people say? They'll all stare at me!"

But they were already staring at her, and they'd do so tonight no matter what she wore, so what difference did it make?

Jenny, who hadn't much use for the *ton*, gave a great sniff of disdain. "Oh, let them all hang! I don't see how it could be any worse than what happened at that last ball."

Both Hyacinth and Jenny glanced down at Hyacinth's feet. She'd spent the week after her disastrous encounter with Lord Chester's pumps hobbling about like a three-legged dog with the help of one of her grandmother's canes.

Even so, she still didn't regret her actions that evening. None of her toes had been broken, and with judicious applications of ice, and days lying about with her feet resting on a stack of plump pillows, the swelling had gone down quickly. She still had a few bruises, and she wouldn't be able to dance tonight, but then no one would ask her anyway, so what did it matter?

At least something good had come out of that debacle. Lord Chester had called on her the day after the ball to offer his apologies, and he'd told her he was leaving London to take a tour of the Continent. Hyacinth was glad of it. Lord Chester was a lovely, decent man, and she hated to see him ruined by an association with Lady Joanna.

"Hmmmm." Hyacinth held out one foot and turned it this way and that, considering. "I daresay you have a point there, Jenny."

Jenny saw her chance, and she pounced. "This deep violet color was made for a lady with your complexion, miss. Why, with your dark blue eyes and fair hair, you'll be mesmerizing!"

Mesmerizing?

Hyacinth turned back to the glass to stare at her reflection. She was well enough, she supposed, but mesmerizing? "Oh, nonsense, Jenny."

Jenny shook her head, her eyes solemn. "It's not nonsense, miss. It's a great pity for such a pretty lady as you to hide as you do. I always said you'd be a belle if you just put yourself forward a bit."

"I've never had any wish to be a belle." That was true enough. She'd never wanted that, and she didn't want it now, but there was something she *did* want.

To make her opinion regarding Brighton perfectly clear to Lachlan Ramsey.

He was going to be furious when she walked into the Sedleys' ballroom this evening, so why not wear the gown? After all, if a lady was going to stage a rebellion, there was no sense in doing it in half-measures. Anyway, hadn't Lachlan complained about English ladies only wearing pale colors?

Jenny turned in a circle, a delighted little sigh escaping her as the violet skirts fanned out around her. "Miss Iris has wonderful taste. This silk is divine, and the cut...well, Mr. Ramsey won't be able to take his eyes off you in this!"

"Mr. Ramsey!" Hyacinth whirled around in her chair to face Jenny, heat flooding into her cheeks. "Why should I care what Mr. Ramsey thinks? That is, if I do wear the gown, it won't be to impress him—" Hyacinth broke off as a knowing grin crossed Jenny's lips. "Oh, very well. It won't be *only* because of him."

"Oh, no. Of course not, Miss Hyacinth. Now, let me see if I can't find the slippers that match the gown." Jenny shot her another sly smile, then disappeared into the wardrobe again, leaving Hyacinth to face her reflection.

Very well, then. She *did* want Lachlan to look at her. She wanted his warm gaze to linger on her, to sweep over her from head to toe as it had in Lord Hayhurst's library. She'd get little enough pleasure from this ball, but if she could steal Lachlan's gaze from Lady Joanna, even if only for the space of a single heartbeat, she'd consider it a resounding success.

Hyacinth titled her head to one side, then the other, studying the lady who stared back at her in the mirror. Blue eyes, pale skin, fair hair—it was the same reflection she'd seen countless times, but something under the surface had shifted.

Perhaps she did want to torture Lachlan just the tiniest bit, but in truth this wasn't really about him at all.

It was about her.

A daring violet gown, an elaborate, eye-catching mass of curls—these things were insignificant. They weren't what mattered. What mattered was she felt...different. She couldn't have explained to anyone—not even her sisters—in what way she'd changed. She knew only that she felt like one of the genies in Monsieur Galland's *Arabian Night's Entertainment*, except now she'd been set free, she didn't know how to get back inside her magic lamp.

Even if she could find a way back in, she wouldn't go.

If she were a foolish or whimsical lady, she might believe Lachlan's kiss had freed her, but she was more practical than she was romantic. No, she'd found her own way out of that lamp, and like most escapes, it had started with a single, courageous step—right into Lady Bagshot's ballroom. Something inside her had broken loose when she'd decided to go ahead with her season, but she'd been hovering on the edge of it since then, caught somewhere between the old Hyacinth and the new.

Or the old Hyacinth, and the real Hyacinth.

But then Isla had said something to her at the Hayhursts ball a week ago... *I've never been very good at doing what I'm told.*

For as long as Hyacinth could remember, she'd done what she was told. *Be careful of your health...consider your delicate nerves...guard against becoming overwrought...*

It had started innocently enough. She was the youngest, and she'd had her share of struggles, especially after her parents died. She was, by temperament, more timid than her sisters, and they were, by temperament, fiercely overprotective. But if her family had been cautious of her, they'd been so out of the deepest, most abiding love, and she was grateful to them.

But this was no longer about love, and it hadn't been for a long time. Her doubt, her hesitation, the way she shied away from people, and avoided attracting any notice...

That was about fear.

It was no longer enough for her. If she was ready to escape her magic lamp and experiment with freedom, it had as much to do with Isla and Ciaran as it did with Lachlan.

Well, perhaps not *quite* as much.

Scowlish. A little smile played at her lips. Oh, he was scowlish, all right. Brooding and gruff, with that insolent dark eyebrow always quirked, and as likely to frown one out of countenance as wish them a good morning.

Of all the people who might have peered around the side of that column and found her cowering there...

Of all the people who might have taken her by the arm and dragged her out...

Of all the people who refused to believe she was better off there...

It had been *him.*

Lachlan was the only person in her entire life who'd ever told her she was brave.

Hyacinth rose and crossed to the bed, where Jenny had laid out the violet gown. The neckline was so low it would raise eyebrows, and she could already tell the bodice would be tight—tighter than any gown she'd ever worn.

She touched a fold of the fluttery silk. It was so fine it felt like mist against her fingertips, and the color made her think of wild Scottish heather in full, glorious bloom.

There'd be no hiding behind a column in this gown. No disappearing. If she chose to wear it, there'd be no turning back once she entered the Sedleys' ballroom.

"Here they are, miss!" Jenny emerged from the closet, waving a pair of violet slippers over her head. "Aren't they sweet, with the pale purple ribbons and all the tiny embroidered violets?"

Hyacinth held out her hands, and Jenny handed her the slippers. "They're...dramatic."

"So is the gown." Jenny gave her a calculating smile, and retrieved the curling tongs from Hyacinth's dressing table. "You can't wear your hair in a simple twist tonight, miss. That gown demands something far more elegant. Ringlets, and trailing curls, with a jeweled headband, I think."

Hyacinth eyed the tongs with trepidation. It would be a lie to say she wasn't terrified—no doubt she'd spend the entire evening shaking in her sweetly-embroidered violet slippers—but if a young lady chose to wear a dramatic violet-colored gown with a tight bodice and scandalous décolletage, what was the sense in quibbling over a few curls?

She crossed back over to her dressing table, and plopped down in the chair. "Very well, Jenny. I leave myself entirely in your hands."

* * * *

Hers wasn't the most daring gown at Lord and Lady Sedley's ball. It wasn't the most fashionable, or the most extravagant, or even the most revealing.

But it may as well have been. Never again would Hyacinth underestimate the uproar a single gown could cause.

If any other lady had been wearing it, it wouldn't have caused the scandal it did, but she wasn't just any lady, and the *ton* couldn't have reacted with more astonishment if she'd strolled into the ballroom wearing only her shift and a pair of dancing slippers.

Every head turned, and a hush followed in her wake as Hyacinth made her way quietly across the floor at her grandmother's side, but she'd hardly taken a dozen steps before the thick silence gave way to furious whispers and audible gasps.

"By Gad, it seems the mouse has a bit of a roar after all, eh, Giles?" remarked one gentleman, nudging his friend in the ribs as Hyacinth approached.

"Long overdue, if you ask me." The other gentleman peered at her, his avid gaze sweeping from her jeweled headband to the toes of her violet slippers. "Lovely. Looks just like her sisters."

If one could judge by their appreciative gazes, the gentlemen heartily approved of her gown, but the ladies weren't so enthusiastic. When she did dare to raise her eyes, Hyacinth found at least a dozen feminine glares directed at her over the top of more than one wildly flapping fan.

"Shameless! As if the girl isn't already notorious enough this season!" hissed one outraged matron, as Hyacinth passed.

"Perhaps that's why she did it," her daughter suggested, giving Hyacinth an appraising look. "She's notorious no matter what she wears, so she may as well wear a daring gown. I think she looks rather dashing," she added.

Hyacinth flushed with pleasure at this unexpected compliment, but alas, her satisfaction was only temporary. It faded the moment they crossed paths with Lady Bagshot, who stood on the edge of the dance floor, her towering yellow turban quivering with outrage as she shot daggers at Hyacinth through her beady brown eyes.

"Shocking!" that lady exclaimed in scathing tones. "I wonder she was permitted to leave the house dressed in such a scandalous manner. Why, I'd sooner face the executioner than I'd allow any granddaughter of mine to parade about at a respectable ball in such a…a…*that gown*! Indeed, I blame Lady Chase for it."

Oh, no. Hyacinth slid a guilty glance at her grandmother, but Lady Chase marched on, her face composed, and her chin high.

When she'd met her grandmother in the entryway to depart for the ball, Hyacinth had been braced for horrified gasps, and a stinging scold that left blisters on her ears. Instead, her grandmother had surprised her. She'd raised her brows, looked Hyacinth up and down, and then poked at a fold of the skirt with the tip of her cane. "Are you *quite* certain you wish to wear *this* gown to the Sedleys' ball, my dear?"

Hyacinth wasn't certain of a blessed thing by then, but she'd swallowed her doubt, and replied with as much bravado as she could muster. "Yes, Grandmother. Quite sure."

"Hmmm." Lady Chase had studied her for another long moment, then she'd nodded. "Very well. Eddesley, have the carriage brought round. We'll need a few extra rugs," she'd added, with a glance at Hyacinth's low neckline. "So Miss Hyacinth doesn't take a chill."

Until now, it hadn't even occurred to Hyacinth wearing the gown might reflect poorly on her grandmother. Oh, *why* had she let Jenny coax her into this? What had she been thinking, engaging in such a reckless stunt? For goodness' sake, she must have lost her wits—

"My dear Miss Somerset!"

Hyacinth's gaze jerked up. They'd made it to the other side of the ballroom and come to a halt in front of Lady Atherton, who raised her quizzing glass to her eyes, and subjected Hyacinth to a long, slow, and torturous perusal.

"Well," Lady Atherton murmured at last, lowering the glass and turning to Lady Chase. "A questionable choice for a debutante, perhaps, but the color suits her, and every young lady should have at least one scandalous gown. Don't you think so, Anne?"

Lady Chase paused for a long moment, then reached for Hyacinth's hand with her gnarled one. "I don't deny it took me by surprise, but I think you look just beautiful, dear. Very much like your mother."

For a moment, Hyacinth was too stunned to speak, but then her eyes filled with tears. Her grandmother could be a fussy old thing, and prone to stern lectures and rigid propriety, but when it came to her love for her granddaughters, she never wavered.

"I-I beg your pardon, Grandmother." Hyacinth squeezed Lady Chase's hand. "I should have asked permission before I—"

"Well, well, of course you should have, but then every lady is entitled to an occasional secret."

To Hyacinth's surprise, both Lady Chase and Lady Atherton cackled at this, but she didn't have time to consider it, because just then a hand landed on her arm, and she turned to find Isla standing there, beaming at her.

"Oh, my goodness, Hyacinth, you look utterly *divine!* Oh, I wish you could have seen Lady Joanna's face when you walked into the ballroom in that gown! As it happens, jealousy and anger turn her complexion a rather unattractive shade of blotchy red. And that odious Miss Tilbury was so shocked she spilled a glass of negus on Lord Clement's new gray coat. He was quite put out about it. Why didn't you tell me you were going to wear that gown?"

"I, ah…well, I didn't know I was, until I…*did.*"

"I'm ever so glad you did! You've put every spiteful gossip in this ballroom in her place tonight. But I must dash," Isla rushed on, breathless. "Lord Sydney has this dance. I just darted away for a moment to warn you about Lachlan."

"Lachlan?" Hyacinth's heart stuttered to a stop, then surged to life again with a painful thud. "What of him?"

"He's, ah…well, he's in a bit of a temper, I'm afraid. We knew he'd be angry to find you were still in London, but the moment he saw you enter the ballroom, a scowl blacker that the depths of Hades spread over his face. I didn't think he'd be *quite* so livid. It's a bit peculiar, isn't it? But I must go. I'll come find you again after the dance."

Isla hurried off without waiting for a reply, which was fortunate, since at that moment Hyacinth couldn't have squeezed a single word through her lips in answer.

Lachlan had caught her eye from across the ballroom, and he looked… *Oh, dear God.*

Isla was right. He was furious, and he was headed in Hyacinth's direction.

Isla met him halfway across the ballroom. She caught his arm and spoke to him for a moment, her lips moving rapidly, but even from this distance, Hyacinth could see Lachlan wasn't listening. He watched her over Isla's shoulder, his dark gaze raising gooseflesh on every inch of her skin.

When Isla fell silent, Lachlan stalked away from her without a single word.

Hyacinth looked to one side, then the other, then behind her, but there was nowhere for her to go, and even if there had been, she wasn't going to run away from him. For better or worse, at least now she had his attention.

She straightened her shoulders, folded her hands in front of her, and waited.

It didn't take long. The ballroom was crowded, but predictably, everyone scurried out of Lachlan's way. Hyacinth had hardly caught her breath before he was standing before her.

He didn't say a word. He paused for a moment, his eyes on hers, and then his gaze drifted upward. A muscle in his jaw jerked as he took in her jeweled headband, the mass of fair ringlets gathered at the back of her head, and the long curls trailing down her face to brush her shoulders.

And then…and then, dear God, his gaze drifted downward.

Slowly, deliberately, those hazel eyes took her in, and he saw everything. The frantic pulse beating at the base of her throat, the flush spreading over her bare neck and shoulders. She'd been obliged to lace more tightly than usual to accommodate the snug fit of her bodice, and now his hot gaze lingered on the high curves of her breasts rising from the clinging violet silk.

Hyacinth couldn't prevent a soft gasp at this blatant appraisal, at the way his lips parted as he skimmed over the trim curve of her waist, the gentle swell of her hips, and lower, over the outline of her legs just visible through the filmy silk. He devoured every inch of her, leaving her breathless, and far warmer than she should be, considering how much of her flesh was exposed.

By the time he'd completed his journey down her body, high spots of color had appeared on his cheekbones. The rapid rise and fall of his chest hinted at something besides anger, but one thing was certain. Whatever else he was feeling, Lachlan Ramsey was angrier than she'd ever seen him.

"What," he growled through tight lips, "Are you doing here, and why are you wearing that gown?"

How dare you...it's none of your concern...you have no right to question my whereabouts or the gown I choose to wear...

Because I wanted you to look at me...

All of these responses flew through Hyacinth's head, but the only one that made it to her lips was, "Don't you like it?"

She cringed at the hopeful note in her voice. She hadn't worn the gown just for him, and yet she couldn't deny she wanted him to like the way she looked. She raised her chin a notch in a rare show of feminine pride.

"Like it? Oh, I like it, *aingeal*. Every man in this bloody ballroom likes it."

Hyacinth's eyes went wide. His lips had gone white, and his voice was a husky rasp. Was he...jealous?

"But that's not what I asked you." He stepped closer, and his hand closed around her upper arm. "I asked why you're here, and why you're wearing *that*."

Her chin inched up. "You were the one who told me to stop hiding behind columns, Lachlan. I'm only following your advice."

A low laugh scraped from his throat, and he drew her closer. "Oh, you won't be able to hide behind a column tonight." He drew his finger down a fold of her gown. "Not without every man in this ballroom following after you. Is that why you're dressed like a Cyprian, *leannan*? Because you *want* them all to gawk at you?"

Hyacinth's mouth dropped open in shock. *Cyprian?*

Hot anger flooded through her, and she jerked her arm from his grasp. "How *dare* you? I don't look like a Cyprian, and the only one gawking at me is *you*."

She was rather proud of this speech—not a single stammer!—but Lachlan's face darkened. "Look around you. There isn't a single man in here who isn't gaping at you, and down to the last one of them, they're wishing they could get their hands on you."

She huffed out a breath. "So what if they are? It's my season, remember? Attracting the attention of eligible gentlemen is rather the point."

"Not this kind of attention. I said I'd watch over you this season, if you recall. Shall I bloody the nose of every aristocrat who's staring at you?" Hyacinth threw her hands up in the air. "You're being ridiculous, Lachlan! No one is staring. I daresay no one's even noticed me—"

"Miss Somerset?"

Hyacinth broke off, and dropped into a hasty curtsey before the tall, fair-haired gentleman who'd addressed her. "Lord Dixon. How do you do?"

She'd met Lord Dixon once or twice before. He was a bit older than she was, and considered very handsome, charming and sophisticated by the ladies of the *ton*. She'd never heard anything to his discredit, but he wasn't the sort of gentleman who frequented debutante balls. Hyacinth couldn't quite hide her surprise at his sudden appearance before her.

"I'm very well, thank you." He nodded briefly to Lachlan, then turned and offered Hyacinth a polite bow. "Would you care to dance, Miss Somerset?"

"Miss Somerset isn't dancing this evening," Lachlan snapped, before Hyacinth had a chance to reply. "She's injured."

He didn't make even the slightest pretense at politeness. Hyacinth shot him a glower that would have felled a lesser man, then turned back to Lord Dixon with an apologetic smile. "I'm afraid Mr. Ramsey is correct, my lord. I injured my foot a week ago, and I'm still unable to dance on it."

"How unfortunate. Should you perhaps be sitting, then? Allow me to escort you to a chair." Lord Dixon smiled again, and offered her his arm.

After a slight hesitation, Hyacinth took it. She couldn't at all account for such sudden and pointed attention from Lord Dixon, but he was the first gentleman to offer her anything other than an insolent sneer since her season began, and she didn't care to stand here and argue with Lachlan about Cyprians and bloody noses. If he wanted a lady to simper and fawn over him, let him go and find Lady Joanna.

"I wish you a pleasant evening, Mr. Ramsey." Hyacinth's eyes met his for a brief second, and a shiver rippled over her skin at the fierce possessiveness glittering in those hazel depths, but before he could offer a single word in response, she laid her hand on Lord Dixon's arm, and let him lead her away.

Chapter Sixteen

"Oh, ah…pardon me. I mistook you for another gentleman."

Ciaran had ambled all the way across the ballroom to speak to him, but as soon as he got close enough to see the murderous expression on Lachlan's face, he turned on his heel to flee.

Lachlan stopped him with a heavy hand on his shoulder. "Where do you think you're going?"

"No place special." Ciaran shrugged Lachlan's hand off. "Just getting my face out of the way of your fist, that's all. You look as if you're about to bloody someone's nose, and I'd just as soon it wasn't mine. I've only just become pretty again after our last brawl."

"It's a ballroom, Ciaran. I'm not going to bloody anyone's nose in the middle of a ballroom. Not yours, anyway." He couldn't say the same for that scoundrel who'd just led Hyacinth away.

"Who, then?" Ciaran turned to see who Lachlan was glaring at, and a knowing grin touched his lips. "Ah. I did wonder if it was like that."

Lachlan snapped his gaze back to Ciaran, bristling. "What the devil does that mean? Like *what*?"

Ciaran rolled his eyes. "Oh come now, Lach. Do you think I haven't noticed the way you look at Hyacinth Somerset? I've seen sheep wear that same pathetic expression, and do you know what always follows?"

"Damn it, I'm not staring at—"

"Lambs, Lachlan. Lambs are what follow."

Lachlan gritted his teeth. Maybe he'd bloody Ciaran's nose, after all. "I told you—I'm not *staring* at Hyacin—that is, Miss Somerset. I told Lady Huntington I'd look out for her, and that's what I'm doing."

Ciaran snorted. "If you mean to look out for her, then you should have advised her to choose a different gown tonight. She looks utterly delicious. Dixon certainly seems to think so."

Lachlan's jaw tightened another notch. Jesus, that gown. How the devil had she gotten out the door without Lady Chase having an apoplexy? He wanted to start at her hems and nip his way up to her bare neck, then tear the gown from her luscious curves with his teeth, and start all over again.

And he wasn't the only one. If Dixon stole another sneaky glance at Hyacinth's bosom, Lachlan was going to bloody more than the man's nose. "Dixon's a blackguard. I don't trust him."

Ciaran shrugged. "Dixon's not so bad. I've never heard any complaints about him, though the gossips have it he's fond of cards, and plays rather deep. Besides, you don't trust anyone, brother."

Lachlan grunted at that. No, he bloody didn't trust anyone, and he had damn good reason not to. He sure as hell didn't trust Dixon, who was leering at Hyacinth as if he wanted to dive into her bodice and stay there for the rest of the night.

"Anyway, you can hardly blame Dixon for having a go," Ciaran added. "She looks...that is, she's very—"

"Tempting," Lachlan said grimly.

"Ah, there's the word I wanted. No chaste pink or white gown tonight, eh, Lach?" Ciaran arched an eyebrow at him. "I'm not complaining, mind you, but why do you think she decided to wear that particular gown tonight?"

To torture me.

She was punishing him, for trying to send her off to Brighton. To teach him a lesson about doubting her.

To make him *see* her.

He'd tried not to. He'd tried to convince himself she was some pure, untouchable being—an angel, rather than a flesh and blood woman, with a woman's desires, and a woman's needs. Under that tight bodice and clinging silk she was still Hyacinth, with all the same sweet kindness that made his heart race and his lungs struggle for breath.

But tonight, she didn't look like an angel. Tonight, she was all woman. Warm, seductive, tempting woman.

Those alluring tendrils of hair teasing at the long, smooth expanse of her throat, her white shoulders rising from the tight embrace of the violet silk, the upward thrust of her breasts, with just the faintest hint of her nipples straining against the flimsy silk...

Lachlan drew a deep breath and tried to will away the blood now surging into his shaft.

That was why she'd worn the gown. To remind him of her soft skin, and her warm, plump lips and wicked, seeking tongue. But it wasn't just the gown, or the arrangement of her hair that made him weak with desire. It was the mysterious, feminine half-smile gracing her lips.

That was no angel's smile.

It was the smile of a woman who knew what she wanted, and had set out tonight to remind him *he* wanted it, too.

He dragged a hand through his hair.

She needn't have bothered. Her scent, the way she'd trembled in his arms, the taste of her on his lips—he could never forget it. Those memories haunted him every moment of every day, until he felt as if he were drowning in them, the water closing over his head—

"Damn it, Lach. Stop gaping at her with that miserable expression on your face. If you want her—and the entire bloody ballroom can see you do—then why don't you tell her? I have a suspicion Hyacinth won't send you away if you do."

Ciaran's last comment hit Lachlan like a fist to the gut. It was bad enough *he* wanted *her*, but to think she might actually want him in return was torture. "I can't tell her, Ciaran. You know it as well as I do."

"No, I don't. I don't know any such thing. If you care for her, and she cares for you, then I don't see what all the fuss is about. You're waffling, brother, when what you should be doing is making Hyacinth yours. Seems to me you're damn lucky to have the chance."

Lachlan didn't miss the trace of bitterness in Ciaran's voice. It was the same bitterness that had been there ever since they left Scotland, with Isobel Campbell's curses still ringing in their ears.

"For God's sakes, Lach. You really have become an Englishman, haven't you? No Scot would stand about like a bloody fool while some other man steals his woman."

Lachlan glanced over at Hyacinth just in time to see her raise her face to Dixon's and offer the man a sweet smile. Lachlan looked away from her, his chest tight. "She wouldn't want me if she knew who I really was. What I'd done."

"Oh, what bloody bollocks. You know it is." Ciaran's voice was hard.

"You didn't see her face the night we arrived, Ciaran. She pointed right at me, and called me a murderer. She was horrified. Worse, she was..."

Frightened of me.

She'd been terrified, as if she thought he was going to lunge for her. Hurt her. She'd shrank away from him, revulsion clear on her face. He still shuddered when he remembered how she'd looked, how just the mere sight of him made her panic.

"Damn it to hell, Lachlan." Ciaran turned on him, his face tight with fury. "She made a mistake, nothing more. She was horrified because she thought you'd done something *you didn't do*."

"But I did do it." Not in the way Hyacinth imagined he had, no, but what difference did it make? He was still a murderer.

"No, you did what you had to do—what any decent man would have done in your place. It went wrong, yes, and that's bloody awful, but it wasn't your fault."

Lachlan turned to stare at Ciaran, and saw the furrow between his brother's brows, the edge of white at his pinched lips. Despite his words, there was a part of Ciaran that still blamed Lachlan for that day, and for everything that had come afterwards.

Perhaps he always would.

"What about the lie, Ciaran?" Lachlan's voice was quiet. "Maybe any man would have done as I did, but a decent man wouldn't have lied about it."

"It's a secret, Lachlan, not a lie."

But Ciaran didn't meet his eyes, and Lachlan let out a short, hard laugh. "It's the same thing."

"We could still tell the truth." Ciaran gave him a hopeful look. "Perhaps it's not too late."

"No, perhaps not."

For the past few weeks Lachlan had been considering telling Finn everything, but he wasn't going to discuss it with Ciaran in the middle of the Sedleys' ballroom. "Isla looks happy tonight," he said, to change the subject.

They both stood for a moment in silence, watching Isla as she twirled across the dance floor in Lord Sydney's arms, her face wreathed in smiles. "She does. Do you think she cares for Sydney?"

"Who can tell with Isla? It would be damn convenient if she did care for him. He seems to admire her, and he's a good sort."

Ciaran nodded. "Sydney's solid. Much better than all these other uptight English prigs."

"Honorable, too, by all accounts, titled, and from a well-respected family. He'd be a good match for her, and a decent husband."

"Yes, but I wouldn't get your hopes up, Lachlan. Isla won't marry without love, and I'm not sure she's in love with Sydney."

Lachlan didn't reply, but watched as Isla made her way through the set. Every now and then she darted a smile in Sydney's direction, but it was a friendly smile only, and Lachlan sensed her attention was elsewhere. Damned if he knew where, though, or on who. Isla made as much sense to her brothers as hieroglyphics carved on a cave wall.

"Speaking of love, Lach, I believe Lady Joanna is looking for you, and I doubt she'll be pleased to find you panting after Hyacinth Somerset. Shall I go and distract her while you, ah...guard Hyacinth?"

Damn it. He'd rather have a tooth pulled than spend another minute with Lady Joanna, but she was Sydney's friend, and Lachlan didn't want to offend her now—not when Sydney could be on the verge of asking to court Isla.

He glanced back at Hyacinth and Lord Dixon, who were chatting amiably with Lady Chase and Lady Atherton. Lachlan couldn't ask for two more formidable chaperones than that pair, and it didn't seem likely Hyacinth would leave their side for the rest of the evening. She couldn't dance, so there was no chance of Dixon trying to manoeuver her onto a deserted terrace when Lady Chase wasn't looking.

Meanwhile, Isla was perfectly mobile, and prone to mischief. There was no telling what scrape she'd get into if Lachlan wasn't there to keep an eye on her.

"No, I'll go. Why don't you ask Miss Atkinson to dance? She's a good lass. God knows the gentlemen pay her little enough attention, for reasons I don't pretend to understand."

"No money. An unforgiveable offense, I'm afraid."

"You don't need a woman's money."

"So I don't, brother, and you're right. She's an agreeable lass, and so are all the other ladies banished to wallflower row. Perhaps I'll dance with them all again tonight." Ciaran ambled off in that direction, his mouth curved in an affable smile.

Lachlan started toward Lady Joanna, but before he'd taken a dozen steps his unwilling gaze was dragged back to Hyacinth. She had her hand on Dixon's arm, and she was laughing at something he'd said, as if she found him utterly charming. A bitter taste coated Lachlan's throat, but he forced himself to swallow it back down.

He hadn't seen a smile on her face at a single ball this season. She'd had precious little reason to be pleased. If Dixon could change that—if he could give her something to smile about—well, only a selfish ass would begrudge her that.

Lachlan turned away, and headed to a far corner of the ballroom, to where Lady Joanna was holding court. He pasted a stiff smile on his face, and tried to forget he wasn't the one who was making Hyacinth smile. He wasn't the one who was making her laugh.

It didn't work.

The next thing he knew, he'd turned around and was marching back the way he'd come, across the ballroom, and back to Hyacinth's side. By the time he reached her, he was in no mood to bother with pleasantries. He took her by the wrist, and tugged her away from Lord Dixon. "A word, Miss Somerset."

"Mr. Ramsey!" She tried to jerk free of his grasp. "What are you doing?"

Behaving like a selfish ass.

* * * *

"I, ah—I beg your pardon, my lord." Hyacinth turned to Lord Dixon, her cheeks aflame. "Please do excuse me for a moment."

Dixon's gaze lingered on the place where Lachlan held Hyacinth's wrist, then rose to Lachlan's face, his blue eyes narrow and calculating. Lachlan tensed, but before he could assess the strange look, Dixon covered it with a charming smile. "Of course."

He bowed to Hyacinth, but Lachlan didn't give her a chance to return the courtesy before he tugged her off to a quiet corner on the other side of the ballroom.

"Columns?" She leaned against the pillar at her back, and raised an eyebrow at Lachlan. "Are you making a joke, Mr. Ramsey? Or are you being intentionally ironic?"

Lachlan didn't answer. He was staring down at her, his throat dry, with only one thought echoing over and over in his head.

Do you know how beautiful you are?

She looked like a butterfly, in her purple gown with the white column at her back, the gauzy silk of her skirts fluttering in a draft of air from a nearby open terrace door. A butterfly or a flower—a hyacinth, like her namesake—slender and vibrant, and with that sweet scent, like wild honey—

"What do you want, Lachlan? You dragged me over here, and now you don't have a single word to say to me?"

He blinked down at her. Damn it, why *had* he dragged her over here? He hadn't thought it out, or considered what excuse he'd offer when he got her alone. He just knew he couldn't bear to see her smile at Dixon again.

She frowned up at him when he didn't answer. "You were terribly rude to Lord Dixon, you know. I'll have to beg his pardon on your behalf now."

Dixon's name on her lips made Lachlan want to slam his fist into the marble column until he'd reduced it to a powder. "What's Dixon want with you?" he growled at last. "I haven't seen him at a single ball so far this season, and yet here he is, come out of nowhere, and he's looking at you as if he's one snap of his jaws away from devouring you."

She glared at him, her color rising. "How should I know what he wants? Oh, wait. I *do* know. He must have seen my gown, and mistaken me for a Cyprian."

Lachlan winced. That had been the wrong thing to say. "I beg your pardon. I never should have said that. You don't look like a Cyprian. You look...very well."

You're far too beautiful, and seeing all these greedy male gazes on you is driving me mad—

"I look *very well?*" She folded her arms over her chest. "Is that what you just said?"

It *was* what he'd said. It wasn't what he thought, but damn it, what was he supposed to say? He'd wasn't the sort of man who could get away with poetic ramblings about butterflies and flowers and honey. He was too big and rough, and...*scowlish.* "Well, yes. You look very well."

This only seemed to incense her further, so Lachlan tried again. "What I mean is, you look...nice."

So tempting, so delicious I can hardly keep my hands or mouth off you...

Her face fell, and she let out a long, weary sigh. "You're really *far* too kind, Mr. Ramsey. May I go back to my grandmother now?"

Back to her grandmother, or back to Dixon? "No. You still haven't answered my question. I was under the impression you were on your way to Brighton, yet here you are. I can't imagine how I could have misunderstood. Can you explain it?"

She shrugged, but her eyes darted guiltily away. "I recall you suggesting a trip to Brighton, but I don't recall ever agreeing to it."

"That wasn't a suggestion, Hyacinth." He leaned in closer, and rested his arm against the column above her head. His mouth was a scant inch from her temple, and he wanted to press his lips to the tiny cluster of curls there. "It was a command. I believe that was perfectly clear."

"The part that isn't clear to me, Mr. Ramsey, is how you can think I'm in any way obliged to follow your commands. I answer to my grandmother, not to you." She lifted her chin, and despite his frustration with her, Lachlan had to restrain a smile. He'd seen both her sisters make that same gesture when they were piqued, but he'd never yet seen Hyacinth do it. It was oddly endearing.

"I see. And what did Lady Chase say, when you told her I *suggested* Brighton? Since you're here tonight, I assume she refused to go. Is that right, *aingeal?*"

She didn't answer, but the guilty flush on her cheek was answer enough for Lachlan. "You never said a word to her about it, did you?" Unable to stop himself, he reached for one of the long, loose curls framing her face, and stroked it with his fingertips. "So devious, Hyacinth. But never mind. I'll speak to her myself."

He started to pull away, but Hyacinth's low, calm voice stopped him. "No, you won't, Lachlan."

He raised an eyebrow. "You'll do it yourself, then?"

"No. There's no need to speak to her at all, because I'm not going to Brighton. I'm going to stay in London and finish my season, just as I promised Isla I would."

"Isla will understand if you can't keep your promise—"

"Perhaps she would, but I've a promise to keep to myself, as well, and I won't break it. Not even for you."

He stared down at her, shaken by her sudden intensity. Her face was pale and set, but there was a telltale quiver in her lower lip, and it hit Lachlan right in the center of his chest. He reached for her without thinking, and cupped her face in his hand. "Do you think I want to see you go, *leannan*? I don't. I'll miss you." To Lachlan's shock, his hand was shaking. "But you'll be better off in Brighton. You have to go, for your own good—"

"Stop it, Lachlan."

Lachlan froze. She spoke calmly, but he'd never before heard such aching disappointment in her voice, and it silenced him at once.

She pulled his hand away from her face. "I don't want any more help from you this season. You don't need to worry about protecting me, or watching over me anymore. I'm releasing you from your promise to do so."

Lachlan had withstood dozens of blows to his face in his lifetime, and any number of fists to his gut, but none of them had ever hurt him as much as hearing her say she didn't need him anymore. Thousands of words rushed to his lips—questions, protests, and apologies—but he could only speak one of them. "Why?"

Her eyes were bright with tears, and he watched in horror as one spilled over and ran down her cheek. She didn't bother wiping it away. "Because you lied. You told me if I went ahead with my season, you'd make sure no one hurt me. That was a lie."

"Who hurt you, *leannan*?" But Lachlan already knew the answer.

"You did. The other night, when we were in Lord Hayhurst's library, you told me I was brave. Do you remember that? No one's ever said that to me before. I thought you meant it." She let out a hollow little laugh. "But you didn't, did you?"

He'd meant every word, but how did he tell her it wasn't her bravery he questioned, but his own? How could he explain that for all her supposed timidity, for all her fragile nerves and innocence, and her delicate angel's face, she was far stronger, far braver than he was?

He didn't have the words to tell her that, so he did the only thing he could do. A strange sense of having been here with her before washed over him as his arm fell away from the column, and he stepped back to give her room to pass. They seemed to be always walking away from each other, with a thousand words left unspoken between them.

But he didn't speak them now, and neither did she. She paused, her eyes searching his, but in his own way Lachlan was as good at hiding as she was, and whatever she saw there, it wasn't what she wanted to see.

She slid away from the column, turned her back on him, and walked away.

Chapter Seventeen

The Fifth Ball
*Miss Hyacinth Somerset's company
Is requested at a ball at Lord Pomeroy's townhouse,
On Monday, the 23rd of February
at 8:00 o'clock in the evening,
Bruton Street, Mayfair*

"Lord Pierce kissed me."

Hyacinth had been inspecting the red marks Isla's fingertips had left on her upper arm when Isla had dragged her out to the terrace, but now she jerked her gaze to her friend's face, her mouth falling open. "He did? Where?"

"*Where?* Why, on the lips, of course. Where else?"

"No, no. I mean, where could you have found enough privacy for a kiss?" Every time Hyacinth turned around she caught Lachlan's eyes on her, burning with such intensity, she half-expected to find scorch marks on her gown. He'd kept his distance since their argument at the Sedleys' ball, but he hardly suffered her to stir a step out of his sight. He was nearly as bad with Isla, so how had she managed to get out from under his eye?

"Lord Pierce followed me to the ladies' retiring room, and when I came out he took my arm, and we ducked into the library."

"Indeed?" Perhaps Lachlan had been right when he'd said the library was the first place a rogue intent on seduction would lure his innocent victim. Hyacinth had thought it nonsense at the time, but she'd kissed Lachlan in Lord Hayhurst's library, and now here was Isla with her own tale of debauchery among the tomes.

Except Lord Pierce wasn't a debaucher. If anything, he erred on the side of being too stiff and proper. For him to forget himself so thoroughly could only mean one thing.

Hyacinth grasped Isla's hands, squeezing with excitement. "Oh my goodness, Isla. Lord Pierce isn't at all the sort of gentleman who kisses young ladies in darkened libraries. He must be in love with you!"

She expected her friend to share her delight, but to Hyacinth's surprise, Isla's smile faded, and a troubled cloud passed over her pretty face. "No, he...I don't think he does love me. He, ah...well, the truth is, most of the time he doesn't even seem to like me much."

"But he must, Isla. I tell you, he's as far from a debaucher as any gentleman I've ever known. If he kissed you, it was because he couldn't bear not to." Hyacinth allowed herself a tiny, forlorn little sigh at the idea of a gentleman so smitten he couldn't resist a kiss. What would it be like, to inspire such passion?

"It's a reluctant affection, then. If he does care for me, I suspect he wishes he didn't."

"That's nonsense," Hyacinth said stoutly. "No man could wish such a thing in regards to you. Why, you're lovely, Isla, and so clever and charming."

Isla gave her a half-hearted smile, but she was shaking her head. "Not clever and charming enough to excuse my scandalous connections. As far as the English *ton* is concerned, my father is a scoundrel who stole the Marchioness of Huntington out from under the nose of her lawful husband, and my mother a disgrace to her name and family. Lord Pierce may not be a rogue, but he's also not the sort of man who's likely to overlook such things."

"If he truly loves you, he will," Hyacinth insisted, but there was a thread of doubt in her voice. She didn't know Lord Pierce well, but she did know the *ton*. They'd tolerated the Ramseys so far, but once the novelty of Lord Huntington's Scottish siblings wore off, so might the *ton*'s forbearance.

"I don't know that he *does* truly love me, or even if he loves me at all."

Isla gave a little shrug, as if it didn't matter to her one way or the other if Lord Pierce cared for her, but Hyacinth wasn't fooled. "But you love him, don't you?"

Isla hesitated, but then she held up her hands in a helpless gesture. "I'm afraid I do. Terribly foolish of me, I know, but I seem to be destined for tragic love affairs."

Hyacinth's brow furrowed. "What do you mean? Do you have dozens of tragic love affairs in your past?"

Isla laughed, but she didn't meet Hyacinth's eyes. "Oh, never mind me. I'm just being silly. Let's talk of you, instead. Forgive me for asking, but have you and Lachlan had a row?"

Oh, no. Was it as obvious as that? "We, ah…why should you think we've had a row?"

"Because you haven't spoken a word to each other in a week. Because I've never seen Lachlan more miserable. Oh, and he has a new scowl, too. Did you notice? He only ever uses it on Lord Dixon, and it's a fearsome one. If I saw that scowl aimed at me, I'd flee London, but Lord Dixon hasn't left your side since the Sedleys' ball."

He hadn't. His attentions had been so assiduous, in fact, when he made a passing remark about playing at cards this evening, Hyacinth had come close to shoving him into the card room, just to be rid of him.

"He's enamored of you, Hyacinth, and…oh, but you don't look pleased. Don't you care for him? He's very handsome."

Hyacinth sighed. He *was* handsome. He was also elegant and charming, intelligent, witty, and entertaining, and solicitous of her comfort. He was, in short, precisely the sort of gentleman every young lady on the marriage mart hoped to snare before the end of the season. Her grandmother was delighted with him.

And Hyacinth….wasn't. "He's, ah…well, he's perfectly…that is, he's very…"

"You don't care for him," Isla said, her tone matter-of-fact.

"Well, I wouldn't say that, exactly—"

"Hyacinth Somerset, don't you dare lie to me."

Hyacinth covered her face, but Isla took her wrists and gently lowered them again. "It's all right, you know. You're not in the least obliged to care for him. It often happens that a gentleman's regard doesn't inspire a lady's."

"Or a lady's a gentleman's," Hyacinth muttered, thinking of Lachlan. "What troubles me is I don't know *why* I don't care for him." Lord Dixon was warm without being too heated, polite without being distant, and proper without being haughty. In short, he was the perfect gentleman, and yet...

"There's something about him, Isla. Something….cold? Or manipulative, perhaps? Oh, I don't know. I can't put my finger on it, but it makes the hairs on the back of my neck prickle with warning. I daresay I'm being unfair to him."

"Yes, well, love isn't fair, is it?"

Isla gave a short laugh, but there was such bitterness in it, Hyacinth's eyes widened with surprise. "Isla, what—"

"Listen to your intuition, Hyacinth, especially when it comes to gentlemen. If you feel something is off with Lord Dixon, then it very likely is. If there's one thing I wish someone had told me earlier, it's that."

"Yes, well, perhaps your intuition is a good deal wiser than mine. If you recall, my intuition told me Lachlan was a violent, brutal man—a murderer, for pity's sake, and I couldn't have been more wrong about him, could I? No, Isla. My intuition has already failed me once, with disastrous consequences. I won't trust it again."

"My dear friend, that wasn't your intuition. That wasn't an error in judgment, but a conclusion you drew from the evidence of your own eyes. I've seen my brothers when they brawl. They look like two giant savages bent on killing each other. Dreadful thing to watch." Isla took Hyacinth's hands again, and held them in hers. "There's nothing wrong with your intuition, Hyacinth. There's nothing wrong with *you*."

Oh, how dear Isla was. Hyacinth raised one of her friend's hands and pressed it to her cheek. "There's nothing wrong with you, either, no matter what the *ton* might think about your parents. We need not concern ourselves with their vicious gossip. As for Lord Pierce, what does your intuition tell you about him?"

"He's a good man, Hyacinth. The best of men, but he's…in the end, I'm afraid he's not meant for me."

Isla tried to smile, but she looked as if her heart would break, and a fissure opened in Hyacinth's own heart. "Don't give up on him yet. Perhaps all it needs is a bit more time."

"Perhaps. I suppose we'll see, won't we?" Isla released Hyacinth's hands and turned toward the door that led back into the ballroom. "Shall we go back? Lady Joanna dragged poor Lachlan off to dance, but he'll be looking for us as soon as she releases him from her clutches."

"Does she ever?" As far as Hyacinth could tell, Lady Joanna had sunk her talons deeply into Lachlan, and it wasn't clear he even wanted to get free.

Isla grinned. "Oh, every now and then he squirms loose. Are you coming?"

The last thing Hyacinth wished to see was Lachlan dancing with Lady Joanna. "Yes, in a moment. Just another breath of air, and I'll follow you."

Isla nodded, then she slipped back into the ballroom, leaving Hyacinth alone on the terrace. She stood for a long moment, staring into the dark garden below, a rueful smile rising to her lips as she recalled how dull she'd thought her season would be. Everything had become so twisted and tangled she couldn't see how it would ever come right again, but it certainly hadn't been dull—

"You look pleased, Miss Somerset. Has something in the garden amused you?"

Hyacinth turned just as Lord Dixon came through the door and joined her at the wall. Her first instinct was to move away from him, but instead she forced a polite smile. He hadn't done a single thing to earn her wariness, and she could hardly advocate for more time for Lord Pierce without offering Lord Dixon the same courtesy.

"No, the gardens are dark and deserted, I'm afraid. The windy weather has frightened everyone away."

"Not you." He inched a little closer, then leaned down and braced his elbows on the top of the wall, his forearm touching hers. "I do hope you aren't chilled."

She was tempted to jerk her arm away from his, but she remained where she was. If she was going to flinch away every time a gentleman touched her, she may as well go back to hiding behind columns. "Oh, I'm not as delicate as you imagine, my lord."

Lord Dixon smiled at her. "But you look so delicate, rather like a porcelain doll."

No doubt he meant this as a compliment, but Hyacinth had to resist the urge to roll her eyes. Perhaps someone should hint to Lord Dixon young ladies didn't care to be compared to lifeless toys.

Perhaps *she* should.

But Hyacinth held her tongue, and Lord Dixon took this as an encouraging sign. "I find it very fetching, Miss Somerset." His voice lowered to a husky murmur, and he drew closer. "I find *you* very fetching."

"You're kind, my lord, but I'm afraid I must ask you escort me back into the ballroom at once." Hyacinth's instincts were warning her to back away from him, but when she retreated, he followed her. Before she knew it, they'd moved outside the rectangle of light streaming through the glass door, and into a shadowy corner of the terrace.

He fingered a loose lock of her hair, his eyes gleaming with desire. "Now, Miss Somerset. You've no need to be afraid of me. I simply want to see if your skin is as soft as it looks."

"You forget yourself, my lord. Now let me pass, if you please." Hyacinth put every bit of command into her voice she could muster, but Lord Dixon only chuckled, then raised his hand and brushed the back of his knuckles across her cheek.

Hyacinth gasped with outrage, and batted his hand away.

"Shhh," he crooned, as if he were soothing a naughty child. "I'll let you pass, of course. I only wanted a private moment to tell you you've bewitched me. I flatter myself my tender sentiments are returned, and I wish to formally court you."

Court her? Returned his sentiments! Why, they hardly knew each other! No man was so easily bewitched by a lady. Now that lady's fortune, on the other hand....more than one fashionable London gentleman found English pounds mesmerizing enough.

Hyacinth's heart was racing now, and she drew a deep breath to calm it. "I thank you for your kind attentions, my lord, but it's far too early in our acquaintance for me to agree to a courtship."

He peered down at her in genuine surprise. "I'm astonished to hear you say so, when you've so particularly encouraged my attentions these past weeks."

Hyacinth gaped at him, amazed. Why, the conceit of him! Only a man of extreme arrogance could have interpreted her politeness as romantic encouragement. "If I have encouraged you, Lord Dixon, I can only offer my sincerest apologies. I never intended for my actions to imply anything more than friendship."

Now she was finding it rather a struggle to remain friendly, given her newfound, implacable loathing for him.

But he only shrugged, as if her feelings on the matter were of little consequence. "A great many successful marriages are founded on friendship, Miss Somerset. Friendship and desire," he added, trailing his fingers down her neck.

"I do *not* desire you, Lord Dixon, and I'm afraid your behavior this evening has put an end to any chance of a courtship between us." She squirmed away from his groping fingers. "I insist you unhand me at once, and let me pass." Hyacinth was truly distraught now, but her voice remained calm and even, and in some distant part of her brain, she marveled at it.

Lord Dixon's brows lowered, and his face hardened. "I'm very sorry it should have come to this, Miss Somerset, but you've left me no choice. If you refuse my offer, I'm afraid I'll have to make London unpleasant indeed for your dear new friends, the Ramseys."

Hyacinth stared up at him in confusion. She was quite sure he'd just threatened her, but she couldn't make any sense of his meaning. What did the Ramseys have to do with Lord Dixon courting her? "I don't understand."

A cold smile stretched his lips. "Ah, you don't know, do you? I thought as much. The Ramseys have been keeping a secret from you and your family, Miss Somerset, and it's a rather ugly one. Ugly enough to end Miss Ramsey's season, and ensure none of the Ramseys will ever be welcome in another London drawing-room. Perhaps not even the Marquess of Huntington's. I don't know him well, but I understand the marquess is a bit touchy about certain things. I doubt he'll take kindly to being lied to."

Hyacinth's wits had scattered like a flock of birds, but she managed to raise her chin and glare at Lord Dixon. "I don't take kindly to it either, my lord, and I think you're lying to me right now."

He laughed. "No, I'm afraid not. I had the story word for word from a distant cousin of mine who lives near Lochinver, where the Ramseys were born and bred. Remote place—quite wild, really. It's a miracle their tale ever made it as far as London. No doubt they thought it wouldn't. But you still look as if you don't believe me, Miss Somerset. Why don't you ask them yourself? I warn you, though, it's a horrifying tale. Best for all concerned if it never sees the light of day. But of course that's up to you."

Hyacinth's head was spinning. Why, Lord Dixon was mad, utterly mad. There was no other explanation—

But then she froze as something Lachlan had said to her that night in Lord Hayhurst's library came back to her.

If you knew what I'd done, all I've done...

For a moment, she was too stunned to utter a word.

Lord Dixon mistook her silence for acquiescence, and a satisfied smile crossed his lips. "Ah, I knew you were a clever girl."

A clever girl...

Yes, she *was* clever—far cleverer than he imagined. Far too clever to allow herself to be coerced into a courtship, much less a marriage, but she had no intention of saying so until she knew more about the Ramseys' allegedly shocking, ruinous secret.

For his part, Lord Dixon seemed to consider the matter of their courtship settled. "Tell me, Miss Somerset." He lowered his face so his mouth hovered over hers, his eyes gleaming with triumph. "Are you lips as soft as your skin?"

Hyacinth jerked her head to the side, and slammed her palms against his chest in an instinctive bid to shove him back, but he was far larger and stronger than she was, and she found herself scrabbling at any part of him she could reach in a desperate effort to fend him off. She'd managed to grasp his waistcoat when all at once he was yanked aside, and she was left clutching at empty air.

"You've made a mistake, Dixon." The voice was low, harsh and furious, and so was the vicious wrench that sent Lord Dixon across the terrace and into the opposite wall.

Hyacinth staggered, but she caught herself before she fell, and looked up in time to see...

Oh, dear God.

Her eyes widened at the savage look on Lachlan's face as he advanced on Lord Dixon. "Lachlan, wait!" She leapt forward and grabbed his arm, and Lord Dixon wisely took that moment to stumble to his feet.

"Did you touch her, Dixon? Did you *dare?*" Lachlan's voice was low and controlled, but there was no mistaking the icy menace there. It was far more terrifying than if he'd fallen into a rage.

Lord Dixon seemed to agree, because he lost no time hurrying toward the door to the ballroom. "It's none of your concern, Ramsey," he spat, as soon as he'd put a safe distance between them. "But if you must know, Miss Somerset has just agreed to accept my courtship."

Oh, no. Hyacinth's eyes dropped closed, but they flew open again when she felt the muscles in Lachlan's arm go rigid under her fingers. She didn't release him, but gripped harder, certain he wouldn't risk hurting her by yanking his arm away.

"I see. Did you mistake Lord Pomeroy's terrace for your bridal bed?"

Lord Dixon bristled. "Now see here, Ramsey—"

"You'll take care not to make that mistake again, Dixon, if you want to live to see your wedding night."

That threat was more than enough to scare off a braver man than Lord Dixon. He tugged his waistcoat down with a sharp jerk, and bowed to Hyacinth. "I bid you good evening, Miss Somerset." But when he straightened, his gaze caught hers, and there was no mistaking the warning there.

A chill shot down Hyacinth's spine. Dear God, he was utterly serious. Whatever secret he had, he was certain it would ruin the Ramseys, and he wouldn't hesitate to use it. Hyacinth thought of Isla, of the way her eyes lit up when she spoke of Lord Pierce, and a cold, tight feeling squeezed her chest.

"Are you all right?"

Hyacinth jerked her attention back to Lachlan. He was standing before her, his chest heaving as he struggled to regain his composure.

"Yes, I…yes, I'm quite all right."

Lachlan dragged his hands down his face, and when he looked at her again, she was shocked to see how pale he was.

"Hyacinth, you can't *ever* let any man lead you out onto a dark terrace alone, especially a man like Dixon. Even if you are courting," he added, his voice hoarse.

"I—" It was on the tip of Hyacinth's tongue to say she hadn't agreed to a courtship, and never would, but something made her hesitate. If Lord Dixon truly did have a terrible secret about the Ramseys, she'd do whatever she could to stop him from telling it.

Short of marrying the scoundrel, that is.

But a courtship—Lord Dixon assumed she'd agreed to it, and as long as he thought so, he'd keep quiet about whatever rumor he'd heard.

Provided it *was* a rumor. If it was the truth...

What then? Hyacinth drew a deep breath and fought back the panic that threatened to engulf her. "I didn't come out to the terrace with him, Lachlan. I came out with Isla. Lord Dixon must have followed me."

This didn't seem to reassure Lachlan, who regarded her with bleak eyes. "Dixon's not like Lord Chester, Hyacinth. He's not your friend. You've got to be on your guard against him. Swear to me you won't go off alone with him again. He's...I don't trust him."

Nor should you.

But Hyacinth didn't say this. She only nodded. "I won't do so again. I swear it."

"This...courtship." Lachlan bit off the word, as if it tasted foul. "Does Lady Chase know of it? Have you written to Finn?"

"No!" Oh, this would become an awful tangle indeed if her family got involved. Whatever it was she intended to do, it had to be done quickly. "It's a recent development only, and I, um...well, I'd just as soon keep it to myself for now."

"You haven't told *anyone*? Not even Isla?"

Hyacinth bit her lip. "No, only you, but I will tell Isla." She had quite a lot to say to Isla, and if what Lord Dixon claimed was true, to hear even more from her in return.

Lachlan's jaw ticked. "A day at most, Hyacinth, then you either tell Lady Chase, or I will."

"Yes, of course. I promise. Lachlan? Is there something...?"

Oh, she wanted so badly to ask him if he was keeping something from her—from all of them—but her mouth refused to form the words. Lachlan was no liar. If he was hiding something, she knew with all her heart he was doing it to protect someone. Perhaps he was wrong to do so, but he would only ever hide something if he believed he had to.

He raised an eyebrow at her. "What is it?"

"Nothing. I just—I'm sorry we argued at the Sedleys' ball. It seems I was wrong about not needing your help, after all. I'm glad you came after me tonight."

He took a step closer to her, his eyes going soft as they met hers. "I'll always come after you, *leannan*, and not because I don't think you're brave. I do." A faint smile twisted his lips, and he reached out and tugged gently at a stray curl resting against her shoulder. "You're the bravest English lass I know."

Hyacinth flushed with pleasure. "I am? Do you know a great many?"

"No. Only you and your sisters. But they're both fierce enough."

"They are, indeed," Hyacinth agreed, her lips twitching.

He held out his arm to her. "Let's find the others. I've had enough of this ball."

Hyacinth nodded and took his arm.

They'd made it halfway across the terrace when she realized she had something tucked into her other hand. She opened her fist, surprised she'd just now noticed it, and glanced down at the object resting in her palm.

It was a small bit of paraffin wax, one end of it worked into a point, rather like a pencil.

She blinked down at it in confusion. Where in the world had it come from? She certainly hadn't had it when she came out to the terrace, so where—

Lord Dixon's waistcoat.

She'd grabbed at his waistcoat to push him away, and at one point she'd gotten her hand into the small pocket. She'd been in a panic, clutching at whatever she could reach, and she must have snatched the odd bit of wax without realizing it. When Lachlan shoved Lord Dixon back, she'd pulled it free.

There was no other explanation for it—nowhere else it could have come from.

She snapped her fist closed, hiding the wax in her palm.

Ciaran had said something about Lord Dixon's gaming, hadn't he? She wracked her brain, trying to remember.

Lord Dixon plays deep, and wins often.

She peeked down at the wax again, her stomach twisting. Not one in a hundred ladies would understand what that bit of wax meant, but Hyacinth was one of the few who did.

Last year, when she'd been in Brighton, she'd become friends with a young lady who'd confided to Hyacinth that her brother had nearly been killed in a duel that past spring, after he'd been caught marking cards. He'd done it by drawing a pattern of lines on the backs of the cards to indicate the number and suit. The lines were invisible to the naked eye, but if one knew they were there, they could see the patterns when the light hit the cards at a certain angle.

He'd drawn the lines with a tiny bit of wax he kept hidden in his palm.

Hyacinth stared down at the wax, her breath catching hard in her chest. She could think of only one reason a gentleman would keep a bit of wax secreted away in his waistcoat pocket.

Lord Dixon was a card cheat.

Chapter Eighteen

Hyacinth had been pacing from one end of the drawing-room to the other, waiting impatiently for Isla to arrive, but when the door opened at last and she caught sight of Lachlan entering the room on his sister's heels, her face fell.

Dash it. She'd invited Isla for a teatime chat under the guise of discussing their gowns for Lady Entwhistle's ball this evening, but what she really intended to do was pry the Ramseys' terrible secret out of her. That is, if such a secret even existed. But she wouldn't be able to wrestle a single word out of Isla with Lachlan hovering about.

Lachlan noticed her reaction, and paused in the doorway to raise an eyebrow at her. "You don't look pleased to see me, Miss Somerset."

Heat flooded Hyacinth's cheeks. "No, that's not so, Mr. Ramsey. I just, ah…well, I can't help but remember the last time you assisted us with our ball gowns. I seem to recall a discussion about some housekeeper's lace night caps, and there was something else as well, having to do with 'stringy white bits.' Yes, that's what it was."

"That was Ciaran," Lachlan protested.

"Oh, never mind Lachlan, Hyacinth. We won't be obliged to listen to his opinions regarding lace trimmings, because he isn't staying. He and Ciaran have another appointment this afternoon. Go on, then." Isla made a shooing motion toward the door, then plopped down on the settee. "Now, Hyacinth, about that jonquil silk gown we discussed. I think—"

"Before you two delve into the merits of jonquil silk, I need a word with you, Miss Somerset."

Hyacinth, who was certain Lachlan wanted to discuss Lord Dixon, was tempted to refuse. All it would take was one searching look from those hazel eyes, and she'd be in danger of telling him everything. She'd have a mess on her hands, indeed. Lachlan would go after Lord Dixon at once. She simply couldn't run that risk—not until she learned if Lord Dixon truly did have a secret that could ruin the Ramseys.

Lord Dixon was a cheat, after all. Why shouldn't he be a liar, as well?

Still, she could see by Lachlan's expression he wasn't going to accept a refusal. "Yes, all right."

He led her to the library, closed the door behind them, and eased her back against it. "You didn't tell me the truth about what happened between you and Lord Dixon on the terrace last night. I couldn't sleep, thinking about it."

He was worried for her? Hyacinth's heart threatened to pool into a warm puddle at her feet, but she forced a casual shrug. "I'm sorry you were concerned, but really, there's nothing at all to worry about."

His eyes narrowed, and a growl of impatience rose from his chest. "Don't lie to me, lass. I saw your face when I came out onto the terrace last night. You were frightened. He said or did something that scared you. Tell me what it was."

"Nothing. There was nothing, I swear it." Hyacinth held his gaze, and prayed he wouldn't notice the guilty flush on her cheeks. "He, ah, took me by surprise, that's all."

"If that's all it is, why haven't you told Lady Chase he's asked to court you? Why hasn't *he* asked her permission? Damn it, he followed you out onto that terrace last night. He waited until you were alone and unprotected, and then he pounced on you."

Lachlan took her shoulders in his hands, his face twisted with anger and….dear God, was that fear?

"He could have hurt you," he rasped.

He could hurt you as well, and I can't let him.

His fingers tightened. "Hyacinth? Tell me the truth. Christ, for all I know, he *did* hurt you."

"No. He didn't. Lachlan, listen to me. If anything was amiss, I-I'd tell y-you." She swallowed, but she could still taste the lie on her tongue, and Lachlan's eyes were still shadowed with worry.

Hyacinth didn't know what to say to convince him, but she couldn't bear to leave him in anguish, so she did the only thing she could think of. She cupped his face in her hand, and stroked her thumb across his cheek.

His eyes drifted closed. Lachlan sighed, and let his forehead rest against hers. "Nothing can happen to you, *aingeal*. If you were hurt, I don't know how I'd ever…"

He trailed off with a shake of his head. She stroked her thumb over his cheek again, shivering with pleasure at the rasp of his beard against her skin. "Nothing will happen to me. How could it, when you never take your eyes off me?"

Oh, no. *No...*

As soon as Hyacinth said the words, she wanted to sink into the floor. Why, she'd made it sound as if she believed he was enamored of her! Now *he'd* think *she* thought he cared for her, or perhaps he'd think she cared for him, or...well, he'd think *something.* She could hardly tell what anymore, but it was sure to be humiliating, whatever it was.

A furious blush flooded her cheeks, and she looked away, embarrassed. "I-I—that is, what I meant to say is, I trust you to—"

Warm fingers touched her chin, and the next thing she knew she was looking into smoky, heavy-lidded hazel eyes. He lifted her hand to his mouth, and brushed his lips over the backs of her knuckles. "It's true, *leannan.* I can't take my eyes off you."

"You mean in the, um...brotherly sort of way?"

She bit her lip, half-afraid to hear his answer, but the corners of his mouth quirked in that rare, precious smile, and he slowly shook his head. "No. Not in a brotherly way at all."

He brushed his thumb across her lower lip, his breath catching when she parted for him, and then his mouth was on hers, so warm and gentle, teasing and licking at her lips until all that mattered was the sensual glide of his tongue against hers.

But she wasn't supposed to kiss Lachlan, was she? There was some reason she couldn't, she was quite sure of that much, but when Lachlan sucked at her lower lip that way, she couldn't quite recall what it was. It had something to do with Lord Dixon...oh, yes! Lord Dixon was meant to be courting her, and—

"You taste so good, *aingeal*," Lachlan whispered to her between kisses. "So sweet."

...and only a scandalous wanton allowed one man to kiss her while another was courting her. She had to stop kissing Lachlan. She had to push him away, and...and something else...leave the room at once? Yes, she must take herself out of his way, before they gave themselves up to temptation.

But she didn't do any of those things. Instead a tiny sigh escaped her, and she wrapped her arms around Lachlan's neck and pressed her body closer to his, as tightly as she could, so she could feel the solid muscles of his chest against her breasts.

He was murmuring something to her, something about butterflies and flowers and honey, and she was struggling to make sense of his words, but then he slid his mouth across her cheek to nip behind her ear, and whatever he was saying didn't matter anymore.

"Lachlan." She gasped when his mouth moved to her throat, his warm breath caressing her dampened skin as he kissed his way down her neck. He tugged down the sleeve of her day dress to bare her skin, then buried his face in the hollow between her neck and shoulder, his lips tracing the curve there.

"*Lachlan.*" Her breath grew shorter with every touch of his lips. She rose to her toes to sink her fingers into the unruly mass of dark hair at the back of his neck, desperate to learn his every line and texture.

"We can't..." But whatever he intended to say was lost in another groan as she pressed her open mouth to the hollow of his throat. He slid his hands down her back to the curve of her bottom, and lifted her against him. "This is what you do to me," he whispered, as he nudged his hips into hers in a single, restrained thrust. "Do you feel me? Do you feel how much I want you?"

"Y-yes." She felt him, the long, hard length of him pressing into the soft flesh of her belly. He was *so* long and hard, in fact, a wiser woman would have been reduced to maidenly tremors, but instead Hyacinth's core was melting for him, and she had the strangest urge to raise her leg, wrap it around his waist, and—

"Lachlan? Damn it, where are you? I've been waiting an age."

Lachlan froze, his hands still clutching her bottom. "Oh, Christ. It's Ciaran. He's been waiting in the carriage all this time."

Hyacinth knew she should be horrified at the possibility of getting caught with her leg balanced on Lachlan's hip, but to her surprise a choked laugh rose to her lips, and she had to slap her hand over her mouth to smother it. "Oh, dear. He sounds put out."

"He's not known for his patience." Lachlan's mouth curved with a crooked grin as he gazed down at her, then he leaned forward and pressed a quick, hard kiss to her lips.

They waited until they heard the thud of Ciaran's heavy boots pass the library, and then the low murmur of his voice speaking to Isla before they reluctantly broke apart. Lachlan smoothed the neck of her gown back into place, and brushed a few loose strands of her hair back from her face before he cracked the library door open and glanced into the hallway. "He's in the drawing room with Isla. Stay here until you hear him pass, and I'll sneak off to the carriage."

Hyacinth laughed softly, still giddy from his kisses. "If you hurry, perhaps you can convince Ciaran *he's* the one who kept *you* waiting."

He was partway out the door, but he turned back, and before she could say another word he was across the room, standing before her again. He took her face in his hands, and pressed one last long, tempting kiss to her lips. "You and Isla will ride to Lady Entwhistle's ball in Lady Chase's carriage tonight? Ciaran and I will come after our appointment."

Hyacinth nodded, but Lachlan hesitated, his long fingers stroking her cheekbone, his eyes dark with worry again. "You'll stay by Lady Chase's side until we arrive, and won't go anywhere alone with Dixon?"

"No, I-I won't," she stammered, knowing if all went as she hoped it would tonight, she'd be compelled to break her word. Oh, how many times would she be forced to lie to this man?

"Good." He kissed her forehead, and then he was gone.

Hyacinth waited a few minutes until she heard Ciaran pass, then she ducked out the library door and hurried back into the drawing room.

Isla was waiting for her, her arms crossed over her chest. "Well, here you are at last. Where have you been all this time, and...upon my word, Hyacinth, why do you look so odd?"

"Odd? I don't know what you mean."

"Your face is flushed, your hair is in disarray, your skirts are wrinkled, and you look..." Isla's eyes widened. "Your lips are swollen! Oh, my goodness, have you been off somewhere kissing my brother?"

"Hush, will you?" Hyacinth turned back to the door and pulled it closed. "For pity's sake, my grandmother will have an apoplexy if she hears you."

"Oh, but this is delightful!" Isla threw herself onto the settee and patted the seat next to her. "Tell me everything! Well, not *everything*—he's my brother, after all. In fact," she added, with a little wriggle of distaste. "Perhaps it would be best if you told me very little. Oh, dash it, don't tell me anything at all, aside from this. Are you in love with Lachlan?"

Hyacinth sank down onto the settee, her stricken gaze meeting Isla's as several irrevocable truths dawned on her at once. She *was* in love with Lachlan—rather desperately in love—and she was also quite sure he'd lied to her.

"You *are* in love with him," Isla breathed. Her lips curved in a joyful smile. "Oh, Hyacinth, I couldn't be happier. Lachlan's been so miserable since we left Scotland, and he's been forced to endure so much. I know he can be grim and rough, but he's the best of men, truly, and he deserves so much better than what..."

Isla trailed off into silence, her smile fading, and Hyacinth knew then, beyond a shadow of a doubt, that Lord Dixon hadn't lied about the Ramseys. There *was* a secret, and it was bad enough they'd felt the need to hide it.

But secrets were ephemeral things, and now the time had come to tell the truth. No matter how awful it was, Hyacinth intended to have the whole of it before she left this room.

Hyacinth took Isla's hand in hers. "Last night, after you left the terrace, Lord Dixon came out. He found me there alone, informed me he intended to court me, and then he…he tried to take a liberty." Isla gasped, but Hyacinth held up her hand for quiet. "As you can imagine, I rebuffed his advances. But when I made it clear I didn't encourage his suit, he got angry, and he…he made an ugly threat."

"He *threatened* you?" Isla stared at Hyacinth, aghast.

"No, Isla. He didn't threaten me. He threatened *you*. You, and Ciaran and Lachlan. He said he knew a secret about you, and he told me he'd tell it if I didn't let him court me."

Isla's face went deathly pale, and the hand Hyacinth held turned icy cold. Alarmed, Hyacinth scrambled for the tea things to pour Isla a restorative cup, but her own hands were shaking, and the dainty porcelain dishes cracked into each other under her clumsy fingers.

"But I don't understand. How could Lord Dixon possibly know about it? Lochinver is such a small, remote village. How could word have made it all the way to London?" Isla seemed to be speaking to herself now, almost as if she'd forgotten Hyacinth was there. "My mother assured us this wouldn't happen, that this story wouldn't follow us—"

"What story, Isla? You need to tell me the truth, so we can think what to do."

"Oh, Hyacinth." Isla buried her face in her hands. "I never wanted to hide this from you. None of us did, not from any of you, but we were afraid. We'd lost everything. Our mother died, and the people we'd known our whole lives, all our friends—they turned their backs on us. It felt as if we were living in a nightmare. Lachlan saw there was nothing left for us in Lochinver, and he made us leave. Ciaran didn't want to—he's angry about it still—but Lachlan was right, Hyacinth. We had to go. We had no choice. We were never going to be able to have any kind of life there, after it happened."

Hyacinth struggled to catch her breath as panic welled in her chest. Dear God, what had happened? What could have been so awful they'd been forced to leave the only life they'd ever known behind?

Hyacinth pulled Isla's hands gently away from her face. "What happened, Isla?"

Isla drew in a shaky breath, then began to speak. "When I was eighteen, I was betrothed to a young man named James Baird. He was a cousin to a family we'd known all our lives. Lachlan, Ciaran and I grew up with his cousins, and our families were close friends. I thought I knew James, too, but I was wrong."

Hyacinth squeezed Isla's hands, and waited.

"One day, a few months or so before our wedding, we happened to find ourselves alone in the stables after a late ride, and he...he tried to take, by force, that which should only be given to a woman's husband on her wedding night. I suppose he thought he had every right, since we were betrothed." A hard, bitter note crept into Isla's voice. "Perhaps he did. Perhaps if I'd just stayed quiet, and let him have his way—"

"No." Hyacinth clutched at Isla's hands, her grip fierce. "No man has that right."

"He...he was rough, Hyacinth, and I—I was in such shock at his sudden viciousness, I didn't...I hardly know what I did, but I must have screamed, because Lachlan burst into the stables, and when he saw James on top of me, hurting me..." Isla shuddered at the memory, and raised tear-filled eyes to Hyacinth's face. "He yanked James away from me, and shoved him back. Lachlan didn't....he just wanted to get James off me, but James stumbled, and when he fell he cracked his head on a heavy wooden post. He...he died, Hyacinth. He died."

Isla shoulders began to shake with sobs, and Hyacinth, tears now running down her own cheeks, gathered her friend into her arms. For a long while, they sobbed quietly, but at last Isla pulled away, and wiped her hand across her eyes.

"Everyone in the village turned on us after that. All our friends, people we'd known all our lives—they called Lachlan a murderer, and me a whore. My mother—well, she'd never recovered from my father's death the previous year, but she began to fail in earnest after that. I truly believe her heart was broken."

"I'm so sorry, Isla." Hyacinth brushed her friend's tangled hair back from her face with a soothing hand.

"Before she died, she told Lachlan the true circumstances of his birth— that he wasn't our father's son, but the son of the previous Marquess of Huntington. A legitimate son and Finn's brother. Lachlan was shocked and angry, and heartbroken, too, I think. He'd always looked up to our father, and then to find out the man he'd so admired wasn't his father at all, and that he had a brother he'd never met—well, you can imagine how he felt. I loved my mother, Hyacinth, loved her with all my heart, but it was wrong, what she did to Lachlan, and he...I've been so worried for him."

Hyacinth nodded, but inside her chest, her heart was bleeding for Lachlan.

"Lachlan despised being lied to, but he saw my mother's revelations as a chance for a new life, and within a few short weeks we were bound for England. I was relieved, but Ciaran was forced to leave his betrothed, a lady named Isobel Campbell, behind. She'd already broken the betrothal—she was as hateful as everyone else in Lochinver—but despite her betrayal, Ciaran loves her still. He can't admit to himself she doesn't deserve his love, and so he blames Lachlan. It's easier to blame someone you know will never turn their back on you, isn't it? And Lachlan—he blames himself for all of it."

Hyacinth gripped Isla's hand, and choked back the tears gathered in her throat. "So when you arrived in England, you chose to keep it a secret."

Isla turned pleading eyes on her. "Yes. We should never have done so, but you must understand, Hyacinth. Everything we'd ever known, everyone we'd ever loved and trusted—it was all gone in a single instant. After that, we felt we couldn't trust anyone ever again. We thought if Lord Huntington knew the truth about us, he'd want nothing to do with us. We thought he'd send us away, and Lachlan...oh, Hyacinth, he was desperate to give Ciaran and me a new life, to replace the one he thinks he took from us."

Hyacinth nodded, but her hands had gone as cold as ice, and she felt numb all over. What must it be like for him, to carry that terrible weight on his shoulders? He'd been wrong not to tell them the truth, and yet how could she blame him for it? Why should he trust her—or Finn or Iris or any of them—when his own mother had lied to him? When everyone he'd ever called a friend had turned their backs on him?

"Lachlan regrets it now—not telling Finn the truth, I mean. You've all been so kind to us, so welcoming. We made a mistake, and all three of us see that now, but...oh, Hyacinth!" Isla turned an ashen face toward her. "What's to be done about Lord Dixon? I suppose we haven't much choice other than to let him tell the *ton* all he knows."

"No, Isla. We're not going to do that. Not when your family's happiness is at stake."

And my happiness, as well.

Hyacinth couldn't imagine her life without the Ramseys. Isla with her fierce spirit, and Ciaran with his devilish smile...

And Lachlan. Most of all, she couldn't imagine her life without Lachlan.

Isla was shaking her head. "But—"

"Listen to me, Isla. If we can just rid ourselves of Lord Dixon, the secret doesn't have to come out. As you said, Lochinver is tiny and remote. There's very little chance anyone else in London will ever hear of it."

Isla went very quiet, and Hyacinth could see by the sudden pallor on her friend's face Isla understood what she was saying. "If Finn heard of it, do you think he'd send us away?"

Hyacinth hesitated. The truth was, she wasn't sure what Finn would do. He was one of the kindest gentlemen she knew, but he had his own painful past to contend with, and he could be severe when it came to certain things.

Things like secrets, and lies.

If he found out the Ramseys had kept something from him, he'd be furious. Worse, he'd be hurt. He'd feel betrayed. Hyacinth didn't know whether he'd be angry enough to send the Ramseys away. He'd always longed for a family, and she couldn't imagine Finn ever doing anything so cruel and unforgiving, but she didn't know him well enough to be sure of him, and she wasn't willing to risk the Ramsey's future on it.

Lachlan's future. He's already lost so much—

"We can't let you marry Lord Dixon, Hyacinth! The man's a terrible scoundrel."

"He *is* a scoundrel, and worse, too. I've not the least intention of marrying him, I can assure you." Hyacinth thought for a moment, then asked, "Isla, didn't you tell me Lord Sydney's lost a great deal of money to Lord Dixon at cards?"

"Yes. A small fortune. Apparently Lord Dixon is lucky, and clever about his wagers."

Hyacinth hesitated. Once she told Isla her plan, she'd see it through to the end, but that didn't mean she wasn't frightened. She was. Just the thought of being alone with Lord Dixon made her stomach turn, and her flesh crawl with dread.

"It's not cleverness, or luck." Hyacinth reached into the pocket of her day dress and pulled out the piece of wax she'd liberated from Lord Dixon's waistcoat. "He's a cheat."

Isla's mouth dropped open. "How can you know that? And what is that, in your hand? It looks like—"

"It's a bit of wax, pinched into a point at the end."

Isla stared at the wax, her brow furrowed. "Where did it come from?"

"Lord Dixon had it secreted away in his waistcoat pocket. I had a bit of a tussle with him on Lord Pomeroy's terrace, and quite by accident I plucked out the wax." Hyacinth held it up so Isla could see it more clearly. "I can only think of one reason a gentleman would carry wax in his waistcoat pocket, and that's to mark the cards."

"Mark them? How?"

Hyacinth, who'd been prepared for this question, drew a pack of playing cards from her skirt pocket. "Like this." She separated a card from the deck, flipped it over, and drew a single line across the blank white back of it.

Isla was shaking her head. "But you can't see the mark. It's invisible."

"Not if the light is at the right angle. Come see." Hyacinth rose from the settee and went to the window, Isla following her. "If the light catches it just so, the bit where I drew the line is duller than the rest of the card. See?" Hyacinth turned the card this way and that. "If you know what to look for, it's not difficult to see it. When Lord Dixon enters the cardroom, he already has the wax hidden in his palm. As the play goes on, he subtly draws patterns of lines on the backs of the cards to indicate the number and suit. Then lays his wagers accordingly."

Isla stared at her, dumbfounded. "For pity's sake, Hyacinth. You're not a card cheat yourself, are you?"

Hyacinth smiled at that. "No. But you'd be amazed at the odd bits of information one can pick up during six weeks in Brighton."

"Indeed." Isla held out her hand for the card, studied it for a moment, and then handed it back to Hyacinth. "It's clever, isn't it? But how do you plan to turn it to account? No one in London suspects Lord Dixon of being a cheat."

"No, but they might if Lord Sydney, who's lost such large sums to him, happened to discover a piece of wax in Lord Dixon's waistcoat pocket. If such an unfortunate occurrence should happen, and Lord Dixon should be revealed a cheat, I doubt the *ton* will care to listen to any of his stories about the Ramseys, do you? Indeed, he'd likely be obliged to leave London at once, or find himself at the wrong end of an irate gentleman's pistol."

"But how will Lord Sydney get a peek into Lord Dixon's waistcoat? Lord Dixon would have to take it off first, and—" Isla's hand flew to her mouth, and her eyes went wide. "No, Hyacinth."

"There are any number of ways a lady can inspire a gentleman to remove his waistcoat."

Isla buried her face in her hands with a groan. "Lachlan will go mad if he hears of this."

"He won't hear of it. Lady Entwhistle's ball tonight is sure to be a crush, and I think we can manage the thing without being noticed. When Lord Dixon asks me to dance I'll accept, but instead of a quadrille, I'll invite him to join me in the library. When you see me leave the ballroom with him, you'll follow with Lord Sydney, and when you come upon us, we'll take care that Lord Sydney discovers the wax. He'll know what it means at once, I daresay."

"I don't like this. It's far too risky. Why not just tell Lord Sydney about it, and ask him to demand to see inside Lord Dixon's pocket?"

"No, that won't do. What if Lord Dixon doesn't have any wax hidden in his waistcoat pocket tonight? We can't have Lord Sydney imply Lord Dixon's a cheat unless we can be certain of the outcome."

"We can't be certain of that no matter who goes diving into Lord Dixon's pockets! You could risk yourself and your reputation, Hyacinth, only to find his pockets empty."

"His pockets won't be empty." Hyacinth held up the bit of wax in her hand, and met Isla's gaze without blinking. "This will be there."

Isla gasped. "Hyacinth Somerset! Do you mean to say you're going to put that in his pocket?"

"No. I mean to say I'm going to put it *back* in his pocket. It's the only way to be certain he has it when we bring in Lord Sydney as witness."

Isla was gaping at her, mouth open.

"Oh, come now, Isla. Don't look so shocked. It's not as if I'm doing anything dishonest. The wax *belongs* to Lord Dixon. I'm only...giving it back to him."

Isla still didn't look convinced. "Too much could go wrong, Hyacinth. What if you can't lure Lord Dixon to the library? What if I can't get Lord Sydney there in time? What if it's unusually warm, and the wax melts—"

"I thought I was supposed to be the timid one, Isla."

"Timid? No, you're not timid, but you may very well be mad." Isla bit her lip, wrung her hands, and shook her head, but at last, after some final protests and dark predictions of impending doom, she threw her hands into the air. "Very well, then. Tell me what I need to do."

Chapter Nineteen

"Your waistcoat is unbuttoned. Your shirt is untucked, and your cravat looks as if there's a rodent nesting in it. It's odd, Lach, but I don't recall you being in a state of undress when we got into the carriage in Grosvenor Street." Ciaran gave his brother a wide-eyed, innocent look. "Whatever could have happened between then and now, I wonder?"

Lachlan glanced down at himself, hastily shoved the tail of his shirt into his breeches, buttoned his waistcoat, and made a half-hearted effort to smooth his cravat. "I'm not in a state of undress."

Not entirely, anyway.

Ciaran grinned, then leaned back in his seat and stretched his legs into the available space, crossing them at the ankles. "Not for lack of trying."

Lachlan kicked his brother's feet away with a glare, but he didn't reply, because he and Ciaran were *not* going to have this discussion, or any other discussion where Hyacinth's name might be mentioned in the same breath as the word "undressed."

"Well, I'll say this for you, Lach." Ciaran laced his fingers behind his head, flung his elbows wide, and offered Lachlan an idle grin. "I can't fault your taste. Sweetest girl in London, and a beauty, as well."

Lachlan's jaw hardened, but he maintained a stubborn silence.

"But then you've always had a weakness for fair hair, blue eyes, and generous curves."

Lachlan scowled. "Never mind her curves. They're nothing to do with you."

Ciaran shrugged. "To be sure, but then a man can't help but notice them, can he? I'm not the only one who's admired them."

Lachlan's eyes narrowed on his brother's face. "Careful, Ciaran."

Ciaran wasn't in a mood to be careful, and he dismissed Lachlan's warning growl with a casual shrug. "Still, I'm a bit surprised. Hyacinth Somerset doesn't look like the sort who'd rip your waistcoat from your back, but then it's always the quiet ones who—"

In one quick leap, Lachlan lunged across the carriage and grabbed his brother by the cravat. "Don't you *ever* talk about her as if she's—"

"I *knew* it!" Ciaran crowed. He pushed Lachlan off him with one mighty shove, and then pinned him in his seat with a booted foot against his chest. "You're in love with her, and—oh, quit thrashing, will you? Hyacinth is as dear to me as Isla is. I would never insult her, and you bloody well know it."

Lachlan did know it, and yet it still took a dozen deep breaths before he was calm, and could push Ciaran's foot off his chest without leaping for his brother's throat again. At this rate, he'd end up in a duel before the end of the season.

Ciaran was trying to pull the folds of his cravat back into order, but after a few fruitless tugs, he gave it up with a sigh. "Damn it, now you've ruined *my* cravat, as well. You know, Lach, you might have just told me you're in love with Hyacinth, instead of making me tease it out of you."

Lachlan's eyebrows shot up. He couldn't remember the last time he'd confided in his brother. Despite their brawling, they'd always been close, but everything had changed after James Baird's death. Isobel Campbell had turned on Ciaran. She'd broken his heart, and Ciaran, devastated by her betrayal, had turned his rage and despair on one of the only people left in his life he knew would never hold it against him.

His brother.

They'd left Scotland behind, and with it, whatever brotherly affection they'd once shared. It had been lost in a flood of anger and resentment.

On Ciaran's part, that is.

Lachlan had feared their bond was broken for good, but Ciaran asking to share his confidence was a glimmer of hope, at least. Ciaran was a devil, no question. He was unpredictable and irritating, and he had a troublesome habit of planting his fist in Lachlan's face, but Lachlan would just as soon have his brother back, all the same.

Lachlan met Ciaran's eyes. "I didn't tell you because I didn't think you'd want to hear it."

"Yes, well." Ciaran looked away, as if he were suddenly riveted by something outside the carriage window. "I knew you were infatuated with her. Had I known it was more than that, it would have explained a few things."

"What things?" Lachlan's tone was wary.

Ciaran made an impatient gesture with his hand. "Well, for one it would explain why you've been skulking about after Dixon, looking as if you're about to plunge a claymore between his ribs. You're making sure he doesn't lay a hand on your woman."

"Damn right I don't want him touching her, but that's not the whole of it. She's afraid of him, Ciaran. She won't tell me why, but he's said something, done something—something worse than insulting her on Pomeroy's terrace the other night. He deserves a bloody claymore through his ribs for that alone."

"He bloody well does." Ciaran was quiet for a moment, his forehead creased in thought, then he asked, "What do you hope to gain from this meeting with Sydney today, Lach? Sydney's lost a few thousand to Dixon, yes, but he claims he doesn't know the man well. No one does, it seems. Aside from the gaming, Sydney says Dixon keeps to himself."

"Sydney knows more about him than we do." It was true enough, but even so, a bleak sort of exhaustion descended on Lachlan. God, it had seemed a simple enough thing—a London season, to lift Isla's spirits—but somehow it had taken on a sinister cast. Lachlan couldn't shake his dread Hyacinth was going to get hurt.

He and Ciaran passed the rest of the drive to Lord Sydney's townhouse in silence, each of them lost in their own thoughts. Lachlan's were grim, indeed, but his spirits rose a bit when they arrived at Sydney's house in Hanover Square.

"How d'ye do, Ramsey? Ciaran?" Sydney welcomed them with hearty slaps on the back, then led them to a comfortable study, and waved them toward some chairs placed in front of a roaring fire. He brought them each a tumbler of brandy, then poured one for himself.

"Damn good brandy, that." Lord Sydney flopped into a chair, then held his glass up to the firelight to admire the rich color. "So, Ramsey. Your brother tells me you're on the hunt for some information about Dixon."

Lachlan nodded. "I promised Lord Huntington I'd keep my eye on Miss Somerset while she's in London for her season, and Dixon's been hanging about her lately." Lachlan took a healthy swallow of his brandy to chase the taste of Dixon's name from his mouth.

"Yes, I noticed that myself. Can't say I blame him. I've always thought her a beauty, but I keep my distance from her on account of my friendship with Lady Joanna. Don't know what she has against Miss Somerset, come to that. Some foolish nonsense, no doubt, but who knows when it comes to women, eh?"

Lachlan took another deep swallow from his tumbler, and let the warmth pool in his stomach before replying. "Who, indeed? So, what can you tell us about Dixon?"

"Not much, I'm afraid. I've known him since he arrived in London several years ago. Even so, I can't say I know much about him, aside from the fact he's got a good deal more of my damn money than I'd like him to. Lucky at cards, that one, and he turns it to account with careful wagering."

"You mentioned he plays deep," Ciaran prompted. "Five-card loo for the most part, isn't it?"

"Loo, whist, *vingt-et-un*—whatever's on at the time, really. He plays deep, and he always plays—don't often see a cards table in London without Dixon sitting at it. He's smart about it, though. Cautious, I mean. Careful with his bets. Methodical. I suppose I could take a lesson from him." Sydney chuckled with the careless amusement of a gentleman who needn't concern himself much with gaming losses.

Lachlan sipped at his brandy, considering. From what Sydney said, it didn't sound as if Dixon was a reckless man, so why was he trying to rush Hyacinth into a courtship? Why was the scoundrel so bloody sure of her? Hyacinth had been polite to Dixon, but she hadn't encouraged him. Yet Dixon seemed damned confident he'd have her in the end. "I noticed he didn't appear until the season was well underway. Is that his habit?"

Sydney frowned. "No, now you mention it. Never known Dixon to give a toss about the season before. He's not much for debutantes—prefers more sophisticated female company, if you know what I mean. I suppose we all fall into the parson's mousetrap at some point, don't we?"

"Not me." Ciaran took a deep swallow of his brandy.

Sydney laughed. "Oh, I don't know about that. One of those little wallflowers you've been flirting with may catch your eye yet. Always thought it a shame no one's offered for Miss Atkinson. She's a sweet girl."

"I don't flirt with the wallflowers, Sydney. I dance with them, and nothing more."

"We'll see." Sydney chuckled again. "Quite their hero, aren't you? All of them are besotted with you. Not a bad game, really."

"Do you think Miss Somerset could be the reason for Dixon's sudden foray into the marriage mart?" Lachlan asked, bringing them back to the matter at hand. "He singled her out at once, the moment he entered the Sedleys' ballroom."

"Well, yes, but she was wearing that purple gown that night, remember? Good Lord, was she wearing that gown." Sydney sighed, a dreamy look on his face. "More than one gentleman noticed her, and quite right, too. Aside from your sister, I've never seen a prettier young lady in my life."

Lachlan's lips pressed together at the reminder that every single lecherous rake in London had been gawking at Hyacinth in that damn gown. "Had Dixon ever mentioned he admired her, before that night? Had he singled her out in any way?"

"Not to me, and not that I ever noticed. They'd been introduced before, of course, but…" Sydney trailed off into silence, his brow furrowing. "It was rather odd, now you ask, Ramsey. I'd seen Dixon the night before at White's—lost several hundred to him, damn his eyes—and I happened to mention Miss Somerset, though I can't quite recall what…oh, yes. It was about her dance with Lord Chester at the Hayhursts' ball." Sydney shook his head. "Bad business, that. I haven't seen Miss Somerset dance since then."

"What did Dixon say, when you mentioned the Hayhursts' ball?" Lachlan took care to keep his tone bland, but something was niggling at him. He didn't know what yet, but he felt certain they were circling closer to whatever it was Dixon was hiding.

"Not much." Sydney shrugged. "Just that he thought Miss Somerset had cancelled her season, and gone to Brighton instead."

"What did you tell him?" Lachlan was leaning forward in his chair now, his brandy forgotten.

"Told him she changed her mind, and that she's been at every ball this season so far, with the two of you, and Miss Ramsey. I, ah…" Sydney paused, flushing a little. "I might have said something about Lord Huntington claiming you as his family, and you, Ramsey, being Lord Lachlan now, though you don't go by the title. Not in a gossiping way," he hastened to add, "But more matter-of-fact. Anyway, Dixon turned up at the Sedleys' ball the very next evening. I looked over, and there he was, bowing over Miss Somerset's hand. Curious timing, that."

Ciaran and Lachlan glanced at each other.

"Yes, very curious," Lachlan muttered, finishing the rest of his brandy in one swallow. It was even more curious when one considered Dixon was pressing for a courtship a mere few weeks later, and a secret courtship, at that. If Dixon's intentions were honorable, he would have approached Lady Chase or Finn about a courtship first, before he spoke to Hyacinth.

"What about Dixon's family, Sydney? What do you know about them?" Ciaran turned his tumbler in his hand, watching with what looked like lazy interest as the liquor swirled in his glass. But Lachlan knew better. Ciaran's knuckles were white, and his body tense as he awaited Sydney's reply.

"Only that he doesn't have any. Not in London, anyway."

"Where, then?" Ciaran's gaze met Lachlan's over the top of his glass. "English countryside somewhere?"

"No." Sydney brought his own glass to his lips, and tipped the remaining liquor down his throat. "His family is Scottish, I believe, on the mother's side. Dixon's got some cousin or some such way up in the Highlands somewhere."

Lachlan went utterly still, his gaze fixed on the flames dancing in the grate, his ears filled with the hiss and snap of burning wood. He was afraid to move, afraid to look at Ciaran—afraid to do anything that might reveal his sudden, intense urgency.

"Oh?" He managed at last, every nerve in his body straining to keep his voice even. "Where in Scotland would that be?"

"Christ, who knows? He told me once, but..." Sydney blew out a breath, tipped his head back against his chair, and closed his eyes as he tried to recall. "Someplace north. That is, all of Scotland is north, of course, but this was as far bloody north as you can get, on the northwestern coast."

Lachlan gripped his tumbler, and made himself concentrate on the cool, smooth glass under his fingertips as dread clutched at his throat. Jesus, he was one moment away from tackling Sydney and shaking the name out of him.

"Let's see. It's one of those damn tongue-twisting Scottish names, isn't it? Someplace called Ach...Achhilt..."

"Achiltibuie?" Ciaran's voice was low and tense.

"Yes! That's it. Achiltibuie. Remote place, he said."

"Very remote," Ciaran echoed faintly. His face had gone white. "It's the neighboring village to Lochinver, where we grew up."

"Indeed? What an odd coincidence. Dixon mentioned his family is mostly gone, but he has a cousin or two up there he corresponds with."

Sydney rose and wandered over to the brandy decanter, but turned around again in surprise when Ciaran and Lachlan both leaped to their feet. "Are you off, then?"

"Yes. It grows late. It's nearly time for Lady Entwhistle's ball." Lachlan dropped his glass on a side table.

"Is it as late as that?" Sydney retrieved his pocket watch and flipped it open to check the time. "Egads, it is. I'd better dress at once."

"We'll see you there, then?"

Sydney beamed. "Indeed you will. Your sister has promised me her first dance."

Ciaran abandoned his glass next to Lachlan's. "Our sincerest thanks, Sydney. You've been a tremendous help to us."

"Have I, indeed? I can't imagine how, but I'm pleased to hear it." Sydney gave them an affable smile. "Until later this evening then, gentlemen."

Lachlan managed to keep calm until Sydney's butler closed the front door behind them, but then he sprinted across the street toward the carriage, with Ciaran right on his heels, shouting to the driver as he ran. "Lady Chase's, in Bedford Square, and hurry, man!"

The driver's eyes went wide. "Yes, sir. Right away, sir!"

They'd hardly slammed the carriage door behind them before Lachlan was hammering his fist on the roof. "*Go*, damn you."

The carriage screeched away from the curb, the whole equipage rattling as it careened over the rutted street.

Ciaran had thrown himself into the opposite seat, and now his eyes met Lachlan's, stark panic in the blue depths. "Christ. Dixon's bloody cousin will have told him everything. Isla's attack—"

"Except he won't have said it was an attack. That's the part everyone in Lochinver forgets. James Baird attacked Isla. He hurt her, and he would have done worse if given the chance. That part of the story never gets told, does it? No, Dixon's cousin will have written that Isla's a whore, and I'm a murderer."

Ciaran dragged a hand through his hair, his face ashen. "How could this have happened, Lachlan? We were so sure that story would remain buried, and now...Jesus. Finn will hear of it, and how do you suppose he'll react? We lied to him. He'd be well within his rights to toss us all out on our arses."

"He would be." What sense was there in arguing? Ciaran was right. They'd lied, or neglected to reveal an important truth, which was the same thing. Why should Finn excuse them? "I should have told them the truth. Every word of it, right from the beginning."

But he hadn't. He'd held back because of his promise to his mother. He hadn't trusted Finn with the truth, even after Finn had given him every reason to trust him. Now his silence had put Hyacinth in danger. Jesus, he'd never regretted anything more in his life.

If anything should happen to her...

"Lady Huntington, Lord and Lady Dare, Lady Chase...they'll all find out." Ciaran looked dazed, as if the ugliness of it was just now sinking in.

"Hyacinth." She must not know yet. She never would have kissed him with such tenderness in the library this afternoon if she knew the whole story. She'd find out. Once she did, she'd despise him for it—for lying to her—and for denying he was exactly what she'd first accused him of being.

A murderer.

God, the irony was so perfect. Even he could appreciate the beauty of it. What a fool he was to think he could escape his past—escape who he was.

"Dixon's holding this over Hyacinth, Lachlan. He's threatening to tell our secret unless Hyacinth agrees to…Jesus, I don't even know what. Marry him? My God, what kind of man threatens a lady into marriage?"

"The kind with gaming debts? Hyacinth's an heiress. Maybe Dixon's not as lucky with his wagers as Sydney thinks he is."

Ciaran's hands clenched into fists. "I'm going to throttle Dixon."

Lachlan had to fight not to let his head fall into his hands. He was as close to despair as he'd ever been in his life. He didn't give a damn about the secret anymore. Dixon could spread the tale all over London, for all he cared. All that mattered was getting to Hyacinth before Dixon did, because if he'd go so far as to threaten her, then he'd do worse, as well.

So much worse.

And Hyacinth…oh God, she'd fight to protect them. Even if she was furious at him for lying to her, she'd never let Dixon tell their secret if she thought she could do something to stop him.

Before the season started, after their call on Lady Bagshot all those weeks ago, he'd begged Hyacinth never to sacrifice herself for his sake again. He hadn't known her well enough then to realize such a plea would fall on deaf ears, but he knew her now. She'd never let someone she cared for be hurt. Not if she thought she could prevent it. It was simply who she was.

How could he ever have thought she wasn't strong? How could he ever have believed, for a single moment that her rare, pure kindness wasn't the only kind of strength worth having?

An image rose in Lachlan's mind then, of her determined smile as she danced with Lord Chester at the Hayhurst's ball. Then later, her bruised and battered feet, resting in his lap…

Aingeal.

After what felt like the longest drive of his life, their carriage at last rolled to a stop in front of Lady Chase's house. Lachlan knocked, then waited in an agony of impatience for Lady Chase's ancient butler, Eddesley, to open the door.

"Lady Chase." Lachlan didn't stand on ceremony, but pushed past Eddesley and into the entryway. "Is she here?"

"Yes, sir."

Lachlan closed his eyes as a relief so profound it nearly dropped him to his knees surged through him. They hadn't left yet.

"But I'm afraid she's ill, and isn't receiving, Mr. Ramsey."

"Ill? Then where are Miss Somerset and Miss Ramsey? Are they here?"

"No, my lady insisted they attend Lady Entwhistle's ball without her."

"What, you mean they've gone by themselves?" Ciaran's voice was sharp with alarm. "What the devil? Lady Chase sent them off alone?"

Eddesley gave a faint sniff of disapproval. "Certainly not, sir. Lady Atherton is to chaperone them. She fetched them in her carriage a half hour ago."

Eddesley said something else, but Lachlan didn't stay to hear it. He and Ciaran were back in the carriage before the old butler finished speaking, and careening over the crowded London streets to Mayfair, and Lady Entwhistle's ball.

Chapter Twenty

The Sixth, and Final Ball
Lady Entwhistle requests
Miss Hyacinth Somerset's company,
At a ball to be held on Saturday, February 28,
At 6:00 o'clock in the evening,
George Street, Mayfair

It would happen after the first dance of the evening.

Hyacinth and Isla had agreed on that this afternoon, and as it happened, fate approved their plan. They'd anticipated the most difficult part of the scheme would be escaping the ballroom without Lady Chase, Lachlan or Ciaran realizing they'd gone, so they'd come up with a rather complicated scheme involving a torn gown and the ladies' retiring room. As luck would have it, Lady Chase had been obliged to remain at home in her bed nursing a chest cold, and for some mysterious reason, despite the late hour, Lachlan and Ciaran hadn't yet made an appearance in Lady Entwhistle's ballroom.

Now, seeing Lord Dixon's smug expression when she invited him to accompany her to the library, Hyacinth decided it was just as well Lachlan wasn't here. There was less chance of bloodshed if he didn't see that smirk.

"May I assume your invitation tonight means you've agreed to accept my courtship, Miss Somerset?"

"Um, yes. If you like, my lord." Hyacinth hardly spared him a glance. She caught Isla's eye over Lord Dixon's shoulder, and gave her friend a nearly imperceptible nod. Lord Sydney had been a trifle late to the ball this evening, which led to a brief panic on Hyacinth's part. However, he'd arrived before the first dance and led Isla onto the floor, and all was in place, just as they'd planned it.

There was nothing left to do now but take Lord Dixon off to the library, get him to remove his coat and waistcoat, slip the wax into his pocket, then fend off his advances while she waited for Isla to burst in with Lord Sydney, and then reveal the wax to him. All this, while avoiding the notice of the several hundred guests now crowded into Lady Entwhistle's ballroom, all of them on the alert for a delicious scandal.

Of course, this depended on whether Isla could even lure Lord Sydney to the library at all. He was, after all, a gentleman. He might refuse, leaving Hyacinth trapped—alone in the library with a coatless, waistcoat-less, amorous Lord Dixon.

Hyacinth's heart was thrashing with such violence in her chest she was amazed Lord Dixon couldn't hear it. Dear God, she must be mad to consider embarking on such a risky scheme. Under her skirts, her knees were shaking, and her tight corset seemed to have squeezed all the breath from her lungs. Perhaps this wasn't such a grand idea, after all—

"I knew you'd see reason, my dear. It would be a great pity to see a lovely young lady like Isla Ramsey ruined, and I'm afraid the *ton*'s disgust would be nothing compared to Lord Huntington's. He's not the sort of man one lies to, is he? Ah, well. Secrets are ugly things."

Well, how kind of Lord Dixon to remind her how much was at stake, just when her courage threatened to fail her. Hyacinth's spine snapped straight, and the smile she gave him was so cold she was certain frost must be drifting from her lips. "Indeed, there are a great many ugly things in London, my lord."

"And a great many beautiful ones." He trailed his fingertip from her wrist to the pale skin above her elbow length gloves, his avid gaze devouring the curves of her breasts. "I find myself eager to explore them."

Hyacinth glanced over his shoulder again. Isla was fewer than ten paces away, her steady gaze fixed on Hyacinth. Very deliberately, Hyacinth reached out and took Lord Dixon's arm. "The library then, my lord?"

Another satisfied smile curled his lips, and he led her with more haste than was proper to the edge of the ballroom. Within minutes, he'd hurried her down the staircase, and tugged her down a deserted hallway to the library.

The thud of the door closing behind them echoed in Hyacinth's ears like a death knell. Lady Entwhistle's library was on the ground floor, which suddenly seemed to be a very great distance from the ballroom. There wasn't a chance anyone would hear her if she cried out.

Hyacinth shivered, and rubbed her hands over her arms. Lord Dixon noticed, and gave her a predatory leer. "Cold, my dear? I'll soon have you warmed."

Bile rose in her throat at his blatant insinuation, but she choked it down, and turned to him with what she hoped was a convincing smile. "Perhaps you'd be so good as to give me your coat, Lord Dixon." It would take care of one item of his clothing, anyway, and without her having to touch him.

He chuckled. "Oh, you won't need a coat for warmth." To Hyacinth's relief, however, he stripped his coat off eagerly enough, and tossed it over the back of the settee. "There's no need to be shy, Miss Somerset. Join me over here, won't you?"

Hyacinth swallowed, and cast a nervous glance at the door. Had it been five minutes since she left the ballroom? She and Isla had agreed Isla would wait for five minutes after Hyacinth and Lord Dixon left, but good heavens, five minutes suddenly felt like an eternity. Surely, she'd been gone for hours by now? Days, weeks—

"Ah, such a timid little mouse." Lord Dixon beckoned her forward with a wriggle of his fingers, then patted the empty space beside him on the settee. "I won't bite," he added, with a wolfish leer.

Hyacinth shuffled forward and perched on the edge of the settee, her hands folded in her lap, and her back as rigid as a rod of iron. Lord Dixon slid closer, and his heavy hand landed on the back of her neck. It took every bit of Hyacinth's self-control not to squirm away from him, but she gritted her teeth, and managed to remain where she was.

"Just relax, my dear." He stroked her neck for a moment, then without warning his hand slid lower. He curled his fingers into the silk at her shoulder and yanked at her gown. Hyacinth heard a tearing sound as the delicate fabric of her sleeve gave way, and then a rush of cool air on her skin.

He drew in a harsh breath when her skin was bared to his gaze. "Oh, Miss Somerset, how wicked you are, to hide such bountiful treasures under those modest gowns of yours."

Hyacinth squeezed her eyes closed and suppressed a shudder when his wet lips descended to her neck. She'd known these moments alone with him would be awful, and endless. She'd braced herself for it, but she never could have anticipated how wrong it would feel to have any man other than Lachlan whisper to her, touch her. Every inch of her skin was crawling to escape Lord Dixon's pawing hands, every instinct screaming at her to get away from him.

Whereas with Lachlan…her body, her mind, and her heart were in perfect harmony when he touched her. Every part of her clamored for him. From the first moment his hands stroked her skin, she'd wanted to sink into him, drown in him.

Desire as powerful as that, a love so strong it surged through her with every beat of her heart...there was no refusing such a gift, and no going back from it, either. There was no place for doubt, and no room for hesitation.

Hyacinth turned toward Lord Dixon, braced her hands on his chest to steady herself, and slid her palms over the expensive embroidered silk until she found the slit of the pocket at the bottom of his waistcoat. She prodded at it with gloved fingers, the tremor in her hands making her clumsy, but at last she managed to open it just enough to get two fingertips inside. She had the wax ready, and she slid it carefully from the center of her palm to the ends of her fingers, and then, eyes closed and breath held, she gave it a little push with her thumb.

It tripped over the ends of her fingers, and fell into his pocket.

Hyacinth froze, her heart pounding, and waited. If he noticed her fumbling, and reached into his waistcoat pocket and found the wax, there would be no place for her to run—

"Unbutton it." Lord Dixon, who'd clearly mistaken her sudden flurry of activity for an excess of passion, grasped her hands in a hard grip and forced her fingers to the top button of his waistcoat. "Take it off me."

"With pleasure, my lord." Hyacinth couldn't disguise the note of disgust in her voice, but Lord Dixon didn't notice. He clamped his hands around her waist as she made quick work of his buttons, tugged the garment off him, then folded it with great care and draped it over the back of the settee. Another gentleman might have found her concern for his waistcoat odd, but Lord Dixon had long since stopped thinking of anything but satisfying his lust.

A surge of triumph shot through Hyacinth. By God, she'd done it, just as she'd planned, and the worst part was over. Now she simply had to hold Lord Dixon off until Isla and Lord Sydney discovered them. Once Lord Sydney found the wax, they'd be rid of Lord Dixon for good.

Relief poured through her, but as the moments ticked by, one after the next, and Lord Dixon grew more enflamed, and hence more determined to relieve her of her clothing, Hyacinth's elation gave way to alarm.

Where was Isla? It had been ages since Hyacinth left the ballroom with Lord Dixon—years, centuries—a lifetime! Could something have happened to prevent Isla from coming? Dear God, what if she didn't come, and Hyacinth found herself stranded in this remote corner of Lady Entwhistle's house with an aroused lord, and—

Crash! The library door flew open with such force it slammed into the wall behind it, and sent a half-dozen heavy books tumbling to the floor. Hyacinth shoved Lord Dixon away from her and shot to her feet, but as soon as she saw who it was, her legs threatened to give way.

Looming in the doorway, his muscular frame filling every inch of space, stood Lachlan, his hands clenched into enormous fists, and his entire body quivering with rage.

Hyacinth reached up a shaking hand to cover her mouth. "Lachlan, I... this isn't...what are you—"

Her words died in her throat as his gaze swung toward her. The library was dark, but a shaft of light from the open door fell on her, and Lachlan froze, his face going whiter than she'd ever seen it as he took in her disheveled hair, bared shoulder, and crumpled gown.

Very slowly, his head turned toward Dixon, and the look on his face then...

"Lachlan, wait."

Someone grabbed Lachlan's shoulder, and for the first time Hyacinth noticed Ciaran was there, behind his brother, trying to hold him back. Behind Ciaran were Isla and Lord Sydney, both of them peering over Ciaran's shoulder, looking horrified.

"Get off, Ciaran." Lachlan growled, his livid gaze still fixed on Lord Dixon.

"I'm not letting you go until I'm sure you won't kill him." Ciaran's voice was calm, but he was glaring at Lord Dixon, his face twisted with anger and disgust.

"Yes, do calm down, Ramsey." Lord Dixon got to his feet and casually tucked his shirt back into his breeches. "Whatever might happen in private between me and my betrothed is—"

"Betrothed!" Isla squeezed between her brother's large bodies, which were still crowding the doorway, and darted to Hyacinth's side. "That's a lie! Hyacinth would never agree to—"

"...is none of your bloody business," Dixon went on with a sneer, ignoring Isla entirely. "But as it happens, this little assignation was all Miss Somerset's idea. Not quite as innocent as she looks, is she?"

Isla gasped with outrage, and Lord Sydney shoved past Ciaran into the library, his face flushed with fury. "Now see here, Dixon—"

"I changed my mind, Lach." Ciaran's low voice cut through the rising commotion. "Go ahead and kill him."

He released his brother, and in the next breath Lachlan was across the room. Before Dixon could dodge him, Lachlan had wrapped one massive hand around his neck. "I warned you never to touch her again, Dixon."

"*You*, warn *me*? You're in no position to warn me about anything, Ramsey. Rather the other way around, I think, unless you want the secret of your murderous past revealed to Lord Huntington, along with the rest of London. Now, take your hands off me."

Lord Dixon tried to jerk free, but Lachlan wrapped his lordship's cravat around his fist and held him fast. "Go ahead and squeal, Dixon. Go to Lord Huntington, and fill his ears with rumors." He gave Lord Dixon a chilling smile. "Provided you have the breath for it, that is," he added, with another wrench of the cravat.

At last Lord Dixon seemed to realize the precariousness of his situation. His eyes bulged, and he clawed at Lachlan's hand, but Lachlan twisted his fingers tighter around the length of linen, and with one heave, jerked Lord Dixon off his feet.

Dixon made a strangled, choking sound, and his gaze rolled to Hyacinth, then to Isla and Lord Sydney, panic filming his eyes when not a single one of them made a move to defend him.

"Tell Lord Huntington all you know, Dixon. Tell all of London, for that matter—I don't give a bloody damn who you tell, but if you *ever* threaten Miss Somerset again—" Lachlan twisted Lord Dixon's cravat a notch tighter. "Or speak to her—" Tighter still… "Or even *look* at her, I'll finish you."

Lachlan gave Dixon one last hard shake, as if to emphasize his point, and then he released him. Dixon dropped to the floor, gasping and coughing, his hands at his throat.

Ciaran ambled forward, and prodded Dixon with the tip of his boot. "Well, I think that settles it, then. Shall we go? Before long we'll have every gossip in London down here."

Lachlan reached down and grabbed Lord Dixon by his ruined cravat. "Get up, you blackguard," he snarled, hauling Lord Dixon roughly to his feet.

Hyacinth's panicked gaze met Isla's. They couldn't let Lord Sydney leave until he'd found the wax—

"Now. Hurry," Isla muttered, so softly no one but Hyacinth heard her.

"Wait, Lord Sydney." Hyacinth skirted around Lord Dixon, who was still moaning and retching. She snatched his coat and waistcoat from the back of the settee and held them out to Lord Sydney, but before he could take them, Hyacinth let the waistcoat drop to the floor.

"I-I beg your p-pardon." She leaned down and grabbed the waistcoat, taking care to hold it upside down and give it a good shake before offering it to Lord Sydney again.

The bit of wax rolled obligingly from the pocket, and landed near the tip of Lord Sydney's boot.

Neither Isla or Hyacinth moved, or even dared draw a breath.

"What's this?" Lord Sydney reached down and picked up the wax. He studied it for a moment, puzzled, then held it up to the light to get a closer look. "Well, I'll be damned." He turned on Lord Dixon, his face dark with rage. "Not just a debaucher, Dixon, but a cheat as well?"

Lord Dixon made some sort of gurgling noise—a protest, Hyacinth assumed—but it was already too late.

"A cheat?" Ciaran took the piece of wax from Lord Sydney and squinted at it, his brow creased. "What the devil is this?"

"Paraffin wax." Lord Sydney took the wax back from Ciaran and closed it tight in his fist. "For marking cards."

"I never cheated! It's not mine, Sydney," Lord Dixon protested in a scratchy, rasping voice.

"I see. There must be some other reasonable explanation for its presence in the pocket of your waistcoat, then? Christ, I can't believe I didn't realize it sooner. No one's that bloody lucky at cards."

"*She* put it there!" Lord Dixon pointed an accusing finger at Hyacinth.

Lord Sydney let out an incredulous laugh. "Miss Somerset? My God, Sydney. You expect me to believe a gently bred young lady like Miss Somerset knows so much about marking cards she sneaked a piece of wax into your pocket to implicate you? You've lost your bloody wits."

Lord Dixon was growing desperate. "For God's sake, Sydney, why do you think she lured me down here in the first place? Think, man! Do you suppose you stumbled upon us by accident?" He jerked his head toward Isla. "These two planned the entire thing! It's obvious what happened—"

"Are you calling my sister a liar, Dixon?" Ciaran thrust his face into Dixon's. "My sister, *and* my sister-in-law?"

Dixon stumbled back a step. "I—"

"I don't understand, Lord Dixon." Hyacinth clasped her hands in front of her, and looked around the room, her eyes wide. "Why should I wish to put wax, of all things, into your waistcoat pocket?"

Lord Sydney gave a grim laugh. "I suppose your uncommon luck at the card tables is also Miss Somerset's and Miss Ramsey's fault, eh, Dixon?"

"I'm telling you, Sydney, the wax isn't mine!"

Lord Sydney tucked the incriminating piece of wax into his pocket, and studied Dixon for a moment with narrowed eyes. "Very well, Dixon, since you're so insistent upon your innocence, why don't we adjourn to the card room this minute, and you can explain yourself to every gentleman there whose money you've taken. Of course, I'll be obliged to show them this." Lord Sydney patted his pocket. "And to tell them where I found it, but I'm certain they'll all believe you when you claim it was simply a trick of Miss Somerset's and Miss Ramsey's."

Lord Dixon's face grew increasingly pale with each of Lord Sydney's words. He didn't say anything for quite some time, but at last, he shook his head.

"Is that a no, Dixon?" Lord Sydney asked. "Well, how curious that option shouldn't appeal to you. I can't think why you wouldn't choose to clear your good name, but no matter. I have another idea, and perhaps you'll like this one better. What if I take you to your lodgings, allow you fifteen minutes to collect whatever paltry belongings you can't do without, and then see you out of London on the next stage?"

Lord Dixon glanced at Lachlan, then at Ciaran, and then for one long, unnerving minute, he stared hard at Hyacinth, but at last he met Lord Sydney's eyes, and gave a brief nod.

"Ah, good. So glad that's settled. Oh, but one thing, Dixon, before we go. If you did try to return to London, I'd be forced to reveal this business about the wax to my friends. I'm afraid it would get about rather quickly, and would give rise to some unpleasantness. Duels, you know, or worse, perhaps. That would be a great pity, wouldn't it? Now, I've nothing to do with this business between you and the Ramseys—something about a secret, I believe it was? Mr. Ramsey has given his permission for you to spread his family's business far and wide, and that's naught to do with me, but it's odd, isn't it, how rumors tend to breed more rumors? And I've found—perhaps you've found this as well, Dixon—that people are far less likely to believe the word of a cheat."

There wasn't anything Lord Dixon could say to that. He held his tongue as Lord Sydney turned and offered Isla a formal bow. "Miss Ramsey, it was my pleasure to have your company this evening. May I call on you tomorrow, to enquire after your health?"

Isla was beaming at him. "Of course, my lord. I'll look forward—"

"No. I'm afraid that won't be possible."

Every head snapped towards Lachlan.

"My apologies, Sydney, but we're leaving London tomorrow, for Huntington Lodge. My sister will welcome your visit when we return."

"I see." Lord Sydney glanced at Isla. "When will that be?"

"Not before the end of the season."

"What? You mean to say Isla's season is over?" Hyacinth forced herself to face Lachlan. "But—"

"Not just Isla's season." Lachlan's voice was flat. "Yours, as well. Half of Lady Entwhistle's guests saw Ciaran and I burst into the ballroom this evening, and they all witnessed our search for you and Isla. We're not exactly dressed for a ball, and we attracted a lot of attention."

Hyacinth's gaze swept over Lachlan, and for the first time she noticed he was still in the same clothing he'd been wearing when she saw him this afternoon at her grandmother's house. He and Ciaran had come to Lady Entwhistle's in a hurry, then—so much so they hadn't even stopped to change their clothes.

And the way Lachlan had burst into the library, the look of panic on his face...

Dread settled like a stone in Hyacinth's chest. Somehow, Lachlan had found out something about this sordid business with Lord Dixon, and there was no question he'd demand she tell him the rest of it.

"By the end of the evening, every gossip in London will know some sort of scandal took place in Lady Entwhistle's library. Your reputations are ruined." Lachlan took a step toward her, his hazel eyes burning into her blue ones. "When we arrive at Huntington Lodge tomorrow afternoon, the two of you are going to explain to Finn how that happened."

Hyacinth and Isla looked at each other, their eyes wide, but neither of them offered a word of argument. It was plain to see their seasons were, indeed, over. A pang of regret pierced Hyacinth's breast for Isla, and any hopes she may have had of Lord Pierce.

For her own part, Hyacinth felt only relief, but as the heat of Lachlan's gaze seared her, whatever courage had seen her through this evening withered away to nothing.

Chapter Twenty-one

By the time they reached Lady Entwhistle's entryway, the gossip had spread throughout the ballroom. Like most gossip, the tiny grain of truth in every rumor was buried under dozens of lies.

Some had it Isla Ramsey had been stripped down to her corset when she'd been caught in the library with Lord Sydney. Others insisted she'd been fully clothed, but Lachlan Ramsey had fallen into a rage nonetheless, and beat Lord Dixon to within an inch of his life. Still others claimed the whole business was part of a complicated scheme hatched by Hyacinth Somerset to trap Lord Dixon into marriage.

But they all agreed on one thing. Both Isla Ramsey and Hyacinth Somerset were guilty of...well, *something*, and whatever it was, it was dreadfully shocking, and required immediate banishment from proper society.

By the time they reached the carriage, Hyacinth's ears were burning, and she'd never been so grateful to leave a ball in her life. It wasn't until the carriage door closed behind her that she realized there was one thing worse than whispered rumors.

Silence. Deep, profound, condemning silence.

No one said a single word the entire ride to Grosvenor Street. Isla's gaze never strayed from the window. Lachlan sat next to Isla, his face as cold and hard as stone. Even Ciaran seemed at a loss for words, and remained quiet.

Hyacinth, who knew she'd be called upon to explain herself soon enough, spent the time inventing and then discarding explanations, and biting her lip bloody.

Sure enough, when they reached Grosvenor Square and Ciaran and Isla climbed down from the carriage, Lachlan remained where he was. Isla gave Hyacinth one last anxious look before Lachlan pulled the carriage door closed, and he and Hyacinth were on their way to Bedford Square.

They rode in silence. They abandoned the carriage, entered the house, and paused in the entryway, all in silence. Lachlan took her arm and led her down the hallway to the library, and still neither of them said a word.

He waited for her to enter, then closed the door behind them, brushed by her without a glance, and went to stand in front of the fireplace.

Hyacinth waited, breath held, for him to speak, but he stood silently, his back to her, and stared down at the empty grate.

The silence dragged on and on, until at last Hyacinth couldn't stand another minute of it. "Lachlan, talk to me."

"Did you put the wax in Dixon's pocket?" His voice was tight, controlled.

Hyacinth hesitated. She had no intention of lying to him, but it was all so complicated—

"Answer me, Hyacinth. Did you put the wax in his pocket?"

"Yes." She took an instinctive step toward him. "But it was his. I took it from him by mistake, that night on Lord Pomeroy's terrace, and tonight I...I put it back."

His hands clenched into fists. "You lured him to the library, slipped the wax in his pocket, got him out of his coat and waistcoat, then you... *distracted* him until Isla could get Sydney down there to catch Dixon out."

Hyacinth's chin rose, and when she spoke, there wasn't a trace of regret in her voice. "Yes, and I'd do it again if I had to."

Lachlan's back went rigid. "Did you ever think, for a single moment, of what he would have done to you if he'd figured out your scheme?" His voice rose with each word, his tight control slipping. "Did it ever occur to you he might have *hurt* you?"

"But he didn't. He didn't hurt me." She stepped closer to him, and laid her hand on his arm. "Look at me, Lachlan."

The stark anguish on Lachlan's face, when at last he turned to her, made Hyacinth's heart splinter to pieces inside her chest.

"He ripped your gown." He caught the torn bit of silk between his fingers. "*He ripped your gown.*"

Those were his words, but his words didn't matter. Her gown didn't matter. What mattered were the words hidden between the ones he spoke, the fear and love tucked between each syllable.

Hyacinth heard the words he didn't say.

I couldn't bear to see you hurt...

She raised her hand to touch his face. "My gown, Lachlan. Nothing more."

Something flickered in his eyes. She thought he'd take her in his arms then, and every part of her ached to be held by him, to let the steady beat of his heart against her cheek chase away the memory of Lord Dixon's touch.

He didn't. He wrapped his fingers around her wrist, drew her hand away from his face, and stepped back. "I told you never to sacrifice yourself for me again."

"Yes." It was the truth. Hyacinth didn't try to deny it.

His eyes grew darker, and his hands clenched into fists. "Why, then?"

Why. She wanted to say, because it wasn't a sacrifice. She wanted to say, because I'd do anything to keep you from being hurt again. She wanted to say, because I didn't have a choice.

She wanted to say, *you already know why.*

But in the end, she didn't say any of those things. Or perhaps she said them all, just in far fewer words. "Because I love you, Lachlan."

And oh, it was so easy to say it. She'd thought it would be difficult—she'd been afraid she'd hesitate, or stammer—but then those words had been hovering on her lips almost since the first moment she saw him. They'd been poised on her tongue, just waiting for her to speak them aloud.

His mouth opened, and his throat worked, but no sound emerged.

A tremor shot through her at his silence, but she'd said what was in her heart, and she wouldn't take it back, even if she could. Hyacinth gathered her courage, stepped closer, wrapped her arms around his waist, and buried her face against his chest.

He smelled so good, like fresh air and the outdoors, and something else, something earthy, like...heather. Scottish heather, woody and mossy, with just a faint hint of honeysuckle. She pressed her face into his neck, inhaled deeply, and wondered if one could become drunk on a scent.

A scent, or a smile, or a man's gentle hands...

"Go to bed, Hyacinth." He reached behind him, grasped her wrists, and tugged her hands away. "Tomorrow, when we see Finn, you'll tell him the truth, and answer every question he asks. Do you understand me? You won't sacrifice yourself for me—or for Isla or Ciaran—again."

He was staring down at her, his face so hard and still Hyacinth's nerve nearly failed her. The other Hyacinth—the timid one—wanted to run from the room, but she could feel his struggle in the tremble of his body, in every harsh, labored breath he drew.

He wanted her as much as she wanted him, and tonight, that was enough.

"I'm not going to bed." She slid her hands over his chest to his shoulders and worked his coat down his arms. His breath caught when it fell to the floor with a heavy thud, then it stopped in his chest when she loosened the buttons of his waistcoat, dragged it off him, and tossed it to the floor. "Don't." His voice was harsh. He caught her wrists in his hands again to stop her, but Hyacinth heard the pleading note hidden in the gruff command, and she saw the way his eyes darkened as he stared down at her.

He held her fast, refusing to free her wrists, so Hyacinth leaned forward and pressed her mouth to the hollow of his throat. She felt his gasp, the convulsive movement of his throat against her lips as he tried to swallow back a moan.

"Let go of my hands, Lachlan," she murmured against his heated skin.

"No, damn you." He was fighting to catch his breath. "You're not wasting yourself on me."

His words were lost in another gasp as she opened her mouth and grazed her teeth lightly over his throat. "Waste myself? No, Lachlan. It's not a waste to give myself to the man I love."

"No. You can't love me. I won't let you." But even as he protested, his body was straining toward her, every muscle tensed with need. "You can't love me, *leannan*."

She laughed softly as she dragged her tongue around the curve of his ear. She nipped his earlobe, then moved lower to trail hot kisses over the bare skin revealed by the open neck of his shirt. "It's too late, you stubborn, foolish man."

He threw his head back in helpless invitation, a low groan tearing loose from his chest, but a part of him was fighting her still. "No, it can't be too late. I don't…I can't have you."

The broken, despairing note in his voice threatened to tear Hyacinth's heart in two. "You already do."

"No." His fingers tightened around her wrists. She knew he was going to try to push her away, and she knew she couldn't let him. All at once, everything hinged on this moment, but she didn't know what to do, or how to change his mind, to make him understand…

So she did the only thing she could think of. She pressed her lips against the center of his chest, and spoke right into his heart. "I'm yours, Lachlan. How could I not be, when you've the fiercest, most loving heart I've ever known? You're a good man, Lachlan—the best of men, and my heart has chosen you."

He didn't answer, or speak at all, but just when Hyacinth was on the verge of despair, he drew in a long, shuddering breath. His fingers went slack around her wrists, and then his arms closed around her, and he buried his face in her hair.

He held her like that for a long time, neither of them speaking. At last, she raised her eyes to his, and reached up to take his face in her hands. "I want more than just your arms around me, Lachlan. I want all of you."

He leaned over her, his mouth hovering over hers, and Hyacinth opened her lips to him, eager to welcome him inside. His tongue found hers at once, stroking and teasing until she was panting from the delicious torment. She sank her fingers into his thick, dark hair and held him still, her lips clinging to his, her tongue nipping and licking into his mouth to deepen the kiss.

"So sweet, *leannan*," he whispered to her between long, slow, drugging kisses. "Dreamed of holding you like this, touching you...making you mine."

Hyacinth shivered at his hot breath drifting over her throat, the glide of his lips over the sensitive skin of her neck. She writhed and squirmed to press closer to him, to touch her bare skin to his, but she was frustrated by his shirt, and what felt like endless layers of silk gown and boned corset.

"Too many clothes." Her cheeks heated at her own shamelessness, but she grasped a fold of his shirt and tugged it loose from his breeches, then slid her hands up the solid curve of his spine. His skin was warm, and stretched taut over the rippling muscles of his back.

The half-grin she loved so much drifted over his lips, and he reached behind him and pulled the shirt over his head.

"Oh." Her breath caught in her throat when his chest and stomach were bared to her gaze. "You're so..."

She trailed off, because she'd never seen anything as beautiful as he was, and she wasn't sure a woman was supposed to call a man beautiful. She'd known he was strong—a coat, a waistcoat, layers of linen and wool—they couldn't disguise the power of his body, but to see him like this, with those impossibly wide shoulders, the hard planes of his chest, and his smooth, perfect skin stretched over layers of muscle...

She laid her hand against his taut belly. A hoarse groan rumbled in his chest, and his abdomen tensed and jerked at her touch.

Her eyes darted to his face. He was watching her with heavy-lidded hazel eyes. "Do you want to touch me, *leannan*?" he asked, his voice husky, strained.

She watched his face as she let her hand drift lower, her fingers tracing the dark, narrow line of hair on his belly. "Yes. Everywhere."

He took her hand and pressed his lips against her palm in a searing kiss, then without warning he swung her up into his arms, cradling her against his bare chest as he crossed the room and laid her down on a sofa in front of the fireplace.

Then he sank to his knees beside her, and turned her face to his with gentle fingers. He studied her for a moment, then said. "You look nervous, *aingeal*. Do you trust me to take care of you?"

Hyacinth fiddled with a fold of her skirts. "Yes. It's just that...well, you're a large, virile sort of man, Lachlan."

He looked startled at this observation, but then he chuckled. "Have Lady Huntington and Lady Dare explained to you what happens between a man and a woman?"

Hyacinth gave him a shy glance, but he was looking at her with such tender humor, a smile rose to her lips. "A little. Just enough to worry me."

"We'll go slowly, then." He reached down to remove her slippers. "There. Not too terrifying so far, is it?"

"Well, no."

He began to slide the pins from her hair. He was careful, his fingers gentle. He caught his breath when the heavy locks tumbled over her shoulders and down her back. "So beautiful. I've imagined how it would look unbound since the first time I saw you."

"You have?" Hyacinth flushed, her heart leaping with joy. "Truly?"

He laughed softly. "You sound surprised. I wonder what you'd think if you knew what else I've imagined."

He kicked off his boots, then stretched out beside her on the sofa, gathered her into his arms, and caught her hand again. "Touch me, *leannan*." He slid her palm over his bare stomach. "Anywhere you like."

Hyacinth's gaze roved over him, her lips parting at the glorious sight of this man spread out before her. He had a smattering of dark hair across the sculpted muscles of his chest, and lower down, under his belly button—the line of it disappeared into his breeches.

She pressed her mouth against the center of his chest to feel the frantic thump of his heart against her lips, and he cupped his hand around the back of her head, urging her to explore his body.

Encouraged by his breathlessness, she covered his chest with kisses, then slid lower to nip at his belly. Lachlan gasped, his fingers tightening in her hair, his neck arching as his head tipped back against the sofa. "Your mouth feels so good."

He curled her tighter into his side and trailed his fingers through her hair in smooth, steady strokes, catching at the long strands and murmuring with pleasure as the waves fell over his stomach.

Hyacinth's eyes fell half-closed. His touch was gentle, soothing, but she wasn't at all tired. Her body hummed with a strange, restless energy, as if he'd tapped a tuning fork and set it vibrating deep inside her. It was a gentle hum at first, but as he continued to stroke her and she became conscious of the warmth of his chest rising and falling beneath her cheek, it grew until the urge to be closer to him was overwhelming. "Lachlan?"

He swallowed, and squeezed her hip. "Yes?"

"I want to see you...touch you." His breeches rested low on his hips, still covering that most masculine part of him, and Hyacinth's hand drifted lower, her fingertips sliding under the waistband.

A low moan rose in Lachlan's throat. His chest heaved as he struggled to catch his breath, and his shaft twitched and jerked against his breeches, as if it was reaching for her. His hips arched when she loosened the buttons on his falls, then he dragged his breeches over his hips and down his legs, and tossed them aside.

She stared down at him, her lower lip caught in her teeth. The hard, thick length of him was pulsing against the taut flesh of his belly, the flushed tip straining toward his belly button. "You're...it's...it's so *animated*." Faint heat rose in her cheeks at how foolish she sounded, but she hadn't understood until now how alive this part of him would be.

A strained laugh escaped him. "It is *now*."

His words faded into a strangled groan as her hand closed around him. Hyacinth's mouth opened with surprise as she cradled his throbbing length in her palm. His skin here was thin, and softer than she'd ever imagined, but under that hot, silky flesh he was rigid.

"Harder, *aingeal*." Lachlan covered her hand with his, his fingers tightening until she was gripping him much more firmly than she would have dared otherwise. "Stroke me." He moved her hand up, his hips jerking when they reached the tip.

"It's, ah...swelling." Hyacinth's voice was filled with wonder, and her own breath was coming harder as he writhed against her touch, broken moans and endearments falling from his lips as she stroked him.

"Do you want me, *aingeal*?" Lachlan stilled her hand, and pulled himself gently from her grip.

Want him? Her entire body was flushed and aching. She was certain if he didn't touch her soon, she'd explode. "Yes. So much, Lachlan." She fumbled for her skirts, ready to tear her gown off, but he reached behind her and loosened every button himself, and soon the silk of her gown, her fine cotton shift, and her tight corset were just a memory.

Lachlan went still. He didn't take his eyes off her as he eased her back against the sofa, his hot gaze moving over every bare inch. He slowly traced the curve of a breast with one finger, then circled a rosy nipple with his fingertip. "So pretty, *aingeal*."

Hyacinth's lips parted in a soft cry. He was so gentle—just one of his fingers, lightly caressing her breast, but even that simple touch made her want to unfurl for him, to stretch and spread under his hands so she could feel them on every part of her body.

His gaze darted to her face, then dipped back down to her breasts, a masculine smile curling his lips when her skin flushed in the wake of his touch. "You're sensitive here."

She couldn't speak, but he didn't wait for an answer. He brought his hands back to her breasts and stroked his palms over her nipples, gently abrading them, sucking in a harsh breath when they hardened for him. He circled the peaks with his thumbs, his mouth opening when they turned a deep, dark pink. He held her gaze as he lowered his mouth to her breast. He paused to nuzzle her neck and press a kiss over her heart, then his lips were *there*, on her nipple, suckling her.

"*Lachlan.*" Hyacinth's back arched sharply at the exquisite tug and stroke of his tongue. Her hands flew to his head, her fingers clutching at his hair to hold him against her breast. "It's so...*oh*. I-I don't know what to do."

She felt his lips curve against her swollen nipple. "You don't have to do anything, *leannan*. Just let me pleasure you." He gave her nipple a final, teasing lick before kissing his way to the other straining peak to suck it into his mouth. "Let me touch you," he murmured, sliding his hand over her hip. "You're so soft here." He stroked his palm over the skin of her upper thigh in a soothing caress, then he let his hand drift higher, higher...

"Oh, oh..." Hyacinth's breath tore from her lungs in a strangled moan as he opened her with gentle fingers, parting her folds to find the center of her pleasure. Then he was stroking her with his fingertip, his breath hard and fast in her ear, and she didn't try to reason, or to think at all, but arched her hips toward his hand, utterly lost to him.

* * * *

He'd gone mad.

The thought drifted through Lachlan's mind as he kneeled between her legs, but it was snatched out of his head by her breathless whimpers, and the sensation of her warm, damp folds against his fingers.

He stroked and circled and teased at her dewy flesh until she was crying out for him, her fingers tight in his hair, her body arching to get closer to his. His name was on her lips, and she was pleading with him to ease the ache inside her.

And he...

He was going to make her his.

It wasn't why he'd brought her here tonight, to Lady Chase's deserted library. Touching her, kissing her, making love to her—those were dreams only, gifts never meant for a man like him.

Scoundrel, liar, murderer...

He'd been that man for so long, he hadn't believed he could ever be anyone else.

Until her.

Because I love you, Lachlan...

As soon as she said those words, it was as if he'd been swept into a racing current, but instead of drowning, he'd broken the surface, coughing and sputtering, but cleaner than when he'd entered, the ugly stains fading into a distant memory.

He didn't deserve her, yet somehow she was his, and he could no more let her go than he could command his heart to stop beating. It made no sense he should be the one who'd been given the gift of her, unless...

Unless it was because no other man could ever love her as much as he did.

"You're mine now, Hyacinth. I'll never let you go. You're *mine*." He took her lips in a slow, lingering kiss. He was hard and aching for her, and every nudge or shift of his hips brought him closer to sinking inside her tantalizing heat, but he held back, the tip of his cock poised at her entrance, pausing for long moments to kiss her as he cradled her face in his hands.

His mouth was still clinging to hers when he surged into her damp heat. He caught her gasp in his mouth, and then stilled, his body over hers, inside hers, the sensation like nothing he'd ever felt before. Lachlan was no monk—he'd had lovers—but never before had he been inside a woman, and at the same time still desperate to get closer to her. Her arms were locked around his neck, her legs tight around his hips. Her breath was in his ear. He was holding her tightly against his chest, and still, he wanted more of her.

He was *inside* her, and even so, he wanted more.

She touched his cheek to bring his mouth back to hers, and then he was moving—just the tiniest nudge of his hips, restrained and careful, and yet the exquisite pleasure of her slick flesh pulling his shaft deep inside her body tore a helpless moan from his lips. "Ah, *aingeal*. I'll never have enough of you."

"I want all of you, Lachlan." She raked her nails down his sweat-slick back, and the tiny sting and her breathless words made him wild. He began to thrust in earnest, his strokes long and even. He gritted his teeth as he held back his own release, until, at last, at last, she let out a cry and arched against him. Her body pulsed around him, so tight and wet and hot, and he buried his face in her neck, groaning as the astonishing pleasure ripped through him.

They lay in each other's arms afterwards, her head cradled against his chest, his hands toying with her hair until at last their breathing calmed. They might have stayed there all night, but for the chime of the longcase clock on the first floor landing.

Five o'clock in the morning.

Lachlan roused himself, gathered their scattered clothing, and helped Hyacinth back into her gown, resisting the urge to tear it off her again the moment the last button was secured. Instead, he clasped her shoulders and pressed a tender kiss to her lips.

Their night was over. Huntington Lodge, and his reckoning with Finn, awaited.

Chapter Twenty-two

"Of all my five granddaughters, I dared to hope *you*, Hyacinth, might manage to get through your season without a scandal." Lady Chase dabbed at her eyes with the sodden handkerchief she'd been clutching in her fist since they'd left London that morning. "But oh, how wrong I was!"

"Grandmother, I—"

"Luring Lord Dixon into a dark library? Heaven and earth, child! What in the world could you have been thinking? No, no—don't try and answer, for there's naught to be done about it now. Your season is over. You're ruined—and Miss Ramsey right along with you—and there's an end to it. Oh, thank goodness I haven't any more granddaughters, for I daresay I wouldn't survive another season."

Lady Chase buried her face in her handkerchief, and commenced a loud wailing.

Lachlan resisted the urge to slap his hands over his ears. He stood in front of the fireplace, his gaze fixed on Hyacinth. The morning had started badly, and had deteriorated with every mile they'd put between London and Huntington Lodge.

To begin with, Lady Chase had been distressed to discover her granddaughter's season had come to such a sudden, disastrous end. She'd alternately wept and scolded the entire way to Buckinghamshire, until Isla had retreated into a morose silence, and Ciaran began to give way to the restless agitation that usually preceded one of his bloodier brawls.

And then there was Hyacinth.

Before they left Bedford Square that morning, Lachlan told her he intended to take Finn aside the moment they reached Huntington Lodge, and tell him the entire truth about what had happened before they'd left

Scotland. Isla's attack, Baird's death—everything he'd hidden, right down to the last detail.

She had *not* been pleased at this revelation, to say the least, but Lachlan flatly refused to let her carry the burden of his secret. He was done with lies. When her arguments and pleading failed to move him, she'd squeezed herself into a corner of the carriage, turned her face toward the window, and hadn't moved again for the entire ride.

After what they'd shared the night before, Lachlan had had visions of a delightful journey filled with yearning smiles and private touches, but she hadn't looked at him once since they'd left Bedford Square. By the time they reached Huntington Lodge his heart was aching, his muscles were screaming with tension, and he was as ready for a brawl as Ciaran was.

He was in no frame of mind to speak calmly with Finn, but as it happened, he didn't get a chance to say a single word to him. The moment they set foot in the entryway, all hell broke loose.

Lady Chase fell into a fit of hysterics. Ciaran had worked himself into a sudden snit over Isla's part in the Lord Dixon disaster, and Isla, provoked into a fury by Ciaran's scolding, had chosen that moment to burst into angry tears, which sent Lachlan headlong into a temper.

Only Hyacinth was silent, but it was a stubborn, ominous silence.

Finn made several attempts to calm the chaos, but at last he threw his hands up in the air and ordered everyone into the drawing room. Since Hyacinth was the only one of the five of them who wasn't either crying or shouting, he'd asked her for an explanation.

He may as well have asked water to explain why it's wet, for all the good it did.

Lachlan stood in front of the fireplace, his hands clenched into fists, and waited in vain for Hyacinth to tell her family the truth—to confess she'd risked her own safety and reputation to protect him from a secret he never should have kept.

Instead, she perched on the edge of the settee, her back straight and her hands folded neatly in her lap, fixed her wide, guileless blue eyes on Finn, and stubbornly refused to utter a single word in her own defense.

Finn gave her a blank look when she finished her fragmented story. "At the risk of sounding like a half wit, I'm afraid I'm going to need you to explain once again how you and Isla were both ruined in a single evening. Hyacinth? What have you to say?"

Hyacinth was patting Lady Chase's arm, but now her hand went still. "Nothing, except to beg your pardon for my behavior."

Lady Huntington, who'd joined them in the drawing room, exchanged a puzzled glance with her husband, who held his hands out in an uncharacteristically helpless gesture. This uncooperative, stubborn Hyacinth was a new and incomprehensible creature, and neither of them knew quite what to do with her.

"Hyacinth, dear." Lady Huntington crossed the room and sank onto the settee next to her sister. "If you'll only explain to us what happened, perhaps we can help."

Hyacinth didn't reply, but continued to sooth her grandmother as if her sister hadn't spoken.

Damn her. Even now, with Lady Chase's hysterics and Lord Huntington's stern eye upon her, she refused to divulge his secret. With every second that ticked by in silence, the deafening howl building in his chest roared closer and closer to the surface.

A roar of rage, because damn it, he was furious with her for endangering herself for *him*. That trick with Dixon—Jesus, when he thought of what might have happened, the number of ways she could have been hurt, he went wild with rage and panic.

Most of all, it was a roar of love—a love more profound than any he'd ever believed a hard, ruthless man like him could feel. A love that had burrowed its way under his thick skin and into his veins until she lived in every part of him, as essential to him as his blood, and bred into his very bones.

Maybe he wasn't a good man, but he wasn't the sort of man who'd let *anyone*—especially not his woman—take the blame for something he'd done. Damn it, he wanted to protect her, to keep her safe. Didn't she understand that?

"I believe I'll go and lie down now." Hyacinth rose unsteadily to her feet. "I'm afraid the journey from London has left me fatigued."

She gave them all an apologetic smile, but before she could take a step toward the door, Lachlan stopped her. "Do you think I'll let you keep lying for us, Hyacinth? That I'll let you sacrifice yourself to keep our secret?"

She froze at his words. Her back was to him, but he saw her shoulders stiffen just before she turned to face him. "I don't know what you mean—"

"Stop it, Hyacinth." He took two long strides toward her, his entire body trembling with the effort it took not to snatch her into his arms.

Hyacinth and Isla exchanged a single, stricken glance, then Hyacinth's anxious gaze darted from Finn back to Lachlan. "Mr. Ramsey, I can't imagine what—"

"Enough." Lachlan caught her hand in his. "Enough secrets, and enough lies. I came here to tell the truth, and I want you to hear it from my own lips."

Finn huffed out a breath. "I'd like to hear the truth from *someone's* lips, if it's all the same to all of you."

Lachlan led Hyacinth back over to the settee. "Sit down, please."

Hyacinth sank back into her seat beside her grandmother, but her face was pale, and she clenched her hands in her lap as if she were holding herself together.

"Hyacinth didn't lure Lord Dixon into the library on a whim. Her actions were deliberate." Lachlan turned to Finn. "I never would have let her out of my sight if I'd had any idea she would do something so reckless, so foolish—"

"Foolish!" Hyacinth leapt to her feet, angry color rising in her cheeks. "In case you've forgotten, that reckless, foolish plan of mine happened to work!"

"Dumb luck, and nothing more. If a single thing had gone wrong, what do you suppose would have happened, Hyacinth?" The anger and fear Lachlan had been struggling to control rushed back to the surface, making his voice harsh. "What if Isla and Lord Sydney hadn't reached you in time? What if Dixon discovered what you were about? Damn you, he could have hurt you! Do you think I ever could have forgiven myself if he had, Hyacinth? When I first saw you, standing there in that damn library with your torn gown, I thought—" Lachlan dragged a hand down his face, bleak despair chasing the anger from his voice. "Jesus, I've never been more terrified in my life."

Silence descended on the room. Lady Chase's weeping came to an abrupt halt. No one moved or even seemed to draw a breath, until at last Lady Huntington's delicate cough broke the silence. Lachlan came back to himself to find everyone in the room staring at him. Both Ciaran and Isla wore identical knowing grins on their lips, but Lady Chase's mouth had gone slack with shock, and Finn was gaping at Lachlan and Hyacinth in astonishment.

"My goodness," Lady Chase croaked at last, raising a bony hand and pointing at Lachlan. "Mr. Ramsey is…why, I don't know how I didn't see it before, but I believe Mr. Ramsey is in lo—"

"I still don't understand this." Finn shot Lady Chase a warning look, then cleared his throat, and fixed a stern look on Lachlan. "Before I left London, you swore to me you'd protect Hyacinth, but from what I've heard so far, it sounds as if you failed to keep your promise."

Hyacinth had resumed her seat, but now she shot to her feet again. "No, he didn't! Indeed, you're wrong, Finn! He—"

"I did fail." Lachlan met Finn's gaze without flinching. "I never trusted Lord Dixon. I thought he was a scoundrel from the start, but I didn't act quickly enough. By the time I did, Hyacinth had already put herself at risk. I should have stopped it long before then. It's a miracle it didn't turn out worse."

Isla made an impatient noise at that, and every head in the room turned toward her. "I'm tired of you taking blame upon yourself you don't deserve, Lachlan. How could you have stopped Lord Dixon, when only Hyacinth and I knew about his threats? As for his being a card cheat—"

"Threats? *Card cheat?*" Lady Chase fanned herself with her handkerchief. "Oh, my goodness. Someone fetch my smelling salts!"

Lady Huntington and Hyacinth both hurried to tend to Lady Chase. Ciaran turned to Isla with a sardonic, "Well done," and Finn, pushed to the last degree of his patience, thundered over the tumult, "For God's sake, will someone please tell me what the *devil* happened in Lady Entwhistle's bloody library?"

Lady Huntington was waving smelling salts under Lady Chase's nose with one hand, and patting Hyacinth's hand with the other. "I'm certain there's a perfectly reasonable explanation for all of it."

"At this point, I'd settle for *any* explanation." Finn turned his glower on Lachlan. "Well?"

"There is an explanation, but you won't find it reasonable. It begins with a lie I told you when we arrived in London."

It was a bald, abrupt confession, but Lachlan was no longer under any illusions about the damage a secret could cause, both to those who kept it, and those it was kept from. He wanted it out.

Finn reacted much as one might expect when he discovers he's been deceived. His eyes narrowed, and his face hardened. "Very well. What did you lie about?"

"It wasn't a lie!" Isla broke in. "It was, well, we didn't tell you the entire truth about why we left Scotland, but we didn't lie about it, precisely."

"We hid the truth. Same damn thing as a lie, I'm afraid." Ciaran glanced at Lachlan. "But it wasn't just Lachlan who did it. We all did."

"If Ciaran's defending me," Lachlan said, "This must be worse than I thought."

Ciaran shrugged. "We're in it together, Lach. We have been from the start. I believe you've mentioned that a few times since we left Scotland."

"I have. I didn't think you were listening."

Another shrug. "I wasn't. Until now."

A long, silent look passed between them, then Lachlan gave his brother a half-smile, and turned to face Finn again. "My father, Niall Ramsey—" He broke off abruptly, shook his head, and began again. "Niall Ramsey, Ciaran and Isla's father, died last year. Our mother," he included Finn in his glance, "Was never the same afterwards. Looking back, I think we all knew she wouldn't live long after he passed, and she didn't. We buried her less than a year later, but it wasn't just grief over his death than sent her into an early grave."

Finn remained silent, his arms folded over his chest, waiting.

A corner of Lachlan's lip turned up, but his smile was bitter. "Since the night we arrived in London, I've marveled over the irony of it, but in the end it's a simple enough thing. One way or another, our crimes catch up to us."

Finn stared at Lachlan, his face expressionless. "Indeed. What crimes would those be?"

Lachlan wasn't looking at Finn anymore. He was looking at Hyacinth, and his voice dropped to a hoarse whisper. "That first night, you accused me of being a murderer. You were right all along, *leannan*. I *am* a murderer. Before we left Scotland, I killed a man."

Both Lady Chase and Lady Huntington gasped, and their faces went white, but Finn, oddly enough, didn't even twitch. He was watching Hyacinth, assessing her reaction, his eyes narrowed in thought. After a moment, he turned back to Lachlan, an eyebrow raised in question. "It's not as simple as that. Let's have the rest of it."

"Why should you think there's more? Is it so hard to believe I'm a killer?"

"Yes," Finn answered at once. "It is."

Lachlan stared at him, at the brother he hadn't trusted, the brother he'd lied to, the brother he might never have known had circumstances been different, and something cracked open in his chest.

"You're right, Lord Huntington. There is more. Much more." Isla got to her feet to stand beside Lachlan. "It wasn't a murder, but an accident. A terrible accident. Lachlan was protecting me from…well, from someone we thought we had every reason to trust. It's a long story, but for now you only need to understand this man, he…he tried to hurt me. He attacked me. Lachlan heard me screaming, came running, and pulled him off me, but my attacker—he stumbled and fell, and struck his head on a heavy wooden beam on the way down. He died instantly."

For a long moment, the only sound in the room then was the hiss and crackle of the fire, but then Lady Huntington rose to her feet, crossed the room, and put an arm around Isla's shoulders. "Oh, my dear," she murmured, gathering Isla into her arms. "Oh, Isla."

"If you ask me, the scoundrel got what he deserved," Ciaran said. "But the rest of the townspeople didn't share that opinion. Lochinver is a small village. Too small for us, after James Baird's untimely demise. If we hadn't left on our own, I have no doubt they would have run us out, or worse."

"We never would have known any of you then," Isla added softly. "At the time, leaving Lochinver felt like the worst thing that could ever happen to us, but now, well, it's strange, isn't it, the way hope so often lies at the heart of a tragedy?"

Finn had been listening to Isla with a pensive expression, but now his gaze swung to Lachlan. "You mean…"

Lachlan nodded. "It was only after Baird's death that my mother revealed the truth about my parentage. She knew she wouldn't live much longer, and she was desperate for us to leave Lochinver, and start a new life far away from Scotland. What better chance than as the second son of a marquess? If none of it had happened—if Baird hadn't died—I don't think she ever would have told me the truth."

"Jesus," Finn muttered, shaking his head.

"I loved my—*our*—mother, but when I found out the truth, I was angry. To discover the man I'd believed to be my father wasn't my father at all, that Ciaran and Isla weren't my full sister and brother, and I had another brother, one I never knew existed…those lies seemed the worst sort of betrayal to me." Lachlan ran a hand down his face. "Christ, I'm not even Scottish."

"No, you're a bloody Englishman. What could be worse than that?" Ciaran glanced at Finn. "No offense, my lord."

Finn's lip curled in a reluctant grin. "And our mother?"

"Buried in Lochinver, beside Niall Ramsey. I don't suppose we'll ever see their graves again. None of us will ever go back there."

"She made us swear we'd leave the past in Scotland, that we'd never tell anyone the secret about what happened." Isla turned a pleading look on Finn. "She believed it would ruin us wherever we went, that we'd become outcasts, and after what happened there, we believed her. Our friends in Lochinver—we'd known them our entire lives. They were like our family, but after James died…" Isla wiped a tear from her cheek. "They turned their backs on us. We couldn't risk it happening again, not even when we met you all, and found out how kind you are."

"It was a mistake. I thought I was protecting Isla and Ciaran by keeping our secret, but I was wrong, and I…" Lachlan swallowed, but he met Finn's eyes. "I beg your pardon for it. We thought that secret would stay buried, but as I said, our crimes catch us in the end."

Ciaran snorted. "It wasn't our crimes; it was Lord Dixon's bloody cousin in Achiltibuie. As it happened, this cousin had heard the whole story, related it to Dixon in a letter, and Dixon, being the blackguard he is—"

"Saw his chance, and took it. He threatened to expose us unless Hyacinth accepted his courtship. Our secret made her vulnerable—put her at the mercy of an unscrupulous scoundrel like Dixon." Lachlan's tone was grim. "I've no doubt he would have tried to force her into marriage, as well."

"Except he didn't, because Hyacinth wouldn't have it." Lady Huntington was staring at Hyacinth with a wondering look on her face, as if she'd never quite seen her sister until this moment.

"Ah, now we come to it. How, exactly, did you do that, Hyacinth?" Finn fixed Hyacinth with a penetrating stare. "Something about Lord Dixon being a card cheat?"

Hyacinth looked around the room, flushing when she noticed every eye fixed on her. "Yes. He, ah…well, I discovered he was cheating at cards, and so I…arranged to expose him."

Hyacinth said this with the air of one who's done discussing the matter, but Finn was far from satisfied with this explanation. "But how the devil—that is, how could you have discovered he was cheating at cards? Did you see him do it?"

Hyacinth bit her lip. "Um, no. I…oh, very well. I found a bit of paraffin wax in his waistcoat pocket. The tip of it was fashioned into a point, like a pencil, and so I suspected he was—"

"Marking cards." Now it was Finn's turn to stare at Hyacinth as if he didn't recognize her. "But how in the world did you know a card cheat would use wax to mark cards?"

"I heard about it from a young lady I met in Brighton. Do you remember Miss Harrington, Grandmother? Her elder brother was a card cheat."

"Indeed?" Lady Chase looked dazed, and she was still clutching at her smelling salts.

"Well, I'll be damned." Finn grinned. "Those trips to Brighton weren't an utter waste, after all."

Lady Huntington wasn't as amused as her husband. "How in the world did you get your hand in Lord Dixon's waistcoat pocket? And what do you mean, you 'arranged to expose him'? I don't like the sound of this, Hyacinth."

"You'll like the truth even less, Lady Huntington." Lachlan curled his hands into fists, his fingernails cutting into his skin. Damn it, he should have killed Dixon while he had the chance. "She lured him into the library—"

"I didn't *lure* him! I don't even know *how* to lure a gentleman. I simply invited him to accompany me to the library, and—"

"Then she tempted him into removing his coat and waistcoat, and—"

"*Tempted?*" Hyacinth crossed her arms over her chest and glared at Lachlan. "I'm no temptress, Lachlan. You exaggerate!"

But Lachlan, who was wildly jealous and growing more so with every word, only glared at her. "She *tempted* him into removing his waistcoat, but first she made sure to put the bit of wax in his pocket—"

"I didn't *put* it there! That is, I put it *back* where I'd found it the night before. For pity's sake, Lachlan, you make me sound a very villainess—"

"I'll leave it to you all to imagine what a man like Dixon might have done if he'd caught her." Lachlan's voice was rising. "But if that weren't dangerous enough, she then proceeded to *divert* him until Isla could arrive with Lord Sydney."

Ciaran interrupted then, a look of unmistakable pride on his face. "Very clever, really. Sydney had lost thousands to Dixon, you see, so he was an ideal choice to discover the thing. Indeed, it was rather ingenious, if you ask me—"

"No one asked you!" Lachlan stepped closer to Hyacinth and caught her shoulders in his hands. "Damn it, why did you risk yourself like that? He put his hands on you! He *touched* you, ripped the sleeve of your gown—"

"Ripped her gown! Oh, *Hyacinth!* Oh, my goodness." Lady Chase collapsed back against the settee, quite overwhelmed.

"I don't deny it was risky, but Hyacinth was just magnificent, Lord Huntington!" Isla plucked at the sleeve of Finn's coat to get his attention. "Perhaps we shouldn't have done it. I can't deny we didn't escape unscathed, what with the scandal it's caused, but, oh, Lord Huntington! Hyacinth truly has such a sweet, tender heart, and once she saw how things were for us, nothing would dissuade her."

"No one doubts the tenderness of Hyacinth's heart." Without realizing he did it, Lachlan drew Hyacinth closer to him, until he was cradling her against his chest. "She's the sweetest lass in London."

Hyacinth said nothing, but she gripped Lachlan's forearms in her hands, as if to keep him there with her.

"Hyacinth." Finn took Hyacinth's arm and drew her gently away from Lachlan. "Why did you take such an enormous risk? Lachlan's right. This could have gone terribly wrong. Why didn't you simply tell Lachlan, or Ciaran or Lady Chase Lord Dixon was threatening you?"

Hyacinth stared up at him with wide eyes. "Because I was afraid if you found out they'd kept something from you, you might..."

"Yes? It's all right. Just tell me."

Hyacinth glanced at Lady Huntington, who gave her an encouraging nod. "I-I...oh, do forgive me for saying this, Finn, but you've only been married to Iris for a short time, and I don't know you all that well yet, and you're...well, you're quite stern, and I was afraid...I was afraid if you found out the truth, you'd send Lachlan—that is, you'd send all the Ramseys away, and I couldn't bear to...well, I'm very sorry, Finn."

Finn's face softened. "It's all right. There's nothing to be sorry for." He turned to Lachlan, and laid a hand on his shoulder. "You should have told me the truth at once, but we don't withhold forgiveness in this family—not from those who sincerely ask for it, as you've done today. You're my brother, Lachlan, and Ciaran as well, and Isla my sister." For a long moment, Finn stared hard at them. "Do you suppose I couldn't find it in my heart to forgive my own family?"

They'd been offered little forgiveness from those they had a right to expect it from. To have Finn offer it so freely now, even after they'd lied to him, humbled Lachlan. "We were wrong, and we're..." Lachlan cleared his throat. "We're truly grateful for your forgiveness."

"You're a good sort, Finn," Ciaran said. "For an Englishman, that is."

Finn shook his head, a grin playing about his mouth. "Lured Dixon into a library, eh? I'll be damned. That took some courage. Our little Hyacinth—"

"Finn!" Lady Huntington shot him a warning look.

Finn straightened, and cleared his throat. "Oh, right. I mean, that was a very foolish thing to do, Hyacinth. It could have gone terribly wrong. I hope you'll never do something so dangerous again."

"Oh, I don't know. Hyacinth was never in as much danger as Dixon was. Lachlan almost killed him. He hauled him off his feet by his cravat, and dangled him there like a ragdoll until Dixon nearly wet himself. That was a good bit of business, Lach," Ciaran added, nodding approvingly at Lachlan.

"Did he, indeed? That *is* a good bit of..." Finn trailed off with a glance at Iris, and once again cleared his throat. "I mean, that was a very foolish thing to do, Lachlan. It could have gone terribly wrong. I hope you'll never do something so—"

"Oh, for pity's sake, Finn. Do you suppose my memory is that short?" Iris crossed her arms over her chest. "I recall you doing something similar to Lord Claire last summer. It must run in the family—squeezing a man's neck, I mean."

"What, you mean to say you thrashed Lady Joanna's brother?" Ciaran shot Finn an admiring look. "Oh, that's very good, that is. How did you—"

"This is all very well," Lady Chase interrupted, putting aside her hysterics for long enough to fix them all with an irritated scowl. "But what's to become of Hyacinth? Are her heroics to be rewarded with a lifetime of spinsterhood?"

"No. Hyacinth won't become a spinster, Lady Chase."

"Humph. You don't know the *ton* as well as I do, Mr. Ramsey. I can assure you, they aren't likely to forgive a scandalous library assignation."

"The *ton* can do as they please, and so will I. I'm marrying Hyacinth."

A stunned silence followed this announcement, then Hyacinth squeaked, "You're *what?*"

"I was meant to protect you this season. I failed. Now you're left without a proper suitor, your reputation is tarnished, and you've no marriage prospects."

"*Tarnished!* Well, you're quite the hero to take me on then, aren't you?" Hyacinth put her hands on her hips and glared at Lachlan, as if daring him to say another word.

Ciaran glanced uneasily at her. "Um, Lach, I think what you mean to say is—"

"This all came about because of our secret," Lachlan insisted, oblivious to Ciaran's warning. "It made you vulnerable to Dixon. I won't let you suffer for my mistake, Hyacinth."

Hyacinth's cheeks flushed a dull red. "I see. So you'll suffer instead?"

Lachlan blinked at her, surprised at her tone. "Well, yes."

Ciaran hissed out a low breath. "Oh, Christ. The correct answer to that question was *no*, Lach."

But he would suffer, because every single day, when he woke up beside her and basked in her smiles, a part of him would know he'd only won her because his lie had robbed her of every chance at a better husband than he could ever be. For a woman like her, to be forced to settle for a man like him was nothing short of criminal.

Finn glanced between Lachlan and Hyacinth. "Ah, Lachlan, I think what Hyacinth means to ask is…the best marriages are built on…a guilty conscience isn't a good reason to—"

"She's my responsibility now, Finn, and I'm not a man who shirks—"

"Oh, for God's sakes, Lachlan! *No.*" Ciaran buried his face in his hands.

"Damn it, man! Do you care for her, or not?" Finn threw his hands in the air, exasperated.

Lachlan stared at Finn, baffled. "Care for her?" He'd never wanted anyone the way he wanted her. He'd never loved anyone, or even ever hoped to love anyone, as much as he loved her. Wasn't it obvious? "Of course I—"

"You're an *ass*." Hyacinth's voice ricocheted off the wall and echoed through the room like a gunshot.

Lachlan turned to gape at her, his mouth hanging open. "I—what did you say?"

"She said you're an ass," Ciaran offered helpfully.

Hyacinth faced Lachlan, her hands on her hips. "You heard me. You're an *ass*, and I'd rather end a spinster than marry you!"

With that, the meek, the timid, the reserved Hyacinth Somerset, who never dared breathe a cross word to anyone, turned on her heel and stomped out of the room, her back straight, and her chin thrust in the air.

The long, awkward silence that followed was broken by Ciaran, who flopped into a chair, crossed his ankle over his knee, and regarded his brother with a deep sigh. "Well done, Lach. You've just made the kindest, sweetest-tempered lass in all of London call you an ass."

Chapter Twenty-three

Like many young ladies, Hyacinth had dreamed of the day when a gentleman would ask her to marry him. She'd imagined impassioned pleas, promises of undying love and devotion, and her suitor descending to his knees in supplication.

Very well, then. She was guilty of indulging in foolish romantic fancies, but the fact remained not once, in all her fevered daydreams, had she ever envisioned a proposal that included phrases like "tarnished reputation," or "responsibility," or "no other marriage prospects." To be fair, she'd also never envisioned calling her suitor an ass, but, well...

"Insufferable, high-handed, overbearing ass!"

Suffering. Had he actually talked to her of suffering in the same breath he'd offered his hand? Though now she considered it, he hadn't even offered his hand, or bothered to ask for hers, had he? He'd simply announced he would marry her, in the same way one would announce they were taking the last slice of beef at dinner, and then only because no one else wanted it.

That was precisely how she felt right now—like leftover beef. Surely a lady had a right to expect more than *that* from a marriage proposal?

"Argh! What an ass!" Hyacinth seized one of the pillows from the bed and hurled it across her bedchamber. It hit the door just as it was flung open, and it dropped to the floor at Isla's feet.

"Well, I see there's no reason to ask if you're still angry." Isla leaned down, fetched the pillow, and tossed it aside. She crossed the room and stood beside the bed for a moment, arms crossed, her stern gaze fixed on Hyacinth. "This is not how I imagined this moment would unfold."

"Nor I, I assure you! I'm sorry to say so, Isla, but your brother is an ass!"

Isla perched on the edge of the bed with a sigh. "Well, yes, but then he's a man, isn't he? He also happens to be an ass who's madly in love with you, so there's that to consider."

"Love! I don't recall any mention of the word 'love' in that dreadful proposal."

Isla sighed again, and plopped down next to Hyacinth on the bed. "No, but perhaps you *do* recall the way he looks at you when he calls you *leannan*? Or the stark panic on his face when he spoke of Lord Dixon hurting you? I know my brother, Hyacinth. He's not the sort of man given to endearments, nor is he one who easily acknowledges helplessness or terror."

Hyacinth peeked at Isla over the edge of a pillow she was clutching to her chest. "No, I suppose not, but he said—"

"Perhaps you also recall the way you leapt to Lachlan's defense—not just when Lord Huntington accused him of failing to keep his promise, but also when Lord Dixon threatened to expose us. I know you, Hyacinth. You're not the sort of lady given to reckless schemes, nor are you one who courts scandal on a whim."

"The scheme with Lord Dixon was meant to protect all of you, not just Lachlan," Hyacinth protested, but she couldn't quite meet Isla's eyes.

"Ah, yes. Of course, it was. Yet when you were alone in that dark library with Lord Dixon, coaxing him out of his waistcoat, you weren't thinking of either me or Ciaran, were you?"

Hyacinth fiddled with the edge of the pillowcase, then tossed it aside with a sigh. "Oh, very well. No, I wasn't. I was thinking of your gruff, hardheaded, oldest brother. You heard him just now, Isla. He didn't make me an offer from an excess of tender feeling, but from a sense of failure, and grim obligation. He said—"

"Oh, never mind what he said! You should know better than to listen to what men *say*. What they say is of far less importance than what they *do*, Hyacinth." There was a sharp edge to Isla's voice that hadn't been there before. "Lachlan's a man of few words, and most of those are gruff and abrupt, but if you wanted a gentleman with a silver tongue, one who would bombard you with empty flattery, you would have settled for Lord Dixon."

"I don't want that. Do you suppose I can't see Lachlan is ten times the man Lord Dixon could ever be, Isla? Don't you understand? I *love* Lachlan. I've loved him from the first moment…well, perhaps not the first moment I *saw* him. I did mistake him for a murderer that first time, but certainly since then. His rough exterior, the way he growls deep in his chest, his enormous hands—I love everything about him."

Isla reached over and seized Hyacinth's hands. "Then I fail to see the problem. Tell him, and let's get on with a wedding, shall we?"

"The problem is I want him to love me back, Isla."

"He does. You may trust me on that."

"He hasn't said so. You've said so, yes, but…well, that's not the same thing, is it?" Tears stung Hyacinth's eyes. Even last night, when he'd held her in his arms and whispered she was *his*, he'd never said a word about love. "He's gone to great lengths *not* to say it, Isla."

Isla's face softened. "Oh, my dear. Don't you see? He's afraid to say it, because he thinks he doesn't deserve you, and only you can convince him he does. There's a part of Lachlan that still blames himself for the tragedy we left behind us in Scotland. He might always have done so, but for you, Hyacinth. If you can forgive him his past, and love him in spite of it, then he can begin to forgive himself. Don't you see? You're his hope—his *aingeal*."

Hyacinth brushed away the tears on her cheeks. Oh, she wanted so badly to believe what Isla said was true, and that Lachlan really did love her. "Do you truly think so?"

Isla smiled. "With all my heart. Such a love as you and Lachlan have is rare, Hyacinth. Don't toss away such a perfect chance at happiness."

Hyacinth gave Isla a shaky smile. "I suppose the least I can do is give him another chance." She slid off the bed and crossed the room, but hesitated at the door, Isla's final words echoing in her head. "Isla? You never said what happened with Lord Pierce."

"Didn't I?" Isla shrugged, but her lower lip began to tremble. "I sent him a note last night, after Lady Entwhistle's ball. He wrote back at once, and he…he asked me never to contact him again. He was very proper and courteous about it, but whatever was between us is now over. Ah, well. I never had much hope of him, in any case."

Hyacinth's hand fell away from the door. "I don't understand. I was so certain he…did he find out what happened in Scotland, and was angry you'd kept it a secret from him?"

Isla gave a cold laugh. "Oh, no. I don't think he even knows about that. No, it seems my brief sojourn in the library with Lord Sydney shocked him back to his senses. He must have heard the gossip, and assumed the worst. After all, no proper young lady would ever wander off with a gentleman in such a scandalous manner."

"But—"

"No, Hyacinth. I'm glad for it, truly." Isla rose from the bed, looking wearier than Hyacinth had ever seen her. "He can't have cared much for me, can he? Such a man as that would never have forgiven me my past, and since I had no intention of keeping it from him, this break was inevitable. It's just as well it happened sooner rather than later, don't you agree? Though I confess myself surprised Lord Pierce would credit idle gossip over my explanation."

This last was said with some bitterness, and Hyacinth could see Isla didn't wish to discuss it further, but she couldn't let it drop yet—not when Isla's future hung in the balance. "I thought better of Lord Pierce than this. How shall we proceed, then? I'm afraid last night's scandal is too recent to have any hopes for a match for you this season, but perhaps next year—"

"Oh, there's no need to fret on my account. I won't end a spinster, despite Lord Pierce's dismissal. I, ah...I'm going to marry Lord Sydney."

"Lord Sydney!" Hyacinth's mouth dropped open. "When was that decided?"

"He made me an offer several weeks ago, and I wrote him this morning, accepting his proposals. My brothers will have to approve it, of course, but they will, and gladly. Who could object to Lord Sydney? He's a dear man, and a perfect gentleman."

Hyacinth didn't argue that point. She'd always been fond of Lord Sydney, and there was no denying he'd make Isla an excellent match.

But...

"Do you love him, Isla?"

Isla's forlorn little sigh seemed to rise straight from her broken heart. "It's not a love match on either side, but I care for him very much, and I know he feels the same for me. We get on well, and he's...well, he's a dear friend. It's a great deal more than many ladies can claim upon marriage."

Once again, it wasn't a point Hyacinth could argue. It all made perfect sense, and yet that didn't stop her heart from sinking in her chest.

Isla noticed her downcast expression, and let out a sad little laugh. "Oh, don't look so grim, Hyacinth. I didn't have much hope my season would end in a love match. First James Baird, and now Lord Pierce...well, I no longer believe in fairy-tale endings."

They were both quiet for a long while after that, but then Isla offered Hyacinth a wan smile. "Last night, in the library with Lord Dixon—Lord Sydney was marvelous, wasn't he? Once he saw that bit of wax, he simply charged forward, without hesitation, and without question."

"Yes. He was quite heroic."

"Indeed. When he first offered his hand, I told him about my past—the entire awful story. I thought he'd regret his proposals once he knew, and I was prepared to release him, but do you know what he did, Hyacinth?"

Hyacinth shook her head. "No. What?"

"He took my hand, raised it to his lips, and said my past was of no consequence to him. He said he cared only for our future." Isla had been looking off into space, her eyes cloudy as she recalled that moment, but when her gaze shifted back to Hyacinth, they were bright and clear. "What a man says is of far less importance than what he does." Isla repeated her words from earlier, her voice soft. "Do you understand?"

Isla's words, and the brave tilt of her chin made Hyacinth want to burst into tears, but she choked them back, and smiled at her friend. "I do. I understand, Isla."

"Go and find my brother, then." Isla made a shooing motion toward the door. "I daresay he'll make an ass of himself again before it's all settled, but I have great faith in your strength, Hyacinth. I always did."

* * * *

"I don't know why you're still sitting here, Lach. After a proposal like that, I'd be in my bedchamber checking for poisonous snakes between my bedsheets." Ciaran bounced his foot against his knee and studied his brother with an abstracted air.

Lachlan, who was slumped on one of the settees with his head in his hands, didn't bother to reply. He'd made a bloody mess of this, though even now, he couldn't figure out how it had gone so wrong. He'd begun well enough, hadn't he? But then he'd said something about suffering, and Hyacinth's face had turned red...

"Did I...did I really imply marriage to her would be a misery?" Lachlan raised his head from his hands and looked at Ciaran, then Finn.

Ciaran snorted. "Imply it? Oh no, Lach. You didn't *imply* a damn thing. It was more like a declaration, wasn't it, Finn?"

Finn had hurried Iris and Lady Chase from the room, then returned and resumed his post in front of the fireplace. He was standing there now, seemingly at a loss as to what to do next. "Well, it certainly wasn't good, but if it makes you feel any better, Lachlan, I doubt Hyacinth would resort to poisonous snakes."

"Non-poisonous snakes, then?" Ciaran asked.

Finn gave him a doubtful look. "I would say no, but then I never thought I'd hear her call anyone an ass, either."

Lachlan dropped his head back into his hands with a defeated groan.

"Well, he *was* an ass. For God's sake, Lachlan. Anyone can see you're madly in love with Hyacinth, so why not just say it, and have done?

Waffling on about mistakes, suffering, and tarnished reputations? Good Lord, I didn't know whether to laugh or cry. Poor Hyacinth."

Lachlan raised his head again. "Anyone can see I'm madly in love with her?"

Ciaran rolled his eyes. "Look at yourself, man! You're miserable, aren't you? If that's not love, I don't know what is. I'd find it all vastly amusing if you weren't so pathetic."

"And if you weren't in love with her, you'd never have made such a mess of the proposal," Finn added, nodding wisely. "Gentlemen in love always make a bloody mess of everything."

Ciaran raised an eyebrow at Finn. "Indeed? You speak as if you've had experience making a bloody mess of things. Should I be complimenting Lady Huntington on her forbearance?"

"The proposal went well enough. It was everything that came before it." Finn shuddered at the memory. "I had to chase her all over Hampshire, and then she jilted me before she finally agreed to marry me. Twice, in fact."

"Twice! And you a marquess, too!" Ciaran let out a shout of laughter. "Good God. Well, Lach, the Somerset sisters seem to be of a forgiving turn, so perhaps all hope isn't lost. If Lady Huntington could forgive Finn, then surely her sister can forgive you, despite your being such an inconsiderate ass."

Lachlan rose to his feet and began to pace from one end of the room to the other. "But what will I say to her?" He couldn't recall ever feeling so unsure of himself in his life. Bloody noses, black eyes—they were easy enough to manage, but this? It was worse than the time he'd taken a blade a half inch into his chest during a brawl.

Of course, the point hadn't touched his heart, whereas Hyacinth held that surprisingly tender organ right in the palm of her hand.

"Throw yourself at her feet, beg her forgiveness, and declare your undying love, of course." Ciaran waved a careless hand toward the door. "For God's sake, Lach, it isn't that difficult."

"Right." Lachlan wandered toward the door, muttering to himself. "Knees, forgiveness, undying love…"

"Can we listen at the door while you grovel?" Ciaran asked, with a wink at Finn.

"Certainly, if you want your eye blackened."

After Lachlan left, Ciaran and Finn regarded each other in silence for a moment, then Finn grinned. "Having brothers is far more entertaining than I thought it would be."

Ciaran grinned back. "You have no idea."

* * * *

As it happened, Lachlan didn't have to grovel.

But he did sink to his knees. Not because Hyacinth demanded it, but because when he found her coming down the stairs in search of him, led her into the deserted library and looked into the sweetest pair of blue eyes he'd ever seen, he could do nothing else.

Anything less would have been a lie.

She twined her fingers in his hair as he knelt before her. He buried his face against her belly, and tried to put into words how much he loved her. In the end, he said what was in his heart. Ciaran would have been in fits of laugher over his bumbling address, but Hyacinth seemed to like it, and she was the only one who mattered.

"The first moment I saw you, *leannan*, I thought you looked like an angel. You were so beautiful in your white gown, I stopped in the middle of the ballroom to stare at you. Even then, before I'd spoken a single word to you, I knew I'd never seen a sweeter face than yours."

Her fingers tightened in his hair, and her breath caught on a sob.

"But once I knew you, I realized your beauty isn't here." He rose to his feet and traced the back of his hand over the lines of her face. "It's here." He rested his palm against her chest, over her heart. "Your true beauty is in your heart. Your kindness, your strength—they come from here. I fell in love with your heart, *leannan*, and I'm a selfish man, because even though I don't deserve it, I want your heart for my own."

She gazed up into his face with tear-filled eyes. "It's yours. My heart and my love are yours, Lachlan. I can't remember a time when they weren't."

Lachlan brushed her hair back from her face, and caught her tears on his fingertips. "Don't cry, *aingeal*."

A soft laugh escaped her lips, and she shook her head as she rose to her tiptoes to slide her arms around his neck. "Oh, Lachlan, I'm no angel. Someday soon, you'll discover I'm just a flesh and blood woman, one with too many flaws to count. Then what do you suppose will happen?"

He wrapped his arms around her waist and pulled her hard against him, and the rare smile he saved for her alone curled his lips. "You'll always be my *aingeal*. But don't worry, *leannan*. I'm also very, very interested in your womanly flesh. I'm a man, after all."

He lowered his mouth to hers and captured her lips in a breathtaking kiss, and as Hyacinth opened to him, she thought of who Lachlan was—everything he was. An Englishman and a Scot, a brawler with enormous hands and blood on his knuckles, and yet a gentleman still, one who worshipped her with his soft, tender touch.

And hidden inside that massive chest, under the hard muscles and layers of scar tissue over the wounds of his past…

The fiercest, warmest heart she'd ever known.

He was all of those things, but more than anything else…

He was hers.

Author's Notes

The information about card marking is from a book published in 1894, entitled *Sharps and Flats: A Complete Revelation of the Secrets of Cheating at Games of Chance and Skill*, written by John Nevil Maskelyne. This fascinating book details the various tricks cards sharps used to cheat their opponents.

There is some discrepancy concerning the dates playing cards began to feature printed designs on their backs. The wealthy could afford custom, hand-painted cards, but the consensus seems to be that until the Victorian era, playing cards had plain, blank white backs, making it easy for cheats like Lord Dixon to mark them with paraffin wax.

About the Author

Anna Bradley is the author of The Sutherland Scandals novels. A Maine native, she now lives near Portland, Oregon, where people are delightful and weird and love to read. She teaches writing and lives with her husband, two children, a variety of spoiled pets, and shelves full of books. Visit her website at www.annabradley.net.

About the Author

Anna Bradley is the author of The Sutherland Scandals novels. A Maine native, she now lives near Portland, Oregon, where people are delightful and weird and love to read. She teaches writing and lives with her husband, two children, a variety of spoiled pets, and shelves full of books. Visit her website at www.annabradley.net.

Printed in the United States
by Baker & Taylor Publisher Services